Bedding Lord Ned

Books by Sally MacKenzie

THE NAKED DUKE

THE NAKED MARQUIS

THE NAKED EARL

THE NAKED GENTLEMAN

"The Naked Laird" in LORDS OF DESIRE

THE NAKED BARON

THE NAKED VISCOUNT

"The Naked Prince" in AN INVITATION TO SIN

THE NAKED KING

"The Duchess of Love"

BEDDING LORD NED

Published by Kensington Publishing Corporation

Bedding Lord Ned

The
Duchess
of
Love

SALLY MACKENZIE

ZEBRA BOOKS
KENSINGTON PUBLISHING CORP.

http://www.kensingtonbooks.com

ZEBRA BOOKS are published by

Kensington Publishing Corp.
119 West 40th Street
New York, NY 10018

All Kensington titles, imprints, and distributed lines are available at special quantity discounts for bulk purchases for sales
promotion, premiums, fund-raising, educational, or institu-
tional use.

Special book excerpts or customized printings can also be
created to fit specific needs. For details, write or phone the
office of the Kensington Special Sales Manager: Attn. Special
Sales Department. Kensington Publishing Corp., 119 West
40th Street, New York, NY 10018. Phone: 1-800-221-2647.

Zebra and the Z logo Reg. U.S. Pat. & TM Off.

ISBN-13: 978-1-4201-2321-0
ISBN-10: 1-4201-2321-1

First Printing: June 2012

10 9 8 7 6 5 4 3 2 1

Printed in the United States of America

For my agent,
Jessica Faust,
who is in many ways the mother—
or at least the honorary aunt—
of the duchess and her brood.

Chapter 1

A man's pride needs careful handling.
— Venus's Love Notes

Miss Eleanor Bowman stood in the Duchess of Love's pink guest bedroom and stared at the scrap of red silk spilling out of her valise, her heart stuttering in horror. That wasn't—

Her brows snapped down. Of course it wasn't. She was letting her imagination run away with her. The red fabric was merely her Norwich shawl. She distinctly remembered packing it, as she did every year. It was far too fine to wear to darn socks or mind her sisters' children, but it was just the thing for the duchess's annual Valentine party. It was her one nod to fashion, the small bit of elegance she still allowed herself.

She snatched the red silk up again, shook it out—and dropped it as if it were a poisonous snake.

Damn it, it *wasn't* her shawl. It was those cursed red drawers.

She closed her eyes as the familiar wave of self-loathing

crashed over her. She'd made these and a matching red dress to wear to Lord Edward's betrothal ball five years ago, desperately hoping Ned would see her—really see her—and realize it was she he wanted to marry, not her best friend, Cicely Headley. But Mama had seen her first, when she'd come downstairs to get into the carriage, and had sent her straight back to her room.

She glared down at the red cloth. Thank God Mama had stopped her. If she'd gone to the ball in that dreadful dress, everyone would know she wasn't any better than a Jezebel.

It was no surprise Ned had chosen Cicely. She'd been everything Ellie wasn't: small, blonde, blue-eyed—beautiful—with a gentle disposition. And then when Cicely and the baby had died in childbirth . . .

Ellie squeezed her eyes shut again, the mingle-mangle of shame and yearning twisting her gut. She'd mourned with everyone else—sincerely mourned—but she'd also hoped that Ned would turn to her and their friendship would grow into something more.

It hadn't.

She snapped her eyes open. Poor Cicely had died four years ago; if Ned were ever going to propose he would have done so by now. She'd faced that fact squarely when she'd turned twenty-six last month. It was time to move on. She wanted babies, and dreams of Ned wouldn't give her those.

She picked up the drawers. She'd dispose of this ridiculous reminder of—

"Ah, here you are, Ellie."

"Ack!" She jumped and spun around. Ned's mother, the Duchess of Love—or, more properly, the Duchess of Greycliffe—stood in the doorway, looking at her with warm brown eyes so like Ned's.

"Oh, dear, I'm sorry." Her grace's smile collapsed into a frown. "I didn't mean to startle you."

Ellie took a deep breath and hoped the duchess couldn't see her heart banging around in her chest. "You didn't s-startle me." If she looked calm, she'd be calm. She'd been practicing that trick ever since her red silk disgrace.

And what was there to be anxious about after all? The duchess's house parties were always pleasant.

Ha! They were torture.

"I was going to look for you later." Ellie tried to smile.

"Then I've saved you the trouble." The duchess had an impish gleam in her eye. "I thought we might have a comfortable coze before everyone else arrives."

Ellie's stomach clenched, and all her carefully cultivated calm evaporated. There was no such thing as a "comfortable coze" with the Duchess of Love. "That would be, ah"—deep breath—"lovely."

"Splendid! Come have a seat and I'll ring for tea." Her grace grasped the tasseled bell-pull and paused, her gaze dropping to Ellie's hands. "But what have you there?"

"W-what?" Ellie glanced down. Oh, blast. "Nothing." She dropped the embarrassing silk undergarment on the night table; it promptly slithered to the floor. Good, it would be less noticeable there. "I was unpacking when you came in."

The duchess frowned again. "Should I come back later then?"

"No, of course not." There was no point in putting this interview off. The sooner she knew the woman's plans, the sooner she could plan evasive—

She clenched her teeth. No, not this year.

"You're certain?"

"Yes." Ellie moved away from the incriminating red fabric.

"Excellent." Her grace tugged on the bell-pull and sat in the pink upholstered chair, her back to the puddle of silk. "I told Mrs. Dalton to have Cook send up some of her special macaroons. It will be a while until dinner, and we need to keep up our strength, don't we?"

"I'm afraid I'm not hungry." Ellie would almost rather dance on the castle's parapets naked—or wearing only those damn red drawers—than put anything in her mouth at the moment. She perched on a chair across from Ned's mother.

"Oh." The duchess's face fell.

"But, please, don't let me keep you from having something." It was a wonder the woman stayed so slim; she had a prodigious sweet tooth.

Her grace smiled hopefully. "Perhaps you'll feel hungrier when you see Cook's macaroons."

"Perhaps." And perhaps pigs would fly. Ellie cleared her throat. "You had something of a particular nature you wished to discuss, your grace?"

"Yes."

Damn.

No, *good*. Very good. Excellent.

The *ton* hadn't christened Ned's mother the Duchess of Love for nothing; she'd been matchmaking for as long as Ellie could remember, usually with great success. Ellie was one of her few failures, but this year would be different. This year Ellie was determined to cooperate.

"I was chatting with your mama the other day," the duchess was saying, her eyes rather too direct. "She's quite concerned about your future, you know."

Ellie shifted on her chair. Of course she knew—Mama never missed an opportunity to remind her that her future looked very bleak indeed. She'd been going on and on about it while Ellie packed, telling her how, if she allowed herself to dwindle into an old maid, she'd be forced to rely on the charity of her younger sisters, forever shuttled between their homes, always an aunt, never a mother.

Perhaps that's why she'd brought those damn drawers

instead of her shawl; she'd been so distracted, she could probably have packed the chamber pot and not noticed. "I believe Mama likes to worry."

The duchess laughed. "Well, that's what mothers do— worry—as I'm sure you'll learn yourself someday."

"Ah." Ellie swallowed.

Her grace leaned forward to touch her knee. "You do want to be a mother, don't you?"

Ellie swallowed again. "Y-yes." She wanted children so badly she was giving up her dream of Ned—her ridiculous, pointless, foolish dream. "Of course. Eventually."

The duchess gave her a pointed look. "My dear, you are twenty-six years old. Eventually is now."

Ellie pressed her lips together. Very true. Hadn't she just reached the same conclusion?

"And to be a mother, you must first be a wife." Her grace sat back. "To be a wife, you need to attach some gentleman's—some *eligible* gentleman's—regard. I believe you spent a little too much time with Ash last year. That will never do."

"I like Ash." The Marquis of Ashton, the duchess's oldest son, was intelligent and witty . . . and safe.

"Of course you like Ash, dear, but I must tell you more than one person remarked to me how often you were in his company."

Ellie narrowed her eyes. "What do you mean?"

"Only that you appeared to be ignoring all the other gentlemen."

She'd been trying so hard to ignore Ned—to hide how much she longed for him—that she hadn't noticed the other gentlemen. "Certainly you aren't insinuating . . . no one thought . . ." She shook her head. "Ash is married."

The duchess sighed. "Yes, he is, at least according to church and state."

"And according to his heart." Ellie met the duchess's gaze directly. "You mustn't think he encouraged any kind of impropriety. He still loves Jess; I'm sure they'll reconcile."

The duchess grunted. "I hope I live to see it. But in any event, I don't believe anyone truly thought there was something of a romantic nature between you—"

"I should hope not!"

"However people are so small-minded, you know, and they love to gossip, especially about Ash's awkward situation."

"I know." Ellie hated how the marriageable girls and their mamas clearly hoped Jess would magically vanish and thus cease to be an impediment to Ash's remarriage. Some had actually said they doubted Jess existed. "It makes me so angry."

Her grace waved Ellie's anger away. "Yes, well, Ash can take care of himself. What really matters is the fact you *were* ignoring the other gentlemen, Ellie. It quite discourages the poor dears."

Ellie snorted.

Her grace gave her a speaking look. "I assure you most men . . . well, I wouldn't call them timid, precisely, but they hate to be rejected. If you wish a gentleman to court you, you must give him some encouragement—a smile, a look, something to let him know you would welcome his attentions. You cannot be forever scowling and dodging."

"I don't scowl or dodge."

The duchess's brows rose. "No? What about Mr. Bridgeton last year? I was certain you two would be extremely compatible and made every effort to throw you together, but whenever I looked to see how things were progressing, you were chatting with Ash, and Mr. Bridgeton was crying on Miss Albert's shoulder."

Which one had been Mr. Bridgeton? The sandy-haired man with the receding chin or the tall, thin fellow with the enormous Adam's apple? "There was no one crying on anyone's shoulder."

"Figuratively speaking, of course." The duchess shrugged. "I confess Miss Albert was my other choice for him. I do usually have more than one match up my sleeve, you know, since I've found young people can be somewhat unpredictable." She smiled rather blandly. "They married last summer, by the by, and are expecting an interesting event this spring."

Ellie felt a momentary twinge of envy. Mr. Bridgeton— she was almost certain he was the sandy-haired one—had been pleasant. His only fault was he hadn't been Ned.

Well, whomever she ultimately married wouldn't be Ned, either. "Whom have you invited . . . I mean, have you invited any gentlemen that I might . . . er, men who might . . ." Oh, blast, her face felt as if it was as red as those damn silk drawers. "You know."

Her grace beamed at her. "Of course I've invited some gentlemen who might be suitable matches for you."

Ellie willed herself to keep smiling. It would get easier with time . . . it had to. She cleared her throat. Her mouth was infernally dry. "Who?"

The duchess leaned forward. "First, there's Mr. Humphrey. He's a little younger than you and very, ah . . . earnest. He's just inherited a small estate from his great aunt; rumor has it he wishes to start his nursery immediately."

"Ah." Mr. Humphrey sounded terribly dull . . . but dullness was fine. She wanted babies, not conversation. And he apparently wanted babies, too. Excellent.

"And then there's Mr. Cox. He's one of the Earl of Bollant's brood, the fourth—or perhaps the fifth—son. He's very popular with the ladies and a trifle wild, but he's shown some signs of being ready to settle down. He's to go into the church, so you could be very helpful to him, your papa being a vicar."

"I see." Taking charge of some silly sprig of the nobility was not especially appealing, but the man did have a number of brothers. With luck he would be equally skilled at procreating, though it would be nice to have a daughter or two as well.

The duchess was smiling at her, a rather expectant look on her face. Did she want her to pick one right now?

"I . . . er, they both sound very . . . pleasant, but . . ." *Remember, she wanted children.* "Well, I suppose I will have to meet them."

"Yes, indeed." The duchess glanced at the door. "Ah, here is Thomas with the tea tray."

One of the footmen came in, a large ginger cat, tail high in the air, strolling along behind him.

"Reggie!" Ned's mother bent to scratch her pet's ears. "Did you come for a treat?"

Reggie meowed and butted his head against her hand.

"Cook sent up Sir Reginald's dish, your grace," Thomas said, putting down the tray.

"Excellent. Please give Cook my thanks."

"Very good, your grace." Thomas bowed and retreated while the duchess poured Reggie a generous saucer of cream and put the dish on the floor.

Ellie kept one eye on the cat, lapping delicately, as she prepared the tea. Reggie looked harmless, but he'd caused quite a commotion last year, stealing feathers and other items from the ladies—and at least one of the gentlemen— and hiding them under Ned's bed. He'd even snatched the stuffed pheasant from Lady Perford's favorite hat. Lady Perford had not been pleased.

"Has Reggie given up his thieving ways, your grace?"

"I don't know, as he hasn't had another opportunity to misbehave." She snorted. "As you well know, Greycliffe hates having any of the *ton* underfoot and grumbles from the moment they arrive until the last one departs."

It was true the duke rarely looked happy during the Valentine house parties. "How does his grace bear your London balls?" Ellie asked, handing the duchess a cup of tea. She used to read the London gossip columns, but as she only ever saw Jack, the youngest of the Valentine brothers, mentioned, she no longer bothered.

"With as much patience as he can muster which is not very much, but since people expect dukes to be annoyingly haughty, it just adds to his consequence." Her eyes twinkled as she sipped her tea. "And it makes people toady him all the more which infuriates him further. No, once a month for four months a Season is the very limit of what he can tolerate. And a ball is only one evening. This . . ." She shook her head and sighed. "But it is my birthday as well as the boys', and he knows how important it is to me, so he grits his teeth and endures. You can imagine how much he's hoping Ned will remarry and Jack will wed soon so I have no more need to have these gatherings."

"Ah." Ellie forced a smile. "Yes." She knew the main point of the damn party was to find Ned—and Jack, of course—a suitable wife. "I can see that."

The duchess glanced down at Reggie who was now cleaning his paws. "Greycliffe is actually hoping Reggie pilfers things again. He thought it made the gathering much more interesting."

Interesting was one way to describe the screaming and tears Lady Perford had treated them to upon finding her mangled pheasant.

Ellie took a sustaining sip of tea. She might as well know everything now; it would make it easier to appear composed in company. "And whom have you invited for Jack"—she swallowed—"and N-Ned?"

Damn, her voice cracked. Perhaps the duchess hadn't noticed.

And perhaps Reggie would leap upon the tea table and sing an aria.

At least Ned's mother didn't comment beyond a raised eyebrow. "I'd originally had Miss Prudence Merriweather in mind for Jack," she said, "however the girl eloped with Mr. Bamford three weeks ago. Quite a shock to everyone, but of course I must take it as a blessing. She clearly would not have done for Jack if she was in love with another man."

Her grace sent her a significant, if obscure, look. Ellie took another sip of tea.

"I had to scramble a bit," her grace continued somewhat dryly, "but I found Miss Isabelle Wharton to take her place. I've never actually met the girl, you understand, but my friend Lady Altman says she is quite striking. I imagine Jack would appreciate a lovely bride." She shrugged slightly. "And if the match comes to nothing, well, Jack is only your age. He has plenty of time."

"Yes." Twenty-six was young for a man; it was firmly on the shelf for a woman.

"And as for Ned"—her grace shot Ellie another indecipherable look—"I invited Lady Juliet Ramsbottom, the Duke of Extley's youngest daughter, with him in mind."

A vise clamped around Ellie's heart. Stupid. A duke's daughter was an excellent choice for a duke's son. She nodded and took a larger swallow of tea. If only there was some brandy at hand to flavor it.

"Frankly, I hope to see you and Ned married this summer."

Ellie choked—and made the unpleasant discovery that it was possible to snort tea out one's nose.

"Oh, dear." The duchess leapt up and slapped her on the back. "Are you all right?"

Ellie, gasping, fished her handkerchief out of her pocket

and waved her hand, trying to get the duchess to stop pounding on her. She would be fine if she could just catch her breath.

Of course Ned's mother hadn't meant she hoped to see Ellie married *to* Ned, only that she hoped both their nuptials would happen this summer.

The duchess pounded harder.

"Please," Ellie gasped, "don't—"

Through watery eyes, she watched Reggie abandon his ablutions and head toward . . .

"Ah, ah, ah."

"What are you trying to say, dear?" The duchess paused in her pummeling. If she happened to glance in the direction Ellie's horrified eyes were staring, she'd see Reggie sniffing a pair of red silk drawers.

Ellie sprang to her feet. Panic miraculously cleared her throat. "I'm fine," she croaked. "Wonderful. Fit as a fiddle." She glanced over her shoulder. Now Reggie was batting at the drawers with one paw.

She shifted her position to block the duchess's view.

"I shouldn't tease you, I know," her grace said. Her eyes dimmed and she sighed, shoulders drooping. She suddenly looked every one of her fifty years. "I've certainly learned harping on a subject doesn't get results. If it did, my boys would all be happily married."

"I'm sure they will be, your grace." Ellie impulsively laid her hand on the duchess's arm. She hated to see her so blue-deviled. "Just give them time."

"Time." The duchess bit her lip as if she'd like to say more on that head. She let out a short, sharp breath and shrugged, smiling a little. "It's only . . . well, I'm so happy with the duke. Is it wrong to want that happiness for my sons?"

"Of course not, your grace, but your situation *is* rather extraordinary." The duke and duchess had fallen in love at first sight when they were both very young. Even more unusual, they'd been happily married for over thirty years and, by all accounts, completely faithful to each other. There was probably not another couple like them in all the English nobility.

Ellie glanced at Reggie again. Damn it. Now the drawers were over his head. If he got caught in them . . .

"I know," her grace said. "When I look around the *ton*, I see so many unpleasant unions." She shook her head. "Well, just consider Ash and Jess. They've been separated for eight years now."

Ellie wrenched her gaze away from Reggie's activities. "I'm certain they will reconcile eventually."

"But when?" The duchess's voice was tight with frustration. "Ash will be the duke; the duchy needs an heir, and neither he nor Jess is getting any younger." She frowned. "And I want a grandchild or two before I'm completely in my dotage."

Damnation. Reggie was now coming their way, the silk drawers in his mouth. Ellie took the duchess's arm and started to walk toward the door with her.

"Ash—and Ned and Jack—can manage their own lives, your grace. You must know you've raised them well."

The duchess sighed. "And there's nothing I can do about it anyway, is there?" She paused and glanced around. "Where has Reggie got to?"

"Likely he finished his cream and left," Ellie said. The blasted cat had just passed behind the duchess's skirts and out the door. Where the hell was he going? Certainly not . . . last year he had . . . but he wouldn't this year, would he? "Has Ned"—Ellie caught herself—"and Jack arrived yet?"

"Oh, no. I don't expect them for a while."

Ellie almost collapsed with relief. If Reggie was taking her undergarment to Ned's room, she'd have time to get it back before anyone—especially Ned—found it. "I hope they reach the castle before the storm. Mrs. Dalton was just saying her rheumatism is acting up."

"Oh, dear. Mrs. Dalton's rheumatism never lies." The duchess stopped on the threshold and smiled, her good spirits returning. "Just think! You young people can go on sleigh rides."

"I'm hardly young." At the moment she just wanted to chase down one misbehaving cat.

"Oh, don't be such a wet rag; you'll freeze stiff in this weather." The duchess laughed. "You can make snow angels, and I'm sure the men will get into a snowball battle."

"Everyone will be cold and wet." Ellie did not want to play in the snow. Such activities were for children.

"And there are ever so many games and things we can do inside." Her grace clapped her hands. "You know, I have the greatest hope this will be a wonderful party."

"Er, yes." Just wonderful, though perhaps snow would be better than rain or general February dreariness.

The duchess patted her arm. "And I have great hopes for you as well, dear." She stepped into the corridor. "I'll expect you downstairs in the blue drawing room before dinner. Don't be late."

"I won't."

Ellie watched the duchess walk down the passage—and the moment she turned the corner, she bolted for Ned's room.

Chapter 2

A little dissembling is a good thing.
—Venus's Love Notes

Damn, he was tired, and the blasted house party hadn't even started. Lord Edward Valentine dropped his portmanteau in the entry to Greycliffe Castle and removed his hat.

"Did you have a pleasant trip, my lord?" Dalton, the butler, asked as he shut the front door.

"Tolerable. It looks like snow." And he was getting a headache. He unwound his muffler.

"That's what Mrs. Dalton said this morning, my lord, when she woke with her rheumatism bothering her something fierce. Mark my words, she says, we are going to have a storm. I just hope all the guests arrive before the roads get bad."

"Er, yes. I do hope Mrs. Dalton is feeling more the thing." Ned pulled off his gloves. He'd be delighted if a blizzard kept everyone away.

Why Mama needed to turn their birthday into such a

bloody event was beyond him. Wasn't it enough of a curse that the Valentines had all been born on Valentine's Day? And while Mama couldn't do much about her given name—her papa, a man of the cloth, no less, had saddled her with Venus—she didn't have to embrace the *ton*'s ridiculous nickname for her. But no, the Duchess of Love she was, hostess of monthly Love Balls during the Season and author of a damn scandal sheet, *Venus's Love Notes*. The family was a blasted joke, dredged up whenever things got dull in the gentlemen's clubs.

There was a reason he rarely went to Town.

"Oh, never fear, my lord," Dalton said in a disgustingly cheerful tone. "A twinge of rheumatism and a threat of snow aren't enough to keep my Mrs. Dalton down. No, indeed. She was up with the larks, bustling about and seeing that all is in readiness."

Damn it all, Ned's head was beginning to pound in earnest. He'd go upstairs directly and take some of the powders his man, Breen, had packed before he'd rushed off to attend his ailing mother in Bath.

"Ned!"

Oh, God, speaking of mothers . . . He looked up to see his mama at the top of the stairs, her smile almost blinding. She would want to talk. He did not feel like chatting when he had a headache coming on. "Hallo, Mama."

She hurried down the steps and threw her arms around him so enthusiastically he was forced to take a step back to save his balance. "Ned! I'm so glad you got here safely."

He returned her hug, not that he had any choice. Did she have to be so blasted demonstrative? "Of course I got here safely. Linden Hall is not so far away."

"No, but I am sure it is going to snow, and the roads will be treacherous." She studied his face. "It is so good to see you."

"You just saw me at Twelfth Night." He shrugged out of

his coat and handed it to Dalton. "Less than a month ago. I've not changed."

She continued to examine him, a small frown forming between her brows. He forced himself not to look away. Was she searching for the boy he'd been? She must know that part of him had died with Cicely.

"You need to smile more," she said at last, linking her arm through his.

He grunted. He'd nothing to smile about.

"Will you have one of the footmen bring Lord Edward's things up to his room, Mr. Dalton?" Mama asked.

"Of course, your grace."

"Mama . . ." Ned stopped Dalton with a look. He'd prefer to take his things up himself.

"I'd offer you tea"—Mama started to lead him away from the entry—"but I'm sure you'd rather have brandy."

"Mama . . ." The ache had spread across his forehead. Brandy was not what he needed at the moment.

"Your father's out visiting tenants—some problem with a drainage ditch, I believe. Ash would have gone, but Greycliffe insisted he needed to attend to the matter himself." Mama snorted. "He wanted to avoid the guests as long as possible, of course. They should be arriving shortly, especially if the weather is turning bad. The only person here so far is Ellie Bowman, though being a neighbor and almost family, she hardly counts." Mama smiled broadly as if something amused her. "Ash is hiding in his study."

"Mama." Ned dug in his heels. "Thank you, but I wish to go up to my room now."

She stopped and looked at him again. Her expression of mild annoyance turned quickly to concern. "Oh, you have one of your headaches, don't you?"

Zeus, he hated to be fussed over. "I'm sure I'll be better shortly." He held out his hand for his portmanteau, and

Dalton gave it to him. The butler had better sense than to argue with him.

Mama patted his arm. "Then you must go to your room to rest"—did a vaguely cunning look flit over her features?—"immediately."

Devil take it, what plot did she have afoot now?

"If Sir Reginald's there," Mama said, almost pushing him toward the stairs, "just shoo him out."

"Reggie? Why would he—oh, don't tell me he's up to his old tricks again. But you said the guests hadn't arrived yet." Ned frowned. "Has he started taking things from the servants?"

Mama shrugged. "I have no idea what Reggie's about. He may not even be in your room, though you *are* his favorite. I just thought I saw him—from the corner of my eye, you understand—head in that direction when I was upstairs a moment ago. Now go on." She made a little motion with her hands as if she were shooing him.

Wonderful. He was loved by a thieving cat. "If I find any purloined items, I'll bring them to you. And from now on I intend to keep my door firmly closed."

"You know that won't keep Sir Reginald out."

That was unfortunately all too true. Closed doors, closed drawers, closed cabinets—if Reggie wanted something, he was going to get it. "I think the servants help him."

"Oh, ye of little faith." Mama patted his arm again. "Go rest and we'll see you in the blue drawing room before dinner. If you feel better sooner, I'm sure Ash would welcome you in his study."

"When does Jack get in?"

"Who knows?" Mama sighed. "Jack will come when he feels like it, though I do hope he arrives before the snow."

"I'm sure he will. Jack may be careless, but he's not stupid." He hoped.

Ned started up the stairs. He could hardly wait to get to the solitude of his room. If only he could spend the entire house party there . . .

But he couldn't. He'd vowed this year not to let anger and pain rule him any longer. Cicely and the baby had been gone four years. It was time to cooperate with Mama and find a new wife.

He paused on the steps, waiting for the familiar sense of loss to steal his breath.

It didn't.

Damn. He gripped the banister more tightly and squeezed his eyes shut. His head throbbed. He was losing even the memory of Cicely. Some days he actually had to look at the miniature of her he kept in his pocket to recall her features. Even that terrible moment when her life had drained from her face, their son wax-colored on the bed next to her, strangled by the umbilical cord, had lost its clarity.

What the hell was the matter with him?

His head jerked up. And how in blazes could he forget Mama had eyes and ears everywhere? He glanced over his shoulder. She was no longer in the entry hall, thank God, and Dalton was gone as well. There were no servants in sight. He was safe for the moment.

He started back up the steps. Perhaps he should be thankful his memories were dimming. Life went on, so he must, too. He still needed an heir—ergo, he needed a wife. It was simple logic, a procreative fact. Love wasn't a required part of the equation.

He'd been lucky to have found love once. Many men—especially men of the *ton*—never found it.

He blew out a long breath. So this year he'd marry one of the women Mama had invited for him. She was the damn Duchess of Love after all; she'd been making matches for years, even back before she'd married Father, if Aunt

Aphrodite was to be believed. One of the females at this gathering must be tolerable.

And once he had a wife, if he put his mind—and another organ—to it, he could have an heir on the way before year's end.

He reached the top of the staircase and turned toward his room, rubbing his forehead. This was going to be a crushing headache. It must be the change in the weather—and riding for hours in the bitter cold hadn't helped.

Damn it, now his stomach was churning as well; he'd be lucky if he could eat anything at dinner. He pressed harder against his forehead. He'd take the bloody powders and lay down for a while; perhaps if he did, he'd stave off the worst of the nausea.

God, he hated feeling like an invalid, but—

"Come here, you spawn of Satan."

He stopped dead in the corridor. What the hell? That had come from his rooms. A woman's voice with diction too educated to be a maid's . . . but Mama had said none of the guests had yet arrived. Who could this be—and what the blazes was she doing in his chambers?

No matter, he would send her on her way immediately. Sooner than immediately, if he could.

He lengthened his stride. He was almost at the doorway when he heard an ominous thud as if something heavy had hit the floor, followed by a muttered curse and the hiss of an angry cat.

At least now he knew what had caused her to trespass. Reggie. Perhaps the blasted animal was stealing plumes again. Well, his intruder could take Sir Reginald and whatever plunder he'd accumulated with her when she departed, which would be in about three seconds.

He stepped through the open door. The noise was coming from his bedchamber. He crossed the sitting room, drawing breath to tell the woman in no uncertain terms to leave at once.

He paused on the bedroom's threshold, his jaw dropping. A female posterior, draped in gray poplin, waggled at him from the near side of his bed. A very attractive posterior—not large, but not too small, and nicely rounded.

His headache abated. Apparently lust was almost as effective a medicine as Breen's powders.

"Give me that, Reggie." The woman's words were slightly muffled by his mattress. There appeared to be quite a battle being waged underneath his bed.

Reggie hissed and must have dodged her.

"Oh, no, you don't." She twisted, backing up. Her skirt, caught under her knees, drew tight, outlining her lovely arse in even more detail.

She had a very, very attractive bottom.

His headache was completely gone.

He should say something. It wasn't proper to be observing her when she thought she was alone. He should—

"Oh, damn it." She jerked on her skirt, freeing it and exposing two elegant ankles and a pair of very shapely calves.

Hell, his head wasn't the part of his anatomy aching now.

"Aha! I've got you." She lunged under his bed, almost disappearing entirely. "Ouch!"

Reggie shot out the other side, scrambled up the bedstead, and ran across the coverlet. He had something red in his mouth.

"Reggie!" the woman shouted. "I'm going to skin you alive."

Reggie seemed not the least bit concerned. He caught sight of Ned and trotted over to drop his prize at Ned's feet.

"What have we here?" Ned stooped to pick it up. Red, silk—he shook the fabric out—*drawers*?

"Aaiieee!"

His head shot up as Reggie wisely darted out of the room. A woman—Good God, it was Ellie Bowman!—rushed at him, her eyes on the red cloth in his hands. Her brown hair, normally restrained primly under a lace cap, had escaped its pins and curled wildly around her face and over her shoulders. Her cheeks were flushed and her eyes gleamed with . . . panic?

He stood quickly. Did she intend to tackle him?

She almost did. She tripped over a book—likely the thing he'd heard hit the floor when he was in the corridor— and fell heavily against him. He grabbed her around the waist as her momentum carried them backward.

"Oof!" He came up hard against the wall, Ellie plastered to his front. She was not a featherweight.

Hmm. No, she wasn't. She was soft and round in all the right places. And she smelled fresh and clean and lemony. Her hair tickled his chin, brushed over his hands.

A wisp of desire curled in his gut, and his cock reacted with enthusiasm. He tangled his fingers in her curls, bent his head . . .

Bloody hell, was he mad?

He snapped his head back. This was *Ellie.* Cicely's friend. His friend. He couldn't . . . she wouldn't . . .

He tried to jerk his hips back, but they were trapped against the wall. At least horror was causing his male organ to return to more appropriate proportions. "Are"—he cleared his throat—"are you all right?"

She blinked at him, her eyes oddly unfocused. Her lips curved up in a damn siren's smile, and his idiot cock stirred with interest again.

"Yes. I, ah . . ." Her eyes flew wide, as if she'd suddenly realized she was pasted on him like wallpaper, and she lurched backward. Her voice turned harsh, almost accusatory. "Your mother said you weren't here yet."

He frowned. What was she blaming him for? She was the one in his bedroom—with the red silk drawers he was still holding.

He rubbed the smooth cloth between his thumb and forefinger. Were they hers? Did she have a pair on now? His eyes dropped to consider her—

He jerked his gaze back to her face. "I just arrived."

"Oh." She pushed her hair off her forehead. "Of course." She smiled her normal, placid smile and somehow rearranged her expression so she looked like her calm drawing-room self. "Did you have a pleasant trip?"

This was the same conversation he'd had with Dalton.

He shrugged. "It was cold, but bearable." Truthfully, the raw weather had matched his mood, though now he was feeling distinctly warmer—inappropriately so, given the current location and company, but perhaps not a bad thing if he were indeed determined to carry through with his matrimonial resolution.

The drawers probably weren't Ellie's—though whose could they be? Mama's?

Oh, God, no! How had that thought crept into his brain-box? He'd have to dunk his head in ice water to freeze the notion out.

"Mrs. Dalton thinks it will snow," Ellie was saying, "and her joints are very accurate."

Yes, far better to think of Mrs. Dalton's rheumatism than Mama's—than anything else. "That's what Dalton said."

Ellie nodded. "We can quite plan our day by her aches." She pushed her hair back again, and her composed expression wavered slightly. "I seem to have lost my cap and pins."

He grinned, remembering the scene that had greeted him. "They are probably under my bed."

"Ah." She turned bright red. "Perhaps they are."

He shouldn't tease her, but he couldn't resist. "Do you want me to help you look for them?"

"No!" She swallowed. "Thank you, but that won't be necessary. I have others. You can return them—well, the cap—to me later perhaps."

She was rather attractively mussed, really, more like she'd been as a girl when she and Cicely used to tag along after Percy and Jess and Ash and Jack and him. Cicely had been the quiet, cautious one, very feminine even then, but Ellie had climbed trees and caught fish and tried to do everything Jess and the boys did. More often than not she'd go home with her skirts torn and her hair hanging down her back.

"Here, you have a smut on your face." He reached to rub the spot on her forehead, but she dodged his fingers.

"I imagine I've collected more than one. The space under your b-bed"—she flushed—"is sadly dusty." She picked up the fallen book and put it back on the table; then she started to edge around him. "I'll just go back to my room and put myself to rights."

"Very well. I'll see you downstairs later?"

"Yes, of course. In the blue drawing room before dinner. I imagine everyone will have arrived by then."

Damn. Whom had Mama invited for him? He—

No, he would try to like at least one of Mama's choices. He'd decided. He clenched his hands.

He was still holding the red silk drawers, and Ellie was on the verge of escaping. "Ellie?"

She paused, her weight on the balls of her feet, leaning toward the corridor and freedom. Clearly she wanted to be elsewhere. "Yes?" Even the tone of her voice, short and tight, said she wanted to leave.

Wasn't she at all happy to see him?

He was being ridiculous now, like Mama. He'd seen Ellie at Twelfth Night, though now that he thought of it, he'd hardly spoken to her. She seemed to prefer Ash's company.

She hadn't always. When she was a girl, she'd shadowed him—at least that's what Ash and Jack always said. And she'd been such a good friend to him after Cicely and the baby died. God, he didn't know what he would have done without her calm compassion. But for the past year or two, they'd hardly spoken.

"Did you have a question, Lord Edward?"

He hated it when she called him that. He held up the red silk. "Are these yours?"

"Hiding from Mama and her guests?" Jack asked as Ned stepped into Ash's study. Jack was sprawled in one of the big leather chairs, his leg thrown over its arm, a brandy glass clasped loosely in his fingers. A sling made of cloth to match his waistcoat was abandoned on his chest.

"No more than you are. When did you get in?"

"Just after you, apparently."

Ned frowned as he closed the door behind him. "At least you beat the snow—and shouldn't you be wearing that sling?" It was just like Jack to be so careless.

Jack rolled his eyes. "No, Lord Worry. The sawbones said I was good as new."

"Don't call me that." Jack had teased him with the dratted nickname since they were boys. "Your collarbone can't be healed yet—you broke it just a fortnight ago, didn't you, racing your damn curricle on the ice?"

"Ah, but it turns out it wasn't broken," Ash said from his seat behind his desk, its surface littered with sketches as always. He reached for the decanter. "Brandy?"

"Thanks." Ned's stomach was starting to twist again. He'd taken Breen's powders and lain down, but it hadn't helped. He'd kept thinking about Ellie and those red silk drawers.

Ellie was so . . . well, *ordinary*. Not in a bad way, of course. She was solid and respectable—not at all the kind of woman to wear red silk drawers.

Except apparently she was.

The thought was damn unsettling. Every time he'd closed his eyes, he'd pictured her with that red garment. Not wearing it, of course—that was beyond his imagination. Just holding it. But still, he hadn't been able to get the notion out of his head. It was like seeing a hedgehog with a waistcoat—preposterous.

Perhaps a little distilled medicine would settle his nerves. He glanced at the sketches on Ash's desk as he took the proffered glass. "What's this? Are you planning to build a castle?"

Ash swept the drawings into a pile. "No, I was just keeping busy, waiting for Mama to drag me out to play host, though I'm fervently hoping Father returns in time to do the honors."

"I think you should build the thing," Jack said. "It would make a splendid folly"—he shot Ash a look and then returned to contemplating his brandy—"or playhouse. Remember when we used to pretend to be King Arthur and the Knights of the Roundtable? This would make a perfect Camelot. You should put it on the island in the lake at Blackweith."

Damn. Blackweith was the estate where Jess lived. Was Jack trying to stir up a hornet's nest?

Apparently.

"And speaking of Blackweith," Jack said, "how's Jess doing?"

"Well," Ash said, his face as impenetrable as the fortress he'd drawn, "according to Walker."

Ah, so Ash and his wife were still communicating only

through the estate manager. Ned wasn't surprised. As far as he knew, Ash hadn't spoken one word to Jess since he'd left Blackweith on their wedding night.

"You'll have to do something about her soon, you know," Jack said.

"Jack!" Ned scowled at his younger brother.

Jack shrugged. "It's true. Neither of you is ever in London, so you don't get all the questions—and those are from the more polite members of the *ton*. The rest just whisper among themselves, coming up with the most outrageous tales they can imagine—and they have very lurid imaginations."

"Bloody hell," Ash muttered, his jaw flexing.

Jack's gaze held Ash's. "Your odd marital arrangement has been the topic of gossip for years, Ash, but with you turning thirty, it's literally taken over the betting books. Best odds are you'll start some sort of formal separation proceedings in the next few months, but wagers are evenly split as to whether you'll seek an annulment or a divorce. The supposed grounds run the gamut from insanity to adultery to impotence and, er, worse."

Ash's face had turned red during Jack's speech. He looked very much like he wanted to hit someone. "Damn it all, my marriage is no one's business but mine and Jess's."

Ned hated to pile on, but Jack was right. Ash had to face facts. "You *are* the heir to a dukedom."

Jack nodded. "People are curious, especially since no one has seen you or Jess in Town for ages. And of course all the idiots that come to this annual festivity are quick to report there's never any sign of your wife." He jiggled his foot. "A number of ambitious London mamas have dared be so bold as to ask me if Jess died and no one thought to announce the fact." He shook his head. "Frankly, I'm surprised Mama and Father haven't been more . . . emphatic about the situation."

Ash ran his hands through his hair. "Mama bites her tongue most of the time, though she's taken to throwing me more of those sad, worried looks of hers. Father, however, is becoming more and more pointed in his comments. It's not been pleasant here of late." Ash let out a long breath. "And if what you say is true . . ." He rubbed his face, suddenly looking years older. "You're both right. It's time to resolve the situation. Once this blasted party is over, I'll go to Blackweith."

"If there's anything I can do to help," Ned said, "you need only say the word."

Jack nodded. "You can count on me as well, I hope you know."

"Yes, thank you, but there's nothing anyone else can do."

It was on the tip of Ned's tongue to ask what exactly the problem was, but he swallowed the question—as, he was happy to see, did Jack. It was none of their business, after all. If Ash wanted them to know, he would tell them.

"Hell, I need more brandy," Ash said, filling his glass. "Anyone else?"

They passed around the bottle. Getting drunk before meeting Mama's guests would not be a good plan, but one more glass would only make Ned more . . . relaxed. He took a long swallow and then gestured at Jack. "So if your collarbone isn't broken, why bother with the sling?"

"It saves me from having to caper around ballrooms with feather-headed chits." Jack grimaced. "I expect to make good use of it this visit. Mama's invited Miss Isabelle Wharton."

Ned raised his brows. "Should I know the name?"

"Jack tells me she's notorious in Town," Ash said, sounding much relieved to no longer be the conversation's focus.

"At least among the men," Jack said. "She is twenty-four and desperate. Her two younger sisters have already preceded her to the altar. I've been dodging her for months, and now Mama brings her here." He dropped his head back to stare up at the ceiling. "I'm doomed."

Jack had always been somewhat dramatic.

Ned took another swallow of brandy and steeled his nerves. "And who has Mama invited for me, do you know?"

Jack turned his head to look at him and then looked back at the ceiling. "Ask Ash."

Ned glanced at Ash; he was staring into his brandy as if he'd never seen the amber liquid before.

"That bad, eh?"

Ash coughed and looked at Jack. Neither said a word.

"Come on, out with it."

Ash cleared his throat. "I believe Mama has Lady Juliet Ramsbottom in mind for you."

"Yes?" Ned waited; more silence. His stomach, which the brandy had pleasantly warmed, knotted again. "I am as unacquainted with Lady Juliet as I am with Miss Wharton. Is she dreadful, too?"

"I wouldn't say that." Jack took a sip of his brandy. "I've heard a rumor or two that she has a temper, but she's always very well mannered—almost meek—at society events."

"And . . . ?" He'd decided to keep an open mind about Mama's choice this year, but if Jack and Ash had reservations . . . "Is she walleyed or hunchbacked? Brainless or brash? Does she look like—"

"She looks like Cicely," Jack said, his voice flat.

"Ah." Oh, God. Ned's stomach heaved, but he clenched his teeth and ignored it. "What was Mama thinking?"

"I'm sure she wasn't thinking to replace Cicely," Ash said quickly. "We all know no one can do that."

"Mama probably only thought—if she thought about it at all—that Lady Juliet was the sort of female you fancied," Jack said. "You know—small and, er, doll-like."

Cicely had been a little like a porcelain doll, hadn't she?

No, how could he think that? Cicely had been perfect—though he was determined his next wife would be more robust, larger, better able to survive childbirth.

The hopelessness he always felt at this party descended on him like a thick fog. Even the snap of the logs in the fireplace suddenly sounded glum. And he'd thought this year would be different. "Oh, damn."

"Exactly," Jack said.

Ash passed the brandy decanter again, and they all filled their glasses.

"Mama must be slipping," Ash said. "Dare we hope the Duchess of Love will retire?"

"No bloody chance of that," Jack said. "Invitations to her monthly balls are as coveted as—perhaps more coveted than—vouchers to Almack's. The food is better and Mama serves spirits." He rolled his eyes. "And from what I hear, her infernal *Love Notes* are as popular as ever."

"Good Lord," Ned said. "Have you ever seen a copy?"

Jack looked at him as though he'd just stepped out of Bedlam. "What do you take me for? I'd rather gouge my eyes out with my own thumbs. My friends know they risk meeting me at dawn if they show me even a corner of one page or quote a single word from its contents."

"And they abide by your wishes?" Ash asked.

Jack raised his brows. "I'm accounted an excellent shot. They dare not put it to the test."

"I wish there was as effective a way to persuade Mama to stop writing the thing," Ned said. "And I especially wish she'd quit having this bloody house party."

"Amen!" Ash lifted his glass and they all drank.

Jack slid deeper into his chair. "Just promise me you won't leave me alone with Miss Wharton." He shuddered.

"If I let my guard down for an instant, she'll wrestle me into the most compromising position she can devise."

"Of course," Ned said, "not that I think you'll need our assistance."

Jack closed his eyes. An unfamiliar tightness marred his features. "I wish I were so confident. Miss Wharton is bloody persistent."

"You know, I'm sure Ellie would help," Ash said. "Being female, she can keep a closer eye on Miss Wharton than we can."

Jack sat up, a relieved smile dispelling his uncharacteristic grimness. "Yes, that's it. Ellie's a good sport—I wager she will help." He shot Ned an oddly bland look. "Assuming Mama . . . or someone else . . . doesn't need her."

What the hell was Jack hinting at? He should ask, but he felt oddly hesitant to hear the answer. Planting his fist in Jack's face would be much more satisfying.

Ned kept his hands to himself. "I think I'll go get ready for dinner."

Chapter 3

The meek may inherit the earth, but they don't marry well.

—Venus's Love Notes

Ellie stood in the shadows at one side of the blue drawing room. Her old evening dress was almost the exact shade as the draperies; if she was very, very still, perhaps no one would notice her.

She'd managed to slip into the room behind Miss Isabelle Wharton without attracting a single glance, though that was not so surprising. Miss Wharton was very striking, as the duchess's friend had said, but in a startling rather than beautiful way. The woman was Ellie's height and quite plump, with a mass of bouncing blond ringlets and a green dress so bedecked with bows and ribbons and furbelows that she closely resembled a large, mobile bush. She rustled through the room directly up to Jack where he stood by the fireplace with Ned, Ash, and a small, colorless woman Ellie had not yet met.

Jack was watching Miss Wharton approach as if she harbored a poisonous vine liable to twine its deadly growth around his neck. If he backed up one more step, his coattails would catch fire from the blaze on the hearth.

Ellie was too far away to hear what Miss Wharton said as she reached the group, but whatever Jack replied caused her to laugh. The three men cringed. She did sound remarkably like a drunken donkey, not that Ellie had ever actually heard such an inebriated animal.

Poor Jack. She should go over and join them. She could—

Oh, no, she couldn't. She couldn't go anywhere near Ned now that he knew the red silk drawers were hers.

Dear God, how was she ever going to survive this party?

She wasn't. Yes, she wanted a husband, but perhaps it would be wiser to feign the headache—or the ague or something—and retreat to the vicarage. There was always next year. Twenty-seven wasn't so very much older than twenty-six.

Oh, *why* hadn't she lied and said the dratted drawers weren't hers?

Because she was a terrible liar, that's why. She always blushed and gulped and stuttered. Ned wouldn't have been fooled for an instant. And whose could they be if not hers? None of the other guests had arrived when Ned found her in his room.

What must he think of her?

She closed her eyes in mortification, but that didn't help. Ned's image was burned into the back of her lids—his long legs, narrow hips, broad chest. The lock of chestnut hair that fell over his brow no matter what he did. His warm, brown eyes with their ridiculously long lashes—opening wide with shock as he stared down at her red silk drawers spilling over his fingers.

"Ohh."

She slapped her hand over her mouth and glanced around. Thank God it seemed no one had heard her. She looked over at the group by the fire. Fortunately Ned had his back to her . . . his strong back with his wide shoulders . . .

When she'd tripped over that stupid book and fallen into him, his arms had gone round her like two iron bands, pressing her against him from bosom to hips. There hadn't been an inch of space between them.

She shivered, and an odd thrill twisted in her stomach—or, rather, somewhat lower than her stomach. Her cheeks burned.

She'd never been embraced by a man like that. She snorted. She'd never been embraced by a man at all. She hadn't wished to be. Ned was the only man she'd ever wanted to touch her.

Well, that would have to change.

Damn Reggie. He'd best not cross her path any time soon or she *would* skin him and use his fur for a muff. At least she wouldn't have to worry about the blasted drawers making another embarrassing appearance. She'd stuffed them into the back of her clothes press and shut the door tight. As soon as she got home to the vicarage, she'd snip them into tiny little pieces and throw them down the privy hole.

"Ah, there you are."

"Eek!" Ellie jumped and jerked her head to the left—the duchess was standing not two feet from her. "Oh, you startled me, your grace."

"That's quite apparent. What are you doing over here—trying to hide in the curtains?"

"Ah." That's exactly what she'd been trying to do, as Ned's mother must know, but Ellie would never admit it. "Er, no, I was just . . ." What? Best change the subject. "Have the guests all arrived safely?"

"Yes, thank heavens. Lady Juliet was the last." The duchess shook her head, sending the purple plume in her hair dancing—she'd better be sure to keep her feather away from Reggie. "I swear the snow was coming down horizontally when she struggled into the castle."

"I must agree with her grace—"

Ellie just then noticed there was a man standing at the duchess's side—a small, mole-like fellow with tiny, watery eyes, thick spectacles, an enormous nose, slightly buck teeth, and no chin.

"—as I was out in it and I will tell you the weather is positively dreadful, perhaps the worst weather I've ever been in and I've been in a lot of weather. I hope it's not unmanly of me to admit that it gave me quite the scare. My horses slipped and slid the whole way from London so I was certain my coachman, who is exceedingly skilled with the ribbons or I would never keep him on, would end us in a ditch, but thankfully he didn't. Still just walking to the castle door soaked me through, my greatcoat was no protection, don't you know. So it will be a wonder if I don't catch my death."

Ellie blinked. She'd swear the man hadn't taken but a breath or two during his entire speech.

The duchess laughed. "I hope you remain among the living, Mr. Humphrey." She threw up her hands in mock distress. "And where have my manners gone, you may ask? I've completely neglected the introductions, which was my point in coming over. Ellie, this is Mr. Lionel Humphrey; Mr. Humphrey, Miss Eleanor Bowman, whom I must say I quite look upon as a daughter."

The mole bowed. "So pleased to make your acquaintance, Miss Bowman; her grace has told me such wonderful things about you, I almost feel as if I know you, but of course I don't, so I'm anxious to spend some time conversing with you, if I may."

"Ah." Was it possible to drown in a flood of words? "Yes. Of course. It's, ah, a pleasure to meet you, too, sir." She swiveled her eyes to Ned's mother; the duchess smiled blandly, inclining her head toward the mole as if to say, go on, take advantage of this opportunity.

Ellie bit her lip. *This* was one of the men the duchess thought might be a good match for her?

Something odd twisted in her stomach, but it wasn't at all the same feeling she'd had when she'd been thinking of Ned. This sensation was more akin to revulsion.

She gave herself a mental shake. She had no time to be picky. She was twenty-six years old. Anything in breeches must be appealing. If her goal was to be a mother, the only qualification a gentleman need have was a working male organ.

Her stomach knotted at the thought of allowing Mr. Humphrey close enough to employ that organ. If only she'd encouraged Mr. Bridgeton last year . . .

There was absolutely no point in entertaining such thoughts. Mr. Bridgeton was no longer available; Mr. Humphrey was, and he was here before her. She would try to look beyond his rather unappealing façade. He might have a heart of gold, after all. Certainly someone must find him worthy of their regard. His friends. His mother . . .

"You two get to know each other." The duchess beamed at them. "I'm afraid I must go—I see my dear Greycliffe has finally consented to join us."

The duke was indeed standing in the doorway, scowling.

Ellie resisted the urge to grab the duchess's sleeve. "Then you'd best catch him before he decides to take a tray in his room."

The duchess laughed. "You know him too well, my dear."

She did. She knew and liked both Ned's parents and his brothers—

She could not let her thoughts travel that direction.

The mole—no, *Mr. Humphrey*—was bowing. "Do not tarry a moment longer, your grace; you can leave Miss Bowman safely in my charge. I will take the greatest care of her."

Ellie bit back a spurt of exasperation and willed her eyes not to roll. What in the world did Mr. Humphrey imagine could happen to her in the duke's drawing room? She should tell him exactly—

No, no, she should not. She swallowed and forced herself to smile. She wanted a baby, so she needed a husband. She must try to like this mol—this *unmarried*, *available* man.

"Have you been to Greycliffe Castle before, Mr. Humphrey?" she asked as her grace went off to greet the duke. A stupid question. If he'd ever been here, she'd know it. No one visited the castle without the news flying through the village, and since the duke did not like to entertain, there weren't that many guests to gossip about.

Mr. Humphrey's nose twitched. "No, but I must say it is very impressive. The house, the grounds—well, I wish I could see the grounds, but with the snow and wind it is quite impossible; still I am sure they must be very pleasant in better weather."

He leaned forward a little which put his nose on level with her bodice—fortunately all her dresses had very high necks—and raised his eyebrows significantly. "I don't know if her grace mentioned it, but I've just come into a substantial inheritance. My poor old great aunt went aloft a few months ago, and, being without children of her own, left the whole to me. A tidy property in Devon—nothing as grandiose as Greycliffe Castle, of course, but quite snug and rather beautiful if I say so myself." He cleared his throat and waggled his eyebrows. "I'm on the lookout for a wife, don't you know, to manage the house and give me"—his eyebrows almost jumped off his forehead—"my heir and spare."

His nose twitched again; it must be some sort of nervous tic, not that he appeared the least bit discomposed.

"I hope you don't mind my speaking plainly, Miss Bowman, but I assume a woman of your advanced years would be awake on every suit. No need to beat around the bush as if you were some young shrinking violet."

"Ah." Her first urge—to reply using her knee to great advantage—would not be appropriate for the duchess's drawing room. And if the man should somehow redeem himself, she didn't want to injure the one part of him that was of the most use to her. "How nice that you've come into some property, sir, but you must regret the manner in which you received it. Please allow me to express my condolences. I'm so sorry for your loss."

"My loss?" Mr. Humphrey blinked at her, his small mouth agape.

"Your great aunt, sir. I'm sorry for her death." Especially since it was the poor woman's departure from the world that had caused Mr. Humphrey to be invited to this party.

"Oh." He nodded, but failed to look at all sorrowful. "Yes, it was very sad, but she was quite old. She had over eighty years in her dish; everyone said it was just a matter of time." He leaned close again; Ellie kept from leaning away only by the most determined exercise of will.

"Many thought my cousin Theo would get her estate, since it was widely believed Aunt Theodora favored his mother over mine—Aunt Winifred even named Theo Theodore to curry favor—but all Theo got was a collection of china cats. I believe—and Mama agrees with me—that old Aunt Theodora finally got sick of Winifred toadying to her and hit on me because she hadn't seen me or Mama in years, though of course if I'd known I'd have a chance at her estate I would have visited, but perhaps it all turned out for the best, don't you think?"

"Er, yes." For Mr. Humphrey; not for poor cousin Theo.

Perhaps Mr. Cox would appear in the drawing room soon; even a noble sprig would be better than this wretched weed.

No, no, no! She could not rule out Mr. Humphrey so quickly. He might merely be an acquired taste. The house party was just beginning. She would reserve judgment—or at least try to.

Mr. Humphrey tugged on his waistcoat. It was hard to imagine the man was only twenty-five; he was already going to fat. "So of course when the Duchess of Love extended this invitation, I accepted immediately. Her grace is such a successful matchmaker, you know, and it will be so much more efficient to obtain a wife now without having to waste time and money on a Season." His nose twitched again, this time clearly in distaste. "Young girls can be so silly, having their heads turned with balls and fancy clothing, when their real duties in life are to bear children, keep their households running smoothly, and see that their husband is well cared for, don't you agree?"

"Er, yes." Sadly, she did agree.

Mr. Humphrey pushed his spectacles back to the bridge of his nose. "Splendid. I could tell you were a sensible woman the moment I saw you, Miss Bowman, and while I know it's too early to speak—"

Good God, the man wasn't going to propose now, was he? It was one thing to admit to practicality, but quite another to dispense with even the slightest whiff of romance.

"—but I must say you've given me reason to hope—"

"Sir, we've just met!"

"—that you will make me the happiest of—"

"Mr. Humphrey!" He was like a runaway horse.

"—men"—Mr. Humphrey smiled—"shortly."

She must remember she couldn't afford to be choosy. She wanted children; her window of opportunity was fast closing. Mr. Humphrey was willing and male.

And she wasn't *that* desperate. She hadn't even met Mr. Cox. "Mr. Humphrey, you presume too much."

"Ah, yes, I know. It's early days yet." He winked one of his squinty, little eyes at her. "As long as we understand each other."

"We do *not* understand each other!" Ellie took a deep breath. She must remember she did not want to burn any bridges. Mr. Cox might be worse. "I mean it is indeed early days—far too early for me—or either of us—to have formed an opinion about . . . anything."

"Oh, I don't know." He gave her a very odd look which in another man she might describe as a leer. "I like what I see. And you?"

"Me?"

He pulled on his waistcoat again. "Do you like what you see?"

"Ah. Er. Well."

"Speechless, eh?"

She nodded. It seemed the only response.

"I often have that effect on women." Mr. Humphrey's narrow lips twisted into a self-satisfied smirk.

"And what effect would that be?" Ned said from behind her.

Ellie spun around, catching her heel in her skirt. She would have fallen if Ned's hand hadn't shot out to grasp her elbow, steadying her.

She shook off his hold immediately; she couldn't risk falling under his spell again. "You shouldn't sneak up on people that way, Lord Edward."

He gave her a puzzled, almost hurt, look, but his face hardened when he shifted his attention to Mr. Humphrey. "Is this man annoying you, Ellie?"

Oh, dear, his voice had that edge to it. Even as a boy, he'd fly to defend whomever he believed to be the injured party in a confrontation. If he thought Mr. Humphrey had insulted her, he could make things very unpleasant.

Lovely. That would be all they needed—Ned and the mole getting into a drawing room brawl, though given the vast difference in their size and strength, the battle wouldn't last long.

"Of course not. This is Mr. Humphrey, Ned. He has just inherited an estate in Devon." She turned back to the mole. "Mr. Humphrey; Lord Edward."

"So why isn't he in Devon?" Ned said, looking at the mole as if the man was indeed a member of the vermin class.

Mr. Humphrey's face turned an unpleasant shade of white, and his small eyes grew as wide as they could behind his spectacles. His Adam's apple bobbed spasmodically.

"Because your mother invited him to the house party, of course," Ellie hissed. "And I'm sure she expects you to make him feel welcome."

"Not if he's insulting you."

"He's *not* insulting me."

Mr. Humphrey finally found his voice. "Of course I am not insulting Miss Bowman, Lord Edward. On the contrary, I was about to"—*Oh, God, the man could not mean to tell Ned he was going to*—"offer her the honor of being my—"

Ellie trod as hard as she could on Mr. Humphrey's foot. "Ouch!"

"Oh, I'm so sorry, sir." She refused to look at Ned. "I can't believe I was so clumsy."

Mr. Humphrey smiled, though his expression looked a bit forced. "Quite all right, my dear." She could feel Ned bristle at the "my dear." "No harm done. As I was saying—"

Thank God the duchess came back then; she'd sent the

duke, a large glass of Madeira in hand, off to join the party by the fire. "Ned, I see you've met Mr. Humphrey."

"Yes." Ned sounded rather surly.

His mother beamed at him. "Splendid. Then if you'll excuse us, I should make Mr. Humphrey known to the others." She took the mole by the arm. "This way, sir."

Mr. Humphrey was no match for the duchess; he meekly allowed himself to be led away.

The moment the fellow was out of earshot—not that Ned gave a damn whether Humphrey heard him or not—Ned turned to Ellie. "That idiot wasn't proposing to you, was he?"

Ellie flushed. "N-no."

"But he's going to, isn't he?"

Ellie wouldn't meet his eye. "Perhaps."

"Good God, he just met you."

She glanced up at his face and then quickly away. "Maybe he was taken with my great beauty."

He heard the sarcasm in her tone and opened his mouth to continue the joke, but something about the way she was holding herself so stiffly stopped him.

What was the matter? Cicely had been very sensitive—he'd learned to choose his words carefully with her—but this was Ellie. He and she had joked and teased about everything for years, like brother and sister. Ellie didn't care about things like physical beauty. Just look at the dress she was wearing. It would be hard to find a plainer gown or one that hid her figure more completely. It had long, puffy sleeves and a neck up to her chin, for God's sake.

But then there were those red silk drawers . . . Was she wearing them now?

And had he lost his mind completely? Next thing he

knew, he'd be imagining Ellie as an opera dancer or some such thing.

"Here come Percy and Lady Ophelia," Ellie said.

"Oh, blast." He turned to see his brother-in-law—short and wiry and as dark as Cicely had been light—and the fellow's light o'love, Lady Ophelia Upton, headed their way. This was going to be infernally awkward. "Why does Mama invite them every year?"

Ellie looked at him as if he were a halfwit. "Because Percy is Cicely's brother and lives nearby, of course, and Ophelia is his"—she flushed slightly—"good friend." She shrugged. "It's not as if he wouldn't notice if he was left off the guest list. He knows when your birthday is; he knows your mother always holds this house party; *and* his butler is the cousin of one of the Greycliffe footmen."

Ned grunted. All true, unfortunately.

He'd never liked the fellow even when they were children—none of them had. Percy was Ash's age and had always been a sneak and a bully. But the man was Cicely's brother, so once Ned had married, he'd tried to keep his opinions to himself—not always with success. Percy had been the root of his infrequent arguments with Cicely, arguments that always left her in tears and him feeling like the biggest brute in Christendom.

And then the month after Cicely died, Percy wrote asking for money. He'd sent him some, because he was certain that's what Cicely would have wanted. And then Percy wrote again and again, damn regularly these last few years. Finally, Ned had had enough. He'd sent him a check at Christmastime with notice it was the last farthing Percy would ever get from him. He'd burned every one of Percy's letters since—and there had been many in the short time since the holiday—without bothering to open them.

He didn't expect his brother-in-law to be happy to see him. "Good evening, Lady Ophelia. Percy."

Ophelia smiled at him, but Percy didn't.

"Edward." The word was encased in ice. Percy gave him his shoulder and smiled at Ellie—the annoying half-smile that always made Ned want to punch him in the teeth. "My dear, it's been too long."

Ellie nodded to Ophelia. "You just saw me last week in the village, Percy, if you'll remember. I was buying ribbon, and you were buying snuff."

Ned grinned. Ellie was too smart to be taken in by Percy—of course, she'd grown up with him, too. She knew how oily he was.

"Must you always be so prosaic?" Percy said waspishly.

"I suppose so. I certainly can't see any reason to talk nonsense with you—nor can I imagine why you'd wish me to do so."

"It's merely polite conversation, as you'd know if you'd ever been to London."

"And as *you* know, Percy, it's highly unlikely I'll ever go to Town, so I think I can save myself the worry of what might pass for polite talk there."

Ophelia frowned. "Surely you want to go to London some day, Ellie," she said, "to see all the sights and attend the balls and parties."

Ellie shrugged. "I've found it best not to wish for what I can't have."

Now why the hell had she glanced at him? Ned couldn't take her to Town—not that he ever went himself, but showing up with an unrelated female in tow would set the gossips into a flutter as wild as if Reggie were to drop into a flock of starlings. He turned to Ophelia. "I hope the weather didn't make your trip too arduous."

Ophelia smiled. "Oh, no. I was fortunate to stay nearby last night."

Probably in Percy's bed.

She put her hand on Percy's arm. "I'd hate to miss the Duchess of Love's annual party."

"Oh? I would be happy to miss it." Ned would give anything to be back in his study at Linden Hall, a glass of brandy by his elbow, a good book in his hands, the fire crackling in the hearth.

"What, Lord Edward," Percy said, "don't you like having us all here to celebrate your birthday?"

"Not particularly." *And especially not you, you whoreson.*

Why did Ophelia waste her time with Percy? Her father, the Earl of Brambril, had been dodging duns for years, so one would think his daughter would look for a man with money, not a ne'er do well like his brother-in-law. Even though her reputation was decidedly soiled, her birth—the daughter of a penniless earl was still the daughter of an earl—would make her appealing to many men. She was still attractive, though age was beginning to make its mark. Ned didn't remember seeing the lines at the corners of her mouth and eyes last year.

There was a stir at the drawing room door and Dalton stepped into the room. "The Countess of Heldon," he announced. "Lady Juliet Ramsbottom; Mr. Harold Cox."

"Wonderful," Mama said, dragging Father over to greet the newcomers. "Welcome to Greycliffe."

"How . . . interesting that they arrived together," Percy said.

Ophelia frowned at him. "Oh, hush, Percy. They likely met in the hall when they came downstairs."

What the hell were they talking about? Not that it made any difference. Percy and Ophelia were always gabbing about some *on dit* that Ned couldn't care less about. He never knew any of the subjects of their chatter.

But this time was different—one of their subjects might become his future wife. At the moment, he could only see

Lady Heldon and Cox. The woman must be Lady Heldon since she looked nothing like Cicely. She had dark hair and heavy-lidded, bedroom eyes; full lips, very red against her pale skin; and extremely large—

He shifted his attention to Cox. The man was a typical London buck—coat, cravat, and pantaloons all the *dernier cri*, dark blond hair cut in the latest style. All he needed to complete the picture of a town beau was to observe them through his quizzing glass—which he did at that moment.

Ned glanced down at Ellie to share the joke.

She was staring at Cox with an extremely determined look. Damn. What was she thinking?

"There's Juliet," Ophelia said.

Ned looked back at the group—and felt as if he'd taken a direct hit to his chest. The rest of the room faded away, and all he could see was the exquisite, fairy-like woman smiling up at Mama. Cicely.

All the pain and loss and love he'd felt for his wife— everything he'd thought he'd finally put behind him— flooded out of the dark place he'd forced them, bringing the prick of tears to the back of his eyes.

This wasn't Cicely. It *wasn't*, but . . .

Even Percy sounded a bit awed. "It is amazing how much Lady Juliet looks like my poor sister, isn't it?"

Chapter 4

Sometimes you need to be daring.
                                        —Venus's Love Notes

Thomas raised his brows as he removed Ellie's un-
touched bowl of soup. She'd been to dinner at the castle
often enough that the blasted footman knew Cook's turtle
soup was one of her favorites. She just had no appetite this
evening.

"Did you encounter any difficulties with the snow on
your way down from London, Mr. Cox?" she asked, turning to the dinner partner on her right. Mr. Humphrey, on her
left, was busy rescuing the last mouthful of soup before sur-
rendering his bowl.

"Hmm?" Mr. Cox was staring across the table at Lady
Juliet.

The woman *was* lovely. She was small and fine-boned
with perfect features, silver blond hair, and large, long-
lashed, deep blue eyes. She looked very much like Cicely,

only perhaps prettier, and at the moment she was gazing at Ned as though he were a god.

And he was looking at her as if she were the answer to his prayers.

Damn.

Ellie glanced at the duchess, sitting to Ned's left. If her grace were Sir Reginald, she'd be purring.

Ellie gritted her teeth. "Did the snow make your travel difficult?" she asked Mr. Cox again. She was clearly wasting her time with him—he was besotted with Lady Juliet. She should pursue Mr. Humphrey instead.

Her stomach knotted.

She reminded her stomach she was already twenty-six years old. She wanted children.

Squinty-eyed little mole children?

Ahh.

No wonder she had no appetite.

"Not at all." Mr. Cox had finally managed to tear his eyes away from the object of his affections. He bent his lips into a polite smile that didn't even begin to reach his eyes. "I rode down on horseback. I found the cold and snow rather . . ."—he glanced back at Lady Juliet as if he couldn't help himself—"appropriate."

"Yes, it *is* February, isn't it? I suppose we should expect winter weather."

That profound observation did not require a reply; Mr. Cox merely nodded.

She should definitely concentrate on Mr. Humphrey. There must be something appealing about him or he wouldn't have been invited . . . unless the duchess recognized Ellie was past her prayers and should be ecstatically grateful to wed any male willing to have her.

Which Mr. Cox, no matter how physically attractive, wasn't. Had her grace not been aware of the man's feelings? He was looking back at Lady Juliet again.

She must have been—the Duchess of Love was awake on all suits. Therefore, there must be some impediment keeping Lady Juliet and Mr. Cox from marrying, though if there was, it seemed rather cruel to dangle the unattainable under the man's nose.

Hmm, Lady Juliet *was* ignoring him; perhaps that was the problem—that she didn't return his regard, a sadly common problem at this party. If so, Mr. Cox might be willing to take Ellie as his second choice. Not a very palatable thought, true, but then he was *her* second choice as well. And odds were his children would be vastly more attractive than Mr. Humphrey's.

"But snow is much pleasanter than rain and mud," her grace said, turning her attention their way and reviving the weather topic. "Don't you agree, sir? It's so much prettier and far more entertaining. Ellie and I were just saying that earlier today, weren't we, Ellie?"

Oh dear, Ned's mother had that mischievous gleam in her eyes again. "I believe *you* were saying so, your grace."

"Of course I was." The duchess leaned closer and waggled her brows. "I ask you, sir, what could be better than slipping through the quiet snow with"—she transferred her gaze to Ellie—"a beautiful lady snug under a pile of furs?"

Ellie was going to expire of mortification, falling nose first into the roast hare Thomas had just placed in front of her. One would think the Duchess of Love would have more finesse. At least Mr. Cox appeared to be taking the woman's heavy-handed efforts in good spirit.

"I can't think of a thing, your grace." His pleasant tone sounded as forced as his smile, but at least he was making an effort to be sociable.

"Splendid." The duchess beamed at him and then at Ellie. "We shall get our two horse-drawn sleighs out as soon as the snow has stopped. And we have sledges, too, for the intrepid among you, and a lovely sledding hill"—she turned toward her son—"isn't that right, Ned?"

Ned looked up—clearly with great reluctance—from his conversation with Lady Juliet. "Isn't what right, Mama?"

"That we have an excellent hill for sledding. You must remember how you and the other boys used to spend hours on the slope by the pond after a good snowfall."

"Yes, of course I remember, but—"

"Ellie and Jess and Cicely would come, too," Jack said from his seat on the other side of Lady Juliet. The duchess's parties were always very informal; talking across the table was not only tolerated, it was encouraged. "Cicely didn't sled—she always moaned about the cold and went home early—but Ellie and Jess did. They were fearless."

"Fearless, Lord Jack?" Ellie smiled pleasantly—she hoped. She'd really prefer to pick up the hare's leg from her plate and wing it at him. Since they were eating in one of the smaller dining rooms, she might be able to hit him. His announcing she'd been a complete hoyden in her youth wouldn't help advance her marriage hopes—of course, her tossing food wouldn't help, either. "I believe plaguy is what you called me."

"Of course I did. You kept trying to steal my sledge."

In her defense, she hadn't had much choice—Papa didn't think sledding was an appropriate activity for a girl, so she hadn't had a sledge of her own. And of course he'd been right. She should have gone home with Cicely. Jess had been different—she hadn't cared what anyone thought, and it had been clear for as long as Ellie could remember that Jess would marry Ash.

"I just wanted to borrow it," she said.

"All the time."

"As I remember," Ash said, "Ellie usually got the sledge when she wanted it."

"Only because she was bigger than I was then." Jack

nodded at the duke. "And because Father would have caned me if I'd rubbed her face in the snow as I'd wanted to."

"Indeed I would have." The duke raised his brows. "As it was, I had to remind you on more than one occasion that a gentleman does not fight with a lady."

"I had no idea I was causing such difficulties." Perhaps if she apologized, Jack would drop the subject. "I'm so sorry."

"Oh, don't be, my dear." The duke smiled down the table at her. "I thought it good for Jack to learn at an early age how to deal with a strong-willed young woman. It's a skill I'm certain has served him well."

The duchess laughed. "Very true."

"I don't know, Father. I haven't had any other female try to steal from me or hit me with a snowball." Jack turned back to her. "I warn you, Ellie, that I throw much harder now, so beware if we get up a snowball fight during this party."

"Yes, indeed. Do take care, Miss Bowman." Miss Wharton's voice had an unfortunate nasal quality to it besides being overly loud. "Lord Jack boxes with Gentleman Jackson himself. He's quite the Corinthian; everyone in London says so."

"I'm sure Ellie knows I wouldn't actually pelt her with snowballs, Miss Wharton." Jack's words had a sharp edge, but it was impossible to tell if Miss Wharton noticed, as Mr. Humphrey chose that moment to open his verbal floodgates.

"Miss Wharton, while I'm confident Miss Bowman appreciates your concern, I feel certain that she is fully aware, being much older and wiser today than she was when she was a child, that even if she once was so bold and reckless as to fling a snowball at Lord Jack, such an activity now that she is a grown—or may I even say a mature—woman is completely unsuitable not to say inadvisable." His nose twitched as if to punctuate his speech, and he turned to Ellie. "Am I not correct, Miss Bowman?"

Ellie drew in a breath. Mr. Humphrey was right by her side; the hare's leg, still uneaten, was on her plate. She wouldn't even have to throw it . . .

Bashing a potential suitor over the head with part of her dinner would not endear her to the man. Remember, she wanted children. "Er . . ."

"You are indeed right, sir," Jack said, taking advantage of her momentary speechlessness. "Ellie's turned into a proper stick-in-the-mud."

Jack, however, was not a potential suitor. If she couldn't fling her food at him, perhaps she could pour a cup of tea over his head later.

"Remember the time Ellie insisted on going over the jump you built, Ash?" Percy had decided to join the ridiculous conversation. Ellie glared at him; he flicked his eyes at her and then concentrated on Ash. "It must have taken fifteen minutes to dig her out of that snow bank."

Ash nodded. "I remember."

Jack laughed. "How could anyone forget? You screamed like a banshee, Ellie. You had snow in your mouth when we finally pulled you free."

"How . . . brave of you, Miss Bowman." Lady Juliet looked down at her plate in a pretty show of feminine meekness. "I'm sure I would be far too timid to attempt anything so frightening."

Mr. Cox made an odd noise, a cross between a laugh and a snort. He was looking at Lady Juliet with an oddly cynical expression.

"As well you should be," Ned said quickly. "Ellie is far more robust than you." He threw her an inscrutable look. "But Mr. Humphrey is right; she wouldn't do such a thing now that she is past girlhood."

"Aha! There's a challenge if ever I heard one," Jack said.

"What say you, Ellie? Are you going to prove me and Ned wrong? I will even lend you my sledge to do so."

"No, thank you."

"Oh, come now, Miss Bowman." Lady Heldon's voice was rich, deep for a woman, and vaguely scandalous—the sort of voice Eve must have used to persuade Adam to eat the apple in the Garden of Eden. "I quite look forward to watching you show the Valentine men—and the rest of us—how to go on, don't you agree, Ophelia?"

"Yes." Lady Ophelia turned to the duke. "Please add your entreaty to ours, your grace."

"Oh, no. I hope I have more sense than to try to tell a grown woman how to behave."

"Exactly." The duchess leaned forward, her eyes twinkling. "Perhaps I shall race you, Ellie. I haven't gone sledding in years."

Ellie almost choked on the bite of hare she'd foolishly tried to eat. Mr. Humphrey put up his hand as if to slap her solicitously on the back, but she shifted away from him.

"Race her?" The duke's eyebrows shot up. "You are not flying down a hill on a sledge, my dear duchess."

"Oh?" The duchess's eyebrows went up as well. "Didn't you just say you had more sense than to tell a grown woman what to do?"

"Er, yes, but I wasn't referring to you." Clearly the duke saw trouble ahead, but he was a brave man with a strong will.

The duchess's eyebrows disappeared into her coiffure.

"I merely wish you to remain safe, my dear. You are not as young as you once were."

The duchess's chin hardened. "Neither am I dead."

"Not yet."

They looked at each other in silence for a moment, and then the duchess smiled. "I'll be careful."

The duke grunted.

"Anyone care to lay a wager?" Jack asked. "Who will win the great race of this year's Valentine house party—the Duchess of Greycliffe or Miss Eleanor Bowman?"

"Jack!" Ellie took a breath; shouting was no more appropriate for a respectable woman at the dinner table than flinging food. She turned to the duchess. "Your grace, I do not intend to go sledding."

"Oh, pooh, don't be a spoil-sport, Ellie," the duchess said. "I think it will be great fun."

Mr. Humphrey cleared his throat. Dash it, what was the man going to say now?

"Far be it for me to presume to offer you guidance, your grace, but I will confess to being concerned for your safety; however, I know I need not worry as you are sure to be ruled by the duke's judgment, just as Miss Bowman has been persuaded by, if I may say so, my superior male counsel."

Ellie's jaw dropped as she swiveled her head to stare at the man. The entire table had gone silent.

"What?" He looked around. "Did I say something untoward?"

"Not if your goal is to have your head bitten off, chewed thoroughly, and spat out on your boots," Jack said, never one to mince matters.

"On second thought, your grace," Ellie said, showing her teeth to Mr. Humphrey in what might have been a smile but wasn't, "I believe I *will* join you on the sledding hill."

"You aren't actually going to sled, are you, Ellie?" Ned asked as he took a cup of tea from her. He glanced back at Lady Juliet sitting with Percy and Ophelia, and his heart shifted.

She was so like Cicely. He knew—his head knew—she wasn't Cicely, but his heart apparently didn't care.

And did it really matter? She made him feel strong and protective again.

Mama thought she was a good match for him, and Mama was the Duchess of Love. He should rely on her judgment, especially as he actually wanted to do so for once.

If only Lady Juliet weren't so small . . . but the accoucheur had told him Cicely's death hadn't been caused by her size, that even large women sometimes died in childbirth. Perhaps—

"Yes, I am going to sled."

"What?" His attention snapped back to Ellie. Her face had the closed, sulky expression he hadn't seen since childhood. "Don't be ridiculous."

Ellie's brows snapped down to meet over her nose.

All right, perhaps he'd been rather blunt, but, blast it, she *was* being ridiculous.

Ellie's chin was up now. "I really don't see what concern it is of yours, Lord Edward."

He struggled to hold onto his temper. "It's my concern because I care about you, Ellie. You must know I think of you as the sister I never had."

Ellie's eyes widened. She looked as if she might cast up her accounts all over his shoes.

He stepped back slightly.

"I am *not* your sister."

"Good God, don't shout." What the hell was the matter with her? Ellie was at heart a reasonable person; she must just be in an odd pet this evening. Perhaps it was an unfortunate time of the month. Cicely had sometimes acted a touch irrational when her courses were coming on.

He glanced around. No one seemed to be paying them any attention, except Mama who smiled and waggled her fingers at him. Did she want him to get back to Lady Juliet? He would in just a moment. He looked forward to it. Lady Juliet wouldn't rip up at him like a harridan.

"And I certainly do not consider you my brother."

That hurt. He'd thought they were close, closer than just good friends. In these last hellish years, she'd been his one constant, his calm port in the storm of grief and guilt raging within him.

He must remember that soon he would have a wife to confide in instead. "Sledding is for children, and you are no longer a child."

"I'm glad you noticed." There was a hint of sarcasm in her voice, but also a slight tremble as if she was holding back some stronger emotion. "But I believe I saw you and Jack—and even Ash—sledding at Christmastime, and you are older than I."

She had. Jack had been the instigator that time as well, assisted by one—or two or three—too many glasses of brandy. They'd been sitting in Ash's study, watching the last few flakes meander lazily through the air, when Jack had got the notion they should take out the sledges for a run or two before dark.

Ned had resisted at first, and he'd complained all the way to the sledding hill, but once he was flying down the slope, the wind snatching his breath, the cold stinging his cheeks, his bad humor had shattered and fallen away. He'd felt alive again, as if his heart had not died with Cicely, but had only been encased in ice. That was when he'd begun to hope he might find the will to wed again. "That's different."

"I don't see how."

His head was beginning to throb again, damn it. "You're a female. Your skirts could get caught in the runners."

"And so I'll end up inelegantly sprawled in the cold, wet snow. I'm hearty. I'll survive."

And why the hell did he have a sudden vision of those skirts flying up to reveal a pair of red silk drawers?

He rubbed his forehead and pressed his temple, but that didn't help. "You could break your leg—or your neck."

"And I could trip and fall into the fire walking over to the hearth or"—she waved her teacup at him—"scald myself right here before your eyes."

She was being purposely obtuse. "What of your reputation? Lady Heldon and Ophelia will spread the tale far and wide."

Her lips twisted in disdain. "My reputation can survive one little sledding adventure. Remember I've just turned twenty-six; I'm hardly a girl. And how shocking can it be? Your mother plans to join me."

"Father will never allow it."

Ellie raised one brow. "I think the duchess will do exactly as she wishes."

Ellie was probably right. "Even so, my mother is married. She doesn't have to worry about giving suitors a disgust of her. You do."

Two spots of red bloomed on Ellie's cheeks. "Oh?"

The sharpness of her voice made him pause, but only briefly. "Yes. If you wish to attach a man's regard, you must behave in a more circumspect manner." He frowned. "That is, in your normal manner."

Her teacup clinked into its saucer, and he flinched. "Careful. I believe Mama is rather fond of that pattern."

She ignored him. "I wouldn't say my 'normal' behavior has been very successful. In case it has slipped your notice, I'm still a spinster."

He tried to rein in his temper, but he wasn't completely successful. "From what Mama has hinted to me, you could have been married several times over if you'd stopped hiding with Ash and encouraged the men she's invited to these blood—blasted parties for you."

Her cheeks turned an even deeper red, almost as red as those red silk drawers . . .

Was she wearing them now?

His gaze dropped to the relevant area of her person. But

why would she wear such a scandalous bit of fabric under such a formless, matronly dress?

He snapped his eyes back up to her face. That was not his concern—and thinking about it made his head ache more.

"Then I suppose I'd best go further my acquaintance with Mr. Cox or Mr. Humphrey," she said. "Please excuse me."

She moved to step past him, but he touched her arm to stop her. "What's the matter, Ellie? You really aren't your-self this evening."

She bit her lip, and then shook her head and looked away. "Or perhaps I finally am."

She stepped around him. She didn't go over to Cox or Humphrey, but instead stopped to study the portrait of the first Duke of Greycliffe—a painting she'd seen countless times before.

What the blazes was wrong with her? Ned rubbed his forehead again. He felt all topsy-turvy, as if he'd landed in Bedlam.

He glanced over at Lady Juliet; she met his eye and smiled. At least some female was happy to spend time with him.

He would let Mama worry about Ellie.

Chapter 5

A pinch of jealousy thickens the broth.
—Venus's Love Notes

Could her situation get any worse? She'd vowed this year to accept the fact that Ned considered her merely a friend and not hope for more, but deep in her heart, no matter how much she tried to deny it, she *had* hoped. And now . . .

Dear God, he thought of her as a *sister*.

Ellie's stomach tightened into a hard knot, and she felt lightheaded, as if she might swoon. She tried to take a deep breath. She needed to appear calm, placid—as Ned had said, she needed to behave in her normal manner, her mask firmly in place, especially after just having spoken with him. The duchess, for one, was certain to guess exactly what had overset her, and Ellie did not care to reveal her feelings any more than she already had.

She took another breath. She would be fine. She—

"Miss Bowman?"

"Eep!" She jumped. Mr. Cox was standing right beside her.

"Forgive me for startling you." Mr. Cox's voice was grave, but his eyes twinkled. He inclined his head toward the painting. "Were you transfixed by this fellow's sartorial splendor?"

"What?" She looked at the portrait. The first Duke of Greycliffe—attired in an enormous lace ruff, a garish doublet, ballooning breeches, white clocked stockings, and high-heeled shoes with enormous pom-poms—glowered down at her. "N-no. I confess I wasn't looking at the painting at all."

"That's good then. I was afraid you admired his elegance." Mr. Cox grinned. "I can't say I'd care to have to rig myself out in such finery—especially the shoes."

Ellie smiled back at him. He was the image of male perfection; any sensible woman would fall immediately in love with him.

Many sensible women had—though not, it would seem, Lady Juliet. And not, unfortunately, Ellie. No matter how attractive Mr. Cox was, her heart refused to beat faster at his attentions. He was not Ned.

Ned who was so unimpressed with her feeble charms that he viewed her as a sister, blast it.

"The shoes *are* remarkable." Perhaps she just needed to try a little harder to find Mr. Cox appealing. "As you can see, the first duke was very fond of fashion. He reputedly cut a wide swath among the ladies of his time, leaving behind many broken hearts."

Mr. Cox shook his head. "Amazing. He looks the veriest popinjay, doesn't he? But I confess we've got a similarly attired peer or two hanging on the walls at home." He chuckled. "I imagine they would be equally horrified at my plain garb."

He spread out his arms slightly as if asking Ellie to survey his attire, so she did—not that she hadn't already noted how well his coat and breeches fitted him. Unfortunately, her admiration was mostly academic.

Still, she did feel *some* admiration. He was certainly much more appealing than Mr. Humphrey. And if there was something keeping him and Lady Juliet apart, then he and Ellie might be able to rub along tolerably well—well enough to produce a few children.

She smiled, trying her best to flirt. "I think I could make some pom-poms for your shoes, if you like."

"No, thank you." He offered her his arm. "Will you take a turn around the room with me instead?"

In past years, she would have declined and hurried off to hide in conversation with Ash. She glanced over to where Ash stood with Jack, Miss Wharton, and Lady Heldon. He—and Jack as well—looked as if they would eagerly welcome her if she tried to join them. She should—

She should walk with Mr. Cox. As Ned had pointed out, she might be married now if she'd only cooperated with the duchess's past efforts. Married, and perhaps already a mother.

She wouldn't waste another minute. She placed her hand on Mr. Cox's sleeve. "I would be delighted to do so, sir. It is too bad it is so snowy out; the Greycliffe gardens are very pleasant, even in winter."

And if they could stroll outside, she could get away from the duchess's far too interested gaze. Ned's mother was sitting with the duke, Miss Mosely—the mousy woman who'd been standing by Ash before dinner—and Mr. Humphrey, but she was smiling and nodding at Ellie, completely ignoring whatever Mr. Humphrey was holding forth about. In point of fact, Miss Mosely was the only one listening to the man—the duke was busy consulting his pocket watch, likely calculating how much longer he had to endure before the duchess would let him escape.

"I believe her grace mentioned your father is the vicar," Mr. Cox said as they passed the scowling portrait of the second duke. "Did you grow up here?"

"Yes. This has been Papa's only living—he was one of the duke's school friends and came here as soon as he was ordained."

This was her home—Greycliffe and the vicarage—the only home she'd ever known. If she married—*when* she married—she'd have to leave it all behind. She might never again see the duke, the duchess, Ash, Jack, Ned—

She wouldn't think of that. She forced herself to smile. "You will undoubtedly consider me the greatest rustic, sir, for I've never traveled beyond the parish boundaries."

He raised his eyebrows. "Not even to London?"

She shook her head. "No. Papa couldn't afford a Season, especially with four daughters to launch. The duchess offered to sponsor me, but I didn't want to be so beholden to her."

That hadn't been her real reason. She hadn't cared to go husband hunting in London because the husband she'd wanted was here at Greycliffe—or Linden Hall once Ned attained his majority and the duke gave him that unentailed property.

She'd always wanted to see Linden Hall, but there'd been no reason to do so. If Cicely had lived, she could have visited . . .

Perhaps that would not have been a good notion.

Mr. Cox's right eyebrow rose higher. "That was exceedingly generous of her."

It had been, but the duke and duchess *were* generous. "Why are you surprised? Papa and the duke are friends—Mama and the duchess as well."

They paused under the gloomy gaze of the third duke. She looked up at the man's pursed lips and flaring nostrils—

she'd often teased Ned about how dyspeptic his ancestors appeared.

"I'm just not used to peers thinking of anyone but themselves," Mr. Cox said.

"Oh?" Ellie looked back at him; his attention had wandered to Lady Juliet who was sitting with Percy, Ophelia, and Ned—though it looked as if all *her* attention was on Ned. She laughed very prettily at something he said, and it felt like a knife twisted in Ellie's gut. She wrenched her eyes back to Mr. Cox—he was still observing Lady Juliet.

"The duke and duchess are the only peers I know," she said, "and the duke didn't expect to inherit—the title was thrust on him when he was thirteen—so I suppose he might have a different attitude than someone born and raised to his position."

Ned must be serious about Lady Juliet if he was willing to subject himself to Percy's company a moment more than absolutely necessary. And his expression when he looked at her—intent yet tender—was exactly the one he'd always had when he'd looked at Cicely.

Ellie's stomach sank so low she risked tripping on it.

"Peers, in my experience, can be quite unreasonable." Mr. Cox managed to return his attention to Ellie. "The title tends to go to their head. But I shouldn't be surprised the duke and duchess are different. It was clear at dinner that they consider you almost a daughter."

"Yes." Ellie had always been happy about that—she'd equated daughter with daughter-in-law in her private thoughts—but now that she knew Ned looked on her as a sister, the idea was far less appealing. "I was often underfoot. As you must have gathered, we all played together as children."

He stopped in front of a sketch of the castle with the gardens in bloom—it was one of Ash's—and pulled out his quizzing glass to examine it. "So you know Lord Ashton, Lord Edward, and Lord Jack well."

"I suppose so"—*like brothers, damn it*—"though Ash is the only one who lives here now. Lord Jack is mostly in London, and Lord Edward has his own estate."

Mr. Cox nodded and put his quizzing glass back in his pocket. "Ashton and Lord Edward never come to Town, do they?"

"No, neither of them cares for London."

"Perhaps they went more frequently when they were married?"

Ellie frowned at Mr. Cox. "Ash *is* married."

"Yes, well, I meant when they were with their wives— did they make a practice of taking their ladies to Town?"

Why was Mr. Cox interested in this topic? Ash and Jess had separated the day they wed, but if Mr. Cox didn't know that, Ellie wasn't about to tell him. And Cicely had been with child by the time she and Ned came home from their honeymoon. "No, but I don't believe Jess or Cicely cared about going to London. They never talked about wanting to visit Town when we were growing up."

"They didn't dream about their Seasons?"

"I think they were quite content to be here in the country." Which is exactly where she wouldn't be once she wed. Well, she might be in the country, but not this part of it. She would have to leave to go to her husband's house and live among strangers. A whisper of panic brushed down her spine.

But there would be children—her children. She must focus on that.

"Tell me about your home, sir." If she knew a few details, perhaps she could persuade herself that moving would be an adventure.

"I don't really have a home, Miss Bowman. I have

bachelor's lodgings in Town, but as the fifth son I am very much on my own."

"The duchess said you were to enter the Church."

Mr. Cox smiled, but his eyes were decidedly bleak. "That's certainly what my mother wishes. I wanted to enlist in the army, but my father refused to buy me my colors, and now that Boney's no longer a threat . . ." He shrugged. "Perhaps I *will* join the clergy."

"You shouldn't do so if you can't like the idea." It was not her place to say anything, of course, but Ellie had listened too many times to Papa complain about disinterested clergymen to keep silent.

"I have to do something, Miss Bowman. I'm not a wealthy man." He hesitated, and then said, his voice a bit harsh, "I'll confess to you that I am very interested in steam locomotives, but some people feel any involvement in such enterprises stinks of trade." He looked at Lady Juliet again—

Good heavens, Lady Juliet was glaring at *her*. And Ned was frowning at her as well. What on earth was the matter with them? She hadn't exchanged two words with Lady Juliet, and she'd been doing exactly what Ned had suggested, behaving in a perfectly unobjectionable manner with a possible suitor. She frowned back at Ned. "Many things are changing in today's world, Mr. Cox."

"May I have your attention, please?" the duchess said, clapping her hands. She'd joined the group with Ash and Jack, leaving the duke, trying unsuccessfully to hide his yawns, with Mr. Humphrey and Miss Mosely. "Miss Wharton has offered to sing for us, and as I'm sure there must be others of you who are willing to do so as well, we are going to adjourn to the music room."

The duke leapt to his feet to escort his wife—and escape Mr. Humphrey and Miss Mosely.

Ellie would prefer to adjourn to her bedchamber and pull

the coverlet over her head, but it was too early for that, and, much as she wished otherwise, she had a potential husband to charm. She smiled and let Mr. Cox lead her into the music room. Hopefully, Miss Wharton's singing voice was better than her speaking voice.

Ned sat next to Jack and watched Miss Wharton ready herself to perform. She'd tried to get Jack to accompany her on the pianoforte, but he'd hidden behind his sling—and then grabbed Ash and Ned to guard his flanks the moment she went to the front of the room. The woman would have to sit elsewhere when she finished.

He switched his attention to Cox, also up in the front of the room. The man was too damn pretty and polished, and he was sitting far too close to Ellie, just about whispering in her ear. He'd been paying her marked attention in the drawing room as well, taking her apart from the others. What was he up to?

He'd best not be trifling with Ellie's affections. If Cox thought no one here was looking out for her interests, he was very much mistaken. Ned's fingers curled into fists. How he'd like to feel his knuckles collide with Cox's nose, crunching bone and flesh, sending blood dripping over the reprobate's snowy white cravat . . .

Jack elbowed him in his side. "Stop growling."

"What?" Ned scowled. "I'm not growling."

"You are. I heard you quite distinctly."

"You need to clean the wax out of your ears."

"If I had wax in my ears, I wouldn't have heard you."

Ned tightened his fists. Perhaps he'd tap Jack's claret instead.

Ash leaned over. He'd won the chair by the wall, so he could be free of Lady Heldon. "What are you two arguing about?"

"Nothing." Ned glanced at Lady Juliet on his other side. He should be conversing with her, but her attention also appeared to be focused on Cox. She did not look happy.

She must have encountered the villain in London; he would ask her about the man's reputation as soon as Miss Wharton was done singing. If it was unsavory, he'd have a word with Father. Mama quite obviously was capable of making mistakes—look at that clod pole, Humphrey.

"Ned was growling," Jack said.

Ned snapped his head back to glare at Jack again. "For the last time, I was *not* growling."

"I know what I heard. You were glowering at Cox, flexing your fingers, and growling."

"If we weren't in Mama's music room, I'd show you growling."

Father, sitting in front of them, twisted around and raised his eyebrows. "I don't know what you are hissing about, but you will have to settle it later. Miss Wharton is about to begin."

Mama had coerced Percy into playing the pianoforte for Miss Wharton, so at least the accompaniment would be tolerable. For all Percy's faults, he was an excellent musician. He struck the opening chords. Father turned forward, and Ned, after giving Jack one last pointed look, sat back in his seat.

He wished *he* had a copious supply of earwax. If Miss Wharton's singing was anything like her speaking voice, he would need it. He cringed—surreptitiously, he hoped—as she opened her mouth.

A surprisingly sweet sound emerged.

His was not the only sigh of relief, all quickly muffled or turned into discreet coughs. Miss Wharton appeared not to notice. She sang without faltering in a pure soprano, seemingly caught up in the music, and she blushed very prettily at the enthusiastic applause when she finished.

"At least you'll have some entertainment if the girl succeeds in marrying you," he murmured to Jack.

"Very amusing. I am not that fond of music, as well you know."

"She is looking for a seat," Ash said. "Should I give her mine?"

Jack raised his brows, though his eyes looked slightly desperate. "So you can sit next to the Widow Heldon?"

It was Ash's turn to look hunted. "Ah, yes, perhaps I'll stay where I am."

"I don't know why you're concerned about the woman, Ash," Ned said. "She can't trap you into anything. You're already married."

Ash picked an invisible bit of lint off his pantaloons. "My life is complicated enough; I don't need any more entanglements."

The only entanglement Ash had was Jess, who lived a two-day ride from Greycliffe and whom he hadn't seen or communicated with directly for eight years. As far as Ned knew, Ash lived like a monk. Not that it was any of his business. Ash was welcome to do as he pleased—assuming Father and Mama would tolerate it.

Not for the first time Ned thanked God he wasn't the heir. People said Father was far more understanding than most dukes, which was probably true. He'd inherited the title by accident when his uncle and cousins were killed in a fire. But he'd been Greycliffe for almost forty years now and had put a lot of effort into the duchy—the older tenants often said how much things had improved since Father became duke. He could not like Ash's odd marital situation throwing the succession into doubt.

And speaking of succession, *he* would like to have a son to succeed him at Linden Hall. He should be wooing Lady Juliet, not squabbling with Jack.

He turned to her. In profile, she didn't look so much

like Cicely, especially at the moment. She was clapping halfheartedly, her mouth turned down, her jaw hard while she stared at . . . he followed her gaze. Cox.

Why the hell was she looking at that fellow again?

"I think Miss Wharton acquitted herself quite well, don't you?" Ned asked.

Lady Juliet dragged her eyes back to him. "I'm sorry— what did you say?" She blushed slightly. "I'm afraid I wasn't attending."

"I said I thought Miss Wharton sang well."

"Oh, yes." Her eyes drifted back to Cox. "She has a very nice voice."

"Indeed she does." He addressed her profile again. "I wonder whom my mother will coerce into performing next."

"Hmm?"

Clearly Lady Juliet's attention was not going to be easily pried away from Cox. She was frowning again. Was she afraid the fellow would do her some insult? He'd damn well better not try. "Has Cox been annoying you, Lady Juliet?"

"What?" She snapped her gaze back to him. Her color fluctuated from pale to flushed; her tongue darted out to moisten her lips. "No, of course not. I've hardly spoken to him."

"But he's distressed you in some way."

She shook her head and looked down at her hands; her fingers were twisting her skirt into pleats. She stopped them and smoothed out the cloth. "No. How could he have? I said I'd hardly spoken to him."

She was lying. "Here, yes, but what about before? Did he trouble you in London?"

"No." Her mouth flattened into a tight, thin line. "Why are you so persistent, Lord Edward?"

He should leave it, but he couldn't. "I don't wish you to be uncomfortable. If—"

"I'm not uncomfortable."

He still didn't believe her. "There are other women here

who might be at risk if the man poses some threat." Damn it, Cox was leaning too close to Ellie again. "Miss Bowman, for example. She's a childhood friend; I would hate for any harm to come to her."

Lady Juliet's brows arched. "I'd have thought Miss Bowman old enough to choose her own"—she smiled, though not very pleasantly—"acquaintances. She certainly looks as if she is well past the first blush of youth."

"Well, of course Miss Bowman knows her own mind, but she's led a rather sheltered life." Ned frowned. Was Lady Juliet criticizing Ellie? He didn't care for that—nor did it speak well of the girl that she had so little concern for a fellow female. However, she *was* young—he'd have to ask Mama just how young—and sometimes young women, especially beautiful young women, needed a few years more experience to sympathize with the less fortunate. Cicely had . . . well, he'd been young, too, so he could hardly criticize Cicely. "Miss Bowman's not used to dealing with men of Cox's stamp."

Lady Juliet's beautiful little chin tilted up. "Your mother—the Duchess of *Love*—invited Mr. Cox, so I hardly think you need worry. And what harm can he do in your father's house, under your mother's nose?" The slight edge in her voice indicated she knew the answer quite well. Cox could steal Ellie's good sense and break her heart.

Well, if Lady Juliet wouldn't tell him about Cox, he'd ask Jack. In fact, he should have thought about that at once—likely would have if they hadn't been arguing. Jack would have heard if Cox was a bounder. He started to turn to his brother, but stopped when Mama spoke.

"That was splendid, Miss Wharton. You have such a lovely voice."

Miss Wharton blushed. "Thank you, your grace." She smiled, looked around the room, and focused on Jack.

Jack smiled back at her and muttered, "If either of you

offer her your seat, I swear I will fill your boots with snow or, better, toss them into the deepest drift I can find."

"Take my seat, Miss Wharton," Mr. Cox said, standing.

Miss Wharton, looking a little deflated, bobbed her head and sat.

Ned felt a twinge of conscience. He'd just been mentally taking Lady Juliet to task for a lack of sympathy. "Are you sure—"

"Yes," Jack hissed. "It's better not to encourage false hope, believe me."

"Your grace." Cox smiled at Mama. "May only women sing at this gathering?"

Mama laughed. "Of course not, sir. My husband and sons cannot carry a tune among them, so I forget to ask our male guests to favor us with a song. Would you care to perform?"

"I'd be happy to, if Sir Percy can be persuaded to remain at the pianoforte."

"Percy?" Mama asked.

Percy nodded. "Of course, if I know the music."

"I'm sure you do," Cox said. "I'm going to sing 'Some Rival Has Stolen My True Love Away.'"

Lady Juliet sucked her breath in sharply, causing Ned to glance down at her. If looks could kill, Cox would be breathing his last on the music room floor.

Cox extended his hand to Ellie. "And I hope Miss Bowman will join me."

If looks could kill, Cox would be twice dead. Couldn't the man sing the damn ditty by himself? Ellie blushed and protested a little, but she got up to stand next to the rogue.

The song was the usual sentimental pap about true love. Ellie had a pretty voice, but Cox's baritone was extraordinary, much as Ned hated to admit it. Still, the man was a bit too theatrical for Ned's taste—he held Ellie's hand and gazed down at her through the whole damn thing. And

Ellie, blast it, appeared to be falling under his spell. She blushed from first note to last.

Ned would have to keep a very close eye on her indeed.

Mama sighed and clapped enthusiastically when they were done. "Oh, that was very nice, Mr. Cox. And you sang well, too, of course, Ellie." She smiled at her guests. "Who would like to go next? Don't be shy."

Mr. Humphrey cleared his throat. "I would be happy to oblige everyone with a song, your grace, as I must tell you I am accounted quite the virtuoso at home, always being begged to give everyone another tune until it is almost embarrassing, though I must warn you I did have a bit of a cold a few weeks ago that left me with a nasty cough; however, I believe I am sufficiently recovered to—"

Father rose to save them. "Thank you, Mr. Humphrey, but I'm afraid we must let your voice rest another night." He looked at Mama. "I think our guests are tired from traveling all day, dear duchess. We should let them seek their beds."

Ned watched Cox smile. Bloody hell. The bastard had better not be considering seeking Ellie's bed.

Mama nodded. "I suppose you are right." She smiled brightly at the group. "Off to your rooms, then, and we'll see you bright and early in the morning. I've got many pleasant activities planned."

Mama had barely stopped speaking before Jack shot out of his chair with Ash at his heels; they made their escape, leaving Miss Wharton and Lady Heldon to find their way upstairs on their own. Percy and Ophelia had their heads together by the pianoforte, likely planning an assignation; and Humphrey was standing with Mama, Father, and Miss Mosely, talking their ears off. Father yawned rather obviously, but Mr. Humphrey rattled on.

Ned looked for Ellie; he'd like to have a word with her before she went to bed. He should advise her to be on her guard. He might have encouraged her to entertain Mama's matches, but he'd never intended for her to throw herself into the lion's den. Not that she would ever enter a man's room, of course, but this man . . . perhaps he should also suggest she lock her door.

She was already walking out of the room with Cox, damn it.

"May I have your escort upstairs, Lord Edward?" Lady Juliet had also been watching Cox and Ellie, but now she smiled up at Ned.

"Of course." He offered her his arm.

She put her hand on his sleeve—and dragged him briskly out of the room to the foot of the stairs. Cox and Ellie had just started up.

"I am so looking forward to tomorrow, Lord Edward," she said rather loudly. "Do you have any idea what your dear mother has planned?"

Had Cox's back stiffened? "No," Ned said quietly. "My mother is completely unpredictable."

For some reason that sent Lady Juliet into peals of laughter.

A few steps above them, Ellie stumbled slightly. Cox steadied her. "You have a beautiful voice, Miss Bowman," he said. His voice wasn't as loud as Lady Juliet's, but it carried very well.

Ned strained to hear Ellie's reply. Lady Juliet didn't give him the opportunity.

"Do you think we'll take the sleighs out tomorrow?" Lady Juliet's voice dropped lower and acquired a sultry note. "I would love to share a fur blanket with you, Lord Edward."

Cox's back definitely stiffened at that, and he paused as if he were going to turn around. What the hell was going on?

At least it was clear Lady Juliet was not afraid of Cox.

"We will have to wait for the snow to stop," Ned said. "O'Leary, the head groom, will not want the horses out if the conditions aren't safe for them."

"Oh, pooh." Lady Juliet stuck her lower lip out in what she must think was a fetching pout, but her eyes slid back up to Cox. "Well, then I suppose I shall have to be patient, shan't I?"

"As shall we all." Ned glanced down to see if this odd little drama was being observed. Lady Heldon smirked at him from the bottom of the steps. Damn.

Cox and Ellie finally reached the bedroom floor and turned down the corridor. Fortunately, Mama had put Ellie in a room close to Ned's; he'd deposit Lady Juliet and then be certain Cox made his way promptly to his own bedchamber before he retired himself.

He stopped at Lady Juliet's door to bid her good night while trying to watch Ellie and Cox unobtrusively. Lady Juliet was not so cautious. She simply stood and stared, so Ned joined her. The show was better than a damn farce.

"You have such a lovely voice, Miss Bowman," Cox said rather passionately. The man knew he had an audience. "I thoroughly enjoyed singing with you."

"Thank you." Ellie glanced at Ned and Lady Juliet and then pushed open her door. "Good ni—"

Cox captured her hand, lifting it to his lips. "I felt such a connection with you when our voices joined."

Lady Juliet hissed.

Ned agreed with her. The urge to punch Cox in the nose returned tenfold. How could the man spout such ridiculous drivel with a straight face? Ellie must have more sense than to be taken in by it.

And Cox had bloody well better not try joining anything besides his voice with Ellie.

Ellie darted another glance at them and then tugged her fingers free. "Yes, thank you, I enjoyed singing with you, too, sir. Now if you'll excuse me, I find I'm quite tired. Good night." She stepped into her room and shut her door firmly in Cox's face. Ned wanted to cheer.

Cox stared at the closed door for a moment, and then turned and started back toward them.

Suddenly Lady Juliet was smiling up at Ned. She, too, sounded rather passionate. "Thank you so much for your kind escort, my lord. It was delightful sitting with you in the music room, and I look forward to seeing you"—she flicked her eyes at Cox and dropped her voice again— "later."

Cox's face darkened so he resembled a thundercloud— or a man bent on murder, preferably Ned's.

Bloody hell. Ned was not going to get caught up in whatever little game these two were playing. "In the morning," he said firmly. "I will see you in the morning, Lady Juliet."

He bowed and stepped aside so Cox could pass. The man glared at him, and then gave Lady Juliet a hard look before proceeding to his room. Lady Juliet smiled at Cox's back and then closed her door.

Ned strode down the corridor. Perhaps he should rethink his pursuit of Lady Juliet. She obviously had some feelings for Cox—and Cox had some feelings for her.

He paused as he passed Ellie's door. Should he warn her? He could knock—

He heard a step behind him and glanced over his shoulder. Lady Heldon had reached the floor. He'd better keep moving. The woman wouldn't understand that since he and Ellie were almost siblings, his talking with her in her bedchamber would be unexceptional. Not that he'd ever done such a thing, of course.

When he got to his rooms, he found the door ajar. Damnation! He was certain he'd shut it firmly when he'd left earlier. Could . . . no, this couldn't be happening again. He stepped inside. "Reggie!"

"Merrow!"

Blast it all. "You'd better not be up to your thieving tricks again or I'll toss you out the window into the snow."

He strode through his sitting room to his bedroom. There was Reggie, sitting on his bed, casually licking his hind leg.

"Did one of the maids let you in?"

Reggie paused, blinked at him, and then transferred his attention to his other hind leg.

"You'd better hope I don't find anything under this bed."

And damn it, now he was reduced to talking to a cat.

He got down on his hands and knees and reached into the murky space. Confound it, Reggie *had* been sneaking around the guest rooms. He dumped the plunder onto the coverlet: three white plumes, a gray kidskin glove, a small enameled snuffbox with a very naughty picture on the lid, a jeweled hairpin, and something that looked suspiciously like a false calf.

"How the hell are we going to return all this? Reggie—oh, damn."

Reggie jumped off the bed, revealing he'd been lying on yet another purloined item—a pair of red silk drawers.

Chapter 6

Find a way to haunt a man's thoughts.
—Venus's Love Notes

"It's still snowing. No sleigh rides today." The Duke of Greycliffe let the curtain fall over the window and padded back to the ducal bed. "How do you propose to keep your guests out of trouble, my dear duchess?"

"They're your guests, too, Drew," Venus said, "and—ack!" She scooted away from him. "Kindly keep your feet to yourself. They are blocks of ice."

Drew grinned as he reached for her again. "But isn't that why I have a lovely wife in my bed—to warm my feet when they are cold?"

"No. Definitely not. I—umm."

Drew was nuzzling her neck, just where she most liked it. She shivered—and not from the cold. Even after thirty years of marriage, she still craved her husband's touch.

But she must remember she had a house full of guests.

"I thought I'd send them hunting in the dungeon. They— ohh." Drew's fingers tweaked one of her nipples.

"Whatever for? They'll just find a lot of cobwebs—and perhaps a mouse or two." His lips feathered over her throat while his clever fingers moved to her other nipple.

"Not if we hide things for them to discover." That felt so good. "And I'll send Reggie along to take care of the m-mice." But it would feel better naked. She tugged on his nightshirt. "Take this off."

"Aren't you afraid I'll catch a chill?"

She heard the laughter in his voice. "No." She tugged again. The damn man was not helping. "I'll keep you warm."

"But you complained so vociferously about my cold feet."

"Drew . . ." She would teach him to tease her. She darted her hand up his leg and wrapped her fingers around—

"Ah." His voice hitched. "Perhaps you are right."

"Of course I am." He was growing thicker and longer. She never ceased to be amazed by this organ. She stroked it, and he drew in a sharp breath, closing his eyes briefly.

"Yes, I am definitely too warm," he said. "However, if you wish me to shed this annoying nightshirt, you'll have to let go."

Venus sighed. This was fun—but it would be much more fun when they were skin to skin. "Very well."

The second her fingers left him, he had his nightshirt over his head and sailing through the air. Her nightgown followed in short order—just as their door started to open.

"Tsk." That was Mary's voice coming from the corridor. "They're at it again, Timms, and at their age. We'll have to come back later."

The door closed, and presumably Venus's maid and Drew's valet went away.

"Oh, dear, Mary will give me that look of hers when she

comes in later." Venus chewed her lip. "Perhaps we *should* get out of bed. What if our guests are up?"

"Then they can amuse themselves—and Mary gives you that look every morning." Drew's hand was moving in a very interesting direction.

"Well, she does think it highly improper that we sleep in the same bed. You know it would suit her notion of my consequence much better if I used the duchess's bedroom and you only visited me occasionally."

"Yes, but it wouldn't suit my notion of comfort. Damn consequence! I refuse to be Greycliffe when I'm in bed with my wife." He kissed her belly and trailed his fingers lower.

Venus wiggled, panting slightly. Oh, just a little lower. A little . . . yes, there. And then his tongue . . .

It was still early. Most of their guests were used to London hours. She and Drew had time to—ohh.

This wouldn't take long; she was desperate for him. She tugged on his hair.

He grinned. "Impatient, dear duchess?"

"Yes." She tugged again. "Very."

Drew was most obliging. He knew exactly what she liked, and when he came over her and into her, she anticipated the explosive pleasure and yet was as thrilled as if it was her first time.

Well, more thrilled. She'd had no idea what to expect the first time. That had been outside on the hard ground, and it had hurt. She had to admit experience, a bed, and a closed door greatly improved things.

"Mmm." She wrapped her arms around him. She never wanted to let him go.

"You are always a delight, my dear duchess." He was a little breathless.

She smiled and kissed his cheek. The first time had been wonderful—if painful—but all the other times since had deepened and strengthened her bond with him. They had faced life side by side. They had gone through sickness and health together; they had shared the joys and worries of raising their sons. Drew knew her better than anyone else in the world—as she knew him.

He turned his head to meet her lips. "Tell Mary you are never sleeping anywhere but here with me."

"I think she knows that after all these years."

This was why she tried to help men and women find their match. This was what she wanted for her sons. Not the physical union—though that was lovely—but this deep sense of belonging to another, this feeling of home and family and connectedness.

Her emotions flooded her as they always did. "I love you, Drew."

"And I love you." Drew kissed her nose and rolled off onto his back. "I love you so much I will endure another day of these annoying people invading my home and my peace."

She laughed and sat up. After the magic came the mundane. She needed to get busy. "Remember that, please. I'm afraid I may need your help more than I usually do this time."

He groaned, throwing his arm over his eyes. "Why do I think this means I will have to involve myself in your matchmaking activities?"

"Because you are very astute."

He moved his arm slightly to glare at her. "*You* are the Duchess of Love."

She grinned back at him and hopped down from the bed. "And you are the Duke of Love."

"I am not. The very thought is revolting."

She scooped up her nightgown and slipped it over her head. "I'm not asking you to do very much."

"Ha! I know you, Venus. You are going to make me

work far more than I wish." He pulled himself up to sit against the headboard, and she was momentarily distracted by his naked chest and shoulders and arms.

"And if you continue looking at me that way," he said, "I'll be forced to haul you back into this bed and"—he waggled his brows—"show you exactly how much I *am* the Duke of Love."

She laughed. "A vain threat. I know you can't do what we just did again so soon."

He chose to look offended. "It's not very sporting of you to say so." Then he grinned. "But you know I can still have you writhing and moaning."

He could, too, and often had. "Don't you dare. I need to attend to our guests."

"And I need to attend to their hostess."

"You *have* attended to me." She moved farther away from the bed to ensure she didn't fall victim to temptation. "Now please pull your mind from between the sheets. We need to discuss this party."

Drew got out of bed to retrieve his nightshirt, and she admired his muscled arse before forcing herself to sit at her dressing table. Her hair looked like she'd been pulled backward through a bramble bush. She picked up her brush.

"You do have an odd assortment this year," Drew said before he threw the nightshirt over his head. "I thought you planned these things carefully."

"I do." Venus sighed and looked in the mirror. Was that another gray hair? "I did. It's just that this group will take a little extra effort."

"I'll say. That Humphrey fellow—"

Venus waved away Mr. Humphrey. "He is not the problem."

"He is if Ellie decides to have him." Drew grimaced. "What a thundering bore. You didn't really think he'd be a good match for her, did you?"

"Of course not. My plans are far more complicated than that. I invited Mr. Humphrey to serve a purpose."

"And does he?"

"I'm not certain." She met Drew's eyes in the mirror. "When one involves oneself in matters of the heart, nothing is clear."

"That I can definitely agree with." He frowned. "And why did you invite Lady Heldon? She's little more than a light-skirt, though I'll grant you that's never kept Ophelia off the guest list. But at least Ophelia limits herself to Percy. Lady Heldon looks to have designs on Ash"—his frown deepened to a scowl—"though what those designs could be is rather a mystery."

"She has her purpose, too."

"If you say so. You are far too deep a player for me. Just tell me what you want me to do."

Venus put down her brush and turned to face him. "Keep an eye out for poor Jack. I'm afraid Miss Wharton *was* a mistake. She is far more desperate than I'd guessed." And then she grinned. "And help me cut out and hide a dozen paper hearts."

Ned frowned at his boots. He was sitting in the drawing room, waiting for the rest of the party to assemble so Mama could reveal the first activity of the day. And there *would* be an activity. Mama did not believe in letting people find their own amusements.

It would have to be something inside. There was no going out. The snow was still tumbling down in thick flakes which the howling wind slapped against the windows and swept into deep drifts.

He slid down on the settee. Why the hell had he chosen this piece of furniture? It was damned uncomfortable. He could sit anywhere he wanted; everyone else was still at breakfast.

He surveyed the available choices. The truth was all the seating options were uncomfortable since Mama had changed the furniture last year. He could switch to a stiff, straight-backed chair, but he should leave those for Jack and Ash. They were the ones seeking to keep females at a safe distance; Ned was supposed to be welcoming women. One particular woman—Lady Juliet.

He closed his eyes, trying to picture the girl, but the only female who popped into his mind was Ellie.

Damn those red drawers.

He'd come down early to give Mama the things Reggie had stolen. At first he'd thought to bring them to the drawing room himself and let their owners simply pick them up off a handy table, but then he remembered the salacious snuffbox and the false calf. The people who belonged to those items might appreciate some discretion. Not that Mama was the soul of that virtue, but it was her party and her thieving cat, so it was her problem.

But the silk drawers . . . He knew whom those belonged to.

He shifted in his seat, but there was no comfortable position to be found.

Perhaps he should have given them to Mama with the rest of the articles. At least then they'd be out of his hands—and he'd had them in his hands rather more than he should have last night. There was something about the smooth, slippery silk—

Blast it, Ellie would be horrified if she knew he'd been fondling her underwear. *He* was horrified. He'd stuffed them into one of his cabinets as soon as he'd realized what he was doing.

How the hell was he going to give them back?

As though his thoughts conjured her, Ellie stepped through the doorway, stopping abruptly on the threshold when she saw him. She looked appalled, damn it. What had happened to their easy, comfortable friendship?

She glanced around the room as if looking for someone—anyone—else to speak to. When she observed they were the only two present, she lifted her chin and approached him.

She was wearing another long-sleeved, high-necked, un-fashionable dark frock. The red drawers could *not* be hers.

But she'd admitted they were.

He'd risen when he'd seen her—he *was* a gentleman, though he wasn't feeling very gentlemanly at the moment. He gave her a curt bow. "Looking for Mr. Cox, Ellie? I'm afraid he must still be abed."

She flushed and scowled at him. "I wasn't looking for Mr. Cox. I saw him in the breakfast room."

"Mr. Humphrey, then?"

"No." She sniffed. "Nor Percy or Jack or Ash or your father—and *certainly* not you."

That hurt, but it also made him angry, and anger was a much safer emotion than . . . whatever the hell he'd been feeling. "You are unpleasantly pert."

"I don't believe I asked your opinion."

He wanted to shake her; instead he clasped his hands behind his back and looked down his nose at her. "You are quite right—you didn't ask. I offered my opinion freely. And here's another bit of free advice—guard your posses-sions more closely."

"Guard my possessions?" She raised her brows, no doubt trying to look haughty, but she couldn't quite manage to mask her confusion. "What do you mean?"

"Reggie has been busy again."

She shrugged. "I know that. Your mother made the announcement at breakfast. She put the things he took on a table in the little yellow salon, and I'm happy to tell you I just checked. Nothing of mine is there."

"Nothing of yours is there because I still have the item in my room."

Now she was beginning to look a little alarmed, though she tried hard not to show it. "You do?"

"Yes. It's of a rather personal and, er, scandalous nature. I thought you might not wish the company to know about it."

Her eyes widened—and then she laughed. "You are teasing me, Lord Edward. I'm sure I don't own anything s-scandalous that Reggie could possibly have taken. The item is probably Lady Heldon's or Ophelia's." She arched a brow. "Or perhaps it is Lady Juliet's."

He hated this false, brittle gaiety. What had happened to her? Ellie had always been direct and truthful. Well, and he supposed he was being rather less than direct himself. "Oh, no, it's yours all right. It's quite distinctive." He paused. His better self insisted he stop, but his better self was easily silenced. "It's very . . . red."

Ellie gasped and turned pale just as Mama and the rest of the party entered.

Mama focused on them immediately. "Oh, there you two are. Having a bit of a tête-à-tête, then?"

"No." Damn it, he felt like a blackguard. It was clear to anyone with eyes that Ellie was upset. "We were just discussing Sir Reginald's bad habits."

"Yes." Ellie gave him a small smile of thanks, which only made him feel worse. "Lord Edward was reminding me to secure my possessions."

Mama laughed. "I'm afraid that's a hopeless task, as nothing is secure from Sir Reginald. I don't know how he does it, but if Reggie wants something, he'll get it."

Humphrey sniffed. "Permit me to say, your grace, that it seems highly unlikely a mere animal could make off with so many objects of such various sizes and shapes. I'm very much afraid one of your guests"—here he looked frowningly at the gathering—"is playing an ill-considered joke on us, and I must register my extreme displeasure at having someone paw through my personal effects."

Ned would wager a goodly sum that the false calf belonged to Humphrey. Hmm. He did look a trifle lopsided.

"Paw is the exact word," Jack said. "Reggie was caught red-handed—or perhaps I should say 'red-mouthed' as that's how he carries his loot—last year. And you may object all you want—Ned objects vehemently when he finds the things under his bed—but Reggie hasn't yet been persuaded to stop."

"I see." Humphrey tugged on his waistcoat. "Well, in that case may I suggest the animal be put out in the stables for the duration of the gathering?"

There was a stunned silence; the duchess stared at Mr. Humphrey as if he had suddenly sprouted a second head.

"It w-would solve the problem," Miss Mosely ventured rather timidly, "w-wouldn't it?"

Her grace transferred her gaze to Miss Mosely. "Sir Reginald," she said, "is a *house* cat."

"But surely for a few days—" Mr. Humphrey stopped and tugged on his waistcoat again as the duchess returned her attention to him.

"Would *you* care to stay in the stables for a few days, sir?"

"Er, no, of course not, but—"

Her grace put up a hand to stop him. She could be quite imperious when she chose to be. "Neither would Sir Reginald."

"Well, I must say if a cat's comfort is more important than . . ." Mr. Humphrey's bluster died under the duchess's unwavering gaze. His nose twitched. "Yes, well, indeed. It is all highly irregular."

Her grace smiled gently. "Duchesses can be 'highly

irregular,' Mr. Humphrey. It's one of the perks of the position."

"At least you aren't as irregular as the Earl of Landly, your grace," Mr. Cox said. "You know he dresses his poodle in a velvet suit and assigns him his own footman."

The duchess snorted. "Poor Landly is daft—and Reggie would never stand for such nonsense."

The duke chuckled. "Whoever tried to get Reggie into any clothes at all would have his hands and face slashed to ribbons for his efforts."

"Exactly." The duchess glanced at Mr. Humphrey. "Reggie doesn't suffer fools gladly."

Mr. Humphrey sputtered, but for once held his tongue.

"Obviously, Humphrey has yet to meet Sir Reginald," Ned muttered.

Ellie bit her lip and whispered back. "Perhaps it's best they never encounter each other."

Ned grunted. "Reggie has the sense to avoid Humphrey, but I'm not so sure Humphrey is as wise."

Her grace had turned her attention to the entire group. "Please take your seats, everyone, so I can explain today's activity."

Ellie hesitated. She should sit by Mr. Cox and continue . . . well, she wasn't certain what. She'd thought they'd started something last night, but then there'd been that odd trip up the stairs and the man's even odder behavior at her bedroom door. Besides, he was on the other side of the room; it would be more obvious than she cared to be at the moment if she made a point of seeking him out.

She might sit with Mr. Humphrey, but Miss Mosely had already taken a place at his side, likely helping soothe his lacerated sensibilities. Well, sensibilities were better lacerated than hands and face—Reggie would take violent exception to anyone mad enough to try to move him to the stables. And the pain would all be for naught—she'd wager a year's pin money the cat would be back in the castle long before his evictor had closed the stable door.

Ned gestured to the settee he'd been occupying. "Care to join me while we listen to what torture Mama has in store for us?"

"Er, thank you." He *was* standing right next to her—it would be rude to walk away. And if she took this seat, Lady Juliet couldn't—though she saw the other girl had already joined Mr. Cox.

So she sat, and he settled himself next to her.

The settee was far too small. If she reached over just a little, she could put her hand on Ned's thigh.

She laced her fingers in her lap.

"If you've looked out any of the windows," the duchess was saying, "you know the snow is still coming down quite heavily. We don't want to lose any of you in a snow bank or have you frozen into icicles, so we will not be venturing outside today." She smiled at Ellie. "Any sledge races will have to wait."

Did Ned growl?

She ignored him.

"Fortunately," the duchess continued, "I anticipated bad weather, though I'd thought we'd have rain rather than snow. February is so unpredictable, isn't it?"

"Oh yes, your grace," Miss Mosely said. "I had a terrible time deciding what to pack."

Mr. Humphrey cleared his throat.

Oh, no. One would think the man would still be slightly deflated, but apparently not.

"Indeed, I must agree with Miss Mosely as I, too, was forced to spend an inordinate amount of time contemplating what to bring to this delightful gathering. I . . ."

Ellie let her attention wander back to Mr. Cox as Mr. Humphrey droned on. Lady Juliet was whispering to him. Mr. Cox looked bored.

Heavens, why wasn't the man showing more interest? If he truly loved Lady Juliet, he should be delighted she was talking to him. Not that Ellie cared, precisely, but if Lady Juliet married Mr. Cox—and last evening's events suggested she felt some sort of attachment to him—she would not marry Ned. And she shouldn't marry Ned if she didn't love him. Ned had already suffered Cicely's loss; it would be beyond cruel if he had to deal with the pain of an unfaithful, uncaring wife.

Not to mention Ellie wouldn't have to watch him marry someone else again, at least not yet.

"I will admit"—Mr. Humphrey was still going on—"that it is easier for gentlemen to travel than ladies as we don't have to bring the assortment of dresses and spencers and such you lovely ones must carry to dazzle our male eyes; however, we poor men do have to select the proper waistcoats"—Mr. Humphrey had selected a rather bilious green one today—"and transport a vast quantity of cravats in order to appear before you with a suitably arranged creation."

"Yes." It was beginning to look as if Miss Mosely had lost control of her head, she was bobbing it so regularly in her agreement with Mr. Humphrey. "Yes, indeed. My brother always says a man must bring a valise full of cravats when he leaves home."

"Good God," Ned muttered. "Do you suppose Mama would object if I put us all out of our misery by stuffing Humphrey's cravat down his throat?"

Ellie gasped and giggled at the same time, making a sort of strangled gurgle.

"Are you all right?" Ned asked.

"Umm."

Fortunately, her grace had finally wrested the conversation from Mr. Humphrey's deadly grasp. "I'm sure that's all very interesting, but as for today's activity, we—"

"I have a good book," Jack called out, "so don't feel you

need to contrive anything on my account." He'd taken a chair closest to the duchess—and farthest from Miss Wharton. The duke was propped against the mantel nearby.

"And I have some letters that need answering," Ash offered. He'd chosen a chair at a good distance from Lady Heldon.

The duchess frowned at them. "Of course you will wish to put aside your other diversions to participate once you hear what we'll be doing." She paused to smile at everyone. "We're going to have a treasure hunt."

Miss Wharton actually squealed—Ellie wasn't certain she'd ever heard a grown woman make that particular sound—and clapped her hands. "A treasure hunt? How exciting!"

"And what treasure are we hunting?" Lady Heldon asked, interrupting her whispered conversation with Ophelia.

"Coins and bank-notes, I hope," Percy said.

"No, Percy." The duchess frowned at him. "Of course there will be no coins or bank-notes. What are you thinking?"

"That he's so far up River Tick, he'll never find his way home," Ned muttered.

"Shush." Ellie frowned at him—and then jerked her eyes back to the duchess. Why did Ned have to be so damn handsome? Any woman would want to lose herself in his deep brown eyes.

But not she. No. She was done with pining for him.

"My dear brother-in-law must be at very low ebb indeed," he said, "to be so blatant about his interest in the ready."

Ellie darted him a glance. "That's not news. He's been living hand to mouth for years."

Ned's brows rose. "He has?"

"Didn't you know? He traded on his expectations until he inherited and then discovered he was expecting far too much. Apparently his father also let money slip through his fingers like water."

"Hmm. I didn't know that, though I suppose I should have suspected it."

He didn't know because he'd been too enamored of Cicely to notice.

No, that wasn't fair. The rumors hadn't started until after Cicely's mother died—two months after Cicely, when Ned was lost in grief.

"Everyone says Lady Headley held the purse strings," Ellie said. "Once she was gone, there was no stopping Sir Arthur." The kinder souls attributed his sudden wildness to sorrow at the loss of his wife, but given that Percy's father died of an apoplexy nine months later while in bed with two of the maids, Ellie took leave to doubt that.

Ned was shaking his head. "I definitely should have guessed. Percy had been begging money from Cicely ever since we married—perhaps before, for all I know—and once she died, he put the touch on me. I cut him off this Christmas; he must be down to his last farthing now. We'll probably find him looking behind the cushions for spare change."

"So what *are* we hunting, your grace?" Lady Heldon asked again.

The duchess smiled and looked around the room. "In honor of St. Valentine's Day, the duke and I have hidden a dozen paper hearts in the castle's dungeon."

"Paper hearts?!" Percy dropped his head into his hands.

Miss Wharton reacted with more enthusiasm. "A dungeon! A real dungeon?"

"Well," the duke said, "it's really more of a glorified cellar. We use it to store wine—though we did *not* hide any hearts in that area"—he directed his gaze at Percy—"and furniture and other items we don't use at the moment."

"It's quite a hodge-podge, as you might imagine," the duchess added. "Rather dusty, I'm afraid, and a trifle cobwebby. The servants don't clean down there, you understand."

"Are there ghosts?" Miss Wharton looked as if she half hoped the answer was yes.

The duchess smiled. "Not to my knowledge, but with a place as old as the castle—it's been the Greycliffe family seat for almost seven hundred years—it wouldn't be surprising if a spirit or two was in residence."

"Oh, dear. I-I don't believe . . . I mean . . . g-ghosts?" Miss Mosely's voice quavered in alarm.

"If there are any spirits about, I'm sure they're friendly ones." The duke appeared to be trying very hard not to laugh.

"I wouldn't be so certain," Ned muttered. "Hasn't Father looked at the damn ancestors' portraits recently?"

Ellie muffled her giggle.

"Oh, even friendly ghosts . . ." Miss Mosely turned an unpleasant shade of white, prompting Mr. Humphrey to go so far as to pat her hand in a bracing manner.

Ned snorted, though quietly, thank heavens. "That woman should be named Miss Mousely. She's far more likely to encounter a spider than a spirit."

"Please don't say so. I imagine she—and most of the other ladies—would be equally alarmed at that prospect," Ellie said.

He smiled at her. "But not you?"

"Of course not."

"Your grace," Mr. Humphrey said, "I must object to subjecting the ladies to the possible presence of preternatural beings. While I—and I assume your other male guests—would face these creatures without f-flinching"—his voice trembled slightly and he cleared his throat—"if f-forced to do so, I cannot think it wise to risk injuring the delicate sensibilities of the lovely females present by inviting them into an area that might be infested with specters."

The duke stared at Mr. Humphrey as if he were some rare species of beetle. He opened his mouth, likely to put the fellow in his place, but the duchess jumped in before he could do so.

"Oh, Mr. Humphrey—and Miss Mosely—don't be concerned. His grace will be with us, and you know no mere ghost would dare misbehave before the Duke of Greycliffe."

The duke blinked at his duchess. "Quite."

"But what is the point of collecting the hearts?" Percy asked. "There must be a point."

The duchess smiled. "Of course there is. Whoever collects the most hearts will get to take the first sleigh ride."

Lady Heldon frowned and then said what everyone was thinking. "Pardon me, your grace, but that hardly seems worth the effort of venturing into a dank dungeon."

"Dank and dusty," Ophelia said. "I believe I'll stay here and keep my hem clean while the rest of you go looking for hearts."

"We can get up a game of cards." Percy looked around. "Care to join us, Ash?"

"No, thank you." Ash contemplated his mother. "Is the winner to ride alone, Mama?"

The Duchess of Love smiled at her eldest son as if he were exceedingly clever. "No, of course not. He or she gets to choose a companion, so I suppose two people win"—she shrugged—"if the chosen companion is happy with the choice, of course."

There was a moment of silence while everyone digested this bit of information.

Ellie swallowed a sigh. Ned would choose Lady Juliet if

he won, and Mr. Cox would choose—she looked over at the couple on the settee. They were both staring at the duchess.

Would Mr. Cox choose Lady Juliet, too? And that would leave Ned with . . . whom?

"Ah, you should have said so at once, your grace." Lady Heldon stood, shook out her skirts, and threw what was obviously intended as a flirtatious glance at Ash. "Will you lead us down to this dungeon, Lord Ashton?"

"Of course." Ash offered his mother his arm. "May I escort you, Mama? That is if the specter-taming Duke of Greycliffe doesn't object?"

The duke inclined his head as the duchess laughed and put her hand on Ash's arm.

Ned turned to Ellie; well, obviously he had no other choice if he didn't wish to be unconscionably rude.

"Coming?" he asked, offering his arm.

She nodded and put her fingers on his sleeve, on his strong forearm. Her head came only as high as his shoulder.

She felt delicate and feminine for a moment, and familiar, painful longing swept through her. She loved Ned; she'd always loved him and probably always would.

But damn it, he didn't love her, at least not the way she wanted him to.

They were the last to leave the drawing room, and by the time they reached the stairs down to the dungeon, everyone else had vanished.

"People must be eager to begin the game," Ellie said.

"Or to finish it," Ned said. "Here, the stairs are uneven. Let me go first. You can lean on me if you need to."

Ellie watched Ned's broad back move ahead of her as she stepped into the stairwell. She would not touch him if she could possibly avoid it. She put her hand against the wall instead.

Whom would she choose to ride with if she won this

game: the man she loved who thought of her as a sister or the man who'd settle for her if he couldn't have the woman he really wanted?

She stumbled slightly, but caught her balance without having to touch Ned.

She'd choose Mr. Humphrey and hope his incessant, nonsensical chattering put her out of her misery.

Chapter 7

Keep a man guessing . . .
—Venus's Love Notes

Ned hadn't been down in the dungeon for years; he'd forgotten how low the ceiling was. He ducked just in time to avoid banging his head on the lintel as he stepped through the door from the stairs into the cellar. Damn! He'd have to be careful.

"Oh—eek!" Ellie landed hard against his back.

He stumbled forward a step, and then twisted, grabbing her by the shoulders to steady her. Her body brushed against his, her breasts soft against his chest, and he inhaled the clean scent of lemon and soap and woman.

His cock sprang to attention.

He shot his arms straight to hold her away from his misbehaving organ. "Are you all right?"

"I'm fine." She jerked herself free. "I merely tripped on the last step."

"I told you they were uneven."

"Yes, I know. The last one was just deeper than the others."

It was—he'd almost missed it himself. "Be careful—the floor's uneven as well."

"I *know* that. I've been here before."

"Not since you were a girl, unless you've taken to helping Dalton with the wine." They were standing right outside the wine cellar, but Father had been very clear there was nothing hidden among the casks. Everyone else had moved on to the other storage rooms around the corner.

"Of course I haven't been helping Mr. Dalton, but it's not as if any of this has changed since we used to play down here." She looked away. "We should catch up to the others." She took a quick step—and tripped again. He caught her around the waist.

Her slender waist. She had a figure somewhere under this ocean of fabric. As a girl, she'd been tall and willowy. When had she started hiding herself in her clothes?

The damn red drawers popped into his head and the image of how she would look—

What the *hell* was the matter with him?

She slipped out of his hold and started to hurry ahead—and stumbled once more.

"Mama will be very unhappy with me if you get injured while in my care," he said, trying to grasp her elbow. She danced out of his reach, and he lost his patience. "What is the matter, Ellie?"

"Nothing." She wouldn't meet his gaze. "I-I just want to catch up. They might start without us."

"I doubt that." Mama had hit on an inspired way to get them to participate in this silly game. She must know Jack and Ash wanted to be certain they weren't trapped in a sleigh with Miss Wharton or Lady Heldon—and those ladies were equally determined to nab their quarries.

He didn't much care if he won or not; surely he would be

paired with Lady Juliet. Humphrey would likely ride with Miss Mousely—Mosely—and Cox . . .

Ned frowned. Would Cox choose Ellie?

Blast it, he didn't trust the fellow—he was obviously a bit of a rake. Ellie didn't have the experience to deal with a man of his stamp; she might be twenty-six, but she was still as green as grass.

"Why do you wish to find these ridiculous hearts, Ellie?" he asked. "You aren't hoping to capture Cox, are you?" She had spent most of last night in Cox's company, seduced by his pretty face, no doubt.

Oh, damn, she flinched before glaring at him. Had he sounded as if he thought she was out of her depth with Cox? He hadn't meant to injure her feelings.

"I'm merely taking your advice to cooperate with your mother's matchmaking efforts."

He hadn't precisely told her to do that, had he?

"And in any event, your mother and father went to the trouble of hiding the hearts," she said, finally taking his arm. "It would be rude not to show some interest."

They proceeded down the corridor in silence. Ellie might have her fingers on his sleeve, but it felt as if she were separated from him by a solid stone wall. All the easy smiles and relaxed warmth he'd had with her in past years were gone. She was acting like a complete—and unpleasant—stranger.

Perhaps it was just as well. He should concentrate on wooing Lady Juliet. He hated to see Ellie hurt—and he was very much afraid she would be hurt by Cox—but if she didn't want his advice, there wasn't much he could do.

He'd have a word with Jack and Ash, though. She might listen to one of them.

"There you are," Mama called out as they turned the corner and found the group gathered by the door to the first storeroom. "What have you two been up to?"

Something in Mama's tone implied that they had indeed been up to something.

Ellie's cheeks turned bright red, and she whipped her fingers off his arm as if his sleeve had just burst into flames. Zeus, did she have to look so guilty? They hadn't been doing anything but arguing, for God's sake.

"I was merely helping Ellie—I mean, Miss Bowman— navigate the uneven flooring," he said.

"Oh?" Mama raised her brows. "I would have thought you'd have no trouble with your footing, Ellie. You and Ned played down here often enough."

"That was when I was a girl, your grace," Ellie said, "many years ago."

"Not so many." Mama had a definite twinkle in her eye. "Why it seems like it was just yesterday."

Good God, now Mama seemed to be hinting that he and Ellie made a practice of sneaking down into the dungeons for some salacious purpose. "Hardly yesterday," he said. "More like almost twenty years ago."

Mama and Ellie both glared at him.

"Well, it was. Admit it, Ellie. You couldn't have been more than seven or eight—ten at the outside—the last time we were down here."

"You might not have wanted to stress quite how far from girlhood Ellie is," Father murmured.

Apparently Father was correct. Ellie showed him her back. "I believe I did say it was many years ago. Is it time to start the game, your grace?"

Mama looked at Ned reproachfully before she smiled at everyone else. "Yes, indeed. Now that we are all here, the hunt can begin."

Ophelia and Lady Heldon almost knocked Ash down to get through the storeroom door, Miss Wharton close on their heels and everyone else not far behind. Immediately the sound of drawers opening and shutting filled the corridor.

"The hearts are rather cleverly hidden"—Mama had to raise her voice to be heard over the din—"and some have clues written on them, so you'll have to use your heads from time to time."

No one even paused in his or her furious searching.

"The duke and I will meet you at the other end of the storerooms. We don't want to risk giving anyone hints."

Mama and Father moved off down the corridor. Ned waited until Ellie and the rest of the party—led by Ophelia, Lady Heldon, and Miss Wharton, of course—had moved onto the second room before he even stepped out of the passageway.

Ash and Jack were the only ones left. Jack had slipped his arm out of his sling once they were alone and was now pulling drawers out haphazardly while Ash leaned against a hideous wooden chair. Carved serpents frolicked across its back. Not for the first time Ned wondered about the decorating taste of his ancestors.

"Why aren't you looking for hearts, Ash?" he asked. "Think they've all been found already?"

Jack was the one who answered. "No one found anything here, so I'm still hopeful." He glanced at Ash. "Why aren't you looking? Resigned to cuddling with Lady Heldon under the fur rug?"

"Don't be disgusting. I just don't believe a helter-skelter approach is the best plan." Ash shrugged. "I'm trying to think like Mama to figure out where she might have hidden the damn things."

"Now there's a frightening notion," Ned said. "I suspect even Father can't divine the workings of Mama's mind."

The storerooms ran the length of the castle and were a series of chambers crammed full of chairs, tables, clothes, statues, paintings, and other odds and ends. Ned had long ago decided his ancestors never threw anything away; they just consigned it to the dungeon.

He and Ash and Jack—and Ellie and Cicely and Percy and Jess—had never tired of exploring the vast, odd collection of cast-offs. He smiled at the battered, one-armed knight propped against the wall in one corner.

"Ah, here's Sir Gawain," he said. He stepped closer. "And his right arm is still on the floor beside him."

Ash laughed. "Thank God it was his arm and not mine."

Ned nodded. When Ash and Percy had been ten or so, they'd pretended to battle with some staves they'd found against another wall. As too often happened, Percy forgot they were pretending—fortunately Sir Gawain, rather than Ash, had paid the price.

"Our thanks, sir knight," Ned said, and lifted the visor as he'd used to do. A red, heart-shaped piece of paper fluttered out.

"Aha," Jack said from where he was poking into the drawers of a broken washstand. "You've found the first heart. Is there a clue on it?"

Ned turned the scrap of paper over. "No, there doesn't appear to be."

"Too bad. I was hoping—" Jack stopped as they heard a squeal from another room.

"Damn." Ash let out a long breath. "Which female was that?"

"Unfortunately for me, it sounded like Miss Wharton. She makes a rather distinctive sound." Jack closed the last drawer and moved away from the washstand. "You know, Ash, I think Ophelia is helping Lady Heldon."

"I'm afraid you're right. Percy probably put her up to it for Lord knows what purpose." Ash's voice was calm, but

Ned heard the current of anger running deep in it. While none of them liked Percy, Ash truly detested the fellow. "But as you keep pointing out, I'm already married, so the widow can't do much more than annoy me. Miss Wharton, however, does seem determined to make you her husband."

"Don't I know it," Jack said glumly.

"Here." Ned handed Jack the paper heart. "You need this more than I do."

"I've found one; I've found one!" Miss Wharton plucked a paper heart from the jaws of a snarling lion epergne and performed a squealing pirouette, knocking a large, hideous, blue and red china dog with her elbow.

Ellie lunged and caught it before it plunged off the edge of the table.

"How exciting." Miss Mosely put down the brass candlestick she'd been examining and sighed. "I wish I could find a heart."

"Now, now, Miss Mosely," Mr. Humphrey said, "do not despair. We are only just beginning the game—I have no doubt you'll be successful, too." He pushed the garish yellow sofa he'd been looking behind back against the wall and nodded at Miss Wharton. "Well done, Miss Wharton."

"Yes, indeed. Brava!" Percy clapped slowly and a bit mockingly, Ellie thought, but he was also smiling. Miss Wharton grinned back at him, far too excited to notice any sort of criticism.

"I've always loved treasure hunts." She stuffed the heart in her pocket. "They are so much fun." She almost ran to the next room; Mr. Humphrey and Miss Mosely followed at a slightly more sedate pace.

"Such exuberance!" Lady Heldon raised an eyebrow. "I almost feel as if I'm back among the nursery set."

Ophelia sniggered. "Miss Wharton is far too old for the nursery."

"Indeed," Lady Heldon said. "There's a reason—or should I say many reasons—that she finds herself on the shelf."

"I don't know, Miranda," Percy said. "I find her enthusiasm refreshing."

Lady Heldon stared at him and then shrugged. "I can't believe I heard you correctly, Percy—the girl's worse than the greenest debutante. However, that's neither here nor there. At present she is very determined and either very good at searching or very lucky. We need to do better if I'm to get Lord Ashton into that sleigh with me."

"Keep your voice down, Miranda." Percy glanced at Ellie; she pretended to examine the china dog. There was a large ridge around its middle—ah, yes, she remembered. It was hollow inside.

Lady Heldon sniffed. "Very well. I don't know why we are standing here talking anyway. Come on." She strode into the next room.

Now why did Percy care if Lady Heldon rode with Ash? Ellie watched him and Ophelia leave, and then glanced over at Mr. Cox and Lady Juliet on the other side of the room to see if they'd overheard the odd conversation. Lady Juliet was rummaging through a pile of old cooking pans, making quite a racket; Mr. Cox had his head inside a wardrobe. Likely neither had caught Lady Heldon's words.

She should warn Ash, but what would she warn him about? He knew Lady Heldon was pursuing him—everyone did. She hadn't been at all subtle about it, though what she wanted, since he already had a wife, was a puzzle. Perhaps she was just looking for some bed sport, but one would think she'd be more discreet with the duke and duchess observing her. And why Ash? Surely there were plenty of men in London willing to entertain her.

But perhaps the biggest question was why the duchess had invited the woman at all. She must know Lady Heldon's reputation.

Ellie looked back down at the ugly dog in her hands. Ned had hidden a toad in it once when he was eight and she was six. He'd given it to her to open, hoping she'd scream, but she hadn't. Cicely had, though.

She sighed. Even if she found all the hearts and chose to ride with Ned in the sleigh, it wouldn't make a difference. He'd likely discuss staffing issues at Linden Hall or, worse, reminisce about Cicely and their childhood while they were alone together.

"Miss Bowman."

Ellie jumped and almost dropped the dog. Mr. Cox had come up to her while she'd been lost in thought. She definitely needed to start paying more attention to her surroundings. "You startled me."

"My apologies." He bent close, touching her arm. She tried to shift away, but she bumped up against the table.

Smile, she told herself. Flirt. This man could be your ticket to children.

Her body refused to cooperate.

He was handsome, damn it. He'd make handsome children. What was the matter with her?

He was standing far too near as he examined the epergne. His sleeve almost brushed her bodice. She tried to draw a deep breath.

He smelled a bit, er, sour. Not dirty, just . . . unappealing. Perhaps it was the soap he used.

She leaned back a little more and held the dog in front of her like a shield.

"I can see why this object was consigned to the cellar," he said, smiling at her in an uncomfortably intimate way.

"Having a lion snarling at me during dinner would quite put me off my feed."

She should be happy, not uncomfortable. She tried to smile back. "It isn't very attractive, is it?" She glanced across the room to try to get at least the illusion of space and saw the lion wasn't the only thing snarling. Lady Juliet looked as if she would love to tear Ellie limb from limb.

"I don't suppose the duchess would have hidden another heart so close to the one Miss Wharton found," Mr. Cox said, his breath stirring the tendrils of hair by Ellie's ear.

She shivered. His words buzzed and tickled like an annoying fly; she clutched the china dog tighter to keep from swatting him. "No, I don't suppose she would have." Why wouldn't the man step away? She could give him a good shove, but that certainly wouldn't advance her matrimonial aspirations.

More to the point, how could she expect to have children if she couldn't bear to be this close to their potential father? An even greater degree of proximity was required to achieve motherhood, if she understood the process correctly.

"Oh, Lord Edward!"

Lady Juliet's saccharine tone caused Ellie to snap her head around. Ned stood in the doorway, Ash and Jack behind him. Ash's expression was, as always, carefully neutral, but Jack's damn eyebrows shot up as he looked from her to Cox.

Ned simply glared at her, his nostrils flaring as Mr. Cox leaned even closer. She could literally feel the man breathing down her neck.

"I've been wondering where you were," Lady Juliet said, latching on to Ned's arm. "Have you come to help me find some hearts?"

Ned smiled down at her, blast it. "I am happy to assist you in whatever way I can, Lady Juliet."

"Oh, good. You must know everything down here. Where do you think your mother would have hidden the hearts?"

Ned glanced at Ellie again. "Lady Juliet," he said, "believe me when I say I can't begin to comprehend my mother's mind."

"Mama *is* a deep one," Jack agreed, coming over to examine the epergne also.

"Miss Wharton has already found the heart that was between the lion's jaws," Mr. Cox said, shifting a little so Ellie could almost straighten.

Jack nodded. "Doubtless that was the shriek we heard."

"She was very excited," Ellie said. "She—"

Miss Wharton's distinctive squeal sounded again.

"She's found another." Jack scowled at the lion. "She'll have them all in short order."

"She will not. Come along, Lord Edward." Lady Juliet dragged Ned with her. "We may need to skip ahead a room, since Miss Wharton seems to have the devil's own luck. You don't think the duchess did give her some hints, do you?"

"Good God, I hope not," Jack muttered as Ned and Lady Juliet left.

"Since this room seems to have been thoroughly searched, I'll go along as well," Ash said. "Coming, Cox?"

"I suppose so." Mr. Cox offered Ellie his arm. "Shall we, Miss Bowman?"

"If you don't mind, Cox, I'd like a word with Ellie," Jack said. "Alone," he added when Mr. Cox made no effort to move.

Mr. Cox raised his eyebrows. "Oh? Is that quite proper, Lord Jack?"

Jack snorted. "Good God, man, don't be an idiot. Besides the fact that I've got only one good arm"—he gestured toward his sling—"Ellie and I grew up together. She'd not hesitate a moment to box my ears if I did anything to annoy her—or bash me over the head with that china dog she's holding." He looked at Ellie. "Isn't that right, Ellie?"

"I'd be boxing your ears or bashing your head constantly, Jack, if that were true." Ellie laughed. "Go on, Mr. Cox. I don't know what you think could happen within shouting distance of a crowd of people—Miss Wharton has certainly demonstrated how sound travels down here—but I am completely safe with Lord Jack in any case."

"Very well." Mr. Cox bowed and took himself off.

"Zounds, Ellie," Jack said as soon as the man had departed, "you don't mean to have him, do you? He's pretty enough to look at, I suppose—he's quite the dashing devil in Town—but he's damn annoying. A bit of a rogue, really."

"And that's saying a lot, coming from you."

Jack rolled his eyes. "Very funny." His expression grew serious. "I'd have wagered you'd take my boring brother over him."

Heat flooded Ellie's cheeks, and she looked down quickly to avoid Jack's probing gaze. She thought of putting the china dog back on the table, but decided it felt rather comforting and solid in her hands. "It doesn't much matter what I want; Ned's not going to give me the choice." Not that she could be assured that Mr. Cox would offer for her, either.

"I know Ned is a little slow—"

"He told me he thinks of me as a sister, Jack."

"Egad." Jack's jaw dropped.

Ellie tapped it with her finger. "You'll catch flies if you aren't careful."

Jack snapped his mouth closed. "Ned's blockheadedness never ceases to amaze me. The man's as thick as these castle walls."

It was nice to have Jack's support, but Jack couldn't make Ned love her the way she wanted him to.

"And I really think Mr. Cox is more interested in Lady

Juliet than me," she said. There was still Mr. Humphrey, but he appeared to be developing a fast friendship with Miss Mosely. Sadly, it looked as if she would fail yet again to make a match, even with the Duchess of Love's best efforts.

"*That* doesn't surprise me."

So much for Jack's support.

"No, don't look at me like that. There were rumors in Town that Cox asked for the girl's hand, and her father turned him down flat. Apparently the fifth son of an earl isn't good enough for the daughter of a duke."

"Or perhaps Lady Juliet simply didn't wish to marry Mr. Cox. She seems to be interested in Ned." Though there had been that odd scene before they'd all retired last night . . .

No, she would not read anything into that.

"Zeus, yes, she does look determined to ensnare Ned, doesn't she?" Jack shook his head. "Doesn't she realize Ned will bury her in the country? He never goes to London; she's hardly ever out of Town. Cox really will suit her much better."

"But if she loves Ned—"

Jack snorted. "Lady Juliet love Ned? I don't think so. I suspect the only person she loves is herself. Hopefully my beef-witted brother will realize that before he proposes." He cleared his throat. "In point of fact, I always thought you'd make Ned a good second wife, Ellie."

"Ah. Er." Jack hadn't said what she thought he'd said, had he? "But I just told you—Ned thinks of me as a sister."

"I don't believe that for a moment. Oh, he may think he thinks that, but that's only because he hasn't allowed himself to consider you in any other light. He couldn't, could he? You were his wife's closest friend." Jack shrugged. "He couldn't let himself see how eager you were to marry him."

Perhaps she could just expire here in the dungeon. There was so much clutter, no one would notice one mummified old maid added to the disorder. "Oh, no, I—"

"Admit it, Ellie. You've been yearning for Ned ever since

Cicely died." Jack moved a candlestick and looked at her sideways. "And maybe even before."

Her stomach knotted, and for a dreadful instant she was seriously afraid she'd cast up her accounts. If Jack had noticed, the entire neighborhood had. Everyone must have been whispering about her and very likely pitying her. How could she—

No. If everyone had been talking, Mama or one of her sisters would have heard and told her.

"Are you all right?"

She blinked. She'd almost forgotten Jack was there. He was staring at her, his brow furrowed, his eyes dark with concern.

"Yes. I'm f-fine." She looked down at the china dog and took a deep breath. Jack could not know anything for certain. "I never tried to come between Cicely and Ned."

Well, except for the red silk dress, but fortunately no one but Papa and Mama and her sisters had seen that.

"Yes, more's the pity."

"What?!" Ellie jerked—and almost dropped the poor china dog.

Jack shrugged. "I kept hoping until the moment Ned said 'I do' that you'd somehow manage to keep him from marrying Cicely."

She gripped the china dog harder—she had to hold on to something. "But Cicely was perfect for Ned. Everyone said so."

Jack grimaced. "I didn't. I thought her revoltingly namby-pamby. She never had an opinion of her own, except when she insisted on coming back to Greycliffe to give birth. And she brought Percy into the family, who even Ned would agree is a very dirty dish."

Ellie's head was spinning. Jack hadn't liked Cicely? But everyone had liked Cicely. "She couldn't help Percy."

"No, and she couldn't help that her mother was a tyrant and her father a bully. I suppose it's no wonder she was such a bland, insipid creature."

"Ned loved her." Jack was the wild Valentine. Of course he'd find Cicely dull.

"I'll grant you he was besotted. Cicely was beautiful in a fragile sort of way, and Ned was only twenty-two, with no Town bronze. The fact that she was the complete opposite of Jess probably helped, too."

"Jess?" She couldn't follow Jack at all. "What does Jess have to do with it?"

Jack looked at her as though she were a complete widgeon. "Think about it, Ellie. Jess was notoriously strong-willed, and Ash had left her at Blackweith. Their marriage was a deuced disaster. It's no wonder Ned found a quiet, biddable girl attractive."

Ellie shook her head. She couldn't let Jack confuse her. "Ned and Cicely were very happy together."

"Were they?" He shrugged. "Perhaps, but I doubt it would have lasted. They were married less than a year, remember. I'll wager if Cicely had lived, Ned would have grown heartily sick of her."

"No." Jack knew nothing of love—or at least the kind of love that mattered. "You must be mistaken."

"If you say so." He grinned at her. "Frankly, I'm far more interested in my own marital situation than I am in Ned's."

This was a surprise. "You want to marry?"

"No, I most definitely do *not* want to marry—which is why I've come to you."

"Oh." Ellie tasted bitterness. "Yes, I am definitely the expert on not getting married."

"Don't be an idiot. You could have wed many times over if you'd wanted to. I've been at these infernal gatherings; I've watched you hang on Ash's every word. Not that Ash isn't a fine fellow, but he's not *that* interesting."

"But—"

"And I've watched your suitors find solace with other female guests while Mama gnashes her teeth in frustration."

"You're being ridiculous."

"Am I?" Jack raised an eyebrow.

Ellie looked back down at the dog. He was right about her taking refuge in Ash's company, but he must be wrong about the rest . . . though Ned and the duchess had said much the same thing.

"But that's neither here nor there," Jack said. "It's *my* freedom I'm concerned with at the moment. Will you help me?"

She heard the tension behind his banter. "Of course. What do you need me to do?"

"Keep an eye on Miss Wharton. I'm afraid she's going to try to compromise me."

Ellie laughed. "Oh, Jack, you must be experienced at dodging matrimonial-minded misses. You spend almost all your time in London."

Jack grimaced. "Yes, but Miss Wharton is unusually persistent. She's been after me for months and knows all my stratagems." His face took on a hunted look. "And now to be stuck in the castle with her for days, with Mama in matchmaking mode . . . Ellie, I may be reduced to running off into the snowdrifts."

"No one can make you marry Miss Wharton, even if she does compromise you."

He hunched a shoulder. "Yes, but I'd prefer not to be ostracized by the *ton*. Everyone knows Miss Wharton is pursuing me like a hound after a fox, but if her reputation is damaged, society will still lay the blame at my doorstep. It's always the man's fault, you know."

"But your father is the Duke of Greycliffe. Surely that will count for something."

Jack looked appalled. "Good God, Ellie, I'm not going to hide behind Father's title. What do you take me for?" He frowned at her. "I don't want to damage Miss Wharton's reputation or even wound her sensibilities. She's not a bad sort. She only wants what most women do. If I weren't her quarry, I'd admire her determination." He raised an eyebrow. "Frankly, you might do well to take a page from her book. You really would make Ned an excellent wife, and I'd much rather have you in the family than Lady Juliet."

This was definitely not a topic she wished to pursue. "Yes, well, we are discussing your marital issues, not mine at the moment. I suppose the first thing to do is help you find the hidden hearts; Miss Wharton seems to be winning this game so far."

Jack nodded. "She does appear to have quite the knack for ferreting them out, doesn't she? Rather like a pig hunting truffles." He pulled a crumpled red scrap of paper out of his pocket. "I've only got one, and Ned gave me that."

So Ned wasn't scrambling to amass a winning pile of hearts. It wasn't much, but it made her feel happier.

"Perhaps we can add another heart to your collection." She shook the china dog she'd been holding and then lifted off its head. Just as she'd hoped, there was a red heart inside.

"Capital!" Jack plucked the paper out and started to put it in his pocket.

"Wait! I think there's something written on one side."

Jack examined the heart. "So there is." His brows furrowed. "Dashed if I know what it means, though."

"What does it say?"

"Find what once was here and you'll find another heart." Jack shook his head. "I certainly don't remember Mama putting biscuits or other treats in this thing—I only remember it ever being in the dungeon."

Ellie flushed. The duchess couldn't know about the toad, could she? And that poor creature was long gone. So what could . . .

"There!" She pointed to a large, green porcelain frog sitting on the shelf above the pots Lady Juliet had been rooting through earlier.

Jack looked at her as if she'd lost her mind. "Ellie, that hideous object could never have fit inside this equally ugly dog."

"Look at it anyway." Perhaps she'd misunderstood.

Jack reached up to get the frog and let out a long, low whistle. He turned and showed her the bottom of the figurine. Stuck into a hole in its base was a red heart.

Chapter 8

❧❀❧

. . . but don't confuse him too much.

—Venus's Love Notes

Ned glared at the flower-bedecked shepherdess perched on top of the tall cabinet. There was a thin line around her neck as if she'd had an unfortunate meeting with Madam Guillotine; in actuality, she'd taken a glancing blow from a cricket bat when he and Jack and Ash had been playing in the entry foyer one winter's day many years ago. It was amazing the poor girl hadn't shattered into a thousand pieces. Dalton had glued her back together, but she'd never been the same. She'd found her way down here instead of the trash-heap only because she'd been a gift from one of Mama's cousins.

He transferred his glare to Cox, who was currently poking his finger into the coils of a serpent-shaped candelabrum. He'd like to see a nice thin line around that slimy bastard's neck. Zeus, the London snake had been hanging all over Ellie when Ned had come upon them.

What the hell had Ellie been thinking to let the fellow take such liberties? She clearly had no more sense than a flea, and no interest in being guided by his superior understanding, damn it. Well, if Ellie wouldn't listen to him, Cox would. A fist planted squarely in the middle of one's face generally got a person's attention.

"Finally!" Lady Juliet snatched a scrap of red from a pot-pourri vase that looked like a pyramid of elephant trunks. She shot a rather triumphant glance at Cox for some reason, and then waved the heart in Ned's face. "I found one."

He took a step back to avoid being poked in the nose. "I see."

She stuffed the heart in her pocket and threw open a clothes press, diving in to rummage through the items Mama or some earlier duchess had consigned to that dark oblivion. A square of orange fabric flew out and fluttered to the floor. Lady Juliet was as bad as a terrier pursuing a rat.

She pulled her head out of the wardrobe when they heard a familiar squeal.

"Blast, Miss Wharton's found another heart." She frowned at Ned. "And you look like one of the statues your family has dumped down here, Lord Edward. Hurry up and start searching through things, if you please. We can't let Miss Wharton win."

The meek, gentle, quiet Lady Juliet of the drawing room who'd so resembled Cicely had vanished; this new woman was a bit of a shrew.

"Why can't we? I assume she'll choose Jack as her sleigh partner; you aren't interested in my brother, are you?"

Her frown deepened to a scowl. "Of course not—don't be such a chub."

Ned hoped his jaw hadn't noticeably dropped, but he was very much afraid it had.

"Lady Juliet is somewhat, ah, competitive, Lord Edward,"

Cox said. His mouth curled into a faint sneer. "She must win the prize even when she doesn't want it."

Lady Juliet's expression froze for an instant; then she tossed her head before sticking it back in the wardrobe. Her subsequent exhortation emerged slightly muffled. "Don't you be a chub either, Mr. Cox."

"I don't seem to be able to help myself," Cox muttered. He shoved his hands in his pockets and looked back the way they'd come. "Where do you suppose Miss Bowman has got to?"

"I'm sure she'll be along shortly," Ned said. If Ellie won the contest and chose Cox as her partner, he'd have to intervene even though he wasn't really her brother. He couldn't in good conscience let his childhood friend be alone with such a scoundrel, even in public in a sleigh outdoors. A thick fur rug could hide countless liberties.

Cox raised his brows. "I wonder if Miss Wharton knows Miss Bowman is alone with Lord Jack."

Ned's brows dropped. He did not like Cox's tone.

"Why would Miss Wharton care?" Ash looked up from the cabinet he'd been inspecting.

"Yes, what are you getting at, Cox?" Ned would really, really like to punch the man. Perhaps he could manage to knock something heavy over on him. "You act as if there's some impropriety going on."

Cox looked blandly back at Ned. "Lord Jack *is* unwed— as is Miss Bowman."

Ned snorted. "Don't be ridiculous. Jack thinks of Miss Bowman as a sister."

"Perhaps he does." Cox smiled in an exceedingly slimy way. "But how does Miss Bowman view Lord Jack?"

"As a brother, of course." Ned looked to Ash for confirmation, but Ash was fiddling with the cabinet's drawers.

Cox shrugged. "If you say so. It just seems odd to me that a female who is regarded by the Duchess of Love as a sort of daughter would still be on the shelf at Miss Bow-man's somewhat advanced age. In my experience doting mamas are very adept at getting their chicks out of their nest and into some man's home."

Ned tried to loosen his jaw enough to sound civil. "My mother has tried to find a suitable match for Miss Bowman, but Miss Bowman has yet to find a gentlemen to her liking."

Cox raised one of his evil eyebrows. "Or perhaps Miss Bowman has already lost her heart and so no longer has it to offer."

"Oh, for God's sake, Cox, Miss Bowman is not such a die-away miss that she would pine in silence for some fellow, and certainly not for Jack. She's far too practical, isn't she, Ash?" He was going to pummel Cox right here and—no. Mama would be extremely annoyed if he injured any of her guests. Still, she should expect it if she was going to invite so many cod's-heads. "Ash?"

Confound it, why hadn't Ash spoken up? He looked at his brother—Ash's expression was inscrutable, damn it. He couldn't really think Ellie longed for Jack, could he? The notion was revolting.

Ned picked up whatever was closest at hand—a large ceramic bowl as it turned out—and pretended to look for a heart.

He shouldn't be repelled by the thought of Ellie marry-ing Jack, though his stomach still twisted at the notion. But that was just from surprise. Now that he considered it, the match had many things in its favor. Sensible Ellie would settle Jack down, reining in his more outrageous, irrespon-sible starts. She might lure him out of Town with all its vices and back to the country where Ned would see him more often. And he'd see Ellie more often, too. He'd like that. In contrast to the elegant high-strung London ladies—

Lady Juliet being a case in point—Ellie was a relief, as direct and uncomplicated as mutton and ale.

He frowned at the bowl. He'd see considerably more of Lady Juliet than Ellie if Lady Juliet was his wife. And perhaps Ellie wasn't as direct and uncomplicated as he'd thought. There were those red drawers . . .

Another squeal erupted ahead of them. Zeus, Miss Wharton should hire herself out as a finder of lost objects. Her skill—or luck—was incredible.

"Lord Edward!" Lady Juliet, having finally finished exploring the farthest corners of the wardrobe, hauled her upper body out of its musty depths to scowl at him. She had a smut on her nose, and wisps of hair floated before her eyes. She batted them away. "Stop chatting and start looking. Time is running out." She moved on to peer inside a teapot.

His stomach tightened. He'd decided to woo Lady Juliet. He wanted a family; he needed a wife . . . but did he need to be nagged incessantly?

He shook the thought away. She'd been delightful in the drawing room. She'd just got too caught up in the game, that was all. Some people were like that—perfectly pleasant, calm, and amiable until they became involved in a competitive situation. Cox had said as much.

And exactly how well did Cox know Lady Juliet? There was definitely some connection between them. A romantic one? But then why would Mama have invited Lady Juliet as a possible match for him? He'd ask Jack; Jack likely had heard something in London.

Jack and Ellie . . .

Bloody hell, now his head was pounding. He'd need to take more of Breen's powders after this ridiculous heart hunt was over.

"Lord Edward, please! I think you've examined that

bowl long enough." Lady Juliet cast him an annoyed glance; she'd moved on to a soup tureen.

He didn't want to look for silly bits of paper. Mama had outdone herself with irritating activities this year, and the party had just begun.

He bent over to pick up the scrap of fabric that had fallen during Lady Juliet's investigation of the wardrobe. He would just—

Aha. The cloth had come to rest by a pair of andirons that depicted the battle between Saint George and the dragon in gruesome detail. Right by the place Saint George's lance pierced the beast's chest he saw a bit of red. A paper heart.

Should he give it to Lady Juliet? She would certainly expect him to do so.

But Jack needed his help to avoid Miss Wharton and perhaps further his relationship with Ellie.

He cringed. He still couldn't imagine Jack and Ellie together, but perhaps he just needed some time to become accustomed to the idea.

"Have you found a heart?" Lady Juliet asked. "Give it to me straightaway."

He palmed the red paper and stood, holding out the cloth instead.

Lady Juliet's delicate features twisted in disgust. "That's not even red. What were you thinking?"

"It looks a little red," Ash said from across the room.

"It's *orange*," Lady Juliet snapped.

"I don't know." Now that Ned looked at the cloth in the light, it did look somewhat red—probably not when put side by side with the heart that he'd managed to slip into his pocket, but definitely when viewed by itself.

"Well, *I* know." Lady Juliet stamped her small, slippered foot.

"Temper, temper," Cox said.

Lady Juliet turned on him. "Don't you—" She stopped, pressing her lips together.

The man chuckled, though he didn't sound particularly amused. "I think I see steam coming out of your ears, Lady Juliet. Keeping all that anger inside can't be good for you."

Lady Juliet's eyes narrowed and her nostrils flared. For a moment, Ned thought she'd launch herself at Cox and wrap her hands around his neck.

Then she drew in a deep breath and turned. "I think there must be no more hearts to find here, Lord Edward," she said, as if none of the previous conversation had occurred. "Shall we continue to the next room?"

"Er, of course." Ned offered her his arm somewhat gingerly. She took it and smiled up at him just as sweetly as Cicely would have. He heard Cox snort.

He wouldn't give the man the satisfaction of seeing he'd irked him. Clearly Lady Juliet's less than delightful behavior just now could be laid at Cox's door. In fact, it showed she had good judgment. He and she were in complete agreement that Cox was vermin.

The next room was the last, thank God. Father stood by the door as they entered; Mama was at the other end sitting in a chair with startlingly well-endowed harpies supporting its arms.

Lady Juliet went immediately to examine a cabinet.

"Keeping us from going back to look for more hearts, Father?" Ned murmured.

"Not exactly, but I do think it's time this game was over, don't you?" Father nodded to Cox as the man passed by on his way to join Percy, Lady Heldon, and Ophelia.

"Definitely."

"It was somewhat illuminating, however," Ash said, stopping next to them.

Ned frowned. "What do you mean?"

"For one, I find I'm not an admirer of Mr. Cox."

"Nor am I."

Ash smiled. "Somehow I didn't think you were."

"Oh, Lady Juliet," Miss Wharton said. "You can stop looking for hearts now. Miss Mosely discovered the only one in this room, isn't that right, your grace?"

Mama nodded. "We are just tallying up what everyone found. Miss Wharton has four, by far the most."

"Her talent is quite astounding," Lady Heldon said, making Miss Wharton's skill sound vaguely inappropriate.

Miss Wharton didn't hear the criticism. She blushed rather charmingly. "I do like a good treasure hunt."

"And you truly are very good at hunting," Miss Mosely said.

"Indeed, Miss Wharton," Humphrey added, "as I was just remarking to Miss Mosely—who made a very good effort, I must say, though not with as notable results as you, of course, but still she has nothing to be ashamed of—well, no one need be ashamed of his or her efforts—but as I was saying to Miss Mosely, you are to be commended for your truly amazing ability to find hidden pieces of paper."

Mama smiled. "I will have to work much harder if we are to play this game again." She looked expectantly at Lady Juliet. "Miss Mosely and Lady Heldon each found one heart. Do you have some, Lady Juliet?"

"Only one, your grace," Lady Juliet said, shoulders slumping slightly. "And Lord Edward is quite empty handed."

Far be it from him to contradict a lady. He would slip Jack the heart when his brother finally made his appearance.

"Ash?" Mama asked.

"Nary a one," Ash said.

"So that leaves five unaccounted for. Ah, and here are our stragglers."

Ned turned, his eyes going immediately to Ellie's face.

She didn't look as if she were in love with Jack, though he couldn't really imagine what Ellie in love would look like. At least there were no blushes or glowing smiles. She looked exactly as she always looked—calm and practical. Why the hell was he even considering something that bounder Cox had said?

Because Ash hadn't discounted the theory, that's why—but then Ash hadn't concurred, either. Chances were good he'd been thinking about building something and hadn't even heard the conversation.

In any event, he needed to give Jack the damned paper heart unobtrusively—Lady Juliet would not be at all pleased if she saw him slip it to him—but Father was blocking his way. "Ellie," he whispered as she started past him, "wait a moment if you will." He could use her as a screen. Ah, there, Jack was now free of Father.

"What?" Ellie asked, pausing.

Perfect. He smiled at her as he bumped Jack and handed over the scrap of red paper. Fortunately, Jack took it as if he was expecting it. "Mama was just wondering if you have any hearts."

"Yes, Ellie," Mama said. "Did you find anything?"

Ellie looked a bit uncomfortable, but then she'd always preferred not to be the center of attention. She glanced back at Jack and cleared her throat. "I'm afraid I don't have any hearts, but Jack does."

"You do?" Mama grinned. "How many do you have?"

Jack produced a wad of red and separated them out. "I've got five."

"Oh." Miss Wharton couldn't hide her disappointment. "You have won." She smiled hopefully. "Whom do you choose to share your sleigh?"

Jack opened his mouth as if to reply and then paused. "I think I should wait to make that choice, don't you?"

"Excellent!" Mama clapped her hands and sprung out

of her chair. "Keep your options open, and everyone else on tenterhooks." She laughed. "Well, our female guests on tenterhooks, that is, though I suppose the men may care if you steal away their choice."

"It *is* only for one sleigh ride," Father pointed out.

"Yes, that's very true, but one never knows how important one sleigh ride may be. It could mean everything—or nothing."

"As usual, my dear duchess," Father said, "you amaze me with your perspicacity."

Mama laughed. "Oh, now you are teasing me, but it's true. At any moment everything might change." She laughed again. "And at this particular moment I suppose what you'd all like to change are your clothes—or at least brush off any cobwebs that may have had the temerity to attach themselves to your persons—and perhaps rest after all this excitement. So off with you, and we will see you in the drawing room before dinner."

Ned watched Ellie make her way toward the stairs. Cox, the bastard, offered her his arm and she took it without once looking at Jack. And Jack actually went so far as to escort Miss Wharton.

Cox must be wrong. Ellie wasn't in love with Jack. She was still unwed because she'd yet to find a man that suited her.

And yet that didn't quite ring true either.

"So, Lord Edward," Lady Juliet said, dropping her voice and leaning close as he led her out of the dungeon, "whom do you think Lord Jack will choose to ride in the sleigh with him? Miss Wharton clearly hopes it will be she, but I would have wagered my quarterly allowance against that outcome. Yet here he is escorting her now. What can it mean?"

"I have no idea." Ned couldn't remember ever feeling so confused. He did not care for the sensation.

* * *

Jack was wrong. Jack *had* to be wrong.

Ellie perched on the settee next to Miss Wharton and stared into her teacup while everyone chatted around her. They were playing charades; the women had just acted out *Gulliver's Travels* and now the men were off planning their clues.

She'd seriously considered staying upstairs after the hunt in the dungeon and pleading the headache, but she knew the duchess would drag her downstairs no matter how much she protested. And she couldn't hide forever—there were still three more days left to this horrible party.

She closed her eyes briefly. Three days. How was she going to bear it?

She clenched her jaw. Damn it, she was going to get a grip on her emotions, that's what she was going to do. Why was she giving any credence to what Jack had said? Cicely had been perfect for Ned. Everyone knew that. If she hadn't died in childbirth, they would have lived happily ever after.

And as for Jack guessing she loved Ned, that was only a guess. A wild, lucky guess. No one else suspected it; Mama would have told her if she'd heard the slightest breath of a rumor. Ellie swallowed a slightly hysterical giggle. Ned certainly had no notion that she loved him. And even the Duchess of Love must not know—she'd have said something if she did, or at least have worked harder to throw Ellie at Ned's head.

She looked over at Ned's mother, who gave her a broad, unsettling smile in return.

She dropped her gaze back to her tea. Now she was jumping at shadows. If she hadn't had that blasted conversation with Jack, she'd just think her grace was being pleasant.

At least Ned had managed to return her red drawers.

She'd found them tied in a large field handkerchief outside her door when she'd left her room for dinner. She'd put them back in the clothes press, but on a higher shelf this time.

"I love charades," Miss Wharton confided, giving a little bounce that caused Ellie to wobble on their shared seat. "Don't you?"

Ellie smiled. It was a relief to think of something besides herself. Miss Wharton was unfashionably loud and enthusiastic, but there were certainly worse flaws.

"I'm afraid I'm not very good at the game," Ellie said. As she had just demonstrated; she hadn't offered a single clue to help her team act out its title. "But you did an excellent job. I think it was your impression of a gull that caused the gentlemen to come up with the answer so quickly."

Miss Wharton blushed. "I'm much better at acting than guessing, though." She giggled. "How do you think Mr. Humphrey will do without being able to speak?"

Ellie laughed. "I can't imagine." So Miss Wharton had a sense of humor. Jack could do worse.

But he'd looked so unhappy and tense in the dungeon.

Jack might be a bit easygoing and even careless at times, at least according to Ned, and he was certainly annoying, but he had a good heart. And he was kind. And likely capable of falling in love.

If he didn't love Miss Wharton, he shouldn't marry her. And if *she* didn't love Mr. Cox . . .

She took a sip of tea. That was different.

"Ah, here come the gentlemen," the duchess said. "Put on your thinking caps, ladies!"

None of the men except Mr. Humphrey looked at all happy to be there, but at least no one was sporting a fresh bruise. Ellie had been a little worried. Percy had always been adept at needling Ash, and now he was at odds with Ned as well. Not to mention Ned had been giving Mr. Cox some markedly unfriendly looks in the dungeon.

Mr. Humphrey began by holding up three fingers.

"Three words," Miss Wharton shouted, bouncing again.

Ellie juggled her tea cup; fortunately, the saucer had captured the splashes. She quickly put it down on the table by her elbow.

Mr. Humphrey nodded enthusiastically, pushed his spectacles up his nose, and then held up one finger.

"First word!"

He placed his hand on his breast.

"Waistcoat," Miss Wharton shouted. "Shirt, cravat."

He shook his head.

"Chest," Ophelia ventured.

"Broad," Lady Heldon said, snickering. "Muscular. Manly."

Mr. Humphrey shook his head more vehemently and then began patting his chest.

"Hit," Miss Mosely said. "And do be careful, sir. You don't want to injure yourself."

"Slap," Lady Juliet tried.

"Beat," Miss Wharton said. "Pound."

Ellie had no guesses and was getting slightly seasick from all the bouncing. She watched Mr. Humphrey thump his chest. Could she love him?

Her stomach twisted. N-no, probably not.

If she couldn't love Mr. Cox or Mr. Humphrey . . .

She stiffened her spine. She was asking the wrong question. Of course she couldn't love either of the men. She knew that. She wasn't some starry-eyed young girl looking for love. No, she was a practical spinster. She wanted a comfortable, civil arrangement that would give her her own home and children.

Mr. Humphrey dropped his hands in defeat and looked to Mr. Cox who smiled and held his thumbs and index fingers together in the shape of a—

"Heart!" Miss Wharton yelled. "Beating heart. Terror."

She bounced almost to her feet. "I know. *The Mysterious Warning* by Mrs. Parsons. Or perhaps *The Mysteries of Udolpho* by Mrs. Radcliffe."

The men gaped at her. Mr. Humphrey and Mr. Cox shook their heads in unison.

"Oh." Miss Wharton collapsed back onto the settee. "Well, my heart almost pounded out of my chest when I read those novels."

"I completely agree," Miss Mosely said, touching Miss Wharton's knee. "I haven't read Mrs. Parsons's book, but *Udolpho* kept me up all night."

"You must try Mrs. Radcliffe's *The Romance of the Forest* if you haven't already," Lady Heldon said, for once not sounding the slightest bit snide. "I quite enjoyed it."

"And Mr. Lewis's *The Monk*," Ophelia added.

"Ladies," the duchess said, "you may discuss your favorite books as much as you like later, but now the poor gentlemen are trying to have you guess a title, and it is not that of a horrid novel."

"Oh, yes, I'm so sorry," Miss Wharton said. "Please continue."

Mr. Humphrey and Mr. Cox looked at the other men. Percy held up two fingers.

"Second word," Miss Wharton said in a more subdued fashion.

Ellie gripped her hands tightly together. But practicality only went so far. Marriage was not the same as hiring an estate manager or a butler or even sharing a house with a brother or father. No, if she wanted children, she would have to share her body.

Her stomach threatened to climb up her throat.

Could she tolerate Mr. Humphrey or Mr. Cox sufficiently to allow one of them to impregnate her? Her reaction to Mr. Cox in the dungeon had not been encouraging, and as for Mr. Humphrey—no, she couldn't see welcoming the mole into her bed, even with her eyes tightly closed and her thoughts focused firmly on household accounts.

Percy pretended to take off his coat and roll up his sleeves. Then he rubbed his hands, grabbed an imaginary something, and made definite digging motions.

"Dig!" Miss Wharton said.

"Shovel," Ophelia offered. "Excavate."

"Bury," Lady Heldon suggested. "Corpse."

"I know," Ophelia said. "'The Grave' by Robert Blair."

Lady Heldon frowned at her friend. "That's only two words, Ophelia."

"Oh, fiddlesticks! So it is."

Ellie bit her lip. She might be able to adjust to Mr. Cox. At least he was attractive, and if the duchess was correct, many other women had accepted his intimate advances. Perhaps marital relations were like riding a horse—a skill one became better at with practice. She enjoyed riding. She didn't have to love the horse. It was a stimulating physical activity, that was all. And if Mr. Cox had had plenty of practice, he was likely very good at performing the deed.

In time she might be able to manage marital congress with equanimity. She might even hope for a little friendship and some respect. She would be the mother of the man's children, after all.

She studied Mr. Cox, who clearly didn't realize he was being observed. His eyes were on Lady Juliet, his expression tight with longing.

Did it matter if the man she married was deeply in love with another woman if that other woman had chosen someone else to wed? It wasn't as if Ellie had her heart to give either. As long as they were honest with each other so neither was living with false hope, it shouldn't make a difference.

It shouldn't, but somehow it did.

Ash had pretended to misplace a variety of objects, so

the women finally decided the last word was "lost." Jack was now trying once more to get them to guess the first word. He put his hands over his heart, looked at Ellie, and made the most ridiculous, besotted face she'd ever seen.

She'd been striving not to look at Ned, but she couldn't keep her gaze from sliding over to meet his. He must find Jack's expression terribly funny.

He didn't. He was glaring at his brother and then he glared at her. What in the world was the matter?

She looked back at Jack. He waggled his brows at Ned and then looked infatuated again.

"Love," Ellie said. "Oh. It's Shakespeare's 'Love's Labor's Lost,' isn't it?"

Jack staggered theatrically to a nearby chair and collapsed into it. "Yes. I thought you'd never guess it."

"Well done, Miss Bowman." Miss Wharton clapped her on the back and almost spilled the tea Ellie had been unwise enough to pick up again. "And well acted, Lord Jack— and all the gentlemen, of course. Shall we play again?"

"I think I've exhausted my meager acting talents, Miss Wharton," Jack said.

"As have I." Ash looked at his mother. "What do you have planned for us tomorrow?"

The duchess smiled. "Mrs. Dalton—and her prognosticating joints—believes the storm is subsiding, so I think we should be able to go skating and perhaps"—the duchess turned her attention to Ellie—"sledding."

Lovely. Ellie felt Ned's eyes boring into the back of her head, but she refused to turn and look at him. "Splendid. If you'll excuse me, I think I'll go upstairs."

Chapter 9

Men like to be in control.
> —Venus's Love Notes

"I think Humphrey should be compelled to play charades more often," Drew said, loosening his cravat. He'd dispensed with his valet, just as Venus had told her maid she could retire for the night. "He is much more entertaining mute."

"He is, isn't he, poor man." Venus sat down at her dressing table and plucked the pins from her hair.

"You promise me he won't wed Ellie?" Drew was joking, of course, but she could hear a faint note of worry in his voice. "I'd hate not to see her regularly, but I have to consider my hearing—and my sanity." He pulled his shirt over his head, and Venus sighed. He *did* have a most impressive chest and pair of shoulders.

She picked up her hairbrush. "It's impossible to promise anything when one ventures into the realm of the heart, but I think it highly unlikely that Mr. Humphrey and Ellie will make a match of it. She seems much more interested in Mr. Cox."

Drew grunted and came over to take the brush from her. "At least Cox isn't such a thundering jaw-me-dead." He pulled the bristles through her hair. She loved the feel of his hands and the long, firm strokes of the brush. "Though I formed the definite impression his interests lie elsewhere."

"They do." The muscles in Drew's arms and chest flexed as he moved. She could watch him forever. "He's madly in love with Lady Juliet. He asked for her hand a few months ago, but that stiff-rumped father of hers refused. Rumor is he gave Mr. Cox no hope."

A familiar warmth spread low in her belly. Other parts of her were beginning to clamor for Drew's touch.

He snorted. "I'm not surprised. Extley's always been a hard-hearted, granite-headed beef-wit. But Lady Juliet is of age. If she wants Cox, she can just take him." He gave her hair one last long brush. "It looks to me as if she means to marry Ned." He frowned at Venus in the mirror. "Isn't that why you invited the girl?"

"No."

Drew moved his hands to her shoulders, his thumbs massaging the tight spot at the base of her neck. She closed her eyes and dropped her head forward. Mmm. She felt as if she were melting—in more ways than one.

"I invited her so she could realize that she does want Mr. Cox—that she wants him far more than she wishes to please her father or even to live her fairytale notion of what her future should be." She lifted her head to meet Drew's eyes. "Have you noticed the way she looks at him when he's looking at someone else? There is a definite current between them."

Drew grunted. "Yes, but she doesn't seem to realize it—nor does our dunderheaded second son. What if Ned asks her to wed and she agrees?" He lifted his hands and stepped back. "It seems to me you are playing with fire."

Venus shrugged and stood. "I only give people opportunities; whether they take them is out of my control." Though she would admit to herself that she *was* worried. She wanted Ned to be happy, and she was almost certain he would not be happy with Lady Juliet. She sighed. "It is too bad arranged marriages went out of vogue."

Drew pulled her into his arms. "And whom would you arrange for Ned?"

"You know." Venus looped her hands around his neck. "The same woman you would."

Drew rubbed his hands up and down her back, and she wanted to purr like Sir Reginald. "I wish Ned had married her the first time."

"As do I." Venus would only say that to Drew in the privacy of their room where she could be sure no one would overhear. "I loved Cicely—you know I welcomed her into the family just as you did—but I did wish Ned had chosen Ellie. I hope Cicely never guessed."

"I'm sure she didn't."

"She was sweet and she needed Ned, but Ellie will challenge him, if he has the sense to marry her. I think he does love her, he just doesn't realize it yet."

Drew's nimble fingers loosened the fastenings on her dress. "Well at least she's not clinging to Ash this year."

"I told her people had noticed." Venus rested her cheek against his chest. She could hear the steady, comforting beat of his heart. "And I think she's different; I think she's decided she's going to marry even if she can't have Ned."

Drew pulled back and frowned at her. "That doesn't sound good."

"No. I wish I'd known beforehand, but I hope I've made her choices unappealing enough that she won't do something silly."

"Hmph. Humphrey is certainly unappealing, but Cox is a different matter."

"Yes, I know. But he does love Lady Juliet, and I think Ellie sees that."

Drew laughed. "You seem to have filled this party with young people who have very little idea of their true desires."

"Which is so true of most young people." Venus smiled up at him. "But not us. I knew as soon as I met you that I wanted you."

His lips slid into a grin. "I'm not sure that is completely true. I remember you being very angry with me."

She shrugged. "That was only on the surface. Deep down in my heart I knew I loved you." She sighed. "What have I done wrong, Drew? Why don't our sons have the same certainty about love?"

He kissed her forehead. "Perhaps the problem is their lustful male, er, minds keep them from recognizing what is in their hearts."

"But you were male and lustful and you knew."

"My dear duchess, your tense is incorrect. I *am* male and lustful." He brushed her lips with his and then pushed her dress down so it puddled around her feet. "However, I had the benefit of falling in love with a brilliant matchmaker who reads hearts as easily as most people read *The Times*."

"I *wish* I could read hearts so easily." She stepped free of her dress. "Tell me this, since you're an expert in lust: how are we to help Ned recognize he loves Ellie?"

He kissed her jaw. "It might help if she didn't hide herself in those dreadful dresses. We lustful men love our ladies' minds and spirits, but we very much admire their bodies, too." He nuzzled the sensitive place under her ear while his fingers worked the ties on her stays loose. "Perhaps Reggie should steal her entire wardrobe."

She grinned. "That might be beyond even Reggie's skills, but I do believe you've given me an idea."

"Splendid. Let me give you several other ideas." He pushed off her stays and pulled her shift up and over her head; then he cupped her breasts, running his thumbs over her nipples. Liquid desire shot through her.

She suddenly had a very clear idea of exactly how she wished to spend the next hour.

She pulled him over to the bed. "Ellie thinks Ash still loves Jess, by the way."

Drew's brows lowered. "Well, I wish he would act on it then. I would like my heir to get an heir before I go to my reward."

Venus ran her hands over his chest. "Go to your reward?! Nonsense. I'll not hear any talk of departing this earth."

He lifted her onto the mattress. "Confess, Venus. You'd like a grandchild to spoil before you're too feeble to do a proper job of it."

She laughed. "Yes, indeed, but I do not plan on being feeble for many years yet. Are you going into a decline soon?"

"I'll show you a decline."

Drew shed his pantaloons almost as quickly as he had when he was twenty-one and vaulted onto the bed. What followed was a flurry of activity accompanied by laughing, giggling, moaning, and gasping, and then Venus was flat on her back, delightfully satisfied.

"I think there's still some life left in you, your grace," she said.

"Of course there is." Drew flopped down onto the mattress next to her and closed his eyes.

Venus turned to look at him—at the strong planes of his face, his long lashes, his clever mouth. She loved him in so many ways. "Thank you for looking out for Jack today."

He kept his eyes closed. "I suspect his brothers and perhaps Ellie were looking out for him as well. After I passed him the paper heart I'd saved out, Ned slipped him one, too."

"Did he? Excellent. I think it was very good Jack won the game outright rather than merely tying Miss Wharton, as then he'd probably have played the gentleman and let her choose her sleigh partner—which would surely have been him."

"Hmm."

Venus turned over to look up at the canopy. For some reason, she did not feel sleepy at all. "You know, I rather like Miss Wharton now. She may have some rough edges, but she is charming in her own way. She was so enthusiastic about both the treasure hunt and charades. She would make some man a fine wife."

Drew frowned and cracked open an eye. "But not Jack."

"No, not Jack."

"Good. I agree Miss Wharton is an estimable young woman, but I could no more bear an extended visit with her than I could one with Humphrey."

Venus nodded. "True, but she may settle down once she marries. I suspect some of her problem is nervous energy that a husband could manage very well."

Drew's eyes lit with a markedly lascivious expression. "Ah, yes, nervous energy."

"What? Oh!" She giggled. "I didn't mean *that* kind of nervous energy! You've already attended to that."

"I have?" He turned to nuzzle the place under her ear, and then moved his lips slowly down her neck. "Are you sure?"

"Y-yes . . . umm." He whispered kisses up the side of her breast. Oh! All Drew needed to do was touch her, and her body ached for him, even now, after he'd already brought her to completion. His lips were so close to her aching peak. She wiggled.

"Feeling a bit more energy, then?"

"Ah, ah, y-yes."

"Let me help you." He finally latched onto her nipple, and after that, Venus didn't give another thought to her guests.

Ned stared down at the small tent in his coverlet just below his waist.

Damn.

It would be fine—wonderful, actually—if his, er, excitement had been caused by dreams of Lady Juliet, but it hadn't been.

He scowled at the offending protuberance, and it obligingly wilted.

Zeus, he felt more tired than when he'd gone to bed—which wasn't surprising as he'd tossed and turned through one disturbing dream after another. He'd waded through red-walled dungeons, swarms of cats, and writhing masses of serpents. His heart had nearly stopped at one point when he'd seen Ellie sitting on Jack's sledge at the top of a mountain. The snow was too deep and his feet too frozen for him to catch her, so he'd watched helpless as she'd barreled down the slope and into a lake.

But the last dream . . .

Oh, bloody, bloody hell. He banged his head back against the bed's headboard, squeezing his eyes shut, but that didn't help, of course. The image was burned into his brain.

Ellie had been dressed in a silky red gown, dancing and flirting with Jack. Zounds, he still felt a hard knot of anger thinking about it. And then the music had changed to a waltz, and Jack had turned into Cox, and—Ned pressed the heels of his hands into his eyes—Ellie's gown had melted away so all he saw was her lovely cream-colored back and those damn red drawers on her swaying arse.

He jerked his hands away from his face and glared at his coverlet. His damn cock was disarranging it again.

He took a deep breath. No, this was good. It was encouraging. His body had been deeply asleep since Cicely's death, and now it was waking. He just wished Lady Juliet and not Ellie was the cause of the resurrection.

Well, it was resurrection nonetheless—that was what was important.

He threw off his covers and swung his feet over the edge of the bed. In truth, dreams didn't mean anything. He would put them out of his mind. He'd just use the chamber pot, clean up, and then—

What the hell was sticking out from under his bed? It looked like . . . he stooped down. Yes, it was a white feather boa.

"Reggie!" He scanned his room. Where the hell—ah, of course. Reggie had made a comfortable nest in his rumpled coverlet.

The cat lifted his head and blinked at him.

"Reggie, if you've been stealing things again, I swear I'll take you by your tail and fling you out the window into the snow." Of course he'd been stealing things—Ned didn't make a habit of collecting feather boas.

The blasted cat yawned. He knew all too well Ned wouldn't dare harm a single hair on his annoying, thieving body.

Ned plucked the boa off the floor, and then got down on his hands and knees to peer into the shadowy area under his bed.

Reggie had been busy. Ned hauled out a large yellow and green reticule; a pink silk stocking, sadly showing the effects of Reggie's teeth and claws; one pantalets leg with lace trim; and a box of Hooper's Female Pills which he dropped as if scorched as soon as he read the label.

"Bloody hell, Reggie, couldn't you stick to less personal items?"

Reggie was too busy licking his hindquarters to reply.

Ned sat back on his heels. "I suppose I can dump them on the table in the little yellow salon like Mama did yesterday. People may as well get used to checking there each morning for their missing belongings."

Reggie neither agreed nor disagreed. He yawned again, stretched, and jumped down from the bed, walking off at a leisurely pace, tail high, as if he ruled the castle—which in a way he did.

Well, there was nothing to do but gather the things and take them downstairs. Ned scooped them up and—oh, damn.

There on the bed where Reggie had been lying were Ellie's cursed red drawers.

Ellie stared out the window in the long gallery. Mrs. Dalton's rheumatism had predicted the weather accurately once again—the sun was out, the sky was blue, and there wasn't a snowflake in sight. She squinted; it was almost too bright. Evergreen branches bent with the weight of the snow, and the fields spread out smooth and white, marred only by the occasional deer or rabbit tracks, for as far as she could see.

It would be good to get out of the house; perhaps the cold would clear her mind.

She rested her forehead against the cool glass of the windowpane. She needed to think. She'd hardly slept at all last night. Try as she might, she could not muster one iota of enthusiasm for either Mr. Humphrey or Mr. Cox.

Choosing a husband in order to have children had seemed

completely reasonable just two days ago, but now it felt like insanity.

She pressed her head harder against the glass. It *was* reasonable. Marriage would not only give her children, it would give her a home of her own. A place to manage; a place she was needed. "Wife" was a far more desirable title than "spinster." As a wife, she'd be treated as an equal by the neighborhood matrons rather than as an object of pity.

No, as long as the man wasn't cruel—and neither Mr. Humphrey nor Mr. Cox showed any evidence of cruelty—marriage was far preferable to spinsterhood. In the not so distant past, many, if not most, marriages were arranged for practical reasons that had nothing to do with the horribly impractical emotion of love.

She sighed. No matter how hard her mind argued, her heart would not be persuaded.

So was Jack right? Should she pursue Ned as Miss Wharton was pursuing Jack—or would Ned just run as far and as fast as his brother?

She heard heels echoing on the wooden floor behind her and turned. Damn, it was Ned. She didn't want to talk to him right now; her thoughts were too confused.

Her heart wasn't confused, though. It leapt like an eager spaniel at the sight of him and, if she let it, would likely fawn all over his boots. He was so dear to her and so handsome— so tall and broad-shouldered with that lock of chestnut hair flopping onto his forehead. This morning he was dressed simply in buckskin breeches and dark blue coat and waistcoat with an elegantly-tied cravat and . . . a large yellow and green reticule?

"I was hoping I'd find you here," he said, coming to stand beside her and dropping the reticule on the wide windowsill.

"Y-yes." Why in the world did he have a reticule? "I couldn't"—no, no need to let him know she hadn't been able to sleep—"I woke early and thought I'd stretch my legs. It's so quiet and peaceful here."

He smiled. "If you can ignore all the disapproving ancestors glaring down at you from the walls."

She smiled back at him, willing the tightness in her chest to relax. "Oh, they're not as bad as the ones downstairs. And I've always particularly liked the painting of you and your brothers over there." The artist had sat Jack, who must have been around four years old and was clutching a stuffed bunny, in a chair with Ash and Ned standing on either side. "You all look so angelic."

Ned chuckled. "You wouldn't say that if you could have heard the threats and bribes and muffled curses that went along with those sittings. I believe the artist swore off painting young boys as soon as he put the last dab of paint on the canvas."

"Perhaps, but I know your parents must be very glad to have the picture now." Ellie's heart clenched a little every time she looked at it. It reminded her so strongly of their happy, shared childhood. She could see a bit of the man in the boy when she looked at Ned's young face.

She looked at the man before her. And sometimes she could still see a glimmer of the boy in the man.

Ned shrugged and glanced out the window. "It looks like a good day. Mama will be happy her plans needn't be rearranged."

"Yes. I imagine the servants are already preparing for everyone to go skating later."

Ned's face tensed, and he frowned. "Is the pond frozen solid?"

Damn. She could hear the worry tight in his voice. "All but the part by the spring and that will be roped off. You know your father won't take any risks."

Ned's frown didn't relax. "But the ice can be unpredictable. Remember when Ash fell through?"

"Yes, but that was in March when the thaw was beginning. He knew he shouldn't have gone out on the pond." Ned had been the one to pull Ash out; everyone else had stood gaping on the bank. Perhaps that was why he never seemed to enjoy skating. "You worry too much."

Ned's brows snapped down to meet over the bridge of his nose.

She shouldn't have said that—Jack twitted him constantly about his tendency to fret.

"I only worry because too many people around me don't worry enough," he said, "which brings me to one of the reasons I came looking for you this morning."

Oh, blast, here it comes. Maybe she could distract him. "Does it have anything to do with your very lovely reticule?"

"What?" He blinked at her, and then looked down at the purse. He flushed. "No. That is, yes."

"No *and* yes?" She forced herself to smile, hoping she could tease her way out of this certain-to-be unpleasant conversation. She didn't want to argue with him. She was too tired, and her feelings were too jumbled. She could as easily scream like a fishwife, saying things she surely would regret, as dissolve into tears. Neither would serve a purpose and both would be highly embarrassing and unpleasant for each of them. Avoidance was quite clearly the best policy.

"The reticule—or rather, what's in the reticule—is the second reason I sought you out."

Dash it all, that sounded very ominous. She looked at the large, lumpy purse. "Has Reggie been busy again?"

"Yes, he has. I don't see why—" Ned pressed his lips together. "But enough of that. I wish to discuss your ridiculous plan to go sledding."

"Ah." That wasn't completely fair. "It's not *my* plan. Jack is very much to blame." She paused—she should be truthful. "And Mr. Humphrey. If he hadn't been so annoying, I likely wouldn't have agreed to go along with the notion."

But of course Ned did not want to discuss anything—he wanted to dictate to her. "I hope there won't be time—not that I'm anxious to see everyone skating, either—but if for some reason Mama urges you to go flying down the hill on a sledge this afternoon, you must give me your word you will refuse."

She looked at him. She should be angry. She *wanted* to be angry. Anger would help her get through this unwanted conversation, and Ned deserved a few sharp words. He was overstepping his place—in point of fact, he had no place to overstep.

But she couldn't be angry. He was worried and concerned which, though annoying, was also very sweet. "Ned, I appreciate your solicitude, but I can't promise anything. I—"

"Of course you can promise."

She inhaled slowly through her nose. He meant well. She must remember that. "If your mother—"

"Father won't let Mama sled."

She wasn't so certain of that. "Then there's no problem. I will only sled if your mother does."

Ned's brow was still furrowed. Clearly he also doubted his father's ability to restrain the duchess. "But Mama may feel compelled because of you. She will not wish to break what she likely views as a promise. You must withdraw first." He pinned her with determined eyes as if he could force her to do what he wanted just by glaring at her. "You need to be sensible, Ellie."

No good could come from her giving him more power over her. He was not her husband and would never be her husband. She must stop trying to please him. "Your mother is perfectly capable of being sensible as well, Ned. And may I remind you you said your father would keep her from sledding. Since I won't sled if she doesn't, I have nothing to promise."

Ned hunched a shoulder and looked away. "Yes, well, but Mama is sometimes—often—able to persuade Father to let her do things that are ill-advised."

Ellie almost laughed. "Only because the duchess can decide such matters for herself. You don't really think your father should try to control her actions, do you? The duke has far too much sense for that."

She expected him to chuckle and agree, but he didn't.

"I do think it. I mean, Father *should* control Mama." His jaw hardened. "It is for her own good. Her own safety."

"Ned . . ." What did she know? She'd never been married. Still, she couldn't imagine any modern woman letting her husband manage her every action this way. "Surely Cicely didn't let you tell her what she could and couldn't do?"

"Of course she did."

"She did?" Cicely *had* been very biddable.

Ellie's heart sank. If that was the sort of woman Ned wished to marry, she could never be his wife.

"Yes." His eyes were now almost pleading. "About important things, she did. About safety." He swallowed, and his face grew dark with despair. "Except I couldn't keep her safe in the end, could I?"

He blinked and turned sharply to stare out the window. His profile could have been carved from granite.

"Oh, Ned." Ellie reached out to touch his arm.

He didn't look at her, but he didn't shrug off her hand either. "I hated it, Ellie. I hated being so damn helpless."

"I know, Ned." They'd been over this many, many times after Cicely died. "But sometimes things happen that no one can protect against. You know Cicely was happy to be carrying your child."

His jaw hardened even more. "She was afraid." He spoke so low, Ellie would never have heard him if it wasn't so quiet in the gallery. "That's why she wanted to come back to Greycliffe and be close to her mother."

She wanted to wrap her arms around him to comfort him as she had four years ago, but the time for that was past. She shook his arm gently instead. "Of course she was nervous and wanted her mother nearby. That's normal for a first baby. All my sisters were exactly the same way."

He didn't reply. He stared out the window a moment more and then stepped back so she had to drop her hold on him.

"Perhaps," he said. "But the fact remains that while I couldn't keep Cicely safe—and yes, I know you are right about childbirth—I *can* protect you from sledding." He looked quite mulish. "Dead is dead, Ellie, whether from an unsuccessful labor or from colliding with a tree."

She could feel his desperation beating against her. It was unreasonable, but he clearly wasn't reasonable about this. It would be easy to give in—she didn't even want to ride on the stupid sledge—but she felt certain that would be the wrong thing to do.

"But you can't protect me, Ned. In your heart you must know that. Even if I don't go sledding, something else could happen. Life—and death—are unpredictable."

He paled slightly, but his expression remained hard and determined. "You may be right, but that doesn't change the fact that this sledding notion is fraught with danger. I forbid you to participate."

Anger spurted through her, but she forced herself to keep it out of her voice. Ned didn't need to be shouted at. "You can't forbid me. You aren't my husband"—pray God her voice didn't wobble on those words—"nor are you my brother or any relation whatsoever." He opened his mouth as if to protest, but she kept going. "And even if you were, I would not allow you to tell me what to do. I can't. I'm not that sort of person." She swallowed. "I'm not like Cicely."

"Ellie—"

"I know you mean well, Ned, but you can't—and I can't let you—live my life for me."

Ned's nostrils flared and his eyes narrowed. She thought for a moment he would grab her, maybe even shake her, but he didn't. He nodded once. "Very well, I can see there's no reasoning with you."

"Ned . . ." She pressed her lips together. She had more to say on the subject, but it was painfully clear he wouldn't listen, at least not now.

He turned away to pick up the reticule. "To address my second reason for seeking you out this morning," he said, his voice now carefully devoid of all emotion, "as you surmised, Reggie was busy again last night. I'm taking the other items he purloined down to the yellow salon, but this I wished to return directly to you. I suspect you might not have got it yesterday, though I did leave it outside your door."

"Ah." Ellie stared with dread at the green and yellow purse.

Ned shrugged. "I suppose Reggie must have seen it and taken it back." He handed her the reticule. "Please put this downstairs when you've removed the, er, garment inside."

Damn it, Ned couldn't have the red drawers. She'd hidden them in her clothes press, tucked away this time in a place that was impossible for Reggie to reach.

Except it clearly hadn't been impossible. There was a bit of red visible where the drawstrings didn't pull tight. "No, I did get them yesterday. I thought I'd found a safe hiding place for them."

Ned grunted. "Obviously, you didn't. I suggest you find a safer place today." His face had a very odd expression— a mix of disgust, horror, and something else. "I don't care to keep finding them in my room."

Chapter 10

Be certain you can trust a man before you pursue him.
—Venus's Love Notes

Ellie waited until the sound of Ned's heels on the wooden floor had completely died away. He'd taken the staircase that was the most direct path to the bedroom floor; she wanted to be certain he was gone before she followed.

"Oh, Ned," she whispered. She leaned her head against the cool window again. He had no reason to feel guilty; there'd been nothing he could have done to save Cicely. Everyone knew that; even the high-priced London accoucheur he'd brought to Greycliffe to help Mrs. Lexton, the local midwife, had agreed. No one blamed him except himself—well, and perhaps Cicely's mother and Percy. But surely even they'd realized, once their grief had lessened, that Cicely's death was simply a tragic accident. Sometimes the cord got wrapped around a baby's neck; sometimes a mother hemorrhaged.

There were many risks a woman took to have a child, but

women were willing to take them. Ellie would be willing, especially to have Ned's baby.

She straightened, stepping away from the window. But the one risk she wouldn't take any longer was the risk of losing herself. She'd spent too many years already trying to be someone she wasn't—trying to be Cicely—to please Ned. Jack was right: she'd turned into a meek, boring, stick-in-the-mud.

But she wasn't reckless and wild, either—or uncaring. She wouldn't sled today even if the duchess did, not because Ned had ordered her not to, but because she loved him.

She held her breath and listened. Silence. He must be gone now. She could hurry down the stairs and into her room without anyone seeing her. It was still early; likely no one else was up besides the servants. And this time she'd hide the blasted drawers in a place she was certain Reggie couldn't find them.

She was at the top of the stairs when she heard voices.

"I can't believe I turned down an invitation to Hallington's party to come to this insipid gathering. Treasure hunts for paper hearts, charades—good God!"

That was Lady Heldon. She must be standing at the bottom of the stairs two flights down.

"And Pelthurst was going to be at Hallington's, wasn't he?"

Ophelia. What if this hideous reticule belonged to her or Lady Heldon? Ellie couldn't very well return it with the damning red drawers inside, but she had no place to hide them. They were too large to fit in her pocket, and they were so *red*.

She would have to go round by the other stairs, but those would deposit her right outside the breakfast room. If Lady Heldon and Ophelia were already awake, chances were good some of the other guests were up as well. She checked her watch.

Heavens! She and Ned must have spoken longer than she'd thought. It was no longer early—almost everyone must be stirring. She definitely couldn't go by way of the breakfast room. What if she ran into Mr. Cox or Mr. Humphrey?

"Yes, he was, and I can assure you I wouldn't have slept alone last night if I'd been there instead of here," Lady Heldon said. Her voice took on an almost wistful quality. "Pelthurst can be very entertaining—quite inventive, don't you know—and Hallington himself had hinted he might like to join us. I don't often get the opportunity to have two gentlemen in my bed at the same time."

Two gentlemen? Lady Heldon didn't sound as if she meant the three of them would be sleeping, but . . . no, it wasn't possible . . . was it?

And why would anyone wish to be part of such a crowd?

"You were happy enough to have the chance to meet—and seduce—the elusive Marquis of Ashton when I suggested it," Percy said.

What?! Shock, followed immediately by scalding anger, flooded Ellie. She'd always thought Percy had had a special fondness for Jess. Why the hell would he try to tempt Ash to betray his marriage vows?

She dearly wished she had something far heavier than this ugly reticule to drop on the group below her.

"I had no idea how elusive he would be when I charmed the duchess into inviting me." Lady Heldon made a noise of disgust. "He must be a sodomite."

Something *very* heavy.

"Don't be ridiculous, Miranda." Percy sounded annoyed—and nearer.

Oh, dear. She looked over the banister—

And saw their heads far too close below her. Zounds, they were halfway up the first flight; they would reach the landing, turn, and see her in just a few moments. She had to hide. But where? The gallery was bare of any good—ah, now she remembered. The hidey holes. There was one nearby between the statue of Diana and the painting of the second duke's hunting hounds.

One of Ned's ancestors had not wished to see his servants, so he'd had small spaces built into the walls for them to duck into when they saw him approaching. She and Ned and the others had used them to play hide and seek when they were children. A few led to narrow staircases; unfortunately this one didn't, but all she needed was temporary concealment. It must still be here. She'd have heard if the duke had got rid of them.

She rushed to the spot, her fingers scrambling over the wall, searching for a small indentation—barely a dimple—in its surface.

"I'm not being ridiculous," Lady Heldon said. "Why else would Ashton show absolutely no interest in me?"

"Perhaps because he has a more discriminating taste in women," Ophelia said a little waspishly.

Lady Heldon laughed. "Surely you're jesting."

"No, I'm not. Not *all* the males in London are panting after you, Miranda."

Lady Heldon sniffed. "Most are, and those who aren't at least look. Ashton barely glanced at me. Think about it, Ophelia." She sounded slightly out of breath. She—and so Ophelia and Percy—paused in their ascent, giving Ellie a few more precious seconds to search for the door latch.

"It would explain his odd marriage—non-marriage, really—and his hiding himself away in the country. Though I admit I'm surprised there've been no rumors, but then I imagine the duke and duchess have used their influence to quash any tittle-tattle."

Where the hell was the spot that would open the door? Ellie swept her hands lower. Ah, of course! She'd been a child when she'd last hidden here, so the indentation was lower than she remembered. She found it and pressed.

The door opened soundlessly. Thank God! She darted inside.

"I really think it too bad of you, Percy, to persuade me to come here when you knew the marquis wasn't at all interested in what I have to offer." Lady Heldon had started climbing again. "You should try to seduce him yourself."

Percy's voice was louder, too; they must have made the turn and were ascending the last flight. "I told you, Ash is not a sodomite. That predilection is hard to hide. Someone would have seen or heard something, and, believe me, I've asked everyone—discreetly, of course. I've always come up empty."

Ellie tugged the door shut and exhaled. She was finally safe, and not a moment too soon. She heard steps echo in the gallery. They were coming closer . . .

They stopped right outside her hiding place.

"Keep trying, Miranda," Percy said. "I know you'll succeed. You're beautiful, and you certainly know how to tempt a man. You'll bring Ash around."

"I don't know. It's especially difficult with his parents as my host and hostess. I do have some scruples."

Ophelia laughed. "You mean you don't want the duchess, and thus everyone else in society, to give you the cut direct."

"Yes, that's part of it."

It was very cramped in the wall, far more cramped than Ellie remembered. Of course she'd been much smaller the last time she'd been in here.

"I told you this would work better if we were somewhere—anywhere—other than Greycliffe, Percy," Lady Heldon said.

"Ash never goes anywhere but Greycliffe. It had to be here."

"Very well. There's nothing to be done about it now in any event. You just better be sure to get me that invitation to the Humley ball, Percy, in exchange for all my troubles. I was mortified at being excluded last year."

"I will."

Something crawled over Ellie's wrist. She bit her lip to keep from making a sound and swatted at it with the reticule. She didn't mind bugs usually, but bugs she couldn't see were definitely disconcerting.

"I don't know why old Lady Humley dislikes me so."

"Perhaps because you slept with her husband." That was Ophelia.

Lady Heldon snorted. "She should thank me for giving her some relief from Humley's attentions. The man was a complete disappointment—all looks and no skill. I think our encounter was over in less than three minutes."

"The problem was likely that you let everyone know how inept he was," Percy said.

"I only whispered a word in one or two ears. It's my duty to warn other women, don't you think?"

"What matters is what Lady Humley thinks," Ophelia said. "She did not take kindly to being mocked in Mr. Rowlandson's and Mr. Cruikshank's and all the other caricaturists' prints."

"She is oversensitive. It's not as if she were at fault. Everyone knows she's far too straitlaced to have bedded him before she'd wedded him."

Oh, Zeus, now Ellie had to sneeze. She pressed her hand firmly against her nose. If she could hear the conversation on the other side of the wall, Percy and the women would hear her. And Percy had played hide and seek here as a child; he'd guess at once where the sound had come from.

"You're certain you can get me that invitation, Percy?" Lady Heldon said. "Because if you think you can't, I shall plan to be on my way as soon as the roads are passable. If

I leave within a day or two, I should be able to catch the end of Hallington's party."

"I *said* I would get you the invitation."

"I do hope so. I'd hate to see the London caricaturists draw unflattering sketches of you or the Marquis of Ashton, you know." Lady Heldon paused, and Ellie could almost picture her slow smile. "Everyone in London is *so* interested in Lord Ashton. He is such a mystery."

"You'll have your invitation."

"Splendid. Now, if you'll excuse me? This gallery is giving me the headache. I've never seen so many paintings of sour-looking people in my life."

Ellie heard one set of footsteps move away. With luck, Ophelia and Percy would leave, too.

Her luck was in short supply this morning.

"How can you promise Miranda that invitation, Percy? You know both Humley and Lady Humley would ride naked down Piccadilly before they'd let her into their house." Ophelia was almost hissing.

"I'll get it. I have my sources."

"I can't imagine who they can be. And you know Miranda will make good on her threat."

Percy chuckled, though he didn't sound especially amused. "I hadn't thought to inflict the artists on Ash, but that might be a very good idea."

"Are you insane?" Ophelia's voice rose. "If you don't get Miranda that invitation, Ash won't be the one figuring most prominently in the artists' drawings. It will be you and quite possibly *me*." Her voice broke on the last word.

"Now, don't worry, Ophelia. I have everything under control."

"You do? Who is going to get you the invitation?"

Another sneeze threatened Ellie. She squeezed her lips

together and pinched her nose. Oh! Her head felt as if it was going to explode.

"I can't tell you."

"You can't tell me because you don't know."

"That's not true. I'm just not at liberty to mention a name."

There was a pause, and Ellie again hoped they'd leave. Her nose was twitching; this hiding place was dangerously dusty.

"Oh, Percy." Ophelia sounded almost despairing. "Why are you trying to cause problems for Ash? Why do you care about him so much?"

Percy laughed, but there was a thread of something dark in the sound. "I don't care about Ash."

"You do. Sometimes I think he's all you care about."

"You're wrong."

"Then tell me this—are you the reason he and his wife are estranged?"

There was a moment of stunned silence . . . into which Ellie sneezed.

"What was that?"

"What was what?" Percy said. Oh, damn. He must have heard her.

"It sounded like someone sneezed."

Ellie could almost picture Percy looking around the empty gallery. "Who could have sneezed, Ophelia? There's no one here but us. You must have imagined it."

Ophelia sounded angry. "All right, perhaps I didn't hear anything. I certainly didn't hear your answer to my question."

"You must definitely rein in your imagination, my dear. How could I have anything to do with Ash's marital woes? He and his wife have not lived together for years. I'm as innocent as an angel."

"A fallen angel, perhaps." Ophelia's voice grew tighter. "But even if you were to blame, Percy, I could forgive that. It's your current obsession with ruining Ash that I can't forgive."

Percy made a comforting sort of noise. "You are merely overwrought from our unpleasant conversation with Miranda. Go have a calming pot of tea. You'll feel much better."

Ellie held her breath. Were they finally leaving?

"All right"—Ophelia's voice was definitely farther away—"but don't think I'll let this matter drop."

"You must do as you see fit, my dear."

Ellie waited, giving them time to make their way down the stairs. Had Percy somehow caused the rift between Ash and Jess? She couldn't remember anything he'd done, though she'd admit she'd always paid far more attention to Ned than to Percy or Ash back then.

She pressed her ear against the door. Not a sound, thank God. They must be gone. She certainly was more than ready to get out of this dark, narrow space. If she remembered correctly, there was a lever . . . yes, there it was.

She pulled it down and the door swung blessedly open—right into Percy's angry gaze.

Ned sat alone in the breakfast room and stared down at the piles of ham and kidneys and kippers and blood pudding in front of him. Ugh. How the hell had all this food appeared?

He'd selected it from the sideboard, of course. Idiot. He pushed his plate away and took a gulp of coffee.

Hell! The hot liquid scalded his mouth. He spat it out and slammed the cup down on the table, sloshing hot coffee over his fingers.

Could this day get any worse? If only he could go back to bed and start over.

He mopped his fingers with his napkin. He'd definitely mishandled that scene in the gallery with Ellie. He'd known it at the time, but had been powerless to stop himself—which was totally out of character. He was always in control, always measured, calm, and rational.

Ha! He'd been everything but those things with Ellie. And somehow he'd even mentioned Cicely and the baby. Good God, he'd almost cried.

It had been four damn years. He should be over it. Ellie must think him a complete milksop.

He wadded his napkin up in a tight ball. But she'd made him so bloody angry. Just thinking about their conversation—and her obstinacy—caused his head to throb again.

He wasn't asking for anything outrageous. He only wanted to keep her safe, to prevent her from breaking her neck or falling into the pond and freezing to death. Why wouldn't she listen to reason?

He felt so damn helpless.

He rubbed his forehead. Still, angry or not, he should never have been so high-handed with her. Even Cicely might have balked at his manner—well, no, not Cicely. Cicely had always looked to him for support and guidance, the only exception being in her dealings with Percy. Her dependence on him had been . . .

Ah, perhaps he'd admit now that it had been a little overwhelming, but he'd been happy to take care of her. He'd loved her, and she'd needed him. He'd protected her.

Except at the end.

He dug his fingers into his forehead. God, he'd never forget Cicely's eyes when she'd been taken to bed with the baby. They'd been so full of pain and fear, silently pleading with him to help her, to make it all go away. And he hadn't been able to do that. He'd watched her suffer, watched the blood—

He was going to drill his fingers into his brain.

Sometimes he even wished he'd been a coward and done as the accoucheur and the midwife had suggested. They'd wanted him to leave Cicely with them, to go wait outside like a proper, well-behaved husband. Even Cicely's mother, once it was clear things were hopeless, had left. But not Ned.

He couldn't leave Cicely to face all that alone. He might not have been able to help her, but at least he'd been there to witness her suffering and maybe, perhaps, he hoped, give her a little comfort.

But, damn it, sledding was not childbirth, as he'd told Ellie. There wasn't anything necessary about it. To risk death, or at least serious injury, for something so silly and ephemeral as a slide down a hill was madness.

He speared a bit of kidney and brought it to his lips.

Yes, he'd gone sledding at Christmastime, but that was different. He was a man. Well, and he was in control of the sledge. If Ellie were barreling down the hill, he'd have to watch as helpless to save her as he'd been in his nightmare last night—as he'd been with Cicely and the baby.

All he wanted was to keep Ellie safe. What was so wrong about that?

He put the kidney down untasted and closed his eyes, rubbing the spot between his brows. He might as well resign himself to suffering a constant headache during this hellish gathering.

Damn it, what was the matter with him? He'd been completely unlike himself ever since he'd arrived at this damn party. Perhaps he wasn't ready to take a second wife.

"Good morning, Ned. Looks like a beautiful day for skating—and sledding."

Jack was standing in the doorway, grinning. "Blast it, Jack, you're not going to urge Ellie to sled, are you?"

Jack dropped down into the seat next to him. "I think Ellie will make up her own mind. Say, are you going to eat that food?"

"No. Help yourself." Ned pushed the plate over to his brother.

"Wouldn't want it to go to waste." Jack dug into the blood pudding with revolting gusto. "Aren't you hungry?" he asked around a mouthful.

"No."

"Shame. One of the things I most like about coming back to the castle is the meals."

"I would think you'd have more variety in London."

Jack shrugged. "Perhaps, but I like Cook's simple, hearty fare." He grinned. "And there's always lots of it."

Jack had demolished the blood pudding and was now making serious inroads into the kidneys.

Ned felt slightly ill. "I can see where quantity might be important to you."

"You used to be quite a good trencherman yourself, Ned. Want that coffee?"

"No." He passed the cup over. "Be careful. It's hot."

Jack took a sip. "It's not too bad." He turned his attention to the ham.

Ned wished he could be as carefree as Jack. He couldn't imagine what it would be like not to worry about everything. He put his napkin over the spot where he'd spilled his coffee and watched Jack chew.

Was Ellie in love with Jack? And, perhaps more importantly, was Jack in love with Ellie?

When he'd arrived at the castle, Jack had seemed very definite that he did not want to wed, but perhaps that was simply because of Miss Wharton. But if Jack did love Ellie, he could easily escape Miss Wharton's pursuit by announcing the fact. Mama and Father would be delighted.

As far as Ned could tell—not that he was an expert—Jack did not look the least bit in love; he'd even been clowning about it during charades.

Damn, Cox *must* be wrong. And thinking of that bounder . . .

"Do Cox and Lady Juliet know each other well, Jack? I suppose they must, having spent time in London."

Jack popped the last bite of ham into his mouth. "Oh, their connection goes back further than London. Their fathers' principal seats adjoin, so they've grown up together." He looked at Ned. "Rather like you and Ellie."

"And you and Ash and Jess and Cicely and Percy."

"Yes, I suppose so." Jack grinned. "But more like you and Ellie."

Damn it, Jack was playing games again. Best to ignore him. "And are Cox and Lady Juliet especially, er, friendly?"

Jack got up to get more food. The man must have a hollow leg. "Very. Rumor is Cox asked for Lady Juliet's hand, but her father refused. Some say Extley didn't think Cox was good enough for his precious little chick, but others think Extley and Bollant had a falling out of some sort, perhaps a boundary dispute, and that's why he wouldn't give his consent."

"That's unfortunate." He should feel angry or . . . something other than this detached, almost academic interest. "And Cox and Lady Juliet accepted Extley's decision?"

"Lady Juliet did." Jack looked over his shoulder and raised his brow. "She's angling to be your wife, isn't she?"

Ned glared back at him. "But Cox didn't?"

Jack shrugged as he piled his plate with food. "He doesn't have much choice, does he, if Lady Juliet is not prepared to defy her father for him." He paused. "Hey, you missed the beef tongue. Did you know?"

"I saw it. I'm not partial to tongue."

"No? Well, I guess there's no accounting for taste." Jack came back, sat down, and set to eating again.

Was Lady Juliet content with her father's decision? Ned wasn't so certain. More to the point, he'd wager Cox was not giving up, and if the blackguard was still pursuing Lady Juliet, he shouldn't be courting Ellie.

Ned grabbed a cup and poured himself some more coffee, taking a cautious sip first this time. He would just have to keep a very close eye on the scoundrel.

Chapter 11

A new gown can definitely raise one's spirits.
—Venus's Love Notes

"Playing hide and seek, Ellie?"

"Of course not." Damn it, this was very awkward. What believable explanation could she give for being in the wall?

There was no believable explanation. She would simply have to smile and babble.

"I just remembered the secret doors and wanted to see if I could open one. And then I went into the little room and got stuck." That was true, though what had trapped her had been Percy and the women, not the door's latch. Why she'd go inside and close the door; why she'd stay inside when help was just a shout—hardly a shout, even—and a knock away . . .

She simply could not worry about making sense.

He raised one eyebrow, disbelief writ large on his face, but she forced herself to keep smiling.

"One might think you were spying on me," he finally said.

That was funny. "I can assure you, Percy, that I have much better things to do with my time than hide in the long gallery walls, hoping you'll come along and say something interesting."

He didn't laugh in return. "You must have heard our conversation. As I remember, sound travels quite well through those thin hidden doors."

"Um." Hell, she couldn't think of a single convincing lie, not that any of her lies were convincing. Percy had grown up with her; he knew she was a dismal prevaricator. "I wasn't, er, paying that much attention, actually. I've discovered I don't much care for confined spaces."

"Oh? Then I would have thought you'd have pounded on the wall and yelled for help."

"Well, I might have, except I didn't want to embarrass myself, especially in front of Lady Heldon, who I must say I can't quite like. And, yes, I did hear her voice, so I knew she was there." Gad, she was beginning to sound like Mr. Humphrey. Well, if a flood of words would get her free of Percy, she'd produce a deluge. "I thought you'd think I was listening in, which of course I wasn't, and since I was certain you'd move on at any moment, I decided to wait—and, yes, pray a bit, too—until I could emerge alone. I will tell you I was very happy when you finally did leave." She swallowed. "Except obviously you didn't."

Percy's eyes narrowed. He looked quite threatening.

This was ridiculous. Percy might be unpleasant, but he wasn't dangerous, and she was in Greycliffe Castle, not some dark London alley.

"Well, I'm sure I wasted quite a bit of time in that silly hiding place, and I must look a sight. It was very small and dusty. I hope I don't have any spiders crawling in my hair."

She shuddered theatrically. "If you'll excuse me, I'll just be off to tidy—"

Percy's hand darted out, and he plucked the green and yellow reticule out of her fingers. "What have we here?"

Her heart froze. Dear God! Why hadn't she dropped the damn thing when she'd been trapped in the dark? "A-a reticule."

"I *know* that." He jerked the strings open and pulled out the blasted silk drawers. He gave a long, low whistle. "Yours?"

"Don't be ridiculous." It wasn't a lie if she told herself he was asking about the reticule. "You know how Reggie likes to steal things."

"He usually brings them to Ned."

"And Ned brought these to me so I might return them." That was true, too, in a way.

"Really? So you know whom they belong to?"

"N-no." Pray God she didn't look too guilty. And she didn't know who owned the reticule. She must keep that firmly in mind.

"Yesterday the duchess put the items Reggie had snaffled on a table in the yellow salon. That seemed to work perfectly well. Why do you suppose Ned brought these things to you?"

She forced herself to shrug. "I have no idea—I'm not a mind reader. You'll have to ask him." Ned wouldn't betray her—at least, she didn't think he would. Especially not to Percy. He liked his brother-in-law even less than she did, which at the moment was rather a challenge.

"Hmm." Percy looked from the red drawers to her long-sleeved, high-necked, drab-colored gown. "It's rather, ah, stimulating to think of you wearing these"—he held up the drawers—"under that depressing dress."

Her stomach twisted with unease. "Don't be insulting."

"Do you have a pair on now?" There was a nasty, hot look in his eyes.

"Of course not." While she'd never liked Percy very much, she'd never been afraid of him. Now she'd admit to feeling more than a little on edge. "I don't know why you think those scandalous things are mine." She held out her hand. "Now give them—and the reticule—back to me, if you please, so I can be on my way."

Percy slipped his fingers back and forth over the silk. "No. You may have the purse, but I think I'll keep these."

"Suit yourself." Ellie took the reticule. She wanted to snatch the drawers as well, but she had enough presence of mind to realize how odd that would look. "I can't imagine why you would want them." She made herself smile. "I doubt they'll fit you."

"Very funny. They are a form of insurance, of course."

"Insurance? In case all your undergarments suddenly go missing?"

"No." He almost snarled at her. "In case you remember any of the conversation you profess not to have heard and think you should discuss it with anyone. I should be extremely unhappy if that should occur. So unhappy I might be provoked to show Cox and Humphrey and maybe even the duchess these lovely red drawers . . . that you left in my room after a romantic interlude."

Thank God she hadn't yet eaten anything this morning; her stomach attempted to turn itself inside out. "That I left in your room after a . . . a . . ." She swallowed firmly. "No one would believe such an incredible tale."

He dangled the drawers in front of her, yet safely out of her reach. "But I have proof."

"I don't know why you think anyone would believe those are mine. They are far more likely to suspect they belong to Ophelia." She raised her brows. "And I would think Ophelia would be very unhappy with you if you spread such a story. It's not a secret that you and she share a rather, ah, close relationship."

He shrugged. "Ophelia is very understanding. She may even be willing to say she saw you in my bed—that she was there with us. As you say, people know we share many things."

"That's disgusting." And after the conversation she'd just overheard—the one she couldn't admit to hearing—she doubted how understanding Ophelia was feeling at the moment.

He smiled. "You shouldn't discount something until you've tried it."

"I believe I can come to a clear opinion without engaging in an, an orgy!"

"Oh, it's hardly an orgy." Percy laughed. "I'd like to see you at an orgy—I'd wager your eyes would roll back in your head and you'd fall into a fit." He looked at the drawers again. "Or, maybe not."

"I am not going anywhere near an orgy."

Percy was twirling the damn drawers on his finger. Could she grab them and run?

"Hmm. The story might actually raise your value with Cox, you know, but I'm afraid it will put paid to any hopes you might have harbored with regard to Humphrey"—he snorted—"and our dear straitlaced Ned."

She tried to keep the desperation out of her voice. "Percy, you know no one will believe those . . . things are mine." She would cling to that thought like a drowning man clings to the tiniest bit of flotsam.

"I think they will. In fact, I think Ned *knows* they are yours. Why else would he have given them to you instead of putting them downstairs on the table with everything else?"

"He gave me the reticule." She could feel the waves breaking over her head. She was going down; she knew it.

"Are you saying he didn't notice this very shocking, very

red garment inside the reticule? Or—" His eyebrows shot up. "Zeus, have you been frolicking in *his* bed?"

"No!"

Percy's lips slid into an oily smile. "My, my, my. And here I thought Ned was true to my dear departed sister."

"He is." Ellie could barely get the words out. She was shaking, she was so furious. She wanted to slap Percy—no, she wanted to kick him right between his legs.

But she felt panic, too. The damn drawers *were* hers.

Percy nodded thoughtfully. "I suspect this explains his sudden parsimoniousness." He frowned at her. "I'm sure he's told you he used to take his role as brother-in-law seriously, sending me needed funds from time to time, but this Christmas he cut me off. It was quite a blow—put me deep in the dismals, as you may well imagine. I couldn't understand why old Ned would suddenly turn against me"—he looked her up and down—"but now I think I see the reason."

"Percy!" Shouting would not help anything. She swallowed, struggling to get her temper under control. "Will you be sensible? There's nothing between Ned and me."

Percy snorted. "Of course there is. Good God, Ellie, what do you take me for? I've seen how you've cast sheep's-eyes at Ned all these years."

"I-I—" Oh, dear God, so Jack hadn't been the only one to notice.

"You're flapping your chin like a dying fish, my dear. It is not flattering."

Ellie snapped her mouth shut.

"That's better." Percy smirked. "While it was clear to anyone with eyes that you would lie down and let Ned walk over you—or do more interesting things with other parts of his person—"

"Percy!" Who knew it was possible to die of mortification and explode with anger at the same time?

"—I was relatively certain Ned was oblivious to your adoration. Ned is a bit . . . well, perhaps I should be charitable and call him unimaginative." Percy sniggered. "It's been quite entertaining watching you lust after him while he mourned poor Cicely."

Ellie tightened her hands into fists. "How can you be so callous? Not about me—I don't care about that"—which wasn't strictly true, but in this universe of suffering, hers was the least significant—"but didn't you feel some sympathy for Ned? Didn't you mourn Cicely yourself?"

Percy glared at her, a new level of fury flashing in his eyes like lightning. "Of course I mourned my sister. She was one of the two most important people in my life." He took a breath. "And Ned killed her."

Ellie gasped. "Ned didn't kill Cicely."

"No? She'd still be alive if that big, rutting—" Percy pressed his lips together so tightly they formed a white line. He drew in a deep breath through his nose, obviously struggling for control, and then he smiled in a most unpleasant way. "Well, enough of that old story. I'm much more interested in the current tale."

"There *is* no current tale." Clearly there was no point in prolonging this conversation. Percy was completely irrational. "Now give me that ridiculous garment, if you please, and we can both go seek our breakfast."

Percy held the drawers behind his back, safely out of her reach. "Oh, no. As I said, I'm keeping them to ensure you aren't tempted to empty the bag about anything you might have overheard this morning. But now that I think about it, they might prove a good investment as well. I just have to see how things fall out before I know the worth of what I have here."

Ellie had a very bad feeling about this. "You're talking in riddles."

"Am I? Then let me explain. I know you have no money, but Ned is quite plump in the pocket. At the moment he appears to be wooing Lady Juliet. He might be willing— eager, even—to keep her from finding out about the existence of this very interesting nether garment. I would be more than happy to hold my tongue . . . for a price. Or he may even care enough about your reputation to be willing to part with a nice sum to protect it." He grinned. "And since I have such a lamentable memory, one payment will never do. I'll need regular reminders."

"You're a snake, Percy."

He bowed. "Thank you. I take that as a compliment."

"Don't. And your plan won't work, you know. Ned won't pay you."

He shrugged. "I suppose we'll find out, won't we? Nothing ventured, nothing gained, as they say. Now if you'll excuse me, I think I'll go put these in a safe place." He headed down the stairs.

Damn it, she wanted to tackle him and snatch the drawers back, but that would be beyond foolish. He was larger and heavier than she and likely moved faster. She would only get hurt.

She leaned against the wall, listening to his feet echo down the stairwell. She couldn't let him do this to Ned, but how could she stop him?

She closed her eyes. She would begin by telling Ned everything she'd heard this morning. She'd admit the damn silk drawers were hers and tell him she was willing to have Percy shout that fact from the rooftops. Then she would just have to trust her stick-in-the-mud reputation was enough to squash Percy's salacious tales.

She definitely would not be sledding today.

She listened again—it sounded as if Percy was finally gone. Very well. She'd take the reticule down to the yellow salon and then retreat to her room to gather her composure and perhaps have a sustaining cup of chocolate.

Unfortunately, the duchess waylaid her the moment she reached the bedroom floor.

"Oh, Ellie," her grace said, taking her arm, "I'm very much afraid there's been a bit of an accident."

"An accident?" Ellie's throat closed up in panic. "Who's hurt?"

"No, no, not that kind of accident, dear. Thankfully this is just a clothing disaster."

"A *clothing* disaster?"

"Well, perhaps a blessing, really. Come, let me show you." She started down the corridor. "I'm not perfectly sure what got into Sir Reginald."

Reggie was usually very careful—or lucky. Ellie couldn't think of anything he'd damaged in his thievery, aside from the occasional pull in a knit stocking. "Do you know whom the item belongs to?"

The duchess smiled. "You."

They turned into Ellie's room. Reggie sat on the floor by the pink upholstered chair, licking his paws. Next to him was Ellie's pale yellow ball gown covered in dark paw prints as if Reggie had walked through mud before dancing on her dress.

"Oh." Ellie picked up the gown. Not only was the bodice ruined, the overskirt was shredded. Reggie must have tried to sharpen his claws on it. She sniffed. "Do you smell fish?"

"Oh, I don't think so," the duchess said, throwing open the windows. Frigid air swept in along with a dusting of snow. "Maybe you're just smelling what Reggie had for lunch."

It was so cold in the room now, Ellie wouldn't have been able to smell a pig farm. "Perhaps." Not that she'd ever noticed an odor to Reggie before.

She turned the dress over in her hands and her heart sank.

There was no way it could be cleaned and repaired in time for the Valentine birthday ball the day after tomorrow.

"I'm sorry, Ellie." Her grace came over to pat her on the shoulder. "I hope you weren't especially fond of that gown."

"N-no." Of course she wasn't. She hadn't particularly liked it when it was new, two—or maybe three—years ago. But it was the only ball gown she had.

"You must let me make reparations for my pet's misbehavior."

"Oh, no, that's all right. I'm sure Reggie didn't mean to damage the dress."

"Nonsense. Whatever his intentions, the gown can't be worn. I don't suppose you have another?"

"No, but I'll make do with something."

Did the duchess shudder?

It didn't really matter. If Percy went through with his threats, she'd likely not be welcome at the ball.

"I insist you let me have a new gown made up for you," the duchess said. "I won't take no for an answer. I even have some spare cloth that I think will be perfect for you."

"But . . ."

"Ah, here's Mary now. Mary, get Ellie's measurements, if you will."

"But . . ."

"Now don't argufy, Miss Ellie," Mary said. "Ye cannae wear this poor thing—not that ye ever should have been wearing it. It always made ye look consumptive. The wee cat's done ye a blessing."

"But . . ."

Mary gave her a stern look. "Ye need a new dress and that's the end of it. Now do as I tell ye, and I'll make ye something that will have all the gentlemen wanting to dance with ye."

"Yes, do stop arguing, Ellie," the duchess said. "You are just wasting time, you know. Mary and I won't let you out of this room until Mary has your measurements."

"Oh, very well." Ellie knew when she had lost a battle. She let Mary poke and prod and measure her with as much good grace as she could muster.

"There ye be," Mary said finally. "I've got all I need, yer grace. Shall I take that poor rag on the floor with me then?"

"Yes, indeed, and do just throw it out. You can't use it as a guide to fit the new dress."

"I ken that very weel." Mary's brogue often grew stronger when she was experiencing strong emotions. "That sorry excuse for a gown fit Miss Ellie like a potato sack."

Mary bundled the poor, maligned dress up and carried it off with her sewing box.

The duchess grinned. "I can hardly wait to see what Mary makes up for you. I know you'll look beautiful in it." She almost danced out the door.

Ellie glanced down at Reggie. He was snapping up what looked suspiciously like a bit of flounder from where the dress had been lying. "What just happened, do you know?"

Reggie did not reply; he was too busy eating.

"Beautiful day, isn't it, Ned?"

Ned glanced down at Percy. Damn it, his brother-in-law looked bloody happy, always a bad sign. "It's cold, but at least the sun's out."

They were on their way to the pond, following the path the servants had cleared through the snow. Ned had intended to escort Lady Juliet, but Ophelia and Lady Heldon had swept her up with them, obviously so Percy could have this opportunity to accost him.

Ned's mood, which had not been good to begin with, turned darker.

He looked ahead. Everyone was strung out along the path. Mama and Father led the way, and Ash followed with Ellie—at least she wasn't walking with Jack or Cox. Cox was a little behind her with Lady Juliet's group, and, behind them, Jack strolled with Miss Wharton, of all people, and Mr. Humphrey and Miss Mosely. Perhaps Jack felt there was safety in numbers—or that the cold and multiple layers of thick clothing would deter Miss Wharton's matrimonial ambitions. Ned and Percy brought up the rear.

Ned's eyes went back to Ellie. She was laughing at something Ash had said.

She'd been right, of course, when she'd told him he had no authority over her. He wasn't her brother, much as he wished he was.

He frowned. No, that wasn't quite true. He didn't want to be her sibling; he just wanted to keep her safe. Which, as she'd pointed out, he couldn't do even if they *were* related.

He hoped she'd decide not to sled. Surely Father had persuaded Mama to think better of the idea—the insane, foolhardy, madcap—

"She's rather beautiful once you know her secret, isn't she?"

Ned looked back at Percy. What the hell was the man talking about? Oh, right. The woman Ned was supposed to be wooing, though he didn't understand the reference to a secret. "Lady Juliet *is* very lovely."

Percy waggled his brows. "That's not whom you were looking at."

This false joviality was a side of Percy Ned hadn't yet encountered, though it was as unpleasant as all the man's other traits. "I'm afraid I don't follow you."

"Ellie." Percy's damn brows jumped up and down again.

"What about Ellie?"

"Oh, come on, Ned." Percy's elbow dug into Ned's side, though not very far. They were both bundled up against the cold. Still, Ned took the precaution of putting a bit more distance between them.

"I really haven't the slightest clue as to what you might be referring." Not that he liked the notion of Percy talking— or thinking—about Ellie at all.

"Let's just say I have something in my possession that I think you'll be interested in—something you might even be willing to, er, encourage me, in a monetary way you understand, not to mention or show anyone else."

Ned stopped walking, thus forcing Percy to stop as well. "Listen to me, Percy. I have no bloody idea what you're talking about, but you'd damn well better not be maligning Ellie or suggesting that she is anything other than the proper, virtuous young woman that she is."

"Proper and virtuous?" Percy chuckled. "Is that the game she plays when she wears those red silk drawers for you? I do have them, you know. In a safe place, of course." Percy looked toward Ellie. "I must say it is very . . . stimulating to think about what she's hiding under those hideous frocks. It fills my mind with all sorts of intriguing images." He leered at Ned. "Are her legs long, Ned, and does she wrap them around you? Are her breasts plump and tasty?"

"Shut up, Percy." A red haze of fury clouded Ned's eyes. It was a wonder the snow at his feet didn't melt.

"A little angry?" he heard Percy say. "Just remember that if you hit me, as I'm sure you'd like to, everyone will see and wonder at it. I'm afraid I might be compelled to tell them why you so forgot yourself. Sad that it would reveal Ellie's, er, other side, but perhaps poor Cox and Humphrey should know before they continue to pay their addresses."

"You will not sully Ellie's reputation." Ned had to grind the words out through clenched teeth.

"I suppose it might actually improve her reputation—not for marriage, of course, but for other . . . pursuits." Percy sniggered. "At least Jack won't call her a stick-in-the-mud any longer."

"Percy . . ." Did the man not realize how close to death he was?

"I confess I've been wondering something since I found those lovely drawers. You Valentine brothers are so damn close. Do you share? Has Jack had a taste of Ellie, too? And Ash . . . that must be why he doesn't miss Jess or seek out any of the local girls. I'll tell you, Miranda was rather insulted that he seemed uninterested in her overtures, but now perhaps I can reassure her—if you choose not to persuade me to remain silent—that she's not losing her touch. It's just that Ash already has a woman to attend to his needs. It makes perfect sense. He's here all year, as is Ellie."

Ned wanted to pummel Percy into a bloody lump so badly he was almost shaking, but that would only serve Percy's purposes, whatever they might be. Later. He would make Percy pay later.

"If you don't wish to die right now," Ned said, "you'd best take your filthy lies and your filthy self away from me—and away from Ellie."

"Very well, I will—for now. But do think about what I've said, my dear brother-in-law. I'm sure we can come to an agreement that would keep me from mentioning this to anyone. Of course the . . . gift would have to be rather more than you were used to sending me, and you do understand I can't give up the lovely red garment that I have in my possession. But pay me well enough, and no one need ever be the wiser."

"I won't pay you a bloody sou, you bastard."

"No?" Percy shook his head, a false expression of pity on his ugly face. "I thought you cared for Ellie more than that." He shrugged. "But I suppose you're finished with her. Still I would think you'd prefer Lady Juliet not hear the tale. It might persuade her she'd rather not follow my sister into your damn bed." Percy spat out the last words.

He couldn't let Percy go down to the pond now and spread this revolting tale, but he couldn't force himself to agree, even for a moment, to consider Percy's terms. He would just have to beat the man insensate. He could do enough damage to Percy's mouth to make speaking very difficult for the foreseeable future.

He smiled. That was a very pleasant notion.

Percy must have guessed the direction his thoughts had taken, since he quickly stepped out of reach.

"Very well, I can see your emotions are in a bit of a turmoil at the moment, Ned. And I confess I do like Ellie; I wouldn't want to make life unnecessarily difficult for her. I tell you what—I'll give you the rest of the day to consider my offer." Percy waved his hand expansively. "No, I'll even let you sleep on it"—he leered again—"and, perhaps, on Ellie so you can refresh your memory as to her delights. We'll talk in the morning. I'm sure we can reach an agreement then."

Percy paused, perhaps waiting for Ned to concur, but when Ned just glared at him, he shrugged and continued down the hill.

Ned watched him go as he tried to fill his lungs. The cold air hurt, but it helped clear the rage from his mind. He needed to calm down before he joined everyone at the pond.

Percy must have got the blasted red dra—the blasted garment from Ellie in the long gallery this morning. How?

Ellie would never have handed it over willingly. The bastard had better not have hurt her.

Percy had almost reached the pond. The servants had a bonfire burning on the banks—far enough from the ice for safety, he hoped—and some people were gathered there to get warm and drink hot cider. Many had already ventured out to skate. Ellie was one. Ned watched her glide gracefully across the ice with Ash.

Damn it, Percy had done more than anger him—he'd twisted his mind, planting seeds of lust there. He never would have wondered about Ellie's legs or breasts before, but now . . .

He wasn't very experienced with women. He'd married young and been a faithful husband, even though Cicely had been a little reluctant about the marriage act—not surprising as he was so much bigger than she—and then she'd conceived and been sick in the early days and large and uncomfortable later.

And after she'd died, he'd been too grief-stricken to take any of the offers he'd received from the local women. Even if he'd been interested, there was no such thing as anonymity in the country or any way to guarantee he wouldn't sire a by-blow. He didn't want to have to bring a wife home someday to live among former lovers and illegitimate children.

And he'd admit he was afraid of having another woman die giving birth to his child. He wouldn't take on that risk lightly.

But he *was* male. He did have urges—he just shouldn't be having them with regard to Ellie.

He started down the hill. He'd check on the bonfire, though it was too late to relocate it. Still, if it was too close to the ice, he could see people didn't skate nearby. And he would be sure the area by the spring where the ice was always thin was adequately roped off.

He was close enough now to see Ellie smiling at Ash, her cheeks flushed, her eyes sparkling. Need struck him in the gut as hard as he would have liked to have hit Percy.

And then, damn it all, they turned and started skating toward the thin ice. Were they mad?

He started walking more quickly.

Chapter 12

❧⚜❧

Anger is sometimes frustrated desire.
—Venus's Love Notes

Ellie loved skating: She loved gliding with long, strong strokes over the ice, hearing the hiss of her skates, and feeling the cold air rush over her face.

"Happy?" Ash asked.

She smiled up at him. "Yes." Unfortunately she'd be much happier if he were Ned.

She glanced around. Where *was* Ned? He'd been at the back of the group with Percy when they'd left the castle. She'd been more than a little nervous about that, particularly when Ned hadn't detached himself immediately from his brother-in-law, since she could think of only one thing they would have to discuss.

She and Ash skated along the pond's opposite bank and then turned back toward the bonfire. She looked up.

Damn. Ned and Percy had stopped on the hill. Percy was talking; Ned was standing as still as a statue.

She tripped over a small bump in the ice.

Ash steadied her. "Are you all right?"

"Yes." Clearly Percy was wasting no time in putting his extortion plans into motion. She hated that she'd given him anything at all to threaten Ned with. Well, she would speak to Ned as soon as she could and tell him not to agree to Percy's demands, and then she'd admit to everyone that the scandalous garment was hers.

Her stomach twisted. If only she'd never made those cursed drawers. She would destroy them the instant she got home.

Ah, it looked as if Percy had finally concluded his speech. He started down the path to the pond, but Ned stayed where he was.

He must be furious. Why the *hell* did Percy have to be such a thorn in everyone's side?

More couples had joined them on the ice—Jack and Lady Juliet, Mr. Cox and Ophelia, Mr. Humphrey and Miss Wharton, even the duke and duchess—and she'd yet to raise the topic she'd intended to with Ash.

"Let's go over there." She gestured toward the end farthest from the bonfire near the roped off area. She didn't want anyone to overhear what she had to say.

Ash raised an eyebrow, but changed direction without argument.

"I'm sorry I haven't spent as much time talking with you at this party as I usually do," she said as the other conversations faded behind them.

Ash's lips curved up slightly. "Don't apologize. You've been making Mama happy by finally paying some attention to the eligible men she's gathered for you."

Ellie wrinkled her nose. "I'm afraid I'd rather have been talking to you than Mr. Cox or Mr. Humphrey."

He sent her a sidelong look. "Cox and Humphrey aren't the only eligible males here."

"No, but you can't think I'd be interested in marrying

Jack!" She laughed. "Whatever you do, don't mention that notion to him—he'd be horrified."

"I wasn't thinking of Jack."

She looked at him uneasily. "And not Percy either." The thought was nauseating—and, in any event, after Ash heard what she had to say, there might not be anything of Percy left to marry.

He chuckled. "No, not Percy, either. I can see why Mama has been tearing her hair out over you."

She decided to let the matter drop. She needed to discuss Percy's perfidy, not possible proposals, and she wouldn't have that much more time alone with Ash to do so. "Actually, it's Percy I wish to talk to you about."

Ash's expression hardened. "I'd much prefer not discuss him. He quite sours my mood."

It was true Percy's biggest conflicts had always been with Ash—and then Jess would take Ash's side, and Percy would become even angrier.

"I'm sorry, but I think you should know what I overheard this morning." She stopped and turned so she could see if anyone was close enough to eavesdrop.

Percy was still by the bonfire, thank God, talking to Lady Heldon and Miss Mosely, and Ned . . . oh, dear. Ned was striding along the bank, skates slung over his shoulder, glaring at her. He'd likely be out as quickly as he could to tell them to move away from the thin ice. But at least there was no one else about. Miss Wharton and Mr. Humphrey were the only two skaters at all nearby, and they weren't yet in earshot.

She didn't have much time to talk to Ash.

"I'd rather not know," Ash said. "Conversations that include Percy are rarely pleasant."

"But, Ash, he encouraged Lady Heldon to wheedle an invitation from your mother for this party. He wanted her to try to sedu—" She bit her lip. Ash's face was expressionless as if he expected her to say what she was going to say, but she still couldn't say it. "—to try to make you do something you shouldn't. Something Jess wouldn't like."

She thought pain flashed through his eyes, but it was gone before she could be certain. "I very much doubt Jess cares what I do."

"No! How can you say that? Of course she cares. She loves you."

Ash's brow rose, his face as hard as granite. He'd always hidden his feelings much deeper than Ned or Jack. "Oh? She's told you that, has she? Just recently?"

His tone was pleasant, but there was something dark, almost savage, there, too. Ellie sucked in her breath. She was suddenly just a little afraid of him. "N-no."

Ash stared at her a moment more, and then his expression relaxed. "Forgive me. I know you mean well, Ellie, but—" He shook his head. "Just leave it be, all right?"

"But, Ash, I think Percy may have something to do with the problem—whatever it is—between you and Jess."

"Of course he does."

She gasped. "What?"

"You don't think I just—" Ash pressed his lips together, and then smiled and shrugged. "I do thank you for your concern, Ellie, but there's nothing you can do."

Ellie felt as if she'd just had a door slammed in her face, but she refused to give up. "P-perhaps if you talked to Jess—"

Ash put a gloved finger to her lips. "I will. Jack told me that the rumors in London have got out of control now that I'm turning thirty. It's clearly time—past time—to resolve the situation. I plan to leave for Blackweith as soon as this party is over."

"Oh. Well, that's good." Except she felt certain that by "resolve the situation," Ash meant end his marriage, if not legally, then emotionally, and while Ellie might not be able to swear Jess loved Ash, she'd wager every penny she had that Ash still loved Jess.

She looked away over the pond. Ned had his skates on now, but was still on the bank, impatiently talking to his mother. Percy was by the bonfire, and Mr. Humphrey and Miss Wharton—oh, dear.

Miss Wharton was out of control and screaming toward the thin ice. *"Aieee!"* She had a very healthy pair of lungs.

Ash started to turn, but since Ellie was facing that way, she reacted faster. She darted forward.

"What—" Ash reached for her, but slipped on the ice. She was past him in a flash.

"Ellie, don't!" That was Ned. He was worrying again, but he needn't do so. She was just going to push Miss Wharton out of harm's way.

Which she did. Unfortunately, she also tripped on one of Miss Wharton's skates. She stumbled, tried desperately to regain her balance, and fell heavily, sliding under the ropes.

She heard an ominous crack and felt the ice shift.

"Ellie!" Ned sounded as if he were right next to her. He couldn't have got there that quickly.

She raised her head—and felt the ice crack more.

"Don't move!" he shouted, and then his voice grew calm. "Lay perfectly still, Ellie. Put your head back down and stay as flat as possible."

"Oh, Miss Bowman, I'm so—"

"Get back, Miss Wharton. Everyone back to the bonfire." Ned's tone brooked no argument.

"But, Lord Edward," Mr. Humphrey began, "I believe I can—"

"Yes, Humphrey." That was Ash. "We all want to help, and the way we can do that is to go over to the bank as Ned said, thereby taking our weight off the ice and not distracting Ned or Ellie."

"Ah, yes, well, I see that might be a wise decision;

however, I do want to make it perfectly clear that I am more than willing to do whatever I can to assist Lord Edward in his valiant attempt to rescue poor Miss Bowman. I believe . . ."

Mr. Humphrey's voice faded as Ash shepherded him away, thank God. Ellie's heart was pounding, but she kept the rest of her body as still as she could. "N-Ned?"

"I'm lying down on the firm ice, Ellie." His voice was so reassuring. "I'm going to grab your ankles and pull you back. Don't try to help me. As long as you stay flat, you'll be fine."

"Y-yes." She must not panic. Ned was here. He would save her. This would be far easier than the time he rescued Ash. She hadn't fallen into the water . . . yet. "All right."

Ned's large hands wrapped around her ankles. It was a sign of her insane attraction to him that she felt a little thrill. Good God! Here she was, inches from plunging into frigid water, at risk of drowning or freezing to death, and she was thinking how strong Ned's grip was.

Well, perhaps lustful thoughts were better than panicked thoughts.

"I'm going to start pulling now, Ellie. This will go very slowly as it's hard for me to get purchase, and I don't know if your fall damaged the ice on this side of the rope as well. I don't want to risk dunking us both. So be patient—and keep still."

"I-I understand."

"Good. You're doing a splendid job."

She felt Ned tug, and she slipped an inch closer to safety. He pulled again, and she moved a little more. Unfortunately, it felt as if her chemise and dress were not keeping pace. Another tug and she was certain of it. An icy breeze slipped over the back of her calves.

Her blush risked melting the fragile ice under her. "N-Ned?"

He grunted and pulled again. Now she felt the cold air on the back of her knees. "Ned!"

"What *is* it?" He sounded very annoyed.

Couldn't he see the problem? "My skirts are riding up. It can't be quite . . . proper." She felt foolish raising the issue, but she also didn't care for Percy and Mr. Cox and Mr. Humphrey—well, even Ash and Jack and the duke— seeing her legs.

For some reason, she didn't mind so much Ned seeing them. Well, he had no choice, if he was going to save her. She was just being reasonable.

She didn't feel reasonable, though. She felt oddly excited.

"I'm afraid I can't reach them to brush them back in place." Ned's voice sounded slightly breathless—he was probably so angry with her he was having a hard time speaking. "I'm more interested in saving your life than your modesty, Ellie."

"Y-yes. Of course. I realize that. I just thought . . ." What did it matter? This embarrassment was minor compared to what she would feel when Percy flashed her red drawers around the company. "Never mind. Please, carry on."

He tugged again. Soon her thighs would be displayed. She moaned as quietly as she could. At least she was wearing a pair of flannel drawers; she wouldn't be completely naked.

What if she'd been wearing her red silk drawers?

Ohh. She bit her lip.

"Take heart, Ellie. It looks as if Mama has noticed the problem," Ned said. "She's ushered everyone to the other side of the bonfire. Only Ash is left to keep watch if I need help."

"Oh." That was good. She didn't mind Ash seeing her legs so very much. At least he was married, not that she was naïve enough to think that made a lot of difference, but somehow it seemed more respectable.

"I think we're past the most dangerous part now," Ned said, "so I'm going to try to move more quickly. You must continue to lie still, though. Let me do everything. Don't try to get up."

"Yes, I understand." Her waist had reached the ropes. Fortunately when she fell, she hadn't slipped far.

Ned pulled steadily now, and she slid closer to safety— as her skirts slid farther up her legs. Now they were bunched around her waist: her entire backside greeted the afternoon sun. But at least her shoulders were past the ropes.

"I think you're finally off the dangerous ice, Ellie, but don't try to stand yet. I want you to roll toward me, just like we used to do on the lawn in the summer when we were children. Can you do that?"

"Yes, of course."

It took her a moment to get started, but then she was rolling over and over as though she were again tumbling down the grassy hill by the formal gardens while the duke and duchess sat drinking tea and brandy on the terrace.

She bumped into Ned.

"Thank God," he said and threw his arms around her, crushing her against him so she could barely breathe.

She buried her face in his coat and hugged him back. She didn't care that they were both cold and damp and sprawled on the ice; she didn't even care any longer that her legs were exposed to the world. She was safe; she was alive; and, best of all, she was in Ned's arms.

He jerked back. Was he going to kiss her?

No, of course not. He was going to read her a thundering scold.

He pushed himself to a sitting position and then hauled her up beside him, grasping her shoulders.

"What the *hell* did you think you were doing, Ellie? Did you consider for even one moment before you rushed headlong into hare-brained, beef-witted, idiotic action?" His grip was hard; his fingers would have left bruises if it weren't for her thick cloak.

"I was trying to save Miss Wharton."

It was doubtful Ned heard her; he continued his tirade without the slightest pause.

"Oh, no, you didn't think at all. Ash was right there beside you, for God's sake. He should have been the one to do something, not you. And I was on my way to intercept Miss Wharton as well. But it's all of a piece, isn't it? You think nothing of decorum, let alone safety."

"B-but—" She wanted to be angry, but she knew she was going to cry. She bit her lip, willing the tears not to fall.

"I don't know what the hell has got into you, Ellie. You didn't use to be this way." He started to shake her—not hard, but she could tell he was holding back. "And now I suppose you'll risk your damn life again and go barreling down the hill on Jack's sledge and end up on the blasted pond and this time you'll fall through and die."

"N-no. I won't."

"You won't? You *will*. If you'd landed with more force or directly on the thin ice this time, you'd have broken through at once."

"I-I meant I won't sled."

"Well, thank God for that. If—"

"Ned." Ash had skated out to them. "You just saved the girl's life; don't kill her."

Ned glared up at Ash. "I'm not going to kill her." He got to his feet and then pulled Ellie up.

Ash held up his hands. "And don't kill me, either."

"Bloody hell, Ash. You saw what she did."

"Yes." Ash smiled at Ellie, which made her feel a little less like crying. "She thought quickly, acted valiantly, and

I believe saved Miss Wharton's life—or at least saved her from a very uncomfortable dunk in ice water." He smiled. "And I know whereof I speak."

"There is nothing amusing about this." The vein in Ned's temple was throbbing. "Ellie could have died."

Ellie didn't particularly like being discussed while she was standing there, but at the moment being ignored was good. She was still struggling to curb her tears.

"But she didn't die. She's safe, Ned. You saved her. It's over. You can relax. Look, everyone is cheering."

It was true. Now that she was safe—and her skirts were safely where they belonged—the duchess had let everyone come back to stand on the bank at the near end of the pond. They were all—even Percy—shouting and clapping.

"Idiots. Bloody idiots." Ned pushed Ellie toward Ash; she stumbled a little, and Ash's arm came round her to steady her.

"They're clapping for you, too, Ned," Ash said. "Come have some cider and put this behind you."

"No." Ned shook his head. "I can't. Not yet. I'm too . . ." He shuddered.

"Ned." Ellie had finally wrestled her tears down. "I'm sorry."

He shook his head again and stepped back.

"And I won't sled. I promise."

He nodded. "Thank you." His nostrils flared as if he were still struggling to control his spleen. "And I'm sorry for losing my temper just now. I worry—" His mouth tightened.

"I know." She put a hand on his arm. "Thank you for worrying. I don't know what would have happened if you hadn't been there to take charge when I fell."

"Come on, Ned," Ash said. "Let's get off the ice."

Ned shook his head once more. "No." He looked at the people on the bank and backed up another step, slipping free of Ellie's hold. "I need to be alone for a while." He turned and skated off across the pond.

Ellie watched him go, her heart tight. She hated to see him this way. "Ned's right. I shouldn't have done what I did."

"Nonsense." Ash took her arm and started back toward the rest of the party. "I'm quite sure Miss Wharton does not agree." He looked down at her. "I will tell you, though, that you likely took ten years off my life. And I'm more than a little chagrined. Ned was right—I should have been the one going to Miss Wharton's assistance, not you."

"No, Ash. I was facing her; I saw the danger first."

"Well, I'm not going to argue with you; I will save my wits for when I have to face Ned."

Ellie frowned. "You mustn't let Ned browbeat you."

"Oh, Ellie, I'm not afraid of my younger brother," Ash said, laughing. His expression turned serious. "But in this instance, I will have to agree with him."

"But—"

"No, I refuse to brangle with you. Come along now and greet your adoring public."

Ned wanted to rush over the ice as if all the demons of hell were after him, but he'd already created enough of a spectacle for one day. He forced his legs to move smoothly and hold at least a momentary glide.

If only he'd been a little quicker—if only Mama hadn't insisted on talking to him—he would have reached Miss Wharton, caught her, and turned her away from danger before Ellie had even got close. The entire drama would have been avoided.

He closed his eyes briefly. Zeus, he hoped never to live through anything like that again. Just the memory made him feel lightheaded. It had been almost as bad as when Cicely died. His heart had literally stopped when he'd seen

Ellie trip and slide under the warning ropes. And when he'd heard the ice crack . . .

He took a couple deep breaths.

When he'd heard that sound, all the blood had drained from his head and then surged back to try to pound its way out through the space between his brows.

Somehow—he'd no idea how—he'd found a way to remain calm. He'd known he had to move slowly and deliberately, but those minutes pulling Ellie to safety had seemed like hours. No, years.

And then he'd ripped up at her. Damn it, she'd deserved every harsh word, but he could see she'd been close to tears.

He felt like a beast.

He reached the bank and sat on a rock to pull off his skates. Everyone on the other side of the pond was gathered around Ellie, probably telling her what a brave, wonderful thing she'd done.

It *had* been brave—but it had also been incredibly stupid.

Mama was the only one looking his way. He could tell she was worried about him—he could see her tense expression even at this distance. He should walk over, join the group, reassure her.

He could no more do that than he could sprout wings and fly back to Linden Hall.

He stood and brushed snow off his coat. He wished he could fly away, back to the quiet and peace of his estate. His life was so much calmer there. No one bothered him. His servants were all well trained; his tenants happy. He saw that everything ran smoothly so there was never anything to worry about. He anticipated issues and attended to them before they became problems.

Back at Linden Hall, he knew exactly what his day would be like. He knew when and where he had to be at every moment. And when his work was done, he could read quietly in his study, a glass of brandy at his elbow. He could stroll his gardens or ride over his grounds without his heart ever once trying to slam its way out of his chest. There was no thieving cat; no matchmaking mother; no scheming brother-in-law; and, most importantly, no headstrong, misguided, maddening woman.

He liked it that way: calm and quiet and orderly and predictable. He was done with heartache and upheaval. He would marry a nice, well-behaved woman like Lady Juliet and begin filling his nursery.

He started back up the path to the house. Out of the corner of his eye, he saw Jack make a move to follow him, but Ash, thankfully, stopped him. That would earn Ash an ounce of forgiveness, but his elder brother had a lot to atone for. What the hell had he been thinking, letting Ellie go bolting after Miss Wharton like that? Ned flexed his right hand. Perhaps their "discussion" would take place outside. He'd quite like to draw Ash's cork and see his blood decorate the snowdrifts.

His feet crunched over the path. The servants had spread cinders, but already the ground was turning icy. They should put down more so no one slipped when the rest of the party returned later.

He reached the spot where he'd had his unpleasant conversation with Percy and smiled grimly. It looked like he had a busy time ahead of him; he'd use his encounter with Ash as a warm up for his meeting with his brother-in-law. He would keenly enjoy mashing Percy's face with his fist.

It would be better, though, if he could manage to steal back the damn drawers first. Without them, Percy had nothing to hold over Ellie's head. His tale of salacious behavior would be greeted with shocked disbelief and righteous anger—against him, not Ellie, especially after Ellie's recent act of heroism, no matter how stupidly misguided it was.

Hmm. Perhaps he would pay a visit to Percy's room while everyone was still at the pond.

He handed the footman his skates as he came in the house. "The path is getting a bit slippery, Thomas. You might want to spread some more cinders."

"Yes, my lord. I'll see to it straightaway."

Ned nodded and took the stairs up to the bedroom floor, slowing when he reached Percy's door. He glanced carefully in both directions—no one else was in the corridor—and then slipped inside.

Zeus, the place was a pigsty. It was painfully clear Percy had let his man go. Shirts were flung over chairbacks; pantaloons lay like cloth puddles on the carpet; soiled cravats festooned the bedposts; and balled-up stockings lurked everywhere just waiting to be trod upon. How the hell was he going to find something as small as a pair of silk drawers in this mess? At least they were red.

He checked his pocket watch. He would allow himself half an hour. If he hadn't uncovered the garment by then, he would simply get it from Percy after he'd beaten him to a pulp. Now, where to begin?

He opened the cabinet closest to him. Faugh! There was a wadded up condom in the middle of one shelf. Thank God Reggie had had better sense than to pilfer that.

He went through the room as thoroughly as he could. He pulled out drawers, peered into the clothes press, even gingerly picked up the dirty clothes. Nothing. Finally, his allotted time was over; he had to admit defeat. He retreated to his own room, closed the door, and collapsed back against it.

And then images of Ellie—Ellie in those drawers and only those drawers—flooded his imagination.

Bloody hell.

It was all Percy's fault. Percy had made him wonder about Ellie's legs and breasts and body. And then at the pond . . .

It had been bad enough wrapping his hands around her delicate ankles, but he'd been able to focus on his effort to save her life. And, truthfully, lying prone on the ice had also helped control his body's inappropriate reaction. But watching her skirts inch up her legs, seeing bit by tantalizing bit the outline of her calves and thighs and sweet rump . . .

He bent over. His damn cock had gone mad.

He squeezed his eyes closed. How could he have been so terrified and so bloody aroused at the same time? One emotion must feed the other—it was the only explanation for such a ridiculous situation. After all, this was *Ellie*. Good, old Ellie. His childhood friend. His almost sister.

His stomach protested.

Well, perhaps not quite that last. But still—Ellie. Not Lady Juliet, the woman he was supposed to be wooing.

He straightened. It was all very confusing, and his emotions had been twisted enough today. He could feel one of his headaches coming on. He'd just go splash some water on his face, take some of his headache powders, and lie down before dinner. He would have to thrash Ash and Percy later.

Reggie was waiting for him, lounging on his pillow, looking damned pleased with himself.

"Confound it, Reggie, can't you at least confine yourself to the foot of the bed? I don't want to be breathing in bits of your fur all night."

Reggie gave him a reproachful look.

"Yes, I know you're offended, but I need that space." He reached for the cat, but Reggie jumped down first, leaving behind a pair of red silk drawers.

Chapter 13

The path to true love is not without its slippery spots.

—Venus's Love Notes

"I can never thank you enough, Miss Bowman."

Actually, Miss Wharton *could* thank her enough. Once or twice would have been fine; nine times—or was it ten now?—in the space of half an hour were far, far too many.

"It was nothing, really, Miss Wharton. Please put it out of your mind," Ellie said, hoping she hadn't stressed the "please," but worrying that perhaps she had.

Ash's aborted laugh indicated she definitely had.

She, Ash, and Miss Wharton were drinking cider, standing by the bonfire with Mr. Humphrey and Miss Mosely. Ellie looked out over the pond. Jack was skating with Lady Heldon; Percy, with Ophelia. The duchess sent her an apologetic look as she and the duke glided by. She'd love to be out there with the others—away from Miss Wharton. Could she persuade Ash to partner her again?

"But if you hadn't acted so quickly and so bravely, I'm

sure I would have broken through the ice." Miss Wharton shuddered. "And I can't swim."

The inability to swim would have been the least of Miss Wharton's problems. "Lord Edward was right there as well. He would have kept you from getting wet."

Of all the skating couples, Mr. Cox and Lady Juliet were by far the most striking. They moved together so gracefully it was as if they were one body, not two. They must have skated together often.

They swept by close enough for Ellie to see their expressions. Oh! Their eyes were glued to each other's, their faces tight with suppressed passion and longing.

She flushed and quickly looked away. She felt as if she'd intruded on an intensely private moment.

"And really, Miss Wharton," Mr. Humphrey was saying, "I must apologize fervently. You were my partner; your safety was my responsibility." The shock of the near disaster had apparently knocked much of the bombast from Mr. Humphrey's breast.

Miss Mosely jumped immediately to his defense. "Oh, sir, you are too hard on yourself. You must admit Miss Wharton—" Her fierceness suddenly faltered. She flushed. "That is, no offense meant, of course, but you were moving rather rapidly, Miss Wharton."

Miss Wharton nodded. "Oh, yes. My lamentable enthusiasm. At home we race about our pond all the time in the winter, but I am obviously not at home. I should have been more careful." She smiled at Mr. Humphrey. "Please don't blame yourself, sir. My papa has always said I skate like a runaway horse. No one can control me." She looked back at Ellie. "Which is why I must thank you yet again, Miss Bowman, and apologize for being the cause of you putting yourself at risk."

Ellie really wanted to scream. "Yes, well, it is over—*do*

let us say no more about it." Perhaps Miss Wharton would cease if Ellie pointed out not everyone saw her as a heroine in this story. "I will tell you Lord Edward thought I was very much at fault for being so impetuous."

"Oh, I'm sure Ned admired your pluck, Ellie," Ash said. "He just wished you'd let me or him attend to Miss Wharton's rescue."

Miss Wharton's face developed a definite sheen of admiration. "Lord Edward was wonderful, wasn't he? So brave, so manly."

"Yes, yes, Ned is a very good fellow," Ash said dryly.

Ellie turned her laugh into a cough. Was Miss Wharton going to set her cap for Ned now? *That* match would be a disaster even Ned should be able to see a mile away. Miss Wharton's impetuosity would have him in Bedlam before Sir Reginald could lick his ear.

"I wish I could tell him so," Miss Wharton said. She looked around. "Where is he?"

"I believe he returned to the house." Ash's smile was slightly evil. "But I'm sure he'd be delighted to speak to you in the drawing room before dinner."

Ellie coughed again. Delighted? Ned would be mortified.

"And since everyone is safe and dry, and Miss Bowman has begged us to desist, I don't believe we need to belabor the issue any longer," Ash said. He bowed to Miss Wharton. "May I take you out on the ice? I do strongly suggest, however, that we head away from the warning ropes."

Miss Wharton laughed. "I believe you are as brave as your brother, Lord Ashton. Yes, I would be happy to take a turn about the pond with you."

Mr. Humphrey cleared his throat as Ash and Miss Wharton skated away from them. "Ah, and here I am, with two lovely ladies." His nose twitched as he tugged on his coat sleeves and smiled a bit awkwardly. "An embarrassment of riches."

"Oh, please, don't feel you need to keep me company," Miss Mosely said with what sounded to Ellie like false gaiety. "I'm quite content to stay here and watch."

"Don't you skate at all, Miss Mosely?" Ellie asked.

Miss Mosely shook her head quickly. "Oh, no." Her smile wavered. "Miss Wharton's papa may say she skates like a runaway horse; mine says I'm like a terrified snail." She looked down at her hands. "Well, I really don't go out on the ice at all."

"I'm sure you just need some practice." Ellie looked at Mr. Humphrey. He had appeared quite competent when he'd been squiring the wild Miss Wharton. "And perhaps an understanding tutor. Do you think you might be able to help Miss Mosely, sir?"

Mr. Humphrey puffed out his chest. "Yes, indeed. I would be delighted to show you the way of it, Miss Mosely. I will tell you, if I may do so without bragging—I'm saying this only to put your fears at rest, you understand—that I am considered more than a little skilled in this area. If you will only try, I will have you gliding over the ice in no time."

"Oh, I don't know." Miss Mosely was clearly torn between her fear of skating and her desire to have Mr. Humphrey's close attention.

"We will go slowly, and if you fall, I will help you up." Mr. Humphrey grinned, suddenly looking much more attractive. "And you *will* fall, you know. It is part of learning. I've fallen many times myself and, as you see, I've survived the experience."

Miss Mosely smiled shyly. "I *would* like to learn." She put her gloved fingers on Mr. Humphrey's arm—and then looked at Ellie. "Oh, but we can't abandon Miss Bowman." She started to remove her hand.

"Of course you can," Ellie said. "I've had my excitement for today, I hope. I was just on the verge of leaving."

It was clear Mr. Humphrey wished to focus on Miss Mosely, but he was too well bred to give up immediately. "Well, if you're completely certain?"

"Completely." She grinned at them both. "I expect Miss Mosely to report at dinner that she raced Miss Wharton across the pond and won."

"Oh, no." Miss Mosely's eyes widened with alarm. "I couldn't."

"Miss Bowman is merely teasing you, Miss Mosely." Mr. Humphrey gave Ellie a reproachful look. "She has a very active sense of humor. Do not worry. We shall go as slowly as you need."

"Oh, thank you." Miss Mosely gazed adoringly up at him.

Ellie waited until Miss Mosely had stepped gingerly out onto the ice, clutching Mr. Humphrey's arm tightly as if her life depended on it, and then she started back to the castle. Her grace saw her, but only smiled and waved. Ellie waved back.

The Duchess of Love should be very pleased with this house party. Miss Mosely and Mr. Humphrey were certain to make a match of it; Ellie wouldn't be surprised if Mr. Humphrey popped the question before the gathering was over. And even Mr. Cox and Lady Juliet appeared to be on the way to overcoming whatever stood in the way of their marriage.

Of course, if Lady Juliet wed Mr. Cox, she would not be able to marry Ned, and that would disappoint her grace. But Ned's mother would be far more disappointed if Ned married a woman who couldn't sincerely care for him.

Ned deserved happiness after his heartbreak. He should wed someone who loved him wholeheartedly—someone like Ellie.

Ellie trudged up the hill, feeling gloomier with each step.

Her feet crunched on the cold, packed snow. The hiss of skates, the drone of conversation, and bursts of laughter drifted up from the pond.

She stopped and looked back. Miss Mosely had graduated to taking a few tentative steps—oh dear, she just landed on her rump. Mr. Humphrey laughed, and it looked as if Miss Mosely was laughing, too, as he helped her up. Ash and Miss Wharton skated over to offer encouragement.

But love didn't guarantee happiness, did it? Look at Ash. She was certain he and Jess loved each other, yet Ash was miserable. Her gaze drifted over to the duke and duchess skating slow, smooth figure eights. That's what she wanted—the love Ned's parents had, the love Mama and Papa had. A love that lasted.

Tears pricked the corners of her eyes. Damn it, she was so tired of being alone. She'd been determined to find a husband this year. She'd *tried* to do what she was supposed to. She hadn't spent all her time with Ash; she'd talked to Mr. Cox and Mr. Humphrey. She'd even tried to get over her infatuation with Ned. None of it had worked.

What was she going to do? Next year she'd be twenty-seven.

She continued up the hill. She couldn't wait until next year; she would have to beat the bushes closer to home to find a husband. Surely she could flush out some male who wasn't pox-marked or ancient.

A jay screamed overhead; she looked up to see if she could spot it in the evergreen branches.

Of course the problem had never been finding a suitable male; the problem had been her unwillingness to find any male other than Ned suitable.

This was the first year since Cicely's death that Ned had shown any interest at all in the women the duchess invited. He'd never completely ignored his mother's choices—he had better manners than that—but he'd never spent more

time with one than the others. He'd been unfailing polite
and steadfastly remote. But this year he'd singled out Lady
Juliet. Was he finally ready to remarry?

Ah, there was the jay. He flapped among the branches,
sending snow cascading to the ground.

Down in the dungeon, Jack had told her she should show
some determination . . .

Ha! She needed far more than determination—she
needed a miracle. Ned was furious with her; Percy was
going to spread terrible stories about her; and the only ball
gown she possessed was ruined.

She snorted. And now she knew she'd reached the depths
of despair—she was worrying about fashion. Ridiculous!

Thomas opened the door for her when she reached the
castle. "Is the path all right, Miss Ellie? Should I put more
cinders down?"

"It's fine, Thomas. I had no problems."

Thomas peered out the door. "Is the rest of the party
coming soon, then?"

"I don't think so. Everyone was still skating when I left."

Thomas nodded, and then sent her a sidelong glance. "I
believe Lord Edward is in his room, miss."

Why was Thomas sharing that information with her? He
didn't think she'd seek Ned out, did he? "Er, yes, well, thank
you. At the moment I need to put away my coat and make
myself presentable."

She climbed the stairs and walked down the corridor
toward her bedroom.

She did need to talk to Ned about Percy to be sure he
knew not to pay the scoundrel anything. But Ned might feel
he had to do something to protect her in some way. He
would worry. It would be much easier if she could just
make the problem go away.

She paused in front of Percy's door. If she had the red
drawers back, Percy would have no hold over her.

The corridor was empty. She could sneak into his room now; if she found the damn garment, she'd be free.

She stared at the door handle, chewing her lip. But if someone found her in Percy's bedroom, the scandal would be enormous. It would give credence to Percy's lies.

No one would see her. Everyone was still at the pond and likely to be there for a while. Miss Mosely was just getting started on her skating lesson, after all. Even the servants had deserted this floor. And Percy had taken what belonged to her. She would only be taking it back.

She reached for the knob.

"Trust me, you don't want to go in there."

"Eek!" She jumped and spun around. Ned was leaning against the wall. "You scared me half to death."

"Sorry. I thought I'd made plenty of noise walking down from my room, but you did seem lost in thought."

She felt herself flush. "Percy has something of mine."

Ned grinned. "Not any longer."

Relief so intense she thought her legs would collapse washed over her. That was wonderful news—if only it were true. "What do you mean? You can't know what I'm talking about."

"Well, I assume you're referring to these." He held up the damn drawers.

Thank God! She snatched them out of his fingers. "How did you get them?"

"Reggie, of course. Percy is no match for Mama's pet."

"I never thought I'd be happy that cat is such an accomplished thief." She balled the drawers up in her hand. "I will hide them away immediately."

Ned chuckled. "I suspect the only way to keep them safe is to wear them."

She smiled back at him. "I suppose you are right. I'll have to—"

Good God, she wasn't discussing wearing these red silk drawers with Ned, was she?

She felt herself turn as red as the offending garment—and as red as Ned's face now.

"Th-thank you—and please thank Reggie for me." She backed up a few paces. "I'll just put these away now. If you'll excuse me." She turned and almost ran to her room.

"Did you enjoy skating this afternoon, Lady Juliet?" Ned handed her a cup of tea and sat down next to her on the settee. They were in the drawing room, waiting for Mama to reveal what torture she'd planned for this evening's entertainment.

Mama showed no signs of calling them to order yet, though; she was chatting by the fire with Jack, Miss Wharton—who had trapped him for a solid twenty minutes before dinner, thanking him over and over for his part in the afternoon's rescue—Miss Mosely, Humphrey, and Father. Ellie and Cox were sitting a little away from that group with Ash and Lady Heldon.

Ellie was her usual composed self now. She wore a high-necked, long-sleeved gray dress he'd wager he'd seen at this party last year and perhaps even the year before that. No one would ever guess she might have red silk—

He shifted his gaze quickly to Ash. His poor brother had made a serious tactical error by neglecting to claim one of the two available armchairs and so had got stuck sitting on the sofa next to Lady Heldon. In point of fact, he was almost sitting on the sofa's arm now; Lady Heldon kept inching closer, and Ash kept inching away.

As Ned watched, Lady Heldon's hand came to rest on Ash's thigh, and Ash jumped up, splashing some of his brandy on himself in the process.

"It was very pleasant, my lord."

"What?" Ned looked back at Lady Juliet; she smiled at him demurely, her head slightly bowed. "Oh, yes. The skating."

"Though it would have been far more pleasant had you stayed," she said.

"I apologize." He smiled. It was time to get back to his wooing, especially given his reaction to Ellie this afternoon. Obviously his body was telling him it required some marital exercise. "I'm afraid I felt rather cold and damp after having lain on the ice."

Cold and damp did not describe at all how he'd felt. He'd been so angry and aroused it was a wonder the ice hadn't melted under him.

"I hope you'll not take a chill, my lord."

"Oh, have no fear of that. I feel perfectly fine now." His temper—if not his temperature—had cooled remarkably once he'd found Ellie's drawers in his room.

Best not to think about that.

"Are you certain?" The space between Lady Juliet's perfect brows wrinkled in concern. "You suddenly look rather flushed."

"It must be the heat from the fire."

She blinked at him. They were seated as far from the fire as possible; Ned would even admit he'd seen his breath once or twice. Lady Juliet shivered, pulled her warm Norwich shawl a little tighter around her shoulders, and looked rather longingly at the hearth.

"Poor Sir Percy," she said. "I was terribly shocked when her grace announced that he'd fallen down the stairs. At least his injuries weren't serious enough to require the attentions of a doctor." She smiled somewhat archly. "And how kind of Lady Ophelia to offer to keep him company in case he needed nursing."

"Er, yes. Very kind."

"Do you know what happened?"

"I suspect he just missed a step." After Ned had left Ellie, he'd calmed down enough to recognize Ash didn't merit a thrashing. Instead he'd saved all his energy for Percy, dragging him outside shortly after his brother-in-law returned from skating.

Percy would be in much worse shape if he'd put up a fight, but he'd let Ned land any punches he wanted, and then, mopping up his blood with his cravat, had asked him to extend his apologies to Ellie for having threatened her. Apparently her attempt to save Miss Wharton had strongly affected him.

"I hope he's recovered by the ball."

"Yes." There was little chance of that. Ned was fairly certain he hadn't inflicted any permanent damage—he hadn't even broken Percy's nose—but Percy would have two black eyes, a fat lip, and an assortment of cuts and bruises for some time to come.

He racked his brain for another conversational topic. This wooing business was difficult; he hadn't had to do it with Cicely. Cicely had always rather idolized him.

Lady Juliet just stared back at him politely.

Besides the fact that she was very pretty and the daughter of the Duke of Extley, what did he know about the woman? That she was calm and restful . . . except she hadn't been at all calm or restful while searching for hearts in the dungeon. That she looked like Cicely—but she wasn't Cicely.

Did she like turtle soup? The color blue? He had no idea.

More to the point, how much did she like Cox?

"Lord Edward, I've been meaning to commend you on your quick thinking this afternoon," Cox said.

Damn, his thoughts must have conjured the man. Cox was at his elbow with Ellie. It looked as if his time alone with Lady Juliet was over. Just as well. His wooing skills definitely needed polishing.

"Thank you," he said, standing to greet Ellie. From the pointed looks Cox had been throwing him across the dinner table, he'd have expected the fellow to express his disappointment Ned hadn't fallen through the ice rather than compliment him. "I was very happy no one was hurt."

"Miss Bowman was quite brave, wasn't she?" Cox spoke to Ned, but looked at Lady Juliet. Lady Juliet scowled back at him.

"Yes, indeed," Ned said. There was a recklessness about Cox tonight. Had he had too much wine at dinner?

Ellie laughed. "Oh, don't perjure yourself, Lord Edward. You considered me more brainless than brave, and you were right. I should have waited for you to assist Miss Wharton."

"No." He may have given her the impression he felt that way—all right, he probably had felt that way—but now that he was over the terror of seeing her on the thin, cracking ice, he could admit he was proud of her. "I would have wished you'd let me help Miss Wharton, that's true, but you *were* very brave to go to her aid so quickly."

Ellie flushed and gave him an uncertain, oddly hopeful smile.

"Well, *I* would have let you save Miss Wharton, Lord Edward," Lady Juliet said. She gazed up at him, a look of adoration in her eyes that hadn't been there a moment ago.

He shifted his weight. Perhaps it was the set of her mouth or the way her eyes darted to Cox, but he'd swear there was something false about Lady Juliet's expression. And even if she was sincere, did he wish to be adored? Cicely had certainly done so, and it had made him feel strong and invincible when he was twenty, but he was almost twenty-eight now. He knew he wasn't invincible.

He no longer wanted to be cast as the hero of someone else's story. He'd already failed miserably in that role.

"You were so masterful in the way you took charge," Lady Juliet was saying. "It quite gave me shivers."

Cox snorted. "That was probably the cold wind."

Lady Juliet glared at him. "Oh, no, I assure you it was seeing a real man in action."

"Oh? Shall *I* take action, then?" Cox's voice was sharp and tight. Good God, were he and Lady Juliet going to brawl in Mama's drawing room?

"Perhaps we should just take our seats. Miss Bowman?" Ned gestured to the empty chair across from him. Cox took the chair closer to Lady Juliet. A bad choice.

"What action would you take, Mr. Cox?" Lady Juliet leaned toward Cox rather flirtatiously. Perhaps she'd been making a bit too free with the spirits as well.

Cox's eyes dropped to inspect Lady Juliet's breasts.

Ned's gaze slid over to Ellie's bodice. It covered her up to her chin, but there was a delightful swell—

Damn it, he should have hit Percy harder—it was his fault his thoughts were wandering in such an inappropriate direction.

He forced his eyes back to Cox.

"I'd free the princess from her prison," Cox was saying.

What? Were they speaking of fairytales now?

"How amusing. And what if the princess doesn't agree that she's in a prison?"

"Denial is always a prison."

Lady Juliet laughed, but the sound had a hard edge. "Very prettily said, but you are the one in denial. You've convinced yourself your silly dreams are real."

This was getting rather personal, if obscure. He should say something if for no other reason than to remind these two they had an audience. "Ah, I think you might like to—"

Cox ignored him. "Oh, have I? Perhaps, but at least I have the courage to dream of happiness."

The man had definitely had too much to drink.

"Happiness?" Lady Juliet dropped her voice to a loud whisper, making her sound like an angry snake. "Do you think I can be happy as a damn vicar's wife?"

Ned would swear he heard Ellie's jaw drop. He was certain she'd never before heard "damn" as an adjective for "vicar."

"But you know I don't mean to go into the church, Jule. I told you that."

Lady Juliet rolled her eyes. "Oh, no, you're going to invest in steam locomotives or some such ridiculous thing. If I hear about Mr. Trevithick's *Catch Me Who Can* one more time—" She stopped, and Ned could almost hear her teeth gnash. "Your father should be shot for letting you go see it when you were a boy."

Cox leaned forward, sounding perfectly sober now. "It's the future, Jule."

"The future?" Lady Juliet sniffed derisively. "Who would choose noisy, smelly engines over horses?"

"Some of the mines have. I've told you that. Once they solve the problem with the rails breaking—"

"Oh, for God's sake, Harry"—Lady Juliet looked ready to pull Cox's ears—"it's still trade. You're still dirtying your hands."

Cox leaned back. "That's the future, too, Jule." His jaw was set; his eyes, narrowed. "I don't expect your father to see it, but you—" He pressed his lips together. "You're not stupid, no matter how much you like to pretend that you are."

Lady Juliet's face was equally set. "I'm not willing to throw away who I am and the life I was born to."

Cox threw up his hands, surging to his feet. "All right then, Jule, you go on. Play your games. Catch yourself a nice, rich, blue-blooded fellow with a country estate"—he threw a disgusted look at Ned—"and be a damn ornament in his home and his bed. I'm done with you."

"Harry, no." Lady Juliet grabbed his hand. "We can—"

He shook off her hold. "We can't. I've told you I won't share—and I doubt Lord Edward wishes to, either."

Ned heard Ellie gasp.

Cox was almost snarling now. He inclined his head toward Ned. "But why don't you ask him?"

He turned on his heel and strode out of the room.

"Ah." Lady Juliet's face froze as if she just now remembered Ned was sitting next to her. She turned slowly to face him. "Ah." She smiled weakly.

Ned felt he should be angry or at least insulted, but his main emotion seemed to be relief—and amusement. "Cox is right, you know," he said. "Steam locomotives are quite likely the future."

"Ah." Her face was quite pale.

He smiled. "And I won't share."

Chapter 14

❧

Disappointment is sometimes a blessing in disguise.
—Venus's Love Notes

"And here I thought Reggie was going to be the only source of entertainment during this house party." The duke offered the duchess a glass of brandy and sat next to her on the overstuffed sofa in their sitting room, draping his arm along its back. "Today's events have been most exhausting, from Ellie's rescue to Percy's, er, accident to the fireworks in the drawing room after dinner."

Venus grinned. "Yes, things are progressing very well indeed."

Drew's brows shot up. "I doubt your guests will agree with that assessment, my dear."

"Oh, pooh. Maybe they won't now, but they will later." She took a sip of brandy and leaned against Drew's side, laying her head on his shoulder. She loved being close to him like this, talking over the day. "Though poor Percy *is* quite a mess. I assume Ned did the honors?"

"I assume he did since they were having such a heated discussion on the hill earlier, but neither Percy nor Ned offered that information. At least nothing appears to be broken."

"Well, that's good, I suppose. I wonder what it was all about?"

"Usually it's best not to know."

"I'm sure you're right." Venus sighed. "There's something dark and angry driving that boy."

"That's not surprising. His parents were rather nasty."

"They were, weren't they?" She'd often been extremely annoyed with Percy when he was young, but she kept reminding herself of what he had to face every day at home. She could avoid the old baronet and his wife—though not as much as she'd like when they were in the country—but Percy couldn't until he was old enough to go off to London. It would have been a blessing if they'd sent him away to school, but they hadn't.

She frowned down at her brandy. She'd never understood why Cicely had insisted on coming back to Greycliffe to be close to her mother when it was time to have her baby. If it had been Venus, she would have run as far and as fast from Lady Headley as she could.

No, that wasn't fair. She must remember that the love between a mother and a daughter was complicated—and some love was more complicated than others.

"I must say, Venus"—Drew brought her attention back to the present—"I was expecting you to be in a dark mood. Here we are, more than halfway through this party, and it seems that all your matches are coming to naught, with the possible exception of Humphrey and Miss Mosely."

"Oh, Drew, how can you say that?" Venus tilted her head back to look up at him. "This is why no one but me calls you the Duke of Love. You'd never succeed as a matchmaker."

Drew's eyes widened and his complexion acquired a vaguely greenish tint. "Good God! Me, a matchmaker? What a horrible thought."

She giggled. "You know, perhaps you should try it. I'm not sure I've ever heard of a male matchmaker."

"For good reason."

"There are procurers, of course, but that's not the same thing."

"Not at all. You are putting me to the blush, my dear duchess."

Venus laughed again. "And you are telling shocking bouncers, my dear duke."

"I am not." He got up and took her glass. "More brandy?"

"Please."

He strolled over to the cabinet. He was still dressed in his pantaloons, but had shed his coat and waistcoat. Venus admired how his fine lawn shirt pulled tight across his shoulders. He was certainly the duke of *her* love. She'd been so wise all those years ago when she'd decided to marry him.

She snorted. Or lucky. She'd been all of nineteen and a naïve country girl, but still she'd known when she'd met him that Drew was hers.

"So tell me why you aren't in despair." Drew filled her glass and then brought the bottle over to keep near at hand. This time he sat against the arm of the sofa and observed her.

"Because things *are* going splendidly, of course. Much better than I'd hoped—or even dreamed."

Drew choked on his brandy. "Cox's and Lady Juliet's

shockingly public brangle was a *good* thing? Cox tore out of the room as if all the hounds of hell were after him, and not five minutes later, Lady Juliet dashed out sobbing."

"Yes, indeed." Venus could barely contain her delight. She bounced slightly.

Both Drew's brows rose. "Need I remind you that the spectacle was so upsetting you changed your plans for the evening's activities?"

"Fiddlesticks! I didn't change my plans for that reason. With four of the party missing, hide and seek would have been sadly flat, and frankly, I didn't trust Lady Heldon to behave. Did you see how she was almost hanging on Ash?"

"It was rather hard to miss." Drew rested his brandy glass on his knee. "I thought you were more concerned about Miss Wharton and Jack."

Venus shrugged. "I've come to think there's no great harm in Miss Wharton. She's too enthusiastic, but that stems more from awkwardness than predatory intent. I think she might make Percy a good wife."

Unfortunately, Drew had just taken a large mouthful of brandy.

"I'm so sorry," Venus said, handing him her handkerchief. "Did some of it go down the wrong way?"

"And up." He blew his nose. "Warn me next time you intend to say something outrageous."

"But there's nothing outrageous in considering Miss Wharton for Percy."

Drew blinked at her over her handkerchief before blowing his nose once more. "Ophelia may have a different opinion."

Venus sighed. She always hated to see a couple grow apart, but sometimes it couldn't be helped. "No, I think Ophelia may have finally lost patience with Percy."

Drew stuffed her handkerchief in his pocket and gave her

an assessing look, as if weighing the odds she would say something to send brandy up his nose again, before taking a cautious sip from his glass. "How can you say that? She volunteered to nurse him."

"Yes, but she seemed annoyed by it." Venus considered the conversation she'd had with Ophelia before dinner. "Something has changed. She's always been a bit of a sheep about Percy—which is sad, because she is far too old for that and has known him far too long to be blind to his faults—but today I felt she'd given up on him, at least as a possible husband. She acted as if she were grudgingly helping an old friend, not a lover."

"Well, hurrah for her," Drew said. "Percy would try the patience of a saint, and Ophelia is definitely not a saint." He favored her with a long look. "Nor is Miss Wharton. I hesitate to contemplate your matchmaking machinations at all, my love—I know my male intelligence can't fathom their mysteries—but I don't see why you think Miss Wharton would be a suitable match for Percy. Wouldn't that be like tossing a puppy into a lion's den?"

Venus laughed. "No, I don't think so, though I'll grant you I'm not certain yet." She smiled. "Didn't you notice how Percy was rather protective of her in the dungeon yesterday?"

Drew regarded her as if she were a bedlamite. "I did not. I was too busy carrying out the task you'd set me—to see that Miss Wharton didn't trap Jack into an uncomfortable position or amass so many hearts she could have her wicked way with our poor boy in the sleigh tomorrow."

"Then surely you saw how concerned Percy was about her safety when she fell on the ice today?"

"No."

Venus frowned. "Are you certain you didn't notice? It was rather obvious."

"To you, perhaps, but not to me." He shrugged. "We've already ascertained I am not the Duke of Love."

"Yes, I suppose we have." She was often surprised at how a generally astute man such as Drew could be so blind to the emotional side of life—and unfortunately her sons seemed to be cursed with the same failing. "Well, I won't do anything to nudge the two of them together until I *am* certain—I didn't become the Duchess of Love by rushing things. Miss Wharton will be a project for the coming Season."

"Lucky girl," Drew said dryly. "So is it this speculative pairing that has you in alt?"

"Of course not, though it is a pleasant possibility to consider. But no, I have three solid matches I'm expecting to come from this party." She bounced again; she felt she might burst with excitement.

Drew was still looking at her as if she was mad. "All right, I can guess Humphrey and Miss Mosely, but I can't begin to imagine who else you see stepping into parson's mousetrap."

"Mr. Cox and Lady Juliet, of course."

Drew stared at her. "How in the world, after the scene we witnessed this evening, can you think for an instant those two will marry?"

"Because they are obviously terribly in love."

"With the emphasis on terribly."

"Oh, Drew, they are suffering! They want to be together, but there's something keeping them apart, like a splinter festering under the skin. They have to dig it out, and then they will feel much better."

"I was under the impression that the 'something' preventing their marriage was the Duke of Extley."

"Oh, no, I'm sure Extley is merely an excuse. The problem is mostly with Lady Juliet—she's afraid to follow her heart. And Mr. Cox has not been doing a good job of allaying her fears. He is far too practical, though he did sound a bit poetic this evening, didn't he?"

"With his ridiculous talk of princesses and prisons?" Drew shook his head. "I was afraid he'd got into the brandy bottle far too deeply."

"Oh, pish, you can be so prosaic yourself. He's just not used to turning a pretty phrase."

Drew snorted. "If half the rumors in Town are correct, Cox is very skilled with pretty phrases, at least the ones that get him into ladies' boudoirs."

"Yes, but his heart's not been engaged in any of those encounters, just his other amorous organ."

"Venus! You are putting me to the blush again."

She would ignore that ridiculous comment. "No, I think tonight Lady Juliet realized she can no longer take Mr. Cox's affections for granted. Her fear of losing him may finally override her fear of the future she'll have with him."

Venus had hoped things would work out this way—especially after watching those two almost melt the ice when they skated together this afternoon—but encouraging young people to recognize and act upon their feelings was almost as difficult as getting Reggie to do . . . well, anything. "At the very least she must see she's burned her bridges with Ned."

"Thank God for that." Drew frowned. "But then who's your third match? Only Ned and Ellie are left."

"Precisely!" She was grinning so hard her cheeks hurt. "Isn't it wonderful?"

She'd swear she saw hope flicker in his eyes, but of course Drew wouldn't admit it. "Yes, if it actually comes to pass."

"Oh, it will. I know it will. I am sure of it."

"I don't know why you are. Ellie has been here every year, and Ned has yet to show that kind of interest in her."

"But this year is different. This year they are both ready. You must admit Ned has never before singled a woman out like he has Lady Juliet."

"But perhaps he actually wanted to marry the girl and has now had his hopes dashed." Drew sounded as if he was afraid he was correct. "Perhaps now he will be a confirmed bachelor."

"Nonsense. It was clear his heart was never engaged with Lady Juliet."

"Oh? I couldn't tell."

Really, the male lack of imagination was staggering. "He was wooing her with determination, Drew, not delight. Almost with teeth gritted. Exactly as I imagine he might hire a new butler or estate manager." She reached over and shook his knee. "And did you see how angry he was at Ellie today when she saved Miss Wharton?"

Drew picked her fingers up and held them. "Venus, you do know anger and love aren't the same?"

She snatched her hand back. "Of course I do. What kind of fool do you take me for?" Drew could be painfully obtuse on occasion.

"I would never take you for any sort of fool, my dear duchess, but you've just pointed to Cox's and Lady Juliet's remarkable row as a sign of tender feelings, and now you appear to be using the same logic with regard to Ned and Ellie. I can't think of a time you've found angry words particularly seductive."

"Anger isn't seductive, of course. It's merely an indication of strong feelings. Think, Drew. What if I'd been the one trying to save Miss Wharton? How would you have felt?"

He frowned. "Terrified, of course. And, yes, angry."

"Exactly. And I'll wager you wouldn't have felt either of those emotions if it had been Percy who'd leapt to the rescue."

Drew shrugged and looked away. "Perhaps not."

"Of course not. And I can also assure you that once you got me to safety, you'd have castigated me in exactly the way Ned did Ellie."

"I'd be annoyed with anyone who'd taken such an unnecessary risk."

"Yes, annoyed—not furious. Ned was so angry he had to go back to the house by himself."

"But certainly Ned has been angry with Ellie before. I don't see why a little temper this year should be so significant."

"It wasn't a little temper, it was a towering rage." Drew was arguing so hard because he wanted what she was saying to be true, of course. "And I told you—this year's different because they are both finally ready to know their hearts." Venus giggled. "Especially Ned. I can't wait until he sees the new ball gown Mary's made for Ellie."

The very first thing Ellie did when she got back to her room that evening was push the wooden desk chair up against the tall mahogany wardrobe, climb onto the seat, stretch up on her toes, and feel around for—

"Aiee!" She screamed and reared back as her searching fingers encountered fur instead of silk.

Oh, blast, she was going to go crashing to the floor. She teetered on the chair, desperately trying to regain her balance, but it was hopeless. Fortunately, the bed wasn't far behind her; it slowed her progress, but she still landed hard on the carpet. She was going to have a very sore rump in the morning.

"Reggie!"

Reggie peered down at her from the top of the wardrobe, Ellie's red silk drawers dangling from his mouth.

"Damn it, how did you know I'd hidden those up there?"

Reggie didn't answer. He jumped lightly down to the desktop and from there to the floor. Then he came over to drop the drawers in her lap.

He rubbed against her side, and she stroked his back. "You are *so* maddening, you know, but I suppose I do need to thank you for rescuing these from Percy."

Reggie graciously allowed her to scratch his ears.

Ellie shifted so she could lean back against the bed. "What do you make of this party, Reggie? It certainly is more . . . well, I wouldn't call it exciting, exactly. Interesting, perhaps."

Reggie did not dispute her assessment.

"I didn't know where to look at dinner tonight. Mr. Cox glared at Ned and Lady Juliet throughout the entire meal." She paused, picturing the table again. "If you wish to know the truth, I believe Mr. Cox was inebriated. He must have had five glasses of wine at dinner, and he'd already had a glass or two of Madeira in the drawing room—and likely some brandy before he'd even come downstairs."

Reggie turned over so she could rub his belly. He clearly was not interested in Mr. Cox's intemperance.

Ellie ran her fingers back and forth over his soft fur. Dinner had been bad enough, but afterward in the drawing room, when Lady Juliet had—

"Merrow!" Reggie's tail swished, and he caught her with his claws.

"Ouch!" She snatched her hand back. What was the matter with the blasted cat? All she'd been doing was—

Oh, yes. Perhaps she *had* been a little rough. "Sorry, Reggie." She smoothed his fur more gently. "It's just that

Lady Juliet made me so angry. She virtually admitted she planned to cuckold Ned with Mr. Cox. Can you imagine that?"

Reggie yawned.

Well, he *was* a tomcat. Perhaps he didn't find the notion so upsetting. But she did, and she should have said so. It was no excuse that shock had stolen her voice; she should have shaken it off and told Lady Juliet exactly what she thought. Certainly she should have expressed her outrage to Ned when the woman had run out of the room.

But she hadn't. She'd been a voiceless little worm, a mute milk-and-water miss—the woman she'd turned into when Ned had married Cicely.

Reggie gave a warning growl, and she gentled her hand again.

"I'm trying not to be a quiet, meek, old spinster any longer, Reggie. I want to be strong and determined like I was at the pond this afternoon." There she'd taken action instead of standing around wringing her hands, waiting for someone else to do something.

She stroked Reggie's ears. As it turned out, it had not been the smartest thing she'd ever done. She could have ended up cold and wet—or worse. She'd been very lucky Ned had been at hand to rescue her.

But she was still proud of herself. And if she found herself the social equivalent of cold and wet—or dead—by no longer pretending to be someone she wasn't, that was a risk she was willing to take.

She stroked Reggie's side and felt him rumble with satisfaction. Life was so much easier for a cat.

She had two more days before the house party was over and Ned went back to Linden Hall. He couldn't still be thinking of marrying Lady Juliet—he must see that would be a terrible mistake—but if he'd decided it was time to remarry, he would be looking around for another candidate.

He didn't have to wait for next year's party; by next year he could be wed and perhaps a father. There must be suitable women near Linden Hall, or he could even go up to London and shop the Marriage Mart.

If she wanted him, she would have to come up with a way to get his attention and persuade him to consider her matrimonial attributes . . . whatever they might be.

Reggie stood up and stretched. He eyed her drawers.

"Oh, no you don't." She snatched them behind her back—and then sat on them for good measure. "You are not taking these back to Ned."

Reggie growled a bit and batted at her derriere, but she held firm—or, rather, sat firm.

"I mean it, Reggie. Go on." She gave him a gentle push. "You're not getting them from me."

Reggie hissed.

"That's not very gentlemanly, sir." She pushed him again. "You are the Duchess of Love's cat. You must live up to her grace's high expectations." Though Ned's mother likely only expected a high degree of meddling from Reggie, and he lived up to that and then some.

Reggie paced back and forth staring at her rump; she crossed her arms and stared back at him. Finally he gave up and ran behind the wardrobe.

"I'm not going to have you hide back there, Reggie," she called after him, keeping her hindquarters planted firmly on the floor, "and then snatch my drawers when I'm not looking."

Reggie did not reply.

"Reggie!"

Still no answer.

"Here, I'll let you out." She clutched the red drawers and got to her feet, wincing a bit as she straightened. Her poor posterior. She hoped it wasn't all black and blue in the morning, not that anyone would see it. But she would feel it.

She hobbled over to the door and opened it wide enough for a cat to exit. "Come on, Reggie."

Silence.

"Reggie!" She glanced up and down the corridor. Fortunately, no one was around to hear her arguing with the duchess's cat. "Will you come along now?"

She might as well be talking to herself, damn it.

She left the door ajar and limped back to the wardrobe. At least the moving around seemed to be helping her rump recover. "Reggie, I'm going to drag you out of there if you don't come willingly right this instant."

Nothing, not even a hiss of annoyance at being spoken to in such a rude fashion. Oh, well. She'd hear plenty of hissing and complaining when she hauled him out from behind the wardrobe, assuming she could reach him, of course.

She stuffed the red silk drawers into her bodice; she wouldn't put it past Reggie to distract her with a scuffle and then dart off with her undergarment in his teeth. Hmm . . . should she don her gloves? No. Reggie might be annoyed when she evicted him, but she felt certain he wouldn't so far forget himself as to do her any real damage.

She grabbed her candlestick and took a deep breath to prepare for battle. "All right, Reggie, don't say I didn't warn you."

She peered behind the wardrobe, candle held high to illuminate the shadows.

Nothing.

She rubbed her eyes and looked again—still nothing.

"Reggie, where are you?" She bent closer. There was only about a cat's width of space between the back of the wardrobe and the wall, and there was no cat there. Reggie

had vanished. Damn. He must have darted out the other side
when she was opening the door.

She looked under the bed and behind every other piece
of furniture. Then she went back to the wardrobe and stuck
her candle into the gap, moving it up and down.

Aha! There, close to the floor, was a cat-sized hole in the
wall.

She jumped back, almost extinguishing the candle. Had
something—rats came immediately to mind—chewed that
opening? But she'd never seen rats in the castle.

She carefully touched the edge of the hole with her fin-
gertip. It was smooth—obviously man, not rat, made.

Did this mean there was some kind of elaborate cat path-
way in the castle walls? She looked around the room. Ugh.
But at least that explained how Reggie managed to move
through the house so freely.

And how was she to keep her red drawers out of Reggie's
hot little mouth?

Ned had suggested the only solution. She put on her
nightgown and slipped the red silk up over her sore derriere before climbing into bed.

Ned came back to his room very late and very drunk,
carrying a bottle of brandy.

"Oops." He bumped against a table, sending the copy of
Some Useful Thoughts on Estate Management he'd been
reading tumbling to the floor. It was a large tome; it made a
large noise.

"Mer-*row*!"

"S-so sorry, Reggie. Did I disturb your s-slumbers?" He
squinted, closing one eye and then the other. There appeared to be two Reggies on his bed. "Invited a friend in,
did you? Never s-say I interrupted a romantic tryst."

Neither Reggie admitted anything.

"Oh, well." He put the bottle carefully on his desk. "I'm frightfully d-drunk, you know."

He didn't usually drink to excess, but he'd made an exception tonight. He felt he'd earned it. He'd smiled after Cox's and Lady Juliet's appalling performance in the drawing room; he'd smiled through hand after hand of whist even as Miss Mosely, his partner, bungled every damn trick; he'd smiled as Jack made idiotic jokes about his bad luck and Miss Wharton, Jack's partner, crowed over their wins. He'd even smiled under Mama's near constant scrutiny.

"You know, Reggie," he said, draining the last drop of brandy from his glass. "I'm damned tired of smiling."

Reggie yawned.

At least once he'd retreated to Ash's study he could stop. Ash and Jack bloody well hadn't expected him to smile. They hadn't even expected him to talk. They'd just kept his brandy glass filled.

"I've got the best of brothers, Reggie," he said, uncorking the decanter. His glass might be empty, but the bottle wasn't. "Remind me of that when next I'm ranting about them, will you?"

Reggie began cleaning his hind leg.

Ned concentrated on pouring the brandy. Getting the liquid into the glass was surprisingly difficult, but he managed to do it without spilling too much. Then he straddled the desk chair, crossed his arms on its back, and sighed. "You must be as unlucky in love as I am, Reggie. I see your friend has left."

Reggie ignored him.

"You d-do know Lady J-Juliet prefers that b-bounder Cox to me, don't you?"

That registered. Reggie paused in his ablutions long enough to send Ned a look—commiserating or derisive, he couldn't tell.

"The thing of it is I don't mind. Oh, I'll admit it's taken me d-down a peg. I s-suppose I always thought once I found a female I was willing to offer for, she'd fall at my feet." He took another swallow of brandy. "Do you ever feel that way?"

Reggie moved on to his other back leg.

"Well, you're a cat, of course. I s-suppose it's d-different for you. No parson's mousetrap for you to step into."

Reggie's ears twitched at the word "mouse."

"But I need a wife if I want an heir. And I do, Reggie. I want an heir and a spare and a few d-daughters, too, if I can get them." He sniffed. The brandy was making him maudlin. "Hell, maybe it's just as well. Lady Juliet is small like Cicely was. Maybe she'd have trouble in childbirth, too."

He fished the miniature of Cicely out of his pocket and looked at it. Damn, he couldn't get it to come into focus. He leaned over so he could hold it closer to the candle.

Cicely looked so young, hardly more than a girl.

Just as he'd been hardly more than a boy.

She'd died just four years ago, but, through a brandy haze, it felt like a great tragedy that had happened to someone else.

"I don't want to forget, Reggie," he said, sorrow settling heavy in his chest, "but she's slipping away from me, and I have to let go. I know I have to move on, damn it."

He put the miniature on the desk. He must remember there was no hurry to wed. He was only twenty-eight—or would be the day after tomorrow. Now that he'd decided to remarry, he'd start looking around him. Perhaps Ellie would have some ideas.

Stupid! Ellie didn't know any suitable females. She'd never been anywhere but Greycliffe.

Ellie . . .

He took another sip of brandy, holding it on his tongue, letting its fumes fill his mouth and tickle the back of his nose.

Ellie of the ugly dresses and the scandalous red drawers.

Ellie might have been disappointed tonight, too. Cox had been one of her suitors. And it looked very much as if she'd lost Humphrey, as well. Odds were that the rattle-brain was going to propose to Miss Mosely before the house party was over. Well, Ellie should be thankful for that. The man's never-ending bombast would drive her mad in short order.

"Ellie didn't act disappointed, Reggie. She sat through the whole argument between Cox and Lady Juliet without saying a word."

Ellie had always been levelheaded. She'd been a great comfort after Cicely died. He would talk to her tomorrow.

Would she be wearing the red drawers under her primly hideous frock?

He eyed Reggie. "You didn't steal back Ellie's drawers, did you?"

Reggie licked his paws as if to say his hands were clean—or to try to wash off his guilt.

"I'll check, you know." He tipped the bottle to pour more brandy, but nothing came out. Damn. He put it back down on the desk. "All right, Reggie, let's see what you've stolen tonight."

Ned stood—a bad decision. The room started to spin, and his stomach . . .

He dived for the space under the bed. He couldn't give a damn what Reggie had put there. There was only one thing he wanted. Desperately.

He grabbed the chamber pot just in time.

Chapter 15

Love should always be your goal.
—Venus's Love Notes

The red silk drawers felt very, very odd slipping over her skin as Ellie descended the stairs the next morning. The very private part of her that they covered tingled in a most distracting fashion.

She flushed. Perhaps taking Ned's suggestion to wear them so as to keep them safe from Reggie had been a mistake.

"Good morning, Ellie."

Ellie almost missed the last step. She flung out her arm and grabbed the banister.

"Good morning, your grace," she said once her heart had stopped pounding and her breathing was back under control. "Were you looking for me?" Lying in wait, more like—she'd swear the duchess had jumped out from behind the staircase.

Her grace grinned. "No, why would you think that?" She

linked her arm with Ellie's and started toward the breakfast room. "Though I am delighted to see you, of course. Were you going to have something to eat?"

"Y-yes." Though now Ellie wasn't certain her stomach would accept anything more challenging than a bit of dry toast.

"Splendid. I've been hoping to have a comfortable coze with you ever since the party started. Let us hope everyone else has chosen to take breakfast in their rooms."

"Ah." Damn, not another "comfortable" coze. Now she definitely wouldn't be able to swallow a thing. She could only hope the rest of the party had decided to come downstairs. Surely Mr. Humphrey would be looking for something more sustaining than the tea and toast he could get in his chamber.

"Did you know Percy and Ophelia left this morning?" The duchess paused to inspect the painting of the lecherous fourth duke in the entry hall.

"No." Ellie frowned. "I'd have thought Percy would be better today. Perhaps the doctor should have been called."

"Oh, no, I don't believe that was necessary." The duchess shrugged. "Likely Percy felt he'd be more comfortable recovering in the familiar surroundings of his own home."

That was a plumper of enormous proportions. Percy's estate was far too dilapidated and understaffed to provide comfort to a flea let alone an injured man. "Which staircase did he fall down?"

"I really can't say." The duchess tore her eyes away from the lascivious duke and continued toward the breakfast room. "You don't happen to know what he and Ned were arguing about on the way to the pond, do you?"

"No." She had a strong guess, but she wasn't about to mention the red drawers to Ned's mother.

"Hmm." The duchess treated Ellie to a probing look. Ellie turned quickly to examine the painting of the fourth duke's duchess. The poor woman looked tired and sad, which was understandable if even half of the stories about her disreputable husband were true. "Why would you think I'd know, your grace? You should ask Ned."

"Yes, but I doubt he would tell me. It looked to be one of those male disagreements." The duchess raised an eyebrow. "Perhaps over a love interest."

Ellie's jaw dropped and her eyes actually felt as if they were starting from their sockets. "Are you suggesting Ned has a romantic interest in Ophelia?"

The duchess's jaw dropped too; then she laughed. "Oh, dear me, no! Not in a thousand years."

"Then you think Percy is interested in Lady Juliet?" Ellie couldn't make any sense of this conversation.

Her grace shook her head. "Not at all." Her lips slid into a somewhat sly smile. "What did you make of that scene between Lady Juliet and Mr. Cox last night?"

Ellie was delighted to have the opportunity to say what she should have said last night. "It was appalling. I can't quite fault Mr. Cox, since he appears to be suffering from strong emotions—and, frankly, I suspect he was in his altitudes last night—but Lady Juliet—" Ellie pressed her lips together. If Ned's mother didn't know the depths of Lady Juliet's perfidy, she shouldn't enlighten her. "I could not at all like the way she disregarded Ned's feelings."

"Oh, fiddle-de-dee." The duchess flicked her fingers at Ellie and continued on to the breakfast room. "Ned deserves to have his feelings disregarded if he insists on being such a cabbage-head."

This was certainly the morning for surprises. "But I thought you invited Lady Juliet with the express intention of matching her with Ned."

The duchess shook her head. "I don't match people with each other, dear. I simply gather a promising group together and let them match themselves, if they are so inclined." She laughed. "Well, some people need a bit more help than others, but I never do more than nudge, I assure you." Her gaze sharpened. "Not that there aren't times I'd like to take certain people by the shoulders and shake some sense into them."

The duchess hadn't directed that last statement at her, had she? Why? She couldn't complain Ellie hadn't tried to find a match this year. "So you aren't disappointed?"

"Oh, no. I'm delighted, actually—well, cautiously delighted. I'm still not completely convinced Lady Juliet will have the sense to throw her lot in with Mr. Cox, but I do believe last night was a good start. And if, as I suspect, she sought Mr. Cox out after she left the drawing room, it may have been a very good start indeed." The duchess winked. "Mr. Cox struck me as a man who, when his back was finally to the wall, would suspend his notions of propriety long enough to persuade a woman that marrying him would be an excellent decision. But we shall see."

They finally reached the breakfast room. Ellie was greatly relieved to find it was already occupied by Miss Wharton, Miss Mosely, Lady Heldon, and Mr. Humphrey.

"Good morning," the duchess said as she entered. "How lovely to see so many of you here. I thought you ladies might prefer to have chocolate in your rooms."

"Oh, I was too excited to stay abed, your grace," Miss Wharton said. "Even though I didn't win the heart hunting contest, I'm still looking forward to riding in a sleigh."

"It is a delightful activity, isn't it?" The duchess took her place at the table as Thomas brought her her usual selection of food—eggs, ham, toast with marmalade, and tea.

Miss Wharton nodded vigorously. "It is one of my favorite things to do in winter."

"And it's a lovely day, too," Miss Mosely said, tearing her eyes away from Mr. Humphrey for a moment. "The sky is so blue."

"Indeed." Of course Mr. Humphrey couldn't remain silent. "A truly splendid day to be outdoors, your grace, as I was just saying to Miss Mosely. Not that yesterday wasn't delightful as well, but when I looked out my window this morning—I have a view of the front lawns, a very lovely prospect, as I've been meaning to tell you, your grace, so I do apologize for being remiss in not doing so sooner—but as I was looking out my window at the snow and the deer and the birds, I thought to myself what a glorious day it is to go for a sleigh ride."

"Yes," her grace said, "though it is quite brisk out, so you will want to dress warmly."

Ellie took the seat next to Lady Heldon; thankfully, her poor posterior had recovered from her tumble last night and she was able to do so without wincing. She would have preferred to sit somewhere else, but she didn't want it to look as if she was avoiding the woman.

"Good God," Lady Heldon muttered, "all this enthusiasm over a little sleigh ride."

Privately Ellie would agree, but she didn't care for Lady Heldon's tone. "You must have patience with our simple country amusements."

Lady Heldon gave Ellie a sour look. "I prefer other simple country amusements—of which I am getting none, I might add."

Ellie hoped she didn't understand Lady Heldon's meaning, but she was very much afraid she did.

"What interesting things has Sir Reginald found this morning, your grace?" Miss Wharton asked. "It is always so funny to see what he collects." She giggled. "He pilfered one of my stockings the other day."

"I don't know, Miss Wharton." The duchess took a sip of tea. "You know Reggie brings all his treasures to Lord Edward, and I haven't seen my son yet this morning. I'm sure he'll be down shortly."

Ellie's stomach twisted. Ned—

No. Mentally she stiffened her spine. She'd vowed to fight for what she wanted—to fight for Ned—so she would have to actually do so. When she saw him. Today. Likely in just a few minutes.

"Where do you suppose Lord Ashton is?" Lady Heldon asked Ellie, *sotto voce*.

She replied in equally hushed tones, though she couldn't understand why Lady Heldon was whispering the question to her instead of asking the duchess. "He probably ate hours ago and is in his study attending to business."

Lady Heldon chewed her ham thoughtfully. "I take it you and he are"—she paused significantly, raising her eyebrows—"good friends?"

Damn, was the woman insinuating what Ellie thought she was? "Well, we've known each other from childhood, so of course we are friends." She forced herself to smile and tried to change the conversation's direction. "However, Lord Ashton is four years older than I; I believe he used to view me very much as a nuisance."

Lady Heldon snorted. "Well he clearly doesn't consider you a nuisance any longer." She gave Ellie a very sly look. "More a convenience, hmm?"

"Excuse me?"

"Come, Miss Bowman, I've heard the gossip."

"Gossip?" Oh, God, that came out in a guilty squeak, especially annoying as she wasn't at all guilty with regard to Ash. She cleared her throat and frowned. "What do you mean?"

"Surely you must know Lord Ashton's odd marital situation is the talk of London. Rumors of all kinds abound, one of which is that you are his"—another blasted pause—"*special* friend."

Anger bubbled up in Ellie's breast. "I am nothing of the kind. Why would people repeat such malicious twaddle?"

"Perhaps because you've spent the majority of these parties in his pocket, though I will say you are being more discreet this year. Did the duchess finally rein you in?"

Ellie wished now that her plate was piled high with eggs and herring and marmalade so she could upend it in Lady Heldon's lap with good effect. "Lady Heldon, you must not listen to such ridiculous tittle-tattle."

Lady Heldon sniffed. "Where there's smoke, there's fire."

"Not in this case." Ellie tried to keep her voice pleasant. She would take a page from Ned's book. "I assure you Lord Ashton views me as a little sister."

"Does he?" Lady Heldon nodded. "All right. I will say once I saw you I doubted the gossip. I mean, let us be reasonable here. What would a man like Lord Ashton see in a woman like you?"

Fortunately Ellie's jaw was clenched too tightly in anger to drop at Lady Heldon's unmitigated rudeness. "I beg your pardon?"

"Well, of course you must be aware that Lord Ashton is an exceedingly handsome man as well as the heir to the duchy, and you are . . ." Lady Heldon shrugged eloquently.

"The daughter of a country vicar?" Ellie was happy her voice trembled only slightly. She could *not* shout at the duchess's breakfast table. As it was, she felt her grace's eyes on her.

"That, too." Lady Heldon masticated another bit of ham, completely ignoring Ellie's angry flush, and washed it down with a sip of tea.

Ellie knew she wasn't the most beautiful or the most stylish female, but she wasn't a complete quiz . . . was she?

"No," Lady Heldon said, apparently to herself, "my initial theory must be correct." She looked back at Ellie, leaned over, and murmured by her ear, "So I suppose Lord Ashton has many, er, close male friends?"

Ellie leaned back and frowned at her. "I'm sure everyone finds Lord Ashton's conversation intelligent."

"I'm not talking about conversation." Lady Heldon waggled her brows. "Unless you mean a very twisted sort of criminal conversation."

Ellie hoped—probably in vain—that the duchess didn't notice how red she must be. She was mortified and furious simultaneously. However, if she hadn't overheard Lady Heldon, Ophelia, and Percy when they were coming up the stairs to the long gallery, she wouldn't have the vaguest clue as to what Lady Heldon was suggesting. "I assure you, Lady Heldon, that Lord Ashton is faithful to his wife."

Lady Heldon snorted. "And how do you know that?"

"I just do." And yes, she realized how inane and, well, childish that sounded.

Lady Heldon rolled her eyes. "Oh, please, Miss Bowman. No one your age can be quite *that* naïve."

"What are you two whispering about?" the duchess finally asked.

Ellie took a deep breath. She didn't wish to answer; her grace likely wouldn't care for the fact they were discussing Ash, even though Ellie hadn't said anything of a private nature. Not that she knew anything of a private nature to say.

"Lord Ashton," Lady Heldon said calmly, obviously not shy about admitting her interest. Her color was still as normal as—Ellie looked more closely—her rice powder made it. "I was just asking Miss Bowman about his friends. You must know everyone in London is so curious about him and his absent bride."

There was a moment of stunned silence that even Mr. Humphrey didn't dare break. The duchess stared at Lady Heldon as if she were an especially exotic—and unpleasant—type of bug.

Now Lady Heldon did flush. "You know I'm not saying anything that everyone else here isn't thinking, your grace."

Ned's mother raised her eyebrows. She suddenly looked exceedingly haughty, every inch the Duchess of Greycliffe. "Perhaps, Lady Heldon, but everyone else has the good manners to keep their vulgar curiosity to themselves."

Lady Heldon drew in a sharp breath, and then her chin went up. She was obviously made of stern stuff—or else welcomed social suicide. "Until the Marquis of Ashton resolves his unnatural marital situation, curiosity—and much less polite emotions—will run rampant whether or not you, your grace, or any of us likes it."

The duchess's nostrils flared. Ellie had never seen her grace look so angry. She and everyone else at the table, with the possible exception of Lady Heldon, held their breath.

Ned's mother opened her mouth—

"The sleighs are ready," Jack said from the doorway. "Father suggests everyone adjourn to the drawing room." He paused. "I say, did I interrupt something?"

The duchess forced a smile. "Not at all." She looked around the table. "If you would like to follow Jack—"

Everyone shot to their feet.

"—except you, Lady Heldon." Her grace's voice was carved in ice. "If you would remain behind for a moment, I should like to have a brief word with you."

"Don't you love sleigh rides, Lord Edward?" Miss Wharton let Ned help her into the sled.

"Yes, they are very pleasant." Ned went round to the other side, climbed in, and spread the lap rug over them. He would much prefer to be back inside. His stomach was unsettled, his head felt as if all the demons of hell were wielding pickaxes behind his forehead, and the bright sun on the vast expanse of white snow flung shards of pain through his eyeballs. At least the world had stopped spinning.

He would never drink brandy again for as long as he lived which at the moment felt like it would be only the next five minutes.

He picked up the reins, and the horses shambled into motion. He dearly hoped Miss Wharton would be content with a plodding pace, though given her somewhat frenetic approach to life, he doubted he'd be so lucky.

He wasn't.

"Er, do you suppose we could go a little faster, Lord Edward? Lord Jack and Miss Bowman are far outstripping us." She smiled at him. "And I do so love to feel the wind in my face."

He glanced ahead at the red and gold sleigh in front of them. Jack and Ellie had almost reached the woods already. They were laughing about some damn thing. Ellie looked younger and prettier when she laughed.

And then they vanished into the trees.

His stomach twisted; damn this nausea, though this time it didn't feel as if the brandy was totally to blame.

He dropped his gaze back to his lead horse's arse. They had only to do one loop through the park—it would take no more than half an hour, if that. He could manage it.

"Of course we can go faster." He grit his teeth and encouraged his cattle to pick up their pace. His head and stomach protested, but if he focused on the horse's rump directly in front of him and didn't look at the scenery sliding past, perhaps he could avoid disgracing himself completely. Not that there was anything in his stomach to come up, but even a case of the dry heaves was to be avoided if at all possible.

"Our numbers are much diminished," Miss Wharton said.

"Yes." Ned wished they'd been diminished by one more—the lady sitting at his side.

They hit a bump, and he had to swallow determinedly.

He would have dodged this duty if he could have, but he was the only man available for the task. Jack had chosen to take Ellie up in his sleigh, of course—even Ned would admit his brother couldn't very well have selected Miss Wharton, the woman he'd been trying so hard to avoid being alone with all week. Ash was too busy planning a snow fort to even notice the problem, and Humphrey was in deep conversation with Miss Mosely. Cox was nowhere in sight.

"I understand Lady Ophelia and Sir Percy have left," Miss Wharton was saying, "which is quite understandable given Sir Percy's injuries, poor man."

"Yes." Ned didn't feel one iota of remorse. He'd pummel Percy again in a heartbeat, though not today. Today he was most definitely not in plump current.

They reached the trees and slid into the shade. Thank God. The muted light was much easier on his eyes, head, and stomach. He drew in a breath of the cold, pine-scented air and felt marginally better.

"And I haven't seen Lady Juliet or Mr. Cox this morning," Miss Wharton said. "Perhaps they are embarrassed by what happened last night and chose to have breakfast in their rooms, though surely they can't intend to hide there all day."

"I imagine we'll see them eventually." He might be wrong, but he suspected since both of them were missing they were "hiding" in one room and quite likely one bed.

Damn, and now he was thinking of those blasted red drawers again. He definitely needed to remarry soon—his body was demanding it.

"But Lady Heldon was at breakfast," Miss Wharton said. "I wonder what happened to her." He felt her look at him. "She mentioned Lord Ashton's marriage, and the duchess was not pleased. Do you suppose she sent Lady Heldon packing?"

"Probably. My mother does not care to have my brother's marriage discussed."

"That was very clear." She paused and sent him another sidelong glance. "Do you care to discuss it?"

"No."

She nodded. "I didn't think so. Really, it would be a violation of your brother's trust, wouldn't it, for you to discuss his situation? You are very right to keep mum."

He was, but Ash hadn't trusted him with any information, so there was nothing for him to conceal. Just as well. He had absolutely no desire to know the details of his brother's marital troubles, though of course if there was anything he could do to help, he would. Ash knew that.

He guided his horses along the winding road. Why the hell hadn't whichever damn duke had cleared this path made it straight? He hoped Jack was being careful. Jack might be able to drive to the inch, but he was also a bit of a dare-devil. He *had* been racing his curricle on the ice just a fortnight ago, after all.

Ned clenched his jaw. And this time Jack had a passenger. He'd better not take a turn too quickly and slide into a tree or injure Ellie in any way. Ned listened for the scream of horses and the splinter of wood over the jingle of his sleigh's harness and the hiss of its runners over the snow. All he heard was Ellie's and Jack's laughter.

"I will tell you," Miss Wharton said, her voice a bit hesitant, "that Lady Heldon was right in what she said—everyone *is* gossiping about Lord Ashton, and most of the gossip is not nice."

"Oh?" He tried to sound repressive but given the current unsettled state of his stomach, he feared he wasn't very successful. Miss Wharton pressed on.

"Yes. When word got out I'd been invited to this party, people who normally cut me dead encouraged me to find out as much about Lord Ashton as I could while I was here—and then tell them all as soon as I returned." She sighed. "London is not a very kind place, Lord Edward."

"Which is one reason I never go there." Damn, Jack was right. It was indeed time for Ash to settle things with Jess.

"Oh, I *wish* I could stay in the country, too," Miss Wharton said rather passionately, "but Mama and Papa are determined to marry me off, so I must spend most of my time in London until they accomplish that goal."

Ned jerked his eyes away from his horse's rump. This was a surprise. "Don't you wish to be married?"

"Yes, of course I do, but"—she smiled sadly and looked down at her muff—"you may have noticed I'm a bit of a bull in a china shop—or, rather, on the Marriage Mart. I'm too loud and awkward, and I never seem to say or do the right thing." She shrugged. "Mama says I must learn to be better behaved—quiet, demure, perhaps a little bit bored—but I can't seem to manage it."

Miss Wharton's description of her mother's ideal bride sounded rather like Ned's—and surprisingly unappealing when stated so baldly. "I hesitate to contradict your mama, Miss Wharton, but I don't believe you should change your behavior. Think how exhausting it would be to have to pretend to be someone you aren't for the rest of your life."

Miss Wharton laughed. "Oh, Mama doesn't expect me to really change. She just means for me to be a model society miss while I'm trying to catch a husband; once I'm wed, she says I can go on as I please as it will be too late for the poor man to get free." Her voice dropped to just above a whisper. "I suspect that's how she got Papa up the church aisle."

"Ah." He'd never met Miss Wharton's mama or papa,

and, frankly, now he hoped never to have that dubious pleasure. "And are your parents happy together?"

"As happy as most couples of our class, I suppose"—she smiled briefly—"which means not happy at all. Your parents are the exception to the rule, Lord Edward."

He'd known Mama and Father's marriage was unusual, but surely marital bliss—or at least contentment—was still something to strive for. "What does your papa say about all this?"

"Oh, he wants me to marry, too, so I'll be some other man's problem. He's managed to rid himself of Lucy and Becky—my sisters—and I think he's afraid he'll be stuck with me f-forever." Her voice broke on the last word, and she gave a shaky laugh. "And here I am acting improperly again."

He looked up ahead and caught a flash of red through the trees. At least Jack hadn't yet wrecked the sleigh.

Did Ellie's mama and papa feel the way Miss Wharton's did?

"No," he said. "He must be happy that you are a support to your mother."

Miss Wharton snorted. "Hardly. I am a thorn in Mama's side, a constant reminder of her failure to foist me off on some suitable male. Papa says I quite ruin Mama's temperament, not that he's ever liked her temperament very much."

He'd never considered how difficult it must be for unmarried women. Ellie had always seemed content with her situation—except perhaps this year.

Now that he thought about it, he did remember Mama mentioning at Christmas how concerned Mrs. Bowman was about Ellie's future.

Hmm. He was in need of a wife, and Ellie was in need of a husband. Perhaps they could solve each other's problem. They were friends, even though things had been a little unsettled between them recently. And there were those odd red drawers . . .

Something inside him twisted—probably his stomach.

"Nevertheless, Miss Wharton, I still think it would be a mistake to try to pretend to be someone you aren't." *Wasn't that what Ellie had said she'd been doing?* "I'm sure there must exist a man in England who will find your true nature delightful."

"Oh?" She looked at him. "You, perhaps, Lord Edward?" She smiled eagerly. "I would be happy to marry you. I believe I could even come to love you, if you don't mind my being so bold as to say so. Your actions on the pond yesterday were most heroic, and you have been very kind to me just now."

His stomach heaved, and, even though frigid air stung his cheeks, sweat popped out on his forehead. "Well . . ."

She giggled nervously. "I have put you in a very awkward spot, haven't I? I do apologize." But she still looked hopeful.

"Ah." He took a deep breath; the air burned his lungs and cleared the panic from his brain.

He needed a wife, and Lady Juliet was no longer a viable candidate. Miss Wharton might do. He was older now—he didn't require, nor really want, the overwhelming lust he'd felt for Cicely. And in any event, that hadn't survived their wedding night.

But first he must find out if Ellie needed his help.

"We've just met, Miss Wharton. I don't believe it would be wise to make a permanent commitment so soon."

"But I need to marry, Lord Edward. I am running out of time." There was a desperation in her eyes that was rather alarming.

"What do you mean?"

"Before I left for Greycliffe, Mama told me that if I

didn't marry this Season, she and Papa will give me to old Mr. Wattles to be his fourth wife." Panic flickered over her face, and her voice drew tight. "The man is at least sixty and still without a son to inherit his estate."

"I see." So this was why Miss Wharton was so determined to find a husband. "You can always refuse to marry him, you know. The days of parents forcing their daughters to the altar are long past."

Miss Wharton looked at him as if he were a complete cod's-head. "You only say that because you're a man. You have no idea the pressures brought to bear on women to get them to wed." She looked back out over the horses' tails. "If I don't marry this Season and refuse Mr. Wattles as well, my life will be more of a hell than it already is. I wouldn't put it past my father to throw me out onto the street."

She must be exaggerating, but she sounded as if she believed every word she said. He wanted to do something to help.

Perhaps he *should* offer for her. He opened his mouth to suggest it, but then they emerged from the trees and he caught sight of Ellie and Jack again.

He must talk to Ellie before he said anything to Miss Wharton. The conversation might be a little awkward, but he'd always been able to talk to Ellie. He'd see if she were in immediate need of a husband. If she were, he would offer her his services. But if she wasn't, then he could approach Miss Wharton. In any event, there was no need to ask Miss Wharton in haste—she did have some time.

"I suggest you see what happens this Season," he said.

"I don't know why this Season should be any different than the previous seven."

He smiled at her. The cold and their conversation had made him feel almost human again. "Because I suspect this Season the Duchess of Love will be trying to find you a match."

Miss Wharton's expression lightened and she smiled. "Do you really think so?"

"I am sure of it. In fact, I will make a point to mention it to her." He grinned. "Now shall we see if we can catch up to my brother?"

Chapter 16

If opportunity knocks, throw open the door and drag it in.

—Venus's Love Notes

Ellie took Jack's hand and let him help her down from the sleigh. The red drawers under her many layers of clothing slid against her skin, and she shivered.

"Are you cold?" Jack asked, concern softening his eyes.

She flushed. "No." The drawers weren't warm, but somehow they generated an odd kind of heat.

She glanced back at the other sleigh. Miss Wharton was smiling up at Ned as if he were her new best friend—or something more intimate, damn it.

Her stomach tightened. She'd tried to watch them during the sleigh ride, but it had been difficult since Jack's and her sled had been in the lead and she didn't want Jack to notice—she did not care to be teased about this. The few glimpses she'd managed had shown Ned and Miss Wharton in an intense, heartfelt conversation. What had they been talking about?

"I doubt you have to be jealous of Miss Wharton," Jack murmured by her ear.

She glared at him. "I'm not jealous."

He raised his eyebrows and looked amused. Blast it, he must have seen her looking back. Her fingers itched to scoop up a large handful of snow and wash his face for him.

"Of course you aren't," he said. "I don't know what gave me that notion."

"I don't either." She spun away and immediately collided with Mr. Cox, who'd come up to take his turn with their sleigh. "Oh! Pardon me, sir."

"Pardon *me*," he said, grabbing her elbows to steady her.

"No, no, it was my fault entirely. I, er, wasn't paying attention." She stepped back, hoping she wasn't staring. Mr. Cox's expression took her breath away: he was grinning widely, almost glowing with happiness. She glanced over at Lady Juliet, who blushed and looked even prettier than usual. Clearly these two had resolved their differences.

Envy lanced her heart as she watched them climb into the sleigh and drive off, followed by Mr. Humphrey and Miss Mosely in the other sled. Everyone was finding a match—everyone but her.

She turned and strode away, the damn silk drawers teasing her with every step. She was taking them off as soon as she could. Surely if she stuffed them under her mattress, Reggie couldn't steal them again—or, if he did, he'd have to shred them to get them free, which would be fine with her.

"Are you trying to run away from me, Ellie?" Jack asked, grabbing her hand and placing it on his arm.

242   *Sally MacKenzie*

"No." She jerked back, but Jack had her fingers trapped under his. "Let go."

"You don't want everyone to think we've had a spat, do you?"

"Why would they think that?"

"Oh, I don't know. Perhaps because you're glaring at me." Ellie snorted and tugged again.

"Or because you're trying to wrestle free as if you fear I mean to abduct you. I only want to keep you from slipping and falling in the snow."

She tugged once more. "No one is paying us the least bit of attention."

Jack looked heavenward as if the Almighty might be persuaded to drop some sense on her head. "How long have you known Mama?"

"What do you mean?" Ellie felt a sudden trickle of unease.

"She's watching us like a hawk—or, worse, like the Duchess of Love in full matchmaking mode."

Ellie glanced up to the terrace; blast it, the duchess *was* looking their way. "Oh, very well." She bared her teeth in what she hoped looked like a smile from her grace's position. "I'll allow you to escort me, if you insist."

"Thank you." Jack directed their steps toward Ash and his snow fort. Ned and Miss Wharton were already there.

"I must say"—Jack was moving far slower than necessary, clearly intending to share his thoughts with her before they reached the others—"I don't see why you are taking your spleen out on me." He treated her to an uncomfortably probing look. "If you'll remember, *I* urged you to pursue Ned. Since I've yet to see you do so, I'm beginning to conclude you don't want him."

"What? You—"

He tightened his grip on her fingers to stop her protests.

"And if you don't want him, Ellie, don't play dog in the manger. Ned needs another wife; if Miss Wharton will have him, it might not be a bad match." He grinned. "And it frees me from her pursuit."

She was so angry, she couldn't speak. Jack was by far the most annoying man of her acquaintance . . . well, except for his next older brother.

He leaned close. "And if you *do* want him, do something about it, for God's sake, because if you don't, Miss Wharton will, and then you'll be back exactly where you were when Cicely married Ned: outside looking in and miserable about it."

She finally found the breath to hiss at him. "I'd decided to do something about it, you blockhead, but you put paid to that by forcing me to ride with you just now."

"Oh." Jack looked a little contrite. "Well, I couldn't very well have chosen Miss Wharton; that would have been too much like slitting my own throat."

"You could have asked Miss Mosely."

"Yes, but I didn't want to take her away from Humphrey." He grimaced. "And, frankly, I couldn't stomach the thought of spending half an hour alone in her company."

"I would have thought you'd be willing to suffer a little for Ned's sake."

"Yes, but only a little. Half an hour with Miss Mosely is far too much. Admit it, Ellie. I might have fallen asleep and crashed the sleigh, and then where would I be?"

"You'd be in a snowdrift where you belong, freezing your—" She stopped herself in time.

"Temper, temper." He waggled his finger in front of her nose. "I am sorry, but self-preservation will almost always trump brotherly love. I shall try to make it up to you."

"I won't be holding my breath." She looked away from

Jack to find Ned glaring at her. What was *he* annoyed about? She raised her chin as they reached him.

No, she wished to attract the man, not fight with him. "Did you enjoy the sleigh ride, Lord Edward?" How the hell was she supposed to flirt? She tried fluttering her eyelashes.

"Have something in your eye?" Jack murmured.

"No," she hissed while trying to keep a smile plastered on her face. At least Ned had stopped glaring; now he looked merely puzzled.

"It was very pleasant," he said.

"Oh, yes." Miss Wharton nodded vigorously. "It was wonderful. Lord Edward is very good with the ribbons— almost as good as you, Lord Jack."

"Never say it, Miss Wharton! I will have to challenge him to a race, then, to prove my superiority."

Ned snorted. "You'd only prove your reckless stupidity. I'd refuse to race you."

"Come, Lord Worry, don't you wish to impress these lovely ladies and have them swooning in the snow?"

There were going to be bodies in the snow, but they'd be Ned's and Jack's if Ned's clenching fists were any indication. Why did Jack insist on twitting him at every opportunity?

Ellie dug her fingers into Jack's sleeve, hoping to encourage him to stop taunting Ned. "It's far too cold to swoon; I don't care to get all covered with snow." She turned to Ash. He'd already built one wall of the fort up to chest height and was working on a turret. "You're coming along with that quite well."

"Yes, Lord Ashton," Miss Wharton said. "It's wonderful. I've never seen such an impressive snow fort."

It *was* impressive, but then anything Ash constructed was.

He'd built a fairytale castle once when they were children that she and Jess and Cicely had played in for hours—until the boys decided to be French troops and attack. Percy had led the charge and kicked down one of the walls when he'd got close, so infuriating Ash he'd jumped on Percy's back. Then the two of them had rolled around punching each other, taking down the rest of the building in the process.

Cicely had cried for hours, even with Ned and then Percy trying to comfort her, and Ellie had been very sad herself, but Jess . . . Jess had laughed.

Ellie had never been able to tell how Jess felt about anything—except Ash.

"It's not hard to build," Ash said, adding another handful of snow to the turret. "This snow is just the right wetness."

"Oh, I could never manage anything like this," Miss Wharton said, "no matter how good the snow was."

"Indeed," Ned said. "Don't let my brother fool you. He could build a castle out of mashed potatoes."

Jack laughed. "I've seen him do so. Confess, Ash: You'd rather be an architect than a duke."

"Oh, no." Ash smoothed the turret's side. "This is just a hobby. I need something to do to keep myself busy; you know Father doesn't really need my help with his properties."

Ned and Jack exchanged a look, but neither said anything. There was one property over which the duke wished Ash would take complete control—Blackweith, where Jess lived and Ash never went.

"Is the snow also good for snowballs, Lord Ashton?" Miss Wharton asked.

"Yes, indeed. You might wish to begin assembling some,

though I thought once everyone is back, we'd start by building some snowmen we can use for target practice."

"What, no real snowball battle?" Jack asked. "If I can't race Ned, I'd like to knock his hat off."

"I'd like to see you try," Ned said, "especially with your arm in a sling—or have you recovered sufficiently to use both hands?" His voice held a touch of sarcasm.

"I can throw one-handed quite well, but, yes, I believe my other arm is feeling much better. Thank you for your concern."

Ned rolled his eyes.

"I can't imagine the ladies would care to watch you pelt each other with snow," Ash said.

"Oh, I don't know." Ellie would definitely enjoy that. She'd even like to fling a few well-placed snowballs at them herself.

"Oh, Miss Bowman, you must be joking," Miss Wharton said, looking appalled. "I have only sisters, as you may know, so we didn't have snowball fights at home, but I was shocked one winter when my male cousins visited after a snowstorm. They chased and tackled each other, smashed snow into each other's faces, and dropped handfuls of it down each other's backs." She shuddered. "They seemed to enjoy the violence."

Ellie would admit that while throwing a snowball at Jack or Ned would be satisfying, getting hit by one would only hurt. "You are likely right, Miss Wharton." She looked at Ash. "Where do you want us to put the invading army, Lord Ashton?"

"Over there," Ash said, pointing to a treeless patch of snow about twenty yards away. "And look, here are the others now."

The sleighs were indeed drawing up, the couples in each

windblown and laughing. The duke and duchess had come down from the terrace to greet them. Ellie watched Ned's parents pause to talk to each couple in turn, and then the duke helped the duchess into the first sleigh, took the reins from Mr. Cox, and headed off for their turn around the park.

The Duchess of Love must be in alt. This had to be her most successful party to date.

Once the others joined them, they made their way to the mock battlefield. Ellie watched Ned walk with Miss Wharton; her head came just to his shoulder.

It should be Ellie's head by Ned's shoulder, but no—she was stuck with Jack.

"You can still throw a snowball or two at the snowmen, you know, and pretend the fellow you're decapitating is Ned," Jack said.

Ellie snorted. "Or you."

He sighed dramatically. "Oh, ye of little faith. I said I'd make it up to you, didn't I? And I will."

She couldn't prevent a little flutter of hope. "How are you going to do that?"

He shrugged. "I don't know yet. It will be a spur of the moment thing."

"I see." What she saw was she shouldn't rely on Jack for help. But that was fine. Hadn't she decided just last night that she must do something herself if she wanted to marry Ned? The time for being the quiet, dependable, old friend, hoping Ned would see her as something else, was long past.

But what should she do? She couldn't very well tackle him and sit on him in the snow until he agreed to marry her, no matter how much that plan appealed to her at the moment.

"Do you want to make the snowman's head, Ellie, while I work on the body?" Jack asked.

"Very well." She began with a small ball of snow and in

no time had a sizable one. She was enjoying the exertion—
perhaps she'd turn this head into a chest.

She put her own head down and pushed harder, rolling
farther and farther until she bumped up against a dainty boot.

"Oh!" She looked up into Lady Juliet's face; the other
girl was sitting on what could have been the bottom of a
snowman but which had been turned into a chair. Mr. Cox
was about ten feet away, building their snowman by himself.

Lady Juliet pointed back the way Ellie had come. "I believe you've strayed out of your territory, Miss Bowman."

"Er, yes." Ellie looked over her shoulder. She *was* rather
far from Jack. She looked back at Lady Juliet. "Why aren't
you helping Mr. Cox?"

Lady Juliet yawned. "I'm far too exhausted to move."

"But all you've done today is ride around the park in a
sleigh."

Lady Juliet's lips slid into a small, satisfied smile; she
strongly resembled Sir Reginald after he'd consumed a
large saucer of cream. "I didn't get much sleep last night."

"Why—oh." Realization hit Ellie like a punch in the
stomach. Lady Juliet had spent the night with Mr. Cox.

No, she couldn't have. The thought was too shocking—
but for some reason, she felt certain she was right.

Lady Juliet smiled back at her, not embarrassed in the
slightest.

"Well, then, I'll just go back to work," Ellie said. She
was horrified—and horridly envious. Not that she wanted
anything to do with Mr. Cox, of course, but Ned . . .

She pushed her snowball back the way she'd come as
quickly as she could.

"That's far bigger than a head, Ellie," Jack said when she
reached him.

"Then use it for something else." Even she could hear the annoyance in her voice.

Jack's eyebrows shot up, but he didn't comment.

"I say, Jack, can you give me a hand here?" Ned said from a few feet away. He was struggling to lift an extremely large ball of snow. "Miss Wharton was a bit overzealous—she could have stopped when this was half its size."

"Of course. I'll be right there." Jack smiled at Ellie. "Seems like Miss Wharton has taken a leaf from your snowman building book, eh?"

"Oh, stop teasing me." Ellie pushed a strand of hair out of her face. She was feeling terribly out of sorts. She wanted to *do* something. "Here, maybe I can help."

Jack grinned at her. "Maybe you can."

"Jack," Ned said, "this isn't getting any lighter."

"Right."

Ellie was already on her way—stupid, even she realized that. She was nowhere near strong enough. Jack was right behind her. She should just get out of his way.

She was starting to step aside when she heard Jack whisper, "Forgive me." Then she felt a hand on her back and a quick shove.

She went flying straight at Ned.

What the hell was taking Jack so long?

Ned heard something that sounded like an outraged squeak and looked around his ball of snow just in time to see Ellie coming at him.

"Uh!" He dropped the snow and grabbed Ellie, but he had no hope of saving their balance. They fell backward like a tree going down in a storm. *"Oof!"*

At least the snow cushioned their landing somewhat. He

could still breathe if he restricted himself to shallow pants. "Are you all right?"

Ellie gasped and nodded. Likely she'd had the breath knocked out of her as well.

He took inventory. He wiggled his toes, shrugged his shoulders. Nothing felt broken. His rump was sore and would likely be much sorer later, but his back seemed fine. He shifted—oh.

He closed his eyes briefly as lust, finally freed from the shock of his sudden change in altitude, roared through him. Ellie might be covered in a multitude of layers, but he could still feel the imprint of her breasts mashed against his chest and the wide, soft expanse of her hips right above . . . Somehow they'd fallen so her legs were on either side of his and . . .

Oh, damn. Hopefully she'd assume the hard length suddenly pushing up against her woman's place was a rolled up bit of one of their coats. She was quiet; she'd laid her head on his chest, probably still working on getting her breathing under control.

And then everyone else appeared, looming over them with expressions of surprise and concern.

And amusement, damn it. What else should he expect from Jack?

"Need some help?" Jack asked, extending a hand.

At Jack's voice Ellie stiffened and tried to scramble to her feet. Oh, blast! Ned grabbed her hips, pressing them to his to preserve his hope of ever fathering children.

She lifted her head, which had the distracting effect of pressing her more tightly against his cock, and glared at him.

"Sorry," he muttered. "Your knee almost squashed my, er, ah . . . a very sensitive part of me."

"Oh." She turned bright red.

Wonderful. Their audience must be enjoying the show. He'd swear he heard someone—likely Jack—snigger.

"Let me just ease out from under you," he said, lifting her off him. Then he got to his feet and pulled her up. He frowned at Jack. "Did you have something to do with what just happened?"

"Yes," Ellie began, "why did you—"

"Fail to catch you when you slipped?" Jack said. "I'm very sorry."

"Are you both all right?" Ash asked, clearly concerned.

"Yes," Ned said. Well, he shouldn't speak for Ellie. "Are you all right, Ellie?"

She nodded but glared at Jack, who looked back at her with an expression of angelic innocence. Ned frowned. He'd seen that look countless times growing up. Jack was definitely guilty of something.

"You shouldn't be standing here in the cold," Jack pointed out helpfully. "You're both covered in snow and will be damp very soon." He smiled. "You don't want to catch a chill, especially before tomorrow's ball."

Ned would just as soon miss the damn ball, but he didn't want Ellie to get sick.

"Lord Jack is very right, Lord Edward," Mr. Humphrey said. "You can't be too careful. Why, just last winter I was out in the snow and caught a very bad cold that went to my chest and might have carried me off, the doctor said, had it not been for my youth and my hardy constitution. And of course Miss Bowman, being of the delicate sex, must be guarded most carefully by us stronger and more knowledge-able men, so I really must urge you to think of her safety"— he bowed—"or I shall be happy to take it upon myself to escort her to the castle where she may procure dry clothes and sit by the fire with a bracing cup of tea."

Ned felt Ellie bristle. Humphrey's hardy constitution might be more at risk than he knew if she got her hands on him right now. "Very true, Humphrey," he said, ignoring the glare Ellie had now turned on him, "about being cold and damp, that is. I definitely think dry clothes are in order. I assume you can manage without us?"

"Indubitably," Jack said. "And Mama and Father might help once they return from their sleigh ride."

Ash laughed. "Yes, do go ahead. You both look exceedingly bedraggled, and I believe I just saw Ellie shiver."

"I'm f-f-fine," Ellie said, teeth chattering.

"Oh, Miss Bowman," Miss Mosely said, "do hurry inside. I am quite worried for you."

Ned took Ellie's elbow and tugged slightly. She was still glaring at Humphrey—a waste of effort as the man was completely oblivious to her displeasure. He was currently conferring with Miss Mosely about the most efficacious treatment for the ague.

"Then we'll be off," Ned said, tugging again. This time Ellie came along.

"Mr. Humphrey is very annoying," she muttered as they walked away from the group.

"Yes, he is, but he is right in this instance. We do need dry clothes."

"Only because J-Jack pushed me into you."

"What?" He stopped, pulling her to a stop as well. "What do you mean? Jack might be reckless, but he's not insane. He wouldn't do something like that."

She lifted her chin. Her cheeks and nose were bright red from the cold. "Well, he d-did." She swatted impatiently at a strand of hair that had fallen over her face and shivered.

He should be shot for keeping her standing in the cold. He took her arm and started walking again. "We can talk about this later; now we have to get you inside."

"I am not some hothouse f-flower," she grumbled, but she came along.

This was actually a good thing, now that he thought about it. Everyone would be outside for a while, so he'd have some time alone with Ellie—the perfect opportunity to discover if she required a husband.

He stood aside to let her precede him into the house. "Careful, the floor may be slippery."

"I kno—eek!"

He caught her as her feet started to slide out from under her, and for a moment she clung to him. He rather liked the feel of her in his arms.

"Oh." She flushed redder than she'd been from the cold and jerked backward. "I'm sorry."

"It's nothing, Ellie." He extended his arm. "But do hold on. Falling here on the marble will hurt far more than tumbling in the snow."

They made it across the entry and up the stairs to the bedroom floor without further incident. He stopped outside her room. "Meet me downstairs in the library once you've changed, will you? I've a subject I wish to discuss."

She gave him a cautious look and then nodded. "Very well."

He continued to his room to find Reggie sprawled in a patch of sunlight on his bed. Mama's cat did not care to be disturbed; he gave Ned an annoyed look and jumped down, leaving behind a rumpled but empty coverlet.

"No red drawers for me today?" he asked Reggie's departing tail. Reggie ignored him.

Ned pulled his wet shirt over his head. Perhaps Ellie had

taken his advice and worn the scandalous things under her skirts. He still couldn't understand how she'd come to have them. He peeled off his wet pantaloons. They were something a woman like Lady Heldon might wear. Very shocking and . . .

Stimulating apparently. He frowned down at his bouncing cock. Clearly it was past time for him to marry again.

He'd rather wed Ellie than Miss Wharton, now that he considered the matter without Miss Wharton's tale of woe echoing in his ears. He and Ellie had a shared past; he was comfortable with her . . .

He frowned as he buttoned the fall of his dry pantaloons securely over his misbehaving organ. He *had* been comfortable with her, but surely they could be comfortable again. If it was a monthly issue, it would pass, though he'd seen Ellie enough over the years that he thought he'd have noticed if she had regular moods.

He shrugged and pulled a clean shirt over his head. He'd learned once he'd married Cicely that he wasn't ever likely to understand female emotions.

He reached for his cravat. And Ellie would like Linden Hall. It wasn't very far from Greycliffe—she could see her family regularly. And she liked Mama, too. And Mama liked her—she looked upon her almost as a daughter already. In fact, Mama and Father would be delighted, even though Ellie wasn't the match Mama had arranged for him.

He snorted. The Duchess of Love couldn't want him to wed Lady Juliet now that the girl was clearly enamored of Cox—and especially if she and Cox had been doing what he suspected they'd been doing last night.

He paused with his cravat half tied. Why had Mama never thought to match him with Ellie?

He shrugged. She must think, as he had, that he considered Ellie an honorary sister.

He picked up Cicely's miniature from his desk and looked at the young girl in the picture. Surely Cicely would approve as well. Ellie had been her closest friend.

He started to slip the painting into his pocket, but stopped. Even though he was confident Cicely would approve, he probably shouldn't bring her likeness along to his proposal.

He put the painting into his desk drawer and then strode out of his bedroom. He paused with his hand on the door to the corridor. Wait a minute—where the hell was Reggie? He looked around the sitting room. No cat.

Oh well, he had more important things to think about than wondering where Mama's pet had got to. He jerked open the door and hurried downstairs. He needed to see to having some tea ready for Ellie—and brandy for him.

Chapter 17

Men can be such idiots.

—Venus's Love Notes

Ellie frowned at her reflection in the bedroom mirror. Why in the world had Jack pushed her? He hadn't been angry; no, he'd obviously thought he was helping her in some way, making her fall against Ned and land spread out over him like a blanket.

Her face turned redder than her silk drawers, and she squeezed her eyes shut. She was going to spontaneously combust from embarrassment.

She should have been embarrassed out there in the snow, but she hadn't been. Oh, no, embarrassment had been the farthest emotion from her thoughts. She'd been far too overcome by the feel of Ned under her.

He'd felt wonderful, even better than when she'd fallen against him in his room that first day. He was so solid, so hard and broad and male. She'd wanted to burrow into his coat—into him—and stay there forever. She'd completely forgotten they were surrounded by the other members of the house party.

Thank *God* Lady Heldon and Percy hadn't been there to observe her. If they had, the story would be all over the neighborhood already. Of course, it might still spread . . .

She bit her lip and tried to swallow her sudden panic. Surely no one could tell she'd wanted to stay draped across Ned? Yes, she should have scrambled up immediately, but . . . but . . .

She forced herself to take a deep breath.

Everyone must have concluded she'd had the wind knocked out of her. That was it. Or perhaps they'd thought she'd been frozen in shock by it all. Yes, she liked that. The elderly spinster paralyzed by such close contact with a male body.

Or perhaps the moment hadn't lasted as long as she'd thought. Perhaps it had been drawn out only in her mind, like the time between the moment you realize you're going to take a nasty fall and the time you crash into the ground. It seems like forever, but it actually happens very quickly.

She forced herself to smile. She would act as if nothing unusual had occurred. If she behaved as she always did, anyone who did have a suspicion would decide they were imagining things. They would—

Her smile froze. Damn it, had *Ned* been able to tell what she'd been feeling? And when she'd slipped coming inside just a little while ago and grabbed him, had he noticed how tightly she'd clung to him?

Maybe that's what he wanted to talk about in the library.

Oh, dear God.

She'd stay in her room. He couldn't force her to come down. She would merely tell him when she saw him in the drawing room later that she'd been too cold or too overcome by—

No. She wasn't going to hide any longer. If he had noticed, she'd admit it. Hadn't she decided to be strong and decisive and persuade Ned he should consider marrying her? Perhaps she'd even try to flirt with him again.

Hmm, flirting was probably a bad idea. After her feeble attempt outside, she had to conclude she'd no skills in that area. She'd likely do such a poor job of it, Ned would decide she'd taken ill and send for a doctor. She would just have to find the courage to come right out and tell him how she felt.

Gaa! Her stomach threatened to revolt at the thought.

She glared at her middle in the mirror. Her stomach would have to behave. She would take her nerves firmly in hand. She could do this.

Maybe.

No, there was no "maybe" about it. She *would* do it.

She surveyed herself one more time—and grimaced. Her courage would benefit from a more enticing covering. Her dress was a muddy brown that she'd thought would compliment her eyes and hair, but which just made her look like a mound of dirt. And she'd never really noticed how much this frock resembled a burlap sack. Well, at least it was warm.

She couldn't even wear her red drawers to make her feel daring. They were far too wet, so she'd draped them over the desk chair by the fire to dry. They should be safe. She'd had Thomas and another footman shove the wardrobe as close to the wall as possible, so Reggie would have to lose some weight to squeeze through the hole into her room. Once she got back, she'd stuff the drawers securely under the mattress.

She made her way down the stairs to the library, took a sustaining breath, and knocked.

"Come in," Ned called.

She stepped inside and shut the door behind her. It was rather scandalous for an unmarried man and woman to be alone in a room with the door closed, but she was certain no one here would blink an eye. It was just Ned and Ellie, nothing to be concerned about.

She took another deep breath. She must make it something to be concerned about. She must be scandalous, or at least alluring.

Or maybe just direct. Yes. Just tell him what she wanted. This was her golden opportunity.

Ned was standing by the fire next to two leather wing-chairs. He smiled at her. "Oh, good, I was going to ask you to shut the door. I have a proposition to put before you that I don't care anyone overhearing. Come, have a seat."

"Ah." An odd sort of despairing, slightly maniacal laughter bubbled up in her throat, but she swallowed it. Another man—another woman—and a proposition might involve talk of secret trysts and stolen kisses; unfortunately, she couldn't fool herself for even an instant into thinking those notions had crossed Ned's mind. No, likely he only wanted to see if she'd be interested in looking over his plans for his spring plantings.

She joined him by the fire and perched on the edge of one of the chairs. He took the other, crossed his legs, and jiggled his foot.

Hmm. He was nervous, too.

"I had Dalton bring in some tea," he said, gesturing to the tea cart. "Would you care for some?"

Ned wasn't drinking tea. She cleared her throat, gripping

her hands together. "I see you have the decanter there. Might I have a glass of brandy, instead?"

He frowned at her. "Have you ever had brandy?"

Drinking brandy was far too daring an activity for a boring old spinster like Ellie Bowman. "There's always a first time."

"Actually, no, there's not always a first time. I'm quite certain many ladies go to their grave never having tasted the stuff."

She was not going to give in. "But I'm chilled." Whether it was from the cold or nerves, her stomach was certainly shivering. "I've always heard brandy is warming."

"Tea is warming, too."

"But brandy is more warming, isn't it?"

Ned was still frowning at her, damn it. She forced herself to look calmly and determinedly back at him. If he refused to pour her a glass, she'd snatch the blasted decanter from him and get her own drink—even if she had to use a teacup. She needed some liquid courage to get through this interview.

"Very well, I don't suppose one glass will hurt you." He smiled. "And it might help relax you a bit. You seem a little tense."

"I suppose I am." Ha! A *little* tense? That was like saying they'd just had a little snow.

He filled a small glass halfway with the amber liquid and handed it to her. "Just be careful. A little goes a long way."

"I'm sure." Did he think she was a ninny? She might not have had brandy before, but she'd had ratafia and Madeira. She took a sip.

And thought she was going to die. The brandy burned her tongue and her mouth before tracing a line of fire down her throat. "Ah." She swallowed again. "Ah, ah."

Ned reached for her glass. "I *thought* tea would be a better choice."

She leaned away from him, putting one hand up to hold him off while clutching her glass to her chest. "No, I'm fine. I was just a bit, er, surprised."

He sat back, worry creasing his brow. "You don't have to drink it, you know."

"I know. I like it."

One of Ned's damn eyebrows flew up.

"No, I do." Now that the brandy had finally arrived at her stomach, it was making her feel warm and almost happy. Her nerves began to unknot. She took another, more cautious sip and was relieved to find the liquid went down much more easily this time. "See? It just takes some getting used to."

"Well, don't get too used to it. I don't want to have to carry you upstairs because you're too tipsy to manage on your own."

She quite liked the idea of Ned carrying her upstairs. "What was this proposition you wished to discuss?"

"Ah, yes." Ned took a swallow of brandy himself. "I had an interesting conversation with Miss Wharton during our sleigh ride."

Damn, perhaps she didn't want to hear this. She took another sip of brandy. "Oh?"

"Yes. It seems her parents have given her to the end of the Season to find a husband; if she doesn't, they will marry her off to an elderly neighbor."

"Oh, dear." Her heart sank, and she swallowed some more brandy. Ned didn't feel he needed to save Miss Wharton from that fate, did he?

"It is shocking to me that parents can be so unfeeling."

He studied her face. "Your parents aren't pressuring you to wed, are they, Ellie?"

"N-no." She took another sip of brandy. "Though I can sympathize with Miss Wharton. I don't believe Papa cares if I ever marry, but Mama has been reminding me more and more often how, if I insist on remaining a spinster, I'll have to rely on my sisters' charity once she and Papa are gone. It's very depressing."

The brandy had taken away all the shivering and tightness in her stomach. It was even taking the edge off her worry about Ned and Miss Wharton. She felt quite detached, almost as if she was floating.

"So you've changed your mind about remaining single?"

She blinked at Ned. For such a handsome man, he was a bit slow in his understanding. "I never chose to be single. It just happened." She drank some more brandy. "Or, rather, marriage didn't happen. We females don't have a lot of choice in the matter, when all is said and done."

She wasn't being completely truthful, but she wasn't quite ready to tell the entire truth—that he'd been married to Cicely, and there'd been no one else she'd wanted to wed.

Maybe she'd never tell him that—there might be such a thing as too much truthfulness. She should just say that she wanted to dispense with spinsterhood now by marrying him.

She hadn't yet had enough brandy to manage *that* speech.

Ned nodded. "I suppose you are right, but I confess I'd never considered the matter until I spoke with Miss Wharton. I now understand why the poor girl has been chasing Jack so assiduously."

"Yes." Damn it, he *was* going to offer for Miss Wharton. She couldn't let that happen without at least trying to state her case. It wasn't as if he loved the girl, and her impetuosity would drive him mad in short order. He needed a friend—

he needed Ellie—to point out what a mistake he'd be making if he offered for her.

"But you . . . I . . ." *Just say it, you numskull!* "I-I want . . ."

"Yes, Ellie?" Ned leaned forward, looking solicitous, but clearly without the faintest inkling of what she felt for him. "What do you want?"

You. But she couldn't make her lips form that word. She held out her glass instead. "More brandy."

His face wrinkled up as if she were holding out a used chamber pot. "That's not a good idea."

He was likely correct, but she was desperate. One more glass—perhaps one more sip—and she'd be able to find the courage to tell him what she felt. This was no time to be cautious. "Please?"

His frown deepened. "You'll be sick."

"No, I won't." And even if she were, it would be worth it. She eyed the decanter. "Just a little more?"

"Oh, very well, but Mama will be exceedingly annoyed with me if I get you foxed." He filled her glass barely halfway. "And slow down. You are drinking far too quickly."

"Um." She took a sip. "So the, er, proposition you mentioned?" Perhaps she could approach the problem from a different, less obvious angle. "I'm still not clear on what it might be. Does it involve Miss Wharton?" She took a sustaining breath. "And if it does, shouldn't you be speaking to her rather than me?"

"No. Or, rather, not yet." Ned poured himself more brandy as well. "If you decide to accept my proposal, then I've no need to talk to Miss Wharton."

"Er, proposal?" The brandy had definitely gone to her head. Her ears were buzzing. Her heart had lurched into slow, hard thuds, and her lungs were stubbornly refusing to take in air. *Breathe, ninny. He doesn't mean a* marriage *proposal.* "What proposal?"

Ned dropped his eyes to his glass. His shoulders tensed, hunching up closer to his ears, and his foot jiggled faster. He was very nervous.

"We are old friends, are we not, Ellie?"

"Y-yes." She took a gulp of brandy. Where was this conversation going?

He smiled at her fleetingly. "I don't know that I ever said it, but I very much appreciated your support after Cicely and the baby died."

"I was happy to give it." She leaned toward him and touched his knee. "Their deaths were a terrible tragedy."

He nodded. His hand covered hers and her pulse jumped. She loved his touch.

"Yes," he said. "It's taken me a long time to get over it, but I think . . . well, I suppose I'll never be over it completely, but I've decided it's time to remarry."

Her heart leapt up into her throat, and her head began to throb so hard she was afraid it might explode.

Ned was saying something, but she couldn't hear him. She shook her head to clear it.

"No?" He looked surprised and somewhat crestfallen.

"No, I mean I didn't comprehend what you said. I'm sorry." She withdrew her hand and glanced down at her brandy glass, but decided she'd better try to marshal her wits instead of drinking any more. "Was it something about"—she swallowed—"remarrying?"

"Yes." He looked her in the eyes now, so intent and sincere. "I want children, Ellie. An heir and others as well."

"Ah." She wanted children, too, so badly she ached with the desire.

"And I thought—" He glanced down briefly before

meeting her eyes again. "Forgive me if I've misconstrued the situation, but I thought this year you might be open to the idea of marriage."

"Ah." She was such a brilliant conversationalist, but it took all her effort to keep her heart and lungs and ears working. Perhaps Ned *had* meant a marriage proposal.

Would he profess his undying devotion? Would he perhaps *kiss* her?

"This year you haven't stayed by Ash's side as you have in the past, and you've shown at least a little interest in the men Mama invited for you." He frowned. "Though you must have noticed Humphrey and Cox both seem to have found other matches."

Ellie nodded. "It would be hard not to notice." But who cared? She wasn't interested in them; she was interested in Ned, and she'd swear he was on the verge of declaring himself. All her dreams were about to come true.

He smiled. "So I thought since I want a wife, and you appear willing to take a husband, it would be sensible and practical for us to marry."

"S-sensible?" Where were the words of love, the bended knee, the "make me the happiest of men" bit? "P-practical?"

"Yes. I did think to ask Miss Wharton, since she seems to be in desperate need of a mate, but I suspect Mama will make her one of her matchmaking projects this Season. I'm not too worried she'll actually be forced to wed her elderly neighbor."

"Y-you are p-probably right." Surely he'd mention love in a moment. She took a quick swallow of brandy.

"Yes, I think I am." He smiled at her. "And there are so many advantages to marrying you instead. You'll be happier at Linden Hall than I think Miss Wharton would be, even though she did say she likes the country. But still, Linden

Hall is far from her home; it's close to yours. You'll be able to visit your family regularly. And Mama loves you like a daughter already."

"Ah." He was talking about the vicarage and his mama. This couldn't be happening. Her dream was turning into a nightmare.

Be reasonable, a small voice in the back of her mind said. *This is your chance to finally marry Ned.*

Ned was still smiling. "You and I have known each other forever; I think we could rub along fairly well. And as for your marital duties"—*Good God, was he blushing?*—"I hope you won't find them too onerous. Once you are with child, I promise to leave you alone until it's time to try again."

Yes, a nightmare. This was definitely a nightmare. In a moment she'd wake up.

"So what do you say, Ellie?"

Yes, the little voice shouted. *Say yes. Marry Ned. Live happily ever after. This is what you've always wanted.*

But he doesn't love me.

He'll come to love you, the voice said. And then a little nastily, *It's not as if you have anyone else asking. You want children, don't you? This could be your last—your only— chance.*

"Ellie? Will you have me?"

Something elemental and completely irrational surged in her then. The little voice screamed in horror but couldn't stop her. She jumped to her feet. "I wouldn't have you if you were the last man on earth."

And in case he missed her meaning, she tossed the rest of her brandy in his face.

Ned was mopping up when Ash and Jack came into the library.

"What did you do to Ellie?" Jack sounded angry. "We just passed her in the corridor."

"She had her head down and looked to be on the verge of tears." Ash's voice was also harsh. Both his brothers were glaring at him, damn it. "When we tried to stop her to see what the problem was, she dodged us. In fact, she just about ran away. That's not like Ellie."

Zeus, did they think he'd beaten her? "I don't know what's the matter with her. All I did was suggest she marry me." He tried to blot some of the brandy from his cravat, but it was a hopeless endeavor. Likely nothing would get the stain out; he'd have to throw the neckcloth away. "And she threw her brandy in my face in answer."

Jack's eyebrows shot up. "Perhaps she was drunk."

"I don't see how she could have been. She only had one glass." Well, and a few sips more, but not enough to count.

"What were you doing giving her brandy in the first place?" Ash asked, coming over to help himself to the decanter.

"I wasn't trying to get her foxed, if that's what you're suggesting. She asked for some. I tried to dissuade her, but she said she was chilled from her tumble in the snow." Ned shot Jack a pointed look. "I still don't understand how she came to go flying into me. She said you pushed her."

Jack took a glass of brandy from Ash and dropped into the seat Ellie had just vacated. "She slipped."

Ned believed that as much as he believed the moon was made of cheese. "Right."

Jack waved away his obvious skepticism. "I can't understand why Ellie would reject your proposal. She's madly in love with you."

Ned snorted even as an odd flame flickered to life in his

gut. Ellie loved him? No, the notion was absurd. "She has an odd way of showing it then."

"Jack's right." Ash cradled his brandy glass and leaned against the mantel near Jack's chair so they were both facing Ned. "Ellie's been hopelessly in love with you since we were children. Everyone but you saw it."

Ned looked from one to the other. They did not appear to be joking. "You're both mad. Ellie's a friend." He balled up his soiled handkerchief; it would also have to go on the ash heap. "Or at least I thought she was."

Jack snorted. "She feels far more than friendship for you, you blockhead. Why do you think she's ignored all Mama's choices and clung to our married brother here?" Jack grinned up at Ash. "Not that you aren't a fine fellow, of course."

Ash inclined his head. "Of course." He looked back at Ned. "Jack's right. I've spent hours talking to Ellie at these damn house parties, and I've watched how she watches you. It's not mere friendship I've seen in her eyes."

Good God, they couldn't be right. Ellie didn't love him . . . did she?

He felt as if the room was spinning, and this time he hadn't had too much brandy.

But no—she'd said she wouldn't marry him even if he were the last man on earth.

"Perhaps the more important question," Ash was saying, "is what do you feel for Ellie? Do you love her, Ned, or do you really consider her just a friend?"

Ned glared at his brother. "There's nothing 'just' about it. I value Ellie's friendship very highly indeed." He didn't have many friends—perhaps none besides his brothers and Ellie. He was a solitary creature, living a comfortable, but solitary existence.

Which was exactly the way he liked it. His life was orderly and well-planned—just as his next marriage would be. He wanted no unpleasant surprises. No messy emotions like love to shred his heart and destroy his peace.

"Wait a moment." Jack shook his head. "You said you 'suggested' Ellie marry you. You didn't really say that, did you?"

"Of course I did. It's an arrangement that would work to both our benefits." His kaleidoscope of emotions finally settled into the hot colors of anger. A hard knot tightened in his chest. "I don't know why you both are making such a fuss about this. I want children, so I need a wife. Ellie's not married and seemed willing this year to consider changing that state. She *is* twenty-six. She's running out of time."

Why the hell were Jack and Ash both staring goggle-eyed at him?

"Please tell me you didn't say *that* to her," Jack said, horror tingeing his voice.

"What? That I wanted children? I thought she should know that, though I suppose she could easily have inferred it."

Jack shook his head. "No, the part about her age."

"Of course not." Not that he mightn't have got to it if the conversation had progressed. Perhaps he was fortunate that it hadn't—he'd admit Ellie might not have taken that part well. But it didn't matter—she hadn't taken any of it well.

"And the bit about children?" Ash looked almost as if he wanted to laugh. "Did you say that as bluntly to her as you just did to us?"

What the hell was he getting at? "I don't know—perhaps." Ned flushed. "But you can be certain I reassured her that I wouldn't take advantage of my marital rights beyond the necessary task of getting her with child. I'm not a brute, you know."

"No, you're an ass," Jack said, his expression twisting with disgust.

Ned's fingers tightened and his arm muscles bunched, but he took a breath and gathered his composure. He would *not* fling his drink in Jack's face. There had already been too much brandy wasted in this room. "You bloody well had best take that back."

"Why? It's the truth."

Self-control was overrated.

The brandy hit Jack's face a split second before Jack grabbed Ned's shoulders. Then they were both down on the floor trying to land punches.

"Good God, stop! Have you two lost your minds?"

Ned ignored Ash; he needed to focus all his attention on Jack. His little brother was much stronger than he'd been as a boy and far more skilled. At least he was fighting fair at the moment, but Ned suspected Jack had been in more than one scuffle where, by necessity, winning—or survival—trumped obeying any rules.

Something hit his backside hard.

"What the hell?" He jerked his head up to see Ash hit Jack on the leg with the fireplace poker.

"Hey!" Jack kicked out, but Ash jumped back in time to avoid being taken down.

"Good move," Ned said, sitting up. He and Jack both glared at Ash.

"And I'll hit you both again," Ash said, "if you don't stop fighting. You've already broken a brandy glass and that hideous china dog that was on the occasional table."

Jack ran his hand through his hair. His brandy-spattered cravat dangled from his neck. "Mama won't care."

"Perhaps not," Ash said, "but she'll care very much if either of you show up at dinner with a cut lip or black eye."

Ash was correct, blast it. Ned pulled himself to his feet, wincing a little as he straightened. "Where did you learn to fight like that, Jack?"

Jack shrugged—and Ned was delighted to see him wince as well. So he *had* done a little damage. "Gentleman Jackson's mostly and, er, well"—Jack stood—"I don't always stay in the good part of Town."

Ned frowned. "Damn it, Jack, what is the matter with you? Have you a death wish?"

Jack grinned. "Not at all."

He wanted to shake some sense into him, but that clearly was impossible. "Will you at least be careful?"

"I'll certainly try, Lord Worry."

Perhaps he would just hit him again—

Ash stepped between them. "I think you'd both better retire to your rooms and make yourselves presentable," he said. "And do avoid letting Mama see you on your way."

"Gad, yes." Jack grimaced. "I hate Mama's sad, disappointed look. You know the one I mean?"

"Yes," Ash said, ruefully. "I do—all too well."

"Well, you do need to do something about Jess," Jack said, "and the sooner, the better."

Ash narrowed his eyes. "Careful, Jack. You may be a better fighter, but I'm sure I could make you feel some pain."

"Doubtful, old man. You'll be thirty tomorrow, remember?"

Ash grunted. "How can I forget when everyone takes it upon himself to remind me?"

Ned smiled, but he wasn't feeling particularly amused. He headed toward the door. "I'll see you both later, then."

"Ned," Ash called.

He stopped with his hand on the doorknob. "What?"

"Far be it from me to offer any sort of advice on the handling of women—we all know how ironic that would be—but I do think you should consider exactly what Ellie means to you. If you find you love her, tell her. Don't hide behind talk of mutually beneficial arrangements. That's not fair to her—or to you."

Ned just nodded and let himself out, closing the door behind him. He looked up and down the corridor; thank God no one was in sight. Then he started up the stairs to the bedroom floor.

Did he love Ellie?

He loved her as a friend, of course, but did he *love* her?

Panic grabbed his throat, and his chest tightened. He couldn't love her. He couldn't again go through the pain he'd suffered when Cicely died. Far better to marry Miss Wharton—he was certain he didn't love her.

He'd spend some time with Miss Wharton this evening to see if they were at all compatible. If they were, perhaps he would say something to her tomorrow. There was no point in putting it off. The sooner he married, the sooner he'd have his heir.

He just wished he felt a bit more enthusiasm at the prospect.

Chapter 18

Red is the color of love.
                                    —Venus's Love Notes

The Duchess of Love pulled back her bedroom curtains and squinted. The bright sun shining on the snow-covered garden and fields was beautiful but harsh. A herd of deer picked its way through drifts near the pond; a rabbit paused on a garden path. The world looked vast, cold, and quiet.

"Happy birthday, my dear duchess," Drew said, coming up behind her and wrapping his arms around her waist.

"Mmm." It was her birthday and her sons' birthday and the last day of her party, and she was very much afraid she wouldn't get the one gift she wanted more than any other. She'd been so hopeful, but after last evening . . .

"You're unusually pensive." Drew nuzzled her neck. "Still worrying?"

"Yes." She'd fretted half the night, and what little sleep she'd got had been haunted by images of Ned and Miss Wharton exchanging vows in Greycliffe's chapel with Ellie's papa presiding.

Drew turned her to face him. "Stop. Ned's a grown man, Venus. He must make his own decisions."

She sighed and wrapped her arms around him, resting her cheek on his chest. The steady beat of his heart was so comforting. "I know. I just wish he was still a little boy. Life was so much simpler then. I could solve all his problems with a hug and a kiss."

"Not all of them. Remember the nights you spent at his bedside when he had a fever or an earache or a bad cough?"

"Yes." She remembered all too clearly—the agony of seeing any of her sons in pain and being unable to make it go away or, worse, the terror of watching them breathe, hoping each breath would not be their last, bargaining with God to make them better.

"He married Cicely; he'll marry Miss Wharton if he wants." Drew hugged her a little tighter. She knew he wasn't happy about that, either. "We'll survive." She felt him swallow. "I'm sure we'll discover Miss Wharton is a lovely young woman once we get to know her better."

She looked up at him. "Yes, of course." She didn't mind Miss Wharton; she just didn't want her as a daughter-in-law. "But I thought things were going so well between Ned and Ellie, especially once Lady Juliet deserted him for Mr. Cox."

"So did I, but apparently they weren't."

"Something must have happened yesterday afternoon." She frowned, biting her lip. It was all so frustrating. "I asked Jack—I can never get anything out of Ash, you know—but even Jack looked grim and wouldn't say a word."

"Then we will just have to see what happens, won't we?"

She hated to have to wait and see. She much preferred making things happen. "And what about Ellie?"

"Ellie is not your problem." Drew paused while they both absorbed that unpleasant truth. "Although," he said after a moment, "I don't see why we can't persuade the vicar and

Mrs. Bowman to let us take her up to London for the Season. If Ned is to be married to Miss Wharton, Ellie might be willing to come to Town and submit to the Marriage Mart, and surely her mother will be anxious to have her broaden her marital opportunities."

"Very true. I'll speak to Constance as soon as everyone leaves." Venus sighed again. "I know she was so hopeful that this year Ellie would find a suitable husband."

Venus had been hopeful, too, but last night had been dreadful. Ellie had been wan, subdued, and back to her old habit of attaching herself to Ash; Ned had spent the entire evening determinedly—perhaps even grimly—talking to Miss Wharton.

"Perhaps Ellie will find a husband in London," Drew said. "She's a very pleasant woman, and I'm sure once you take charge of her wardrobe, she'll prove to be a very attractive one as well. She has a pretty face; it's just a little difficult to, er, appreciate her full beauty when she hides herself in oceans of fabric."

Venus nodded. "Yes." Then she grinned. She'd forgotten about the dress. She couldn't do that.

"I see you have a plan," Drew said, letting her go.

"I do." She almost waltzed over to her dressing table and started to brush some of the tangles out of her hair. Mary always wanted to braid it before she went to bed, but Drew preferred it loose; of course she was far more interested in pleasing her husband than her maid.

She tugged on a particularly stubborn tangle. She would admit braiding had its advantages sometimes. "I told you I had Mary make Ellie a new ball gown, didn't I?"

"Yes. And I believe you said you'd enlisted Reggie's help in ruining the old one."

"I did." She turned to look at Drew; he was splashing water over his face. "Isn't that ice cold?"

He shrugged and dried his face with a towel. "I don't

mind—it helps me wake up." He hung the towel on the washstand and came over to lean against the bedpost. "You know, I can't imagine Ellie was happy to have her frock destroyed."

"She wasn't particularly, but I think even she recognized the world is a better place without that hideous gown."

Drew's eyebrow flew up. "It can't have been that bad."

"It was. It was the yellow dress—you must remember it."

He frowned. "Wasn't her dress last year yellow?"

"Yes, that's the dress. She wore it last year and the year before last and the year before that. I think it might be the only ball gown she's ever owned, and it always made her look like a faded lemon with aphids crawling all over."

"Oh, right, now I remember." Drew grimaced. "It *was* rather round and fussy."

Round and fussy hardly began to describe that cloth nightmare. All of Ellie's dresses were horrendous, but that ball gown had taken ugly to new heights. "Constance could never understand why Ellie insisted on buying the fabric to begin with, and then why she persuaded the dressmaker to add all those ribbons and flounces—adding insult to injury, Constance always said."

"Hmm." Drew frowned thoughtfully. "Either Ellie has terrible fashion sense or the dress was a kind of public hair shirt."

"Perhaps, but what could Ellie be doing penance for? She's lived a quiet, exemplary life as far as I can tell." Venus wrinkled her nose. "Whenever I had to look at that dress, I felt as if *I* was doing penance."

"So does she like the new gown better?"

Venus stood and almost skipped over to give Drew a kiss on his cheek. "Oh, she hasn't seen it yet. Mary and I agreed that we shouldn't give it to her until the very last minute, otherwise we're afraid she'd find a way to subvert our efforts—wear another dress or find some hideous fichu or shawl to drape around it or . . . or something."

He laughed, cupping her face and brushing her lips with his. "This should be interesting."

"Yes." She was going to be hopeful. Surely Ned wouldn't do anything stupid like offer marriage to Miss Wharton before the ball, and once he saw Ellie in her new dress . . .

"I think this might be a wonderful birthday after all."

Ned scowled at the billiard table as Ellie got ready to take her shot. Jack, with his bloody warped sense of humor, had insisted Ellie and Ned form one team while Jack and Miss Wharton formed the other. They'd been playing for what seemed like forever. It was torture.

Ned had yet to exchange one word with Ellie. They'd carefully stepped around each other, averting their gazes so as not to make eye contact. But he'd studied her when her attention was elsewhere.

She looked horrible, blast it. She was pale and drawn and had dark circles under her eyes. He'd wager she hadn't slept much last night.

Well, neither had he. He'd tossed and turned until his covers were in a complete knot, but at least he'd come to a decision. He was going to ask Miss Wharton to marry him. Ellie had made it clear *she* didn't want him, and, well, he didn't want her either. He felt too much for her. Love, he supposed it was love, but whatever it was, it terrified him. He'd loved Cicely, but this was worse. If he got Ellie with child and she died, he'd die, too.

But none of that mattered. Ellie didn't love him. She'd made that very, very clear. All through the night he'd kept hearing her words, seeing her expression when she'd told him she wouldn't marry him. And then he'd wake up with a jerk, head pounding, stomach churning.

God, it hurt.

But it was for the best. He'd finally reached that conclusion around dawn. He would marry Miss Wharton. He was a little concerned she might feel he was rushing his fences, but there was no point in putting it off. If she accepted him, they could make all the arrangements now, and he wouldn't have to go up to London.

He'd be doing a good deed by freeing her from her unpleasant parents and giving her a home. He'd have to come back to Greycliffe from time to time, of course, but maybe by then this feeling he had for Ellie would have dulled to a manageable—a pleasant—fondness. As if he and Ellie were indeed just friends.

And maybe Ellie would have married and moved away.

He almost doubled over in pain at the thought.

"Ned," Jack said, "have you grown roots over there? It's your turn."

"Right." He stepped up to the table and took his shot, not sparing a moment's thought on it—and then watched in horror as the cue ball barely escaped falling into the right far pocket. Damn it, he didn't want to completely embarrass himself.

Ellie cast him a quick look of surprise—he never bungled his shots so badly. He stared back at her. It wasn't as if he *wanted* to be playing this stupid game, after all. The sooner it was over the better. Then he could get back to his plans for Miss Wharton.

Ellie dropped her gaze to the billiard table, staring at it as if the location of the Holy Grail was hidden in its green baize covering.

"Perhaps you need to focus a bit more on the game," Jack murmured as Miss Wharton got ready to take her shot.

Ned grunted. He'd been on the verge of taking Miss Wharton on a stroll in the long gallery and perhaps asking for her hand in marriage when Jack had caught him and dragged him into the billiard room. In fact now that he thought of it, each time he'd tried to have a private word with the woman, Mama or Father or one of his brothers had prevented him from doing so. That could not be just bad luck.

Apparently Miss Wharton was not much of a billiards player; she *did* pot the cue ball.

"Oh, dear," she said, laughing—though the laughter was a bit strained. She couldn't be oblivious to the tension between him and Ellie. "I'm afraid I always lose at billiards. My sisters used to fight over which one of them would be unlucky enough to have me on their team."

"That's quite all right, Miss Wharton," he said. He certainly didn't care if she was accomplished at billiards or not. He wasn't looking for a wife to play games. He wanted children, and there was no reason to think Miss Wharton would not be able to manage that task.

Ah, but could *he* manage his part of the business?

Heat swept up his neck to his face, and he bent quickly to examine his cue stick. Of course he could. He might not feel any particular, ah, stirrings for her at the moment, but he was male. He should be able to rise to the occasion.

Oh, damn, what a poor choice of words.

"Indeed, Miss Wharton," Jack said, taking his shot, "this is just a friendly game, you know. A way to pass the time until you ladies must off to prepare for tonight's ball."

Ellie paled, but Miss Wharton's face lit up. "Oh, yes. I'm *so* looking forward to it. Her grace said that all the local gentry as well as a number of the *ton* will be here."

Ellie's face turned even whiter, if that were possible. What was the issue? Was she concerned that her parents as well as her sisters and their husbands and everyone who knew her would be here? But they came every year; this year was no different.

"Yes, it will be an infernal crush," Jack said, grimacing. "I confess I shall be glad when it is over."

"Oh, Lord Jack, how can you say that?" Miss Wharton's eyes grew wide with shock as if Jack had just uttered some blasphemy.

"Easily." He laughed. "But I suspect most gentlemen do not enjoy balls to the degree that ladies do." Jack looked over at Ellie. "Your turn, Ellie. See if you can win it, why don't you? Ned here looks like he's ready for the game to be over."

"Oh, no, Jack," Ned said through his teeth, "I'm having a most enjoyable time."

Jack grinned, but Miss Wharton gave him a startled look. Ned tried to make his expression look pleasanter.

"Very well," Ellie said, a spark of animation—or perhaps merely annoyance—in her voice at last. "I will see what I can do."

The cue ball was in an awkward location, so Ellie had to come over to Ned's side of the table to reach it. He backed up and would have moved away completely, but he caught Jack's eye. Damn it, was his brother daring him to stay where he was? He would do so, then. He didn't want Jack thinking he couldn't bear to be close to Ellie.

Except he couldn't bear it. Ellie had to almost drape herself over the table to get the proper angle on her shot; her dress—her ugly, dark gray, shapeless, hideous dress—pulled tight as she leaned over farther, outlining her lovely, rounded, perfect arse. She was well within arm's reach. He could—

He could *not*.

At least Ellie's body blocked Jack's view of Ned's nether regions. He hoped.

He'd suspect she was torturing him on purpose, except he was quite sure she had no idea the effect she had on him. *She* wasn't a Lady Heldon. And, to be fair, he hadn't fully realized it himself until just now. He shifted position and focused instead on Ellie's glossy, brown hair—

That wasn't helping.

He forced his eyes up to contemplate the fifth duke, glowering down from the opposite wall. The man had gone through three wives and sired twelve daughters—and not a single son. The duchy had gone to a nephew that family lore said the old duke detested. No wonder the fellow looked so angry.

"Good job, Ellie!" Jack said.

"Yes, Miss Bowman, that was a wonderful shot." Miss Wharton clapped enthusiastically, seeming genuinely excited at Ellie's skill.

Ellie, glowing with pleasure, looked at him—and her face fell. Damn.

"Well done, Ellie," he said awkwardly. He was very conscious of Jack glaring at him. He hadn't meant to hurt her feelings.

"Yes, well, now that the game is over, I believe I'll go upstairs." Ellie ignored Ned to smile at Jack and Miss Wharton. "There was a problem with the ball gown I brought from home, and the duchess kindly had her maid make up a new one. I haven't seen it yet—I suppose there may still be some adjustments that need to be made."

The clock on the mantel chimed the hour, and Miss Wharton startled. "Oh, look at the time! I'll go up with you, Miss Bowman, if I may." She linked arms with Ellie; he could tell Ellie was a bit taken aback by the gesture, but she managed to return Miss Wharton's smile nonetheless.

"Perhaps you can tell me what to expect," Miss Wharton said, "since you've been to these balls before." She laughed. "I'm sure they must seem completely dull to you, but I confess I'm beyond excited."

"Oh, I don't find them dull at all," Ellie said as she and Miss Wharton left the billiards room.

"You know you were watching Ellie and not Miss Wharton," Jack said as soon as the women had departed.

"Just now?" Ned tried to snort convincingly. "I was watching them both."

Jack's eyebrows lifted skeptically. "If you say so. But I meant during the game."

Ned had been very carefully *not* looking at Ellie—well, except when he'd been looking at her inappropriately. "You are imagining things."

"I don't think so."

"You are." He knew he was lying, but if he said it enough, perhaps it would become true. His feelings were merely a physical response, evidence that his relevant parts still functioned, and he should have no difficulty performing with Miss Wharton.

Unfortunately, his most relevant part cringed at the thought.

A deep frown creased Jack's brow; there wasn't the slightest glint of humor in his expression. "You aren't really going to ask Miss Wharton to marry you, are you, Ned?"

There was no reason to be evasive. "Yes, I am. I decided this morning."

Jack's reaction was not encouraging—his face hardened and he stared at Ned as if he were trying to decide what species of lunatic he belonged to.

He had no obligation to explain himself, but the words insisted on coming out. "It makes perfect sense. I need a wife; she needs a husband."

"But you love Ellie!"

"I—" He wanted to say he didn't, but he was afraid that would be a lie.

"And she loves you."

Now he was on much firmer ground. "I assure you she does not. Didn't I tell you last night that she turned me down?"

Jack snorted and rolled his eyes at the same time. "Of course she did. If your 'proposal' was anything like you described, she probably thought you were intent on hiring a housekeeper—or, worse, purchasing a brood mare."

Surely it hadn't been that bad? "You don't know. You weren't there."

"True. So tell me this: Did you at any point tell her that you loved her?"

There was that damn word again, opening up the terrifying abyss. Ned swallowed and tried to speak calmly. "No."

"Then tell her."

"No."

Jack gripped Ned's shoulder and shook him a little. "You have to."

"I *can't*, damn it." Ned threw off Jack's hold. Bloody panic burst in his chest where his heart should be. "Don't you understand? I loved once—I can't do it again. I can't bear it; I can't face that pain one more time."

"Ned." Jack's eyes were so full of compassion it hurt to look at them, so Ned looked away. "I know I can't really understand. I know that, but I do believe this: You need Ellie—"

"I don't." He couldn't.

"—and she needs you."

"No." He wouldn't listen. Jack had to be wrong.

"At least give her the chance to tell you in so many words that she doesn't love you." Jack's voice grew soft. "I've called you Lord Worry for years, but I never thought to call you Lord Coward."

Ned felt as if he'd taken a flush hit to his stomach. "Damn you, Jack, you can go straight to hell."

Ellie looked out her bedroom window. If she squinted, she could just make out the smoke snaking up from the vicarage chimney. Tonight her family would come to the ball, and tomorrow the duke and duchess would send her home in one of their carriages. She'd pack away her good dresses until next year.

But next year Ned would be married, perhaps to Miss Wharton.

She swallowed. Miss Wharton seemed nice enough. She might make Ned happy. She—

Oh, God. Ellie bit her lip and pressed her forehead against the cold glass of the window, but the tears came anyway. *She* could be Ned's wife. If only she'd said yes in the library yesterday—one word, three little letters—she'd be betrothed right now. The duchess would be pleased; her sisters would be happy—and likely relieved they no longer had to worry about supporting their spinster sister; and Mama . . . Mama would be ecstatic. The duke might very well announce the engagement at the birthday ball, and all the neighbors would congratulate her. And this time next year she might be increasing or perhaps already have a baby to cradle in her arms.

What did it matter that Ned didn't love her? As he'd said, they were old friends. That was more than she had with any other man she might consider marrying—certainly more than she had with Mr. Cox or Mr. Humphrey, not that either of those gentlemen was interested in wedding her any longer. They had both found their matches.

When she'd decided she wanted children even more than she wanted Ned, she'd faced the fact that she likely was giving up all hope of a love match. She'd come to expect exactly what Ned was offering—a sensible, polite bargain. Ned would be kind to her and would love their children. He'd be an attentive, good father. Why the hell hadn't she said yes?

Because she loved him so much she literally ached with it. She'd thought she'd ached for children—this was much, much worse. It was as if a knife had been plunged in her heart and twisted.

Could she bear to live the kind of bloodless existence he described? With another man—yes. But with Ned?

No. It would kill her.

She sighed and pulled her handkerchief out of her pocket. Perhaps she'd been foolish to think she could manage this kind of arrangement at all. She blew her nose. She should resign herself to being a maiden aunt. An eccentric maiden aunt, perhaps. That could be amusing.

The shadows were getting longer; it must be late. She glanced up at the clock. Oh, dear, Mary should be in at any moment with her new dress; she didn't want her to see she'd been crying. That would provoke all kinds of unpleasant comments.

She poured water in the washbasin and splashed it on her face. She'd meant to apologize to Ned this afternoon for throwing her brandy at him. That had been very rude of her. But she'd barely been able to look at him during that dreadful billiards game—and he'd barely been able to tolerate her presence.

She would apologize this evening at dinner or at the ball. She didn't want them to part on such bad terms.

Damn, she was going to cry again.

She dunked her face in the washbasin just as someone knocked on her door.

"Yes? Come in." She grabbed a towel and peered around it as the door swung open, and her grace entered, followed by Mary with her arms full of—God, no!—red fabric.

"Did you think we'd forgotten you, Ellie?" her grace said, beginning to shut the door as Mary laid her burden on the bed. "We—oh, excuse me, Reggie. I almost caught your tail. You'd be very angry about that, wouldn't you?"

Reggie slipped into the room, padded across the floor, and leapt up onto the bed.

"Stay away from Miss Ellie's dress, sir." Mary made shooing motions with her hands. "This one's not for you."

Reggie merely yawned and settled himself on the coverlet a handbreadth from the red—the very, very red—cloth. At least her drawers were still safely stuffed under the mattress. Ellie had checked on them again when she'd got back to her room.

"I hope you don't mind me coming with Mary," the duchess said, "but I couldn't wait to see you in your new gown."

Ellie finished drying her face and put the towel down on the washstand. "It's very red."

"It is, isn't it?" Her grace beamed at her. "Now let's get that frock off you, shall we, so you can try it on."

"I-I don't think I should wear red." The last time—the only time—she'd done so, her mother had sent her directly back to her room. Good God, if she wore this dress, her family would see it, and Mama, at least, would immediately think of Ned's and Cicely's betrothal ball.

"Don't be silly. It will look lovely on you, won't it, Mary?"

"Aye, as we'll see in a pig's whisker if ye'll stop stalling, Miss Ellie." Mary approached her with a look that clearly said she'd not stand for any nonsense.

"Very well." What choice did she have? Her old gown had gone off to the rag heap. She let Mary help her out of her dress and into the new ball gown with as much good grace as she could muster.

"Oh, Ellie!" Her grace clasped her hands in front of her chest delightedly. "You look so beautiful!"

"I-I do?" She was afraid to look in the mirror, but she didn't need the glass to tell her that rather more—*far* more—of her person was exposed than she was used to. The dress's bodice hugged her breasts and left a scandalous amount of her neck and arms uncovered. It was really too bad she'd not managed to pack her Norwich shawl. "Do you have a fichu I can borrow?"

The duchess's smile turned to a scowl. "Definitely not! You are not going to hide yourself under yards of fabric any longer, miss. Now come here and look at yourself."

"Aye." Mary gave her a little nudge. "Go on, do. Looking won't kill ye."

Ellie was not so certain. She stepped reluctantly over to the mirror and forced her eyes to focus . . .

She watched her jaw drop. She did look, if not beautiful, then very pretty. This red dress was much finer than the one she'd made years ago—Mary was a far more accomplished needlewoman and the silk was of considerably higher quality. The cloth fell in shimmering folds from her bodice to her slippers, skimming her hips and swirling around her feet when she moved. And the color . . . Somehow the red made her skin—her vast expanse of exposed skin—glow.

Her face glowed, too. "Oh! Thank you, your grace—and you, too, Mary. The dress is lovely."

Mary snorted. "I'm thinking it's the woman in the dress that's lovely, Miss Ellie."

"Very true, Mary," the duchess said. "Now sit down, Ellie, so Mary can fix your hair."

Ellie did as ordered—she was almost in a trance, she was so bemused at her new appearance—and Mary made short work of pinning up her hair to show off her shoulders and neck even more.

"And now the pearls," her grace said.

"Pearls? What do you—oh!"

The duchess fastened a necklace around Ellie's neck.

"I can't wear these." Ellie lightly touched the perfect strand of milky pearls.

"Of course you can." Ned's mother patted Ellie's shoulder. "You know I've always thought of you as a daughter."

"But . . ." Ellie sniffed.

"Now don't go crying," she said. "We can't have your

eyes matching your dress, can we? Come, stand up and let me look at you one more time."

Ellie got to her feet; the duchess shook her head slowly as if in wonder. "Who would have thought . . ." She grinned. "I'll wager all the men at tonight's ball, my sons included, won't be able to take their eyes off you."

Ellie smiled back. If only Ned . . . but it was too late for that.

"Yer grace, we'd best be getting ye ready," Mary said then.

"Oh, dear, yes. Look at the time! Just give Ellie the gloves, Mary, and we'll be on our way." The duchess almost skipped to the door. "I can hardly wait to see everyone's reaction when you come downstairs, Ellie!"

Mary handed Ellie a pair of long, white kid gloves and then followed her grace out of the room, leaving the door slightly ajar.

Ellie's eyes went back to the mirror. She moved her right arm—and the woman in the mirror's arm moved, too. She touched her face, the pearls at her neck—and the other woman did the same. As unbelievable as it seemed, it must be her reflection.

Reggie's reflection appeared by her feet.

"What do you think, Reggie? Do you recognize me?"

Reggie stretched, looking as bored as only a cat can.

Ellie laughed. "That's put me in my place, hasn't it? I'll just slip on these lovely gloves and—oh." She dropped one.

Before she could even begin to bend down to get it, Reggie snatched it up in his mouth and darted out the door.

She ran after him. "Reggie, blast it. Where are you—"

He was going to Ned's room, of course. She saw him disappear through Ned's door.

Damn.

She looked at the one glove still in her hand. She couldn't

go downstairs with only one glove, and her old gloves would never do.

She glanced up and down the corridor. Deserted. If she hurried, no one need know. But what if Ned came up?

The duchess wasn't even ready yet. Surely Ned would still be downstairs. It would only take her a moment to fetch her glove.

She bit her lip. She had no choice. She *had* to get that glove.

She dashed down the passageway and slipped through Ned's door. There was no point in looking in the sitting room—she knew exactly where she'd find Reggie.

He was waiting for her; she'd swear he was smiling around the glove still dangling in his jaws.

"Reggie, give me that."

He didn't, of course. He disappeared under the bed.

She paused. She hated to disarrange her hair or get her beautiful new dress dusty, but once again, she had no choice. She would just have to go back to her room to try to repair the damage once she'd recovered her belonging.

She carefully raised her skirt so she wasn't kneeling on it and got down on the floor. "Reggie, I swear you're going to pay for this." She crawled partway under the bed.

That was when she heard the door to the corridor close.

Chapter 19

Seduction is a skill anyone can learn.
                                    —Venus's Love Notes

Ned shut the door to his rooms and leaned against it for a moment. Zeus, he wished he could just stay here and skip dinner and the bloody ball. His head was pounding, and the brandy he'd just consumed with Ash in Ash's study wasn't helping as he'd hoped—it just made him muzzy-headed and morose.

He jerked off his coat and waistcoat. He'd drunk more brandy during this blasted party than he had in the whole year previous. He'd swear off the damn stuff when he went home—alone—to Linden Hall.

He ripped off his cravat and walked over to look out the window. The light was flat; dusk was coming on. The landscape looked colorless and cold.

His stomach twisted when he saw a carriage, the first of many, roll slowly up the drive. The guests invited for dinner would come and then, later, those attending only the ball. Shortly the castle would be crawling with people.

He looked longingly at his door again. If only he could lock it and barricade it, but if he didn't appear in the drawing room when it was time to greet Mama's guests, Mama would send someone up to haul him downstairs. He'd best just accept his fate and get ready.

He sat down to wrestle off his boots—and wrestle with the question that had been bedeviling him since the damn billiards game.

Was Jack right—*was* he a coward?

He tugged off his socks and flung them at the settee. Blast it, there wasn't much satisfaction in tossing something so light. They fluttered more than flew and landed limply and soundlessly. His boots now . . . but that would skate perilously close to a temper tantrum. He had more control than that, he hoped.

He stood and pulled his shirt over his head. At least Ash hadn't tried to lecture him—he'd just passed the brandy bottle. Ash had far more experience than Jack with love and the pain it caused.

But Jack had accused him of cowardice.

He blew out a long, angry breath. All right, so he *was* a coward. He'd admit it. The thought of loving someone again, of suffering through all the worry and heartache once more, turned his blood to ice.

He opened his fall and jerked down his pantaloons, kicking them off so he stood in only his drawers.

But Jack was wrong about one thing: Ellie *didn't* love him. Jack hadn't been there to hear her when she'd rejected him and to see the brandy splash over his face and cravat.

However, it was also true Ned didn't love Miss Wharton.

He sighed. It was a good thing his family had conspired to keep him from proposing to the woman today. That would not have been fair to her. He may have decided to avoid love, but she likely had not. She might not expect it; she might be willing to forgo it to avoid marrying the neighbor; but chances were she still hoped for it.

There was no rush. He would talk to Mama and see if she planned to take Miss Wharton under her wing. Surely the Duchess of Love could find her a better match, but if not, he could propose to her once the Season was over. A few months wouldn't make that much difference. He—

He frowned. Had he heard a noise in his bedroom? Oh, God, not Reggie. That was all he needed. It would be infernally difficult to return the cat's plunder with everyone getting ready for the ball and the new guests all over the castle.

He strode into his bedroom. Just as he suspected, Reggie was sitting on his bed—on his pillow, no less—and he had something under him.

"Damn it, Reggie, what have you got there?" He came closer. "At least it's white—it can't be Ellie's drawers."

Did he hear an odd little whimper? He stared at Reggie who just blinked, catlike, back at him.

It must have been his imagination. "So, are you going to give it to me easily, or will I need to fight you for it?"

Reggie was willing to surrender his prize without a battle. He sat up and licked his paws, allowing Ned to pluck the object off the pillow. It was a long, white, lady's glove. Even he could tell it was of very high quality. "Oh, damn, Reggie. I'll wager one of Mama's female guests is looking frantically for this right now."

Was that another whimper he heard? Reggie had now moved on to washing his flank; it seemed unlikely he would have made the sound.

Ned rubbed his forehead. It was a good thing the house party was over tonight. Clearly, he was losing his precarious grip on reality. First thing in the morning, he'd leave for the blessed peace and quiet of Linden Hall. "Have you purloined anything else, Reggie?"

Reggie abandoned his ablutions and grinned—not that cats could grin, of course, but it certainly looked like a grin to Ned. Then he jumped down and ran under the bed—only to come scooting back out, hissing.

"What the hell do you have under there, Reggie?" Ned grabbed an unlit candlestick as a weapon and got down on his hands and knees to peer into the shadowy space. Two eyes peered back at him—eyes in a very familiar face. "Ellie? What are you doing under there?"

"H-hiding."

"From whom?" The only person he could even begin to imagine threatening Ellie was Percy, but Percy wasn't at the castle any longer.

"From y-you."

"What? You're hiding from me under my bed?" That made no sense at all. "Come out of there."

"No, that's quite all right. I'll just stay here until you leave."

Perhaps he wasn't the only one headed to Bedlam. "Don't be ridiculous; you can't stay under my bed. Come along now." He backed away to give Ellie room. Nothing happened. "I'll drag you out, you know, if I have to."

He heard a small growl—he looked over his shoulder, but Reggie had gone, so the noise must have come from Ellie—and then he saw movement. A slim, elegant arm with a small, very red, puffed sleeve emerged followed by a lovely neck and back somewhat obscured by glossy, chestnut hair and a red skirt pulled tight to outline a narrow waist and flaring hips.

"Ellie?" He'd never seen Ellie dressed this way. Where were the dull colors, long sleeves, and high necks?

"Yes, yes, I'm coming. It's not the easiest thing in the

world, you know, to crawl out from under a bed with a ball gown on."

"I can't say I've ever tried it." He would have laughed, but his mouth had suddenly gone dry. Now her skirt had ridden up to expose her shapely calf and ankle. He knew he shouldn't stare, but his self-control had departed with Reggie.

He stood as the last of her finally emerged. "Let me help you up," he said, extending a hand.

"Thank you." She grasped his fingers and struggled to get up, tugging on her skirts to free her feet and then leaning heavily on the bed. When she was finally upright, she looked at him—

"Eep!" Her free hand—the one in a long, white glove— flew up to cover her mouth as her eyes widened and her face flushed to match her dress.

What the hell? He looked down . . .

Zeus, he'd forgotten he was almost naked. Worse, his drawers, the only scrap of fabric on his person, were completely insufficient to restrain his ardent admiration of Ellie's new dress—they bulged alarmingly.

He dropped her hand, lunged for his banyan hanging on the hook behind the door, and thrust his arms into its sleeves. He fumbled to close the clasps down the front—she was still staring at him.

Well, he could return the favor; in fact, he felt quite unable to take his eyes off her.

"Why are you in my room?" Damn, that sounded harsh, but he couldn't help it. His mouth was still infernally dry.

"Ah." She was staring at his throat as if she'd never seen a man's neck before. She probably hadn't. Men's necks were generally wrapped in cravats.

He'd never seen her neck, either, since she chose to hide it with her dresses. He moistened his lips as his eyes traced the delicate line of her throat and collarbone. Was her skin as soft as it looked?

"I-I, er . . ." She closed her eyes and took a deep breath—which made her bodice rise delightfully.

He would never have guessed Ellie had such a slim but well-rounded figure. He'd very much like to see it in far more detail.

No. He would not allow lust to cloud his mind. He searched for some self-control.

Unfortunately, his body was too busy wallowing in desire after so many years of drought to care about self-control.

"I *mean*," Ellie said, her eyes still closed, "isn't it obvious? Reggie stole my glove, and I came to get it back."

"That doesn't explain why you were lurking under my bed." The damn lust made him sound accusatory, even though that was the farthest thought from his mind.

Hell, the only thought in his poor brain box was to lay Ellie down on his bed so conveniently situated behind her and make mad, passionate love to her.

Please God, he had to keep his wits about him. He'd forsworn love, remember? Loving Ellie would bring him too much pain.

And she didn't love him.

His eyes slid over her hair and neck and breasts. Had she actually said that in so many words? Ash and Jack both insisted she *did* love him.

It made little difference. His body had cut all connection to his better judgment. Apparently standing virtually naked with a painfully aroused cock in a bedroom with a beautiful woman—with *Ellie*—did that to him. Try as he might, he could not douse the fire consuming him—only one action would accomplish that.

Not that he had any intention of doing *that* tonight, of

course. Much as he felt like an animal at the moment, he wasn't truly a beast.

Ellie opened her eyes to glare at him. "What, do you think I was planning on leaping out and ravishing you?"

His cock jumped, and he thought he was going to explode. Could she see the need in his eyes? No, probably not. The light was behind him; his face was in shadow.

Her eyes widened when she realized what she'd said, and she slapped her hands over her mouth. "I didn't mean that."

Pity. He would like to be ravished by this new, very alluring Ellie.

Her face was redder than her dress. "I-I was just startled when I heard your d-door close. I didn't think, I just . . ." She swallowed; he watched her throat flex. "It didn't seem like it would be a good idea to be found in your room, though of course no one who knows us would think anything of it." Her voice took on a slightly sharp, sad edge. "I mean I'm only Ellie, after all."

"Only Ellie?" *He* could hear the need in his voice.

He should check the corridor to be certain no one was watching and then send her scurrying back to her room. Surely that was what a gentleman would do. He could talk to her later when they were both—well, when he—was properly dressed.

"Yes." She turned to snatch her glove off his bed. "And since I've now recovered what I came for, I will go back to my room to tidy up. My hair is falling down, and I'm sure I have covered this lovely new dress in dust."

Her hair *was* falling down; he wanted to pluck out her remaining pins and see how long it was. He wanted to run his fingers through it and bury his face in it.

She stepped toward him, but he didn't move.

"You are blocking the door, Lord Edward."

He wouldn't touch her, not yet. He was afraid if he did,

he would lose the slim—very slim—hold he still had on his animal instincts. "Did you mean what you said in the library yesterday?"

Panic flashed across her face, and then her chin tilted up. "About what?"

"About not marrying me even if I were the last man on earth."

"Oh." She cleared her throat. "I may have overstated the case somewhat." She looked down at the glove in her hands—she was running it through her fingers over and over. "And I did mean to beg your pardon for"—she cleared her throat again—"for throwing brandy in your face. That was not well done at all. I don't know what came over me."

"I suspect you were furious at the coxcomb who'd made such a mull of his marriage proposal." He shook his head. Even he couldn't believe now how inept and, yes, insulting he'd been. "I should be the one begging pardon."

She bit her lip and glanced up at him. "Yes, well, let's agree to forgive each other, shall we? Then we can return to our comfortable, old friendship." She started to edge to one side as if she planned to dart around him.

He couldn't let her go now, not with so much left unresolved. He was to leave Greycliffe in the morning; he had to know if he had any chance with her. He put his hand out to touch her arm.

She froze, eyes widening. She looked a bit like a frightened rabbit, but she didn't try to pull away or shake off his hold—not that he *was* holding her. His fingers just lay lightly on her gloveless forearm, on her smooth, soft, warm skin.

He couldn't help himself. His fingers moved of their own volition up and down, never straying higher than her elbow—and then finally clasping her hand and bringing it to his lips. Desire burned in him like a fever. "I don't want to go back to our old, comfortable friendship, Ellie," he said before brushing her knuckles with his mouth.

Ellie couldn't breathe. The glove she'd been holding dropped from her fingers. She'd felt so many things in such a short time: panic, mortification, shock, and something else. Something dark and confusing.

She'd meant to dash back to the safety of her room, but now . . . The touch of Ned's lips flashed like lightning down her arm to lodge in her heart—and an organ somewhat lower in her body. Heat radiated from both locations. She couldn't move. "Y-you don't?"

"No." His eyes, hot and intent, held hers.

When she'd seen him look at Cicely back before they'd wed, she'd thought she'd seen yearning or even worship in his eyes, and she'd dreamt that one day he'd look at her that way. But this . . . this was far more carnal. It made her uncomfortable, as if her skin was too tight and sensitive.

Was this the way a man looked who was bent on seduction?

She swallowed. "What *do* you want?"

"You." His eyes widened briefly as if the answer surprised him as much as it did her, and then his lips slid into a slow smile.

Definitely seduction. She could think of only one cause for this sudden change in attitude. "Because of my new dress?"

Mama had said on more than one occasion that men were far more influenced by their senses than women. Ellie hadn't believed her, but perhaps she should have.

If she'd worn that other red dress to Ned's and Cicely's betrothal ball, *would* Ned have chosen her instead?

No. There'd been far more to Ned's love for Cicely than just physical attraction.

Could there be more between her and Ned as well?

"The dress is certainly very nice," Ned was saying as he traced the line of her bodice, making her nipples tighten into shockingly hard peaks. "But it's not the dress that I want."

But if she couldn't have more—if she couldn't have marriage and happily ever after—would she take seduction?

Of course not! It was wrong. Sinful. Scandalous. Well-bred young ladies—or even old spinsters—didn't participate in such, er, activities . . . whatever they were.

But she'd seen Ned's broad chest and shoulders, his muscular arms. She knew they were there under his banyan. And she felt this hot, throbbing *need*.

She'd just resigned herself to being a maiden aunt, so why not a maiden with some experience? No one need know besides Ned; surely he would keep her secret. And while there was a chance their encounter might result in a child—fear and yearning twisted into a tight knot in her heart—one time would not be so dangerous. It had taken her sisters many tries to become enceinte with their first children.

This was Ned, the only man she'd ever loved. Shocking as it was to admit it, she wanted him so badly she was prepared to do anything to have him even just once.

She'd spent years being a quiet, proper woman, and she had years ahead of her playing that same role. This was her one chance to be wildly improper and let her body rule her mind.

Ned bent his head to whisper by her ear. "No, it's not the dress I want, it's the woman in the dress."

Her need exploded, and the odd, damp place between her legs throbbed to the beat of her heart. The room suddenly felt too warm. Ridiculous! It was February in Greycliffe

Castle, for God's sake. She'd wanted her shawl earlier when she'd been hiding under Ned's bed, but now she wanted to shed her lovely dress and her stays and her chemise to be completely, wonderfully naked.

The thought that Ned was virtually naked under his banyan was torturing her. She wanted to see his chest and shoulders again; she wanted to touch him; she wanted to *feel* him, to put her skin against his. She wanted to experience what her sisters had whispered and giggled about all these years while throwing her pitying looks. She might never be able to acknowledge that she knew what they were talking about, but that didn't matter. She would have this memory to hold in her heart for as long as she lived.

It was the last day of the party, and she was feeling reckless. They weren't expected downstairs for a little while. She would do what she wanted just this once.

"And I want you," she said, reaching for the top clasp on his banyan.

His fingers caught hers—he was frowning. Damn it, Lord Worry—the rational, careful, sensible Ned—had returned. "What are you doing?"

"Isn't it obvious?" She tried to free her hands. "I'm attempting to open these clasps."

He made an odd sound, something between a laugh and a groan. "Well, yes, but—" An annoyingly determined look settled over his features. "That is not a good idea. You should go back to your room."

"I don't want to go back to my room." Blast it, it would help if she had the faintest idea how to seduce someone. At least Ned wasn't dragging her to the door yet.

"What if someone comes in and finds us?"

Fear briefly cleared the lust from her mind. Ned was right. If someone found her here with him, the scandal would be enormous. The duchess would have her thrown out of the castle; Mama would lock her in her room forever. It would be far worse than the last time she'd worn a red dress—

Oh, no. This was not the same at all. "You closed your door, didn't you? I distinctly remember hearing a door shut."

"Well, yes."

"So then we're safe. No one will come in without your permission, even the servants, and they are too busy with the guests arriving to bother you anyway." She smiled. "And if the unthinkable happens, I'll just hide under your bed." Her smile widened. "I've done it before."

Ned's grasp had loosened so she was able to jerk her hands free and get the top clasp open before he stopped her again.

"Ellie, you don't know what you're doing."

She hoped she heard a hint of desperation in his voice. "Then why don't you show me?"

He laughed a bit breathlessly. "That would not be a good idea. Now—"

"Why?" Damn it, Mama—well, perhaps not Mama. That was an unsettling thought. But *someone* should have given her lessons in seduction along with instruction in needlework and household management. Surely this aspect of a man's well-being was as important as having well-kept linens and palatable meals. "Why wouldn't it be a good idea? It seems like an excellent idea to me."

His chin hardened—that was always a bad sign. Once Ned made up his mind, he was almost impossible to persuade. "It is *not* a good idea. I might do something I'd regret later."

Oh, hell, maybe the direct approach was best. "Ned, I *want* you to do something you'll regret later—well, I hope you won't regret it, actually, but I'm sure it's the thing that you think you will." She looked him in the eye. "I want you to take me over to that bed and do whatever it is men do with women in such situations."

His eyes widened with shock, but she didn't care. This was her best chance. She'd be strong and decisive. If she failed, it wasn't going to be from lack of trying. "And I want you to do it *right now*."

She took advantage of his momentary surprise to open three more clasps before he stopped her again.

"I can't." He sounded desperate.

"You *can*." She not only sounded desperate, she *was* desperate.

He glared at her, but she could see his desire battling his conscience. "You haven't agreed to marry me. I won't do anything unless you do."

She didn't want to trap him into something he didn't want—well, at least not something as permanent as marriage. "Come, Ned, I'm not that naïve. You don't ask all the women you take to bed to marry you, do you?"

He flushed a brighter red than her dress, and his glare turned to a scowl. "Yes, I do."

"Oh." Her mouth dropped open. She shouldn't be shocked—she'd have sworn Ned had never been a rake—but she'd always heard men would climb into bed with any woman who offered them the slightest invitation. So if Ned had never . . . that meant Cicely had been the only . . .

He stepped away from her, giving her clear passage to leave. "If you'd hoped for a more experienced husband, you will have to keep looking."

"No, I—"

"I'm sure Mama will be happy to take you to London for the Season." Ned looked away from her. "You should be able to find plenty of men there who are far more skilled in the amatory arts than I."

This was ridiculous. Now she had to deal with Ned's

bruised male sensibilities. Why would he think she'd want to associate with some unknown libertine?

"Damn it, Ned, at least you've done it more times than I have." She crossed her arms to keep from shaking him. "Whatever 'it' is. I do wish you would stop stalling and show me."

He crossed his arms as well. "Only if you swear you'll marry me."

She raised her chin. "I'll marry you only if you swear our marriage will not be some dreadful marriage of convenience. I expect to sleep in the same bed as you and to have you fulfill your marital duties regularly."

Ned frowned. "I'm not sure you should insist on that. You've admitted you don't know what those duties are. You may find you don't like them."

Did he sound a little worried? Perhaps she should be cautious. "Very well, I won't insist on that point now, but I reserve my right to insist later." She grinned at him, hoping her nerves weren't glaringly obvious. "If you will get on with it, I should be able to make a decision shortly."

He didn't grin back. "The first time for a woman can be, ah, somewhat uncomfortable, Ellie."

"Uncomfortable?"

"When the maidenhead tears, it can hurt." He cleared his throat. "There can be bleeding."

This was a bit alarming, but it couldn't be worse than childbirth—not that she would say that to Ned. Rather than making him laugh, it would likely cause him to run from the room. "Very well, consider me warned." She smiled hopefully at him. "Now will you ruin me?"

That was the wrong thing to say as well. His face got that damn mulish look again.

"No. I don't know what I was thinking. We shall wait until we are married." He started toward the door to his sitting room. "That's the proper thing to do—that's what your parents and mine expect. We'll announce our engagement tonight, and then I'll get a special license."

"I don't want to wait." She grabbed the back of his banyan before he could escape. "I promised to marry you; I thought you promised to ruin me."

"Ellie." He turned; she danced out of his reach.

If he took hold of her, her hope of seduction would be over. He'd walk her chastely out of his room and close the door behind her—likely lock it as well. And while she'd have the pleasure of a betrothal announcement at dinner and at the ball, she wanted more. She wanted—needed—something to relieve this odd tension that was so strong it almost made the hairs on her arms stand on end.

She not only didn't want to wait—she couldn't. But how could she get Ned to cooperate?

"Ellie, be reasonable."

"No." If Mama was right and men were ruled by their senses, perhaps she could appeal to Ned on that level. He certainly had liked her new dress.

She backed toward his bed, shedding hairpins as she went, watching his eyes follow her hands. His desire was warring with his conscience again—she could see it in his eyes.

"I can't wait, Ned. I've waited so many years already. I fell in love with you when I was nine. You were a boy—you didn't care or even notice. And then you fell in love with Cicely."

"Ellie."

She heard the pain in his voice, but she couldn't stop. "Please believe me, Ned. I never wanted anything bad for Cicely. She was my friend, and I mourned her death. But I never stopped loving you—I never stopped *wanting* you." She pulled out the last hairpin and shook her head. Her hair tumbled over her shoulders to her waist.

"Ever since your year of mourning was over, I kept

hoping you'd see me as more than a friend." She peeled off the one glove she was wearing.

"Ellie, I—"

"I waited and hoped, but I didn't *do* anything. I was a coward, Ned." She kicked off her slippers.

"No, you—"

He was watching her hair. She would give him something else to look at.

"I *was*, but I'm not now." She put one leg up on the bed-steps. "I don't just want a husband, Ned. I've never just wanted a husband. I've always wanted you." She started sliding her gown up her leg.

"Ellie, you shouldn't do that." Ned's eyes were riveted on her hands as they inched up toward her knee.

"Do you know what you do to me, Ned? Do you have any idea what I'm feeling right now?" Her fingers reached her garter.

"Uh." He swallowed. He might be panting just a little.

She smiled as she untied her garter and dropped it on the floor. Then she slid her stocking slowly down to her ankle and over her foot. Yes, he was definitely panting.

"I'm aching, Ned." She peeled her other stocking off and dropped it next to its mate. "My heart aches for you, but another part of me does, too." She turned to face him. "It's very hot and w-wet and needy."

Ned groaned and closed his eyes. He was still fighting, blast it. What more could she do?

"Please, Ned? I'll beg if I have to."

That did it. He was across the room in one stride. "Ellie," he said. He looked—he sounded—like he was in pain. And then his mouth came down on hers.

Chapter 20

Never be bashful in bed.
—Venus's Love Notes

Ned's mouth crushed hers against her teeth; she made a small sound of protest, and he gentled the pressure at once.

Mmm, that was better. His lips brushed back and forth, making her lips feel swollen and tingly. Her heart stuttered, and the damp place between her legs pulsed. She arched into him, pressing against a very satisfying bulge—until he shifted his hips back.

That would never do. She tried to tug him closer—he resisted her efforts, damn it. Was he still trying to protect her? She didn't want to be protected.

She put her hands on his chest and pushed.

She had to push again to get his attention.

"W-what?" He blinked down at her.

"Time to get this lovely banyan off," she said, reaching for the clasps. She wanted to see—and feel—his chest and shoulders.

His hands covered hers. "No."

She tried to wiggle her fingers free. "What do you mean, no? I thought you'd agreed to ruin me."

He frowned. "Will you stop saying that? I agreed to make love to you, but we don't have to remove our clothing to do that." He cleared his throat. "In fact, perhaps it would be best if we didn't."

She frowned at him. "Best for whom?"

"For you." He cleared his throat again. "I believe it is customary for delicately-bred women not to be subjected to any sort of nakedness during the, er, lovemaking process."

She gaped at him. "You're jesting, aren't you?"

His brows slanted down. "I am not."

"Well, you should be." She went back to trying to open his clasps; he stopped her again.

"Ellie, I think you should allow yourself to be guided by me. I don't want your sensibilities overwhelmed."

She leaned back and looked him in the eye. "Ned, I am twenty-six years old. I may be a virgin, but I'm not some young, frightened miss. I've dreamt of this moment—well, not in detail, of course, since I am sadly lacking in experience—"

"There is nothing sad about that! Of course you don't have experience. You're the unmarried daughter of a vicar."

"Yes, well, all right, I'll grant you that. But I am now going to get some experience, and I mean to get as much as I can. I *wish* to have my sensibilities overwhelmed." She grinned at him. "So please stop trying to protect me."

"But, Ellie, I'm not sure—"

She covered his mouth with her fingers. "*I'm* sure." She moved her hand to cup his jaw. "I promise to ask for my vinaigrette if I feel a swoon coming on."

That got him to laugh. "Very well, but don't say I didn't warn you."

"I won't." She made quick work of his clasps. "And

think how wonderfully superior you'll feel when I finally recover from my faint, and you can say you told me so."

She pushed open the banyan and put her palms flat against the soft brown hair that covered his chest. She heard—and felt—him take a sharp breath; she felt his need beating against her hands with the beat of his heart. It was both frightening and exciting.

"Or perhaps you will be the one swooning," she said.

He laughed breathlessly. "Perhaps."

She ran her hands up over his chest, over the hard smooth muscles, to push the banyan off his shoulders. She couldn't quite manage to get it off his arms, so he helped. While he was occupied with that, she reached for the very interesting protuberance in the front of his drawers.

"Don't touch, Ellie."

"Why? Does it hurt?" It certainly looked like it might. "It's a wonder you can get your breeches on."

"Yes, it hurts." Ned finally parted company with his banyan and dropped it on the floor. "And it is all your fault that I am in such a state."

"My fault?" Ellie watched the thing bounce around. "I don't see how it can be my fault."

"You'll understand shortly. Now we need to get you out of that lovely dress, since you insist on doing this naked. Turn around."

"Very well." She turned to face the bed, presenting Ned with her back.

His fingers skimmed over her arms and shoulders, and she shivered in anticipation.

"Damn fasteners," he muttered. "They're so blasted tiny."

"Careful—don't tear anything." She bit her lip. She shouldn't have said that, but she didn't want the dress ruined, especially as she still needed to wear it tonight.

"Would you rather go downstairs now than risk your gown to my clumsy fingers?"

"No." She glanced back at him—and her mouth went dry at the sight of his neck and shoulders. She turned to face the bed again. "Tear away."

He chuckled. "I would hate to destroy this lovely gown. Let me see . . . ah, yes. Here we go."

It felt as if it took forever. Ned's fingers brushed and fumbled all over her body, until she was so weak with need she had to brace herself with her arms on the mattress. Finally the red dress and her stays lay draped over a chair. She started to turn toward him, but he stopped her, his hands sliding slowly up her legs, higher and higher, over her calves and knees and thighs. They lingered on her derriere and then moved up until she raised her arms and he pulled the chemise off her completely. She was finally naked except for the strand of pearls around her neck.

But her skin wasn't uncovered for long. Ned pressed against her back, one hand cupping her breast, the other tangling in her nether curls and curving over the aching place between her legs. He pulled her against him and nuzzled her neck.

She was trapped between his hands and his chest. The torture was exquisite.

"Perhaps you are right about this nakedness," he murmured, his breath tickling her ear.

"But you aren't naked." She pressed her derriere more tightly against his interesting bulge, still shielded from her by his drawers.

"You think I should remedy that situation?"

"Yes. Definitely. Immediately."

"Very well." He dropped his hands. "If you will give me a moment—"

"Let me." She spun around and grabbed his waistband,

untying its laces and pushing it down . . . "Oh." She cradled the long, thick organ that sprang free. It was smooth and hard and warm—and moved as if it had a life of its own.

Ned made an odd sound—part laugh, part groan—and wrapped his arms around her, pressing her up against him from breasts to knees. "I think," he whispered, "that if you wish to complete your ruination, it's time to go to bed."

She was very, very eager to be thoroughly ruined. "That sounds like an excellent idea."

"Except"—Ned stared down at her, serious now—"you will not really be ruined. If you climb into my bed and let me come into your body, Ellie, you are accepting me as your husband and I am taking you as my wife. We may be anticipating our public vows, but the promises we make to each other here tonight are as binding as if we'd spoken them in church before our parents, our families, and our friends—at least to me."

She was serious, too. "So this is not to be some sensible, practical union?"

He laughed. "I did make mice feet of that damn conversation—I dare not call it a proposal—we had in the library, didn't I? No, our union may be sensible—I'm sure Mama and Father and my brothers think so. And I suppose it is practical. But it is so much more than that." He cupped her face in his hands. "I love you, Ellie. I'd given up hope of ever loving again—no, I'll admit I was terrified of it—and now I find myself so filled with love"—he grinned at her—"I may explode if we don't do something about it very soon. So—will you marry me?"

She, too, was on the verge of bursting with her love for him. "Yes. Yes, of course I will marry you, Ned."

She'd barely got the words out before he'd torn aside the coverlet and lifted her onto his bed. "Then let us proceed with the ceremony."

* * *

Ned knelt next to Ellie and stared down at her. She'd stretched herself out on her back, arms wide, waves of brown hair flowing over his pillow, completely naked except for the single strand of milky white pearls around her neck. Her flawless skin almost glowed against his dull sheets. His heart—and another organ—clenched with love and desire.

She was perfect. She was all that he could ever wish for—his past, his present, and his future.

But what if they made a child tonight? What if in nine month's time—

His cock drooped in despair. How could he risk losing her? He couldn't.

"Are you worrying, Ned?" She gently touched his softened member. "You look . . . sad."

He felt the feather-light touch as though it were a spark. He saw Ellie's eyes widen as his cock stirred, if only feebly. He laughed, but he felt more like crying.

"Perhaps I *am* worrying a little." He cleared his throat. Why be evasive? Ellie knew him too well. "Or a lot."

"Don't." She rested her hand on his thigh. Just having her fingers nearby gave his poor organ hope. "I want children, Ned. I want them so much I was willing to consider marrying a man just to be a mother." She smiled, shaking his thigh slightly, enough to make his hopeful cock move. "But I would much, much rather have your children."

Now her fingers were stroking his thigh, coming very, very close to—

He jerked his attention back to the matter at hand—no, poor choice of words. He forced himself to remember the greater concern, to think with his big, not his little, head.

"But what if you—" He couldn't say it. "What if something bad happens?"

Ellie sat up. His eyes dropped to watch her lovely, small breasts sway with the motion. He might be concerned for her safety, but he *was* male, damn it.

"Ned." She touched his jaw, and he raised his gaze to meet hers. "I can't promise you that nothing bad will happen. Life's not like that. But I'm willing to take the risk. I *want* to so I can hold my child—our child—in my arms."

His cock leapt at that thought, eager to be about the business of giving her what she wanted.

He frowned, ignoring as best he could his thoughtless organ. "I want that, too, Ellie, but I want you more. I love you too much. If I were to lose you, if I'm ever forced to watch you die as I watched Cicely, unable to do a thing to save you—" His throat closed up, and his unruly member deflated to lie cowed and limp between his thighs. Nothing could resurrect the poor thing now.

He was wrong.

Ellie's face hardened with determination. "I love you, too, Ned. I would do anything for you, but I won't let you hide from life."

"You don't understand. You *can't* understand."

"Maybe I can't. But I do understand I spent far too long hoping and wanting and not *doing* anything to make what I wanted happen." She brushed her lips over his. "I'm not going to make that mistake again. You're not leaving this bed until I've thoroughly ravished you."

That made him laugh. "Don't be—Ellie!"

She'd bent her head to kiss his poor organ. He should shove her away. He put his hands on her head to do so, but somehow his fingers got trapped in the silky depths of her hair and ended up holding her where she was instead.

"Does that hurt?" Her whispered words caressed his growing flesh.

"No, but you shouldn't—ohh."

Her tongue flicked out over him.

He couldn't help it—he spread his thighs to give her more room. He tried to remember why she shouldn't do this, but the sensation of her wet tongue stroking him scrambled all coherent thought.

"I'm sure this isn't—" He bit back a moan. "What you're doing isn't p-proper."

She paused and he almost cried. "Don't you like it?" She brushed a kiss over his aching flesh. "This part of you certainly seems to. It's grown large and hard again."

"Ahh . . ."

"I think this will be easier if you lie down." She moved around on the bed so she could push him back onto the pillows.

He was stronger than she; he could easily resist . . . but he obligingly did as she wanted. His little head was in complete control now, standing up eagerly, waiting to see what Ellie would do next.

What she did was straddle his legs, her long hair teasing his skin, breasts dangling over his thighs. And then her mouth went around—

"Ahh." His hips jerked up. *"Ohh."*

He was done with thinking and worrying. Four years of grief and fear and guilt and deprivation flooded him, mixing with overwhelming love.

"Ellie!"

She looked up. "What is it this time?"

"I-I can't wait any longer." It was hard to get the words out.

"Wait?" She looked puzzled. "Wait for what?"

"This." He pulled her up as gently as he could and pushed her onto her back. Then he came above her, trying to maintain some control over his relentless need. "I'm afraid this is going to be quicker than it should be."

Ellie grinned at him. "It can't be quick enough for me. I've waited all my life for you; I don't want to wait a minute more."

He frowned. "I may not be able to be gentle."

"I don't want gentle." She tugged on his head. "Just do it, will you?"

She did sound rather anxious.

He kissed her breast and then licked her nipple. She moaned, and her legs spread wide. That was encouraging. He latched on and sucked, and her head tossed on the pillow, her hands grabbing his hair and holding him to her breast.

He slid his fingers down over her belly to the juncture of her thighs . . . Thank God—if God didn't mind being thanked in such a situation, though Ned did mean it in a most reverential way—she was wet and ready for him. Her hips arched up at his touch, and she rubbed against him. Perhaps she was right—he couldn't be quick enough.

He left her breast and kissed his way down her body, urged along by her lovely whimpers of desire. Her hot, musky scent surrounded him; he slid a cautious tongue into her cleft . . .

"Oh, Ned, oh, oh, please, now, I can't . . . wait . . ." Her hips twisted frantically.

It clearly would be cruel to deny her what she wanted so desperately. And what he wanted, too.

He rose up over her again and slid into her tight, warm body. He tried to be careful. He knew he had to be gentle— he didn't want to frighten or disgust her as he had Cicely. He wanted to show her how much he loved her, but he felt a tidal wave of need battering his control.

He flexed his hips and broke through her maidenhead— and heard her gasp in pain. Damn.

He paused, deflating slightly. "I'm sorry."

She grunted. "Are you done?"

He should be, but the smell and feel of her was too much. He was swelling again. And she did say she wanted children. "Not quite."

He moved as slowly as he could. In and out. In and out.

"Oh." She stiffened a little. "Oh."

Was he hurting her? He stopped though his body screamed go.

Fortunately, Ellie agreed with his body.

"Don't. Stop." She wiggled under him, grabbing his hips. "Go. Faster. Harder."

He flexed his hips again. He tried to pay close attention to her reactions, but he was drowning in his own response. He should . . . ah.

She whimpered and dug her fingers into his arse. "Yes. Oh." Her body grew tighter; she made a desperate little sound—and then her legs jerked. She shuddered, and he felt her pulse around him.

It was too much. He pulled back and thrust deep one last time, spilling his life and his love into Ellie.

He was home.

Ellie wrapped her arms tightly around Ned. She could barely breathe, but she didn't care. She wanted to stay this way forever, Ned deep inside her, his weight pressing her into the mattress. She felt gloriously married, even if law and church might not yet consider her so.

He turned his head to kiss her cheek. "I'm too heavy for you." He sounded as relaxed and dazed as she felt.

"Mmm." He was, but she didn't want to say so.

He lifted himself off her, and she felt chilled and empty until he gathered her up against his side. She rested her cheek on his shoulder and draped her arm across his chest while he grabbed the coverlet with his free hand and pulled it over them.

He kissed the top of her head. "Did I hurt you?"

She heard a thread of worry in his voice. "No." She should be honest. "Well, maybe a very little at the beginning, but it was worth it." She tightened her hold on him and kissed his chest. "It was wonderful . . . better than I could ever have imagined. I want to do it all again."

He chuckled. "Not now. You are likely rather sore."

She moved her legs. "Perhaps a little." But it was a good soreness.

Had they made a child? She wouldn't mention it; Ned would start worrying. She slipped a hand over her belly. She hoped they had, but she'd be happy—very happy—to keep trying.

Ned's fingers combed through her hair. "Next time I promise we'll go slower. I'm afraid I was a bit out of control."

She grinned at him. "You didn't hear me complaining, did you?"

"No." He gave her a slow kiss. "You were a bit out of control yourself. I liked that."

She kissed him back. "I didn't offend your notions of propriety?"

"Not too much." He frowned. "But speaking of propriety, which is a bit ludicrous considering I'm lying naked in bed next to a gently-bred virgin—"

"I'm not a virgin any longer!"

He gave her a quelling look. "—the daughter of the vicar who is not—yet!—my wife, we should get dressed and go downstairs. I expect everyone will have noticed our absence."

"But no one will remark on it. I'm just Ellie, your old friend, remember?" She slipped her hand down his chest and belly, but he caught her before she could reach her goal.

"You are not going to tempt me to more misbehavior."

"Are you sure? I'd much rather stay here with you than go downstairs."

"As would I, but we are going downstairs." He sat up and swung his legs off the bed. "We will get dressed and—oh, damn."

"What is it?" Ellie sat up, too, and pressed herself against Ned's back, slipping her fingers around to—

He grabbed her hands. "*Will* you behave yourself?"

"Must I?"

"Yes. We need to get moving. I should at least offer your father the courtesy of a private meeting to ask for your hand in marriage before announcing our betrothal." He glanced at the clock on the mantel. "If we hurry, maybe I can have a word with him before dinner."

"Or after dinner."

"Oh, no," he said, getting out of bed. "I'm quite sure once everyone sees us, it will be very apparent we need to marry immediately."

"I don't know why." Ellie admired Ned's muscled arse as he strode over to his clothes press.

"Because I am not a lady's maid, and I don't believe we want to call Mary in to get you dressed again." He pulled on a new pair of drawers, scooped her chemise off the floor, and walked back to her. "And stop staring at me as if I'm some special ice you want to lick all—" He closed his eyes as if he were in pain, and she saw the lovely bulge appear in his drawers again. She reached for it—and he dodged her hand.

"Ellie, I love you, I want you, you are the dream I hadn't the courage to dream, but we *have* to go downstairs now."

"Oh, very well." She climbed down from the bed, took her chemise, and slipped it over her head. "But will you promise me I can come back here to sleep tonight?"

"No." He ran his hand through his hair. "I don't know.

We'll see." He pulled on his shirt and breeches and then helped her lace up her stays.

She turned to face him as soon as he was done, and wrapped her arms tightly around him. "I love you, Ned."

He hugged her back. "And I love you, Ellie. Thank you for having the courage to make me see it." He stepped back. "And now we really, really have to go downstairs."

Chapter 21

Love conquers all.

—Venus's Love Notes

"Do you have any idea where Ellie is, your grace?" Constance Bowman asked Venus. Ellie's mother looked around the drawing room again. "I stopped by her chamber when we arrived, but no one was there—except for Sir Reginald playing with a scrap of red silk. I do hope that wasn't Ellie's Norwich shawl."

Venus smiled. "I'm sure it wasn't."

"You are probably right. It didn't look large enough, and I would think Ellie would be wearing her shawl—wherever she is." She glanced at the door and then surveyed the room once more. "It must be almost time for dinner."

"I'm sure she'll be down shortly." Venus raised her brows significantly. "I notice Ned is missing as well."

Constance's eyes brightened. "You don't think they're together?"

"One can hope." And pray, but Venus had discovered

over the years that the Almighty didn't respond to prayers
as promptly or as literally as she'd like. In her opinion, it
was much more efficient to consult a matchmaker for
matters of the heart—not that anyone would say she'd been
at all efficient in settling her sons' matrimonial issues.

Constance sighed and shook her head. "If they are, they
are probably sitting sedately in the library discussing the
weather. Oh, Venus, I don't know what I'm going to do with
that girl. I'd really hoped this year she'd put aside her infatuation with Ned and find a husband, but it looks to me as if
all the men you invited for her have chosen other women—
just like every other year."

Venus patted Constance's arm. "Don't worry. I have a
very strong suspicion that my son and your daughter are not
merely discussing the weather."

Hope bloomed on Constance's face again, though it was
clear she was struggling to keep it in check. "Why would
you think that?"

"Mother's intuition. I've been watching them during this
party." She bent her head closer to Constance's. "*And* I had
Mary make up a red silk dress much like the one you described to me."

Constance's jaw dropped. "You actually got Ellie to wear
something flattering? I've been trying to do that for years,
as well you know."

Venus chuckled. "She didn't have any choice. I, er, persuaded Reggie to ruin that rag she'd brought."

"Well, thank Reggie for me. I *tried* to dissuade her from
choosing that fabric, but she was adamant. And between
you and me, poor Mrs. Wilkins, our dressmaker, has come
to me in tears more than once after fitting Ellie. Frankly, I
think Ellie's been determined to make herself look a fright
ever since Ned married Cicely." Constance sighed. "I
thought I was doing the right thing when I refused to let her

attend their betrothal ball in that shocking red dress, but now I'm not so sure."

"And, as I've told you many times, there's no point in worrying about it—it's water over the dam. Ned was dreadfully in love with Cicely. I'd wager Ellie could have shown up naked, and he wouldn't have noticed."

"Venus! Ellie would never do anything so shocking!"

"No, I know that, but I'm happy to report she was showing a bit more of her old, strong-willed self during this party. I was quite encouraged."

Constance looked doubtful. "I can't imagine Ned wishes to wed a termagant."

"I wouldn't say Ellie was as bad as that, but I do believe Ned needs someone to upend his carefully ordered life and make him feel daring and willing to risk something again." Venus shrugged. "And if I'm wrong and Ellie and Ned don't make a match of it, you know I stand ready to take her up to London for the Season. Don't worry—I'll find her a good husband." Though Venus really, really hoped that would not be necessary.

"But she's *twenty-six*." Constance was actually wringing her hands. "She could hardly be more firmly on the shelf."

"Nonsense. She'll do fine, if it comes to that. Contrary to what you hear in the country, London is not populated only by coxcombs and dandies. There are a few sensible, discerning men still available." She smiled in what she hoped was an encouraging fashion. Where the hell *were* Ned and Ellie? "But let us hope my son proves to be sensible and discerning himself."

"Looking for our second son?" Drew asked, coming up to them. "Good evening, Mrs. Bowman."

"Good evening, your grace. It's lovely to be here as always."

"And it will be even lovelier tomorrow when our London

guests have departed, and we can be at peace again," Drew said, smiling at Constance. "Though I believe we have some more excitement to endure first." Now he was grinning.

Venus grabbed Drew's arm. "You know something—what?"

Drew's brows rose as he put on his haughtiest expression—except his eyes were laughing. "My dear duchess, you are wrinkling my coat."

She shook his arm. "I'll do more than wrinkle your blo"—Drew's glance shifted to Constance, and Venus, recalled to her surroundings, adjusted—"blasted coat if you don't empty the bag immediately."

"Such vehemence."

"Drew, my patience is worn to a thread."

"Yes, your grace, please tell us what you know." Constance sounded as if she were on the verge of falling to her knees in supplication.

Drew bowed. "I apologize for teasing you both. I've only come to report that Dalton just approached your husband while I was speaking to him, Mrs. Bowman, and very discreetly asked the vicar to step into the library. Apparently Lord Edward wished to have a word with him."

Constance almost clapped her hands, but stopped herself right before they made contact. "Oh, that does sound very promising."

"I thought you might wish to make your way to the door," Drew said, "to greet them as soon as they return. I have a feeling it will be a very brief conversation."

Drew was correct. They had no sooner reached the door than the vicar appeared. He had a very odd expression—a mix of delight and disapproval. When Venus looked at the couple standing behind him, she completely understood. Poor Ellie's coiffure was markedly lopsided and her dress looked as if she'd been assisted into it by a dresser who was all thumbs.

As Ned undoubtedly was.

"I am happy to tell you," the vicar said, "that our children will be marrying—as soon as possible."

"Wonderful!" Venus hugged the vicar—he was a bit taken aback by her enthusiasm—and then Drew and Constance and Ned and Ellie. And then she and Constance whisked Ellie away to put her to rights before the formal announcement.

Later Venus stood in the ballroom with Drew at her side and watched Ned and Ellie waltz together for the first time as a betrothed couple.

"Happy, my dear?" Drew asked.

"Very—as I'm sure you are as well."

"I am, but I had complete faith the Duchess of Love would work her matchmaking magic."

Venus snorted. "That makes one of us." Then she smiled. "Have you ever seen Ned look happier?"

"No, but I very much fear Ned's happiness has put Jack back in a dangerous position."

Venus stiffened with alarm. "What do you mean?"

"I believe Miss Wharton took the betrothal announcement hard. She looked almost overcome at dinner."

Venus nodded. "I noticed that, too. I think Ned did raise her hopes a bit—he certainly had me worried he might make her an offer. I am sorry for her, but a union between her and Ned would have been a disaster."

"Yes, but I'm not sure she understands that. In any event, she seems to have returned to her original plan of trapping Jack into a proposal."

"She has?" Venus would do something about that. "Where is she?" she asked as the music drew to a close.

"She's just finished dancing with Mr. Humphrey, but it

looks as if Jack is asking Ellie to stand up with him, so I believe he should be safe for the moment." Drew took her arm and led her out onto the floor. "And since I've instructed the orchestra to play another waltz, I believe this is the perfect time to steal a dance with my wife."

The music started and Venus let herself be caught up in the joy of waltzing with her duke. But not totally caught up. Now that Drew had alerted her to the danger, she was keeping a sharp eye out.

Ah, Miss Wharton was talking to Constance—she seemed to be congratulating her. That was nice. The girl wasn't bad at heart, she just wasn't the girl for Jack. Venus would see what she could do for her this Season. Perhaps not Percy . . . hmm. She must give it some thought.

She watched Mr. Cox waltz by with Lady Juliet, and Mr. Humphrey with Miss Mosely. Her party had been far, far more successful than she had dared hope. But not perfect.

"I wish I could do something about Ash."

"Ash has a wife, Venus. You are a matchmaker, not . . . well, not whatever it is Ash and Jess need."

Drew was right, of course. "I suppose I'll focus on Jack, then."

Drew laughed. "Lucky Jack—I'm not certain he'll thank you, you know. In fact, if he's smart, he'll stay as far away from your blasted monthly Love Balls as he can."

"But—"

Drew laid his finger on her lips. "Put your sons out of your mind for the moment, my dear duchess. Your poor husband wants your attention."

"There's nothing the least bit poor about you, my dear duke, but if you want my attention, of course you shall have it now"—Venus grinned—"and later when I feel like celebrating my successes properly."

Drew's eyebrows rose. "How interesting. I shall see if

my old brain can come up with some appropriately festive ways to help you mark the occasion."

Venus giggled. "I'm sure you can. You are my inspiration in all, my Duke of Love."

Drew treated her to a look of disgust and then swept her, laughing, across the ballroom floor.

Learn how the young, vivacious
Venus Collingswood
came to meet the love of her life
and future husband
Andrew, Duke of Greycliffe,
and got her start as a matchmaker
in this special prequel novella,
printed here in its entirety.

THE DUCHESS OF LOVE

Also available as a Kensington e-book.

Turn the page to begin!

Chapter 1

Venus Collingswood ran into the vicarage and flung open the door to the study. As she expected, Papa, Mama, and her older sister, Aphrodite, were all there reading.

"Papa," she said breathlessly, "did you know the Duke of Greycliffe and his cousin are coming to Little Huffington?"

"Hmm?" The Reverend Walter Collingswood kept his eyes on his book.

Venus turned to her mother. Surely with two unwed daughters, Mama would have heard the news. "Mama, did *you* know?"

Mama turned a page. "Did I know what, dear?"

"That the Duke of Greycliffe and his cousin, Mr. Valentine, are coming to visit now that Greycliffe has inherited Hyndon House." Venus paused before she delivered the most important part. "And neither of them is married."

"Oh?" Mama made a notation on the paper by her elbow. "That's nice."

"Nice?" Venus glanced at Aphrodite. At twenty-three Ditee was Venus's only matchmaking failure, in imminent

danger of becoming an old maid despite Venus's best efforts. Surely she was interested in this news?

Surely not. Ditee was consulting Papa's large Latin dictionary. She likely hadn't heard a word Venus had said.

I swear I'm a changeling, Venus thought. *It is the only explanation.*

"Mrs. Shipley told me Mrs. Edgemoor told her that Greycliffe and Mr. Valentine are expected next week so Greycliffe can inspect the property," she said, refusing to give up. "We should invite them to dinner to welcome them to the neighborhood."

Mama sighed and sat back. "Walter, I am having the devil of a time making sense of this passage."

"I'll take a look at it in a moment, my love."

"Mama!"

Mama blinked at Venus. "I'm sorry, Venus, were you saying something?" She glanced back at her book. "Oh, I have it! Malum is *apple*, not evil. The man threw the ripe *apple*. How silly of me not to have seen it at once."

"I've made the same mistake, Mama," Ditee said, glancing up from the dictionary.

Venus ground her teeth. "I am going out to the road and throw myself under the next carriage to pass by."

"Oh?" Mama chewed on the end of her pencil. "Please tell Mrs. Shipley to put supper back an hour before you go, will you?"

"Yes, Mama."

Venus stepped carefully out of the study. She did not slam the door behind her. She was quite proud of herself.

Mrs. Shipley, standing in the hall, clucked sympathetically. "Deep in their books, are they, Miss Venus?"

"Yes." Venus swallowed. She was going to explode with frustration if she didn't get out of this house immediately. "Mama said to set supper back an hour."

The housekeeper laughed. "I warned Cook when that package of books arrived they'd be in there all night."

Venus smiled tightly. "I believe I'll take Archimedes for a walk."

"Good. He's been trying to beg a soup bone from Cook all morning. She'll be happy to have him out from underfoot."

Venus collected Archie from the kitchen, and they stepped out into the hot afternoon sun. A squirrel scampered by; Archie, barking maniacally, shot off over the broad lawns in pursuit. Venus strode after him.

What was she going to do? Having a duke—and a ducal cousin—fall into their laps was not an opportunity to be missed, yet she couldn't invite them to the vicarage herself. Well, she might try—she wasn't above a little, er, creativity for a good cause—but the fact remained that unless the men appeared in togas and laurel wreaths, no one in her family would notice them.

Her odds of nabbing Ditee a duke were about as good as Archie's for catching a squirrel—zero.

It was a crime. Ditee was at her last prayers, and yet she was by far the most beautiful girl in Little Huffington. Venus had managed to find matches in the admittedly shallow pool of marriageable men for far less well-favored women. Farmer Isley's sister closely resembled his prize sheep, for goodness sakes, and Mrs. Fedderly's niece had an obvious squint, and yet she'd successfully matched them with willing males.

Ditee was sweet tempered, too, as long as you didn't try to take a book away from her. That was the problem. She wouldn't pull her nose out of her Latin tomes long enough to have a conversation with a man, let alone something of a warmer nature. The men had finally given up and turned to younger, more approachable girls.

Not that Ditee noticed.

But if her sister could catch the duke's attention . . .

"I'm sure Ditee would be considered a diamond even in London, Archie," Venus said as the dog, having chased the squirrel up an oak tree, trotted back to her.

Archie, tongue lolling from his exertions, wagged his tail enthusiastically.

"And she is certainly intelligent. Any man must be pleased to have intelligent children, wouldn't you say?"

Archie barked twice in apparent agreement.

"Of course, it would help if he is a bit scholarly himself, but I suppose he'll spend most of his time at his clubs, so that shouldn't make too much difference." But Ditee needed to cooperate in any matchmaking effort; Venus had learned that lesson all too well. What would seduce her sister? Not a handsome face or deep pockets or—

Venus snapped her fingers. Of course—books! "I would think a duke, even if he isn't much of a reader himself, would have an extensive library, wouldn't you, Archie? Owning a vast quantity of books is considered most impressive."

Archie was not interested in books—he'd chewed one as a puppy and been exiled from the house for months. He raced off after another squirrel.

Venus treated herself to a lovely daydream of Ditee walking down the aisle at St. George's, Hanover Square, the *ton*, dressed in the latest fashions, filling the pews and even standing in the back. Not that her imaginings could be very precise. She'd never seen St. George's or any church besides Papa's here in Little Huffington.

If Ditee did marry the duke, she'd spend part of her time in London, wouldn't she? Surely she'd invite Venus to visit. Then Venus could see the museums and the parks and go to the theater and perhaps even a ball or two. She'd not be condemned to live forever in sleepy Little Huffington amid people she'd known her entire life.

Archie had reached the gate to Hyndon House's land and was waiting for her to open it. She paused, her hand on the latch. Old Mr. Blant, the previous owner, had never cared if they trespassed, but the duke might feel differently.

Archie barked and then whined, bumping her hand with his nose. He smelled water.

She'd like to go down to the water, too. It was so hot, and the deep, secluded pond was one of her favorite spots.

Archie jumped up as if to push the gate open himself.

"Archie, your manners! Show a little patience."

Patience was not Archie's strong suit. He got down from the gate, but clearly it was a struggle. His back end wiggled, his front feet danced, and his eyes were bottomless pools of supplication.

The duke was still in London; he'd never know.

"Oh, very well, we'll go in, but before we come again, we must ask Greycliffe's permission."

Archie backed away enough so she could swing the gate open, but the moment there was space for him to squeeze through, he was gone.

Venus closed the gate carefully behind her. She must not get ahead of herself with her matchmaking. She knew nothing at all about Greycliffe. He'd never come to Hyndon House while Mr. Brant was alive, and Mrs. Shipley had not got any details from Mrs. Edgemoor beyond the fact that the fellow was unwed. What if he was Papa's age? She frowned. She couldn't wish for Ditee to marry an old man. Or an ugly one. Or an unrepentant rake.

She heard a great deal of quacking and honking and then a storm of birds erupted from the trees ahead of her. Archie had reached the pond.

She hurried down the rest of the slope and through the woods.

She'd been coming here since she was a girl, but she was always a little surprised and thrilled to step out of the trees and see this perfect jewel of water. The woods ringed it, leaving a grassy bank on which to sit or sun; and on the south and deepest side, a large gray rock sat as if it had been placed there specifically to jump from. Once Papa had discovered the pond, he'd been sure to teach her and Ditee how to swim.

It would be quite peaceful, if it weren't for Archie, romping and splashing in the water. He started toward her.

"Oh, no, you're not going to shake half the pond all over me," she said, dashing for the rock and scrambling up onto it, well out of Archie's reach. After some good-natured barking, he ran back into the water.

She sat down. Even the stone was hot.

When she was a girl, she used to come here often. Before Ditee had become such a bloody bookworm, Mrs. Shipley would pack them both a basket with their lunch, and they'd spend lazy summer days playing in the water, lying in the sun watching the clouds float by, and talking about all sorts of things.

She took off her shoes and stockings and wiggled her toes. She'd dearly love a swim, but she was nineteen now, not nine.

Yet if the duke did bar the gate to his property, this might be her last chance.

It was *so* hot . . .

She looked around. She'd never seen anyone else here. What were the odds someone would appear today?

Close to zero. Certainly good enough to wager on.

She pulled off her bonnet and plucked out her pins, shaking her hair free. She was wearing a simple frock; it took only a moment to have it and her stays off. Then she stood up in her shift and looked down at the deep, cool water. It would feel so good washing over her.

But a wet shift would feel terrible—even worse when she had to put her stays and dress on over it. She didn't have time to lie in the sun and let it dry.

This was a stupid idea. She would get dressed again.

But if it weren't for the shift . . .

Could she . . . ?

She closed her eyes, imagining the cool water rushing over her naked flesh.

No. That was too scandalous.

But Archie didn't care what she wore—or didn't wear— and there was no one else to see.

Archie, obviously sensing he might have company, ran back and forth on the bank, barking encouragement.

Damn it, what was the benefit of living in the middle of nowhere if you couldn't do what you wanted? No one would see her but Archie, and he didn't bear tales—except for the one he was wagging furiously.

Before she could change her mind, she grabbed her hem and pulled off her shift. She threw it on top of her other clothes, turned back to the pond—

Oh! Her ankle twisted slightly, throwing her off balance. Her arms flew out, but there was nothing to hold onto.

She tottered on the edge and then plunged down into the clear, cold water.

Andrew, Duke of Greycliffe, stood with his cousin, Mr. Nigel Valentine, in the entry to Hyndon Hall, their valises by their feet. The housekeeper gaped at them, her face a chalky white.

"Oh, your grace," she said, "I'm so sorry. I don't know how it happened, but I was given to understand you wouldn't be arriving until next week."

She was actually wringing her hands.

She was also addressing Nigel.

Nigel raised a brow and gave Drew a look as if to say, how do we gently correct this person?

In Town everyone knew Drew, of course, but in the country people seemed to forget a duke could be so young. Not that Nigel was old—no one would consider twenty-eight ancient—but it must seem far more ducal than twenty-one.

Drew could powder his hair like Nigel and most gentlemen did. That would make him look older—but hair powder made him sneeze.

"Our plans changed," Drew said, "Mrs. . . . ?"

The woman's eyes darted to meet his. "Edgemoor, sir." She was almost breathless with anxiety.

It sounded odd to be addressed as "sir" rather than "your grace." Odd, but not unpleasant. Ever since he was thirteen and had had the title thrust on him, he'd had the recurring fantasy he would wake up one morning himself again: just Drew, not Greycliffe.

Why not now?

"Please don't be distressed, Mrs. Edgemoor," he said. "The duke knows we came without warning." From the corner of his eye, he saw Nigel's other brow shoot up. "Take your time. Is there a place we can wait and not be in your way?"

"Oh, yes, thank you, sir." She turned to bob a curtsy in Nigel's direction. "Your grace. It won't take long, truly. I've already aired your rooms. If you'll just step into the study," she said as she led them to a pleasant chamber at the back of the house, "I'll have Cook send up some refreshments." She wrung her hands again. "And if you'd like your baggage, when it arrives—"

"That will not be a problem, Mrs. Edgemoor," Drew said. "We don't expect to be here more than a week or so, so we traveled light. All we have are the two bags we brought in."

The housekeeper looked as though she would collapse with relief. "Very good, sir. I'll have Williams, the footman, take them upstairs. Your rooms will be ready as quick as can be."

"Splendid. Thank you, but please don't feel the need to hurry."

Drew smiled at the housekeeper as she curtsyed again and almost ran from the room.

Nigel cleared his throat. "Since when have you taken to referring to yourself in the third person, *your grace*?"

"Shh." Drew glanced over his shoulder. The hall appeared deserted, but it was always best to take precautions. He closed the heavy door and moved toward the windows to look out over the formal gardens and the broad, green lawns that ended at some woods. "I have a plan."

"A plan?" Nigel pulled out his snuffbox and took a pinch. "What kind of a plan?"

"I thought you could be the duke while we are here."

Nigel made an odd, strangled sound and sneezed violently. "Damn it, you need to warn a fellow before you say something so preposterous."

A servant scratched at the door and entered, carrying a tray with bread and cheese and a jug of ale. He looked almost as nervous as the housekeeper and fled as soon as he'd deposited his burden.

Nigel poured a mug and offered it to Drew. "You must be thirsty from the ride. You aren't thinking clearly."

Perhaps he wasn't, but the notion of getting out from

under his title, even for only a few days, was damn appealing. "It shouldn't be difficult to manage."

"Difficult? It's impossible. I won't do it." Nigel drained the mug he'd offered Drew.

Nigel didn't understand. He'd likely never wished to escape his life. "But I might never get this opportunity again."

"I said no."

Nigel's face didn't yet look as unyielding as the cliffs of Dover, so perhaps Drew could wheedle him into agreeing. "It wouldn't be for long."

"No!" Nigel scowled at him. "I don't know why you would want to do something so ridiculous."

To get a brief taste of freedom. "At least think about it, will you?"

Nigel grunted. "Oh, all right."

Drew laughed. "Splendid. I'm off for a stroll. Do you want to come exploring with me?"

"Good God, no. I've just ridden two days to get to this godforsaken place. I intend to rest—and see if the house has something more sustaining than ale in its cellars. But you go ahead. Youth is full of energy." He tossed him some bread. "Here. We can't have you expiring in the fields somewhere."

Drew caught the bread in one hand. "Thanks. I'll see you later."

Nigel snorted. "Hopefully you'll be thinking more rationally then."

Drew grinned and let himself out onto the terrace, taking the stairs down to the gardens. He followed one of the manicured paths away from the house. It was hot in the sun; he'd left his hat on the table in the entry. He should go back.

But it felt good to stretch his legs. He'd walk as far as the woods. He popped the rest of the bread into his mouth and lengthened his stride.

Nigel was likely right—pretending he wasn't the duke was a dunderheaded idea, but damn, he wished he could do it. It might be different if he'd been born to the title, but he'd become Greycliffe courtesy of an early morning fire at one of London's most exclusive gambling hells. His uncle—the fourth duke—his uncle's two sons, and his father had all died in the flames.

He frowned. He'd never forget when word of his sudden elevation spread through Eton. Boys who'd looked straight through him the day before suddenly fawned all over him. Bah. At least it was practice for when he got older and went up to Town. The toadying there was beyond nauseating, and the London women were worse than the men. Whores, actresses, widows, debutantes—they all wanted to get their hands on his purse and, if they could manage it, their name with his on a marriage license.

He was almost at the trees now. Was that barking he heard? And splashing? He grinned. He was hot and sticky. He'd wade into the water and wash the dirt of the road off. He started untying his neck cloth as he followed a narrow path down through the dense pine trees.

Ah, there was a large rock to the side of the path. He sat down to jerk off his boots as likely many men before him had. He could just see the pond through the tree branches; he didn't yet see the dog, but it sounded as if it was having a wonderful time. He couldn't wait to join it.

He shed his coat, shirt, breeches, and drawers quickly and stepped to the edge of the woods. Now he saw the dog, a brown and white mix that was obviously part water spaniel, running back and forth on the bank, barking up at—

He jumped back behind a tree trunk.

The girl hadn't seen him. She was standing on a large rock on the other side of the pond, looking down at the water about ten feet below her, clad in only her shift. Her long chestnut brown hair fell in waves to her waist, hiding her face.

She'd best take care or she would fall.

Concern tightened his gut. She didn't intend to jump, did she? He should stop her, but catching sight of a strange, naked man coming out of the woods might well frighten her into losing her balance. What should—

Bloody hell.

The girl was pulling off her shift.

His jaw dropped as another part of him sprang up. His eyes followed the cloth up her body past the well-turned ankles; the long, pale thighs; the lovely nest of curls, so dark against the white of her belly and hips; and the slim, curved waist to stop at the two small, round, perfect breasts almost hidden by her hair.

The pond water had better be ice cold or he'd never get his breeches back on.

She turned to throw the shift behind her, and he got a glimpse of her lovely, rounded arse.

Zounds, he was going to die of lust.

And then she turned back and wobbled. Her arms flew out—Good God! She was falling.

He sprinted for the pond, hitting the water at the same time the girl did.

Chapter 2

❧

Venus managed to right herself as she fell so she went into the pond feet first. She plunged down, the water rushing over her skin. It felt wonderful—exciting and a bit sinful.

But she needed to breathe. She kicked and pulled, stopping her descent and making her way back to the surface. Her hair wrapped around her like weeds. She fought through it, but by the time she popped up above the water, her lungs were screaming for air. She opened her mouth—

"Aa-urg!" And took in water. Something strong and hard had grabbed her waist. Her heart flashed into a wild, mad beating. She was going to be pulled back under. She clawed at the thing.

It was an arm—a rock-hard, muscled, naked, male arm. It hauled her up against an equally hard, naked chest.

Oh, God! If she didn't drown, she'd be raped.

She thrashed and kicked, but she couldn't move. She was pinned to the villain as if by an iron band.

"Steady," an educated male voice, slightly breathless,

said by her ear as they moved toward the shore. "I've got you. You're safe."

Safe? Ha! She renewed her efforts to break free.

"Stop struggling," he said, annoyance sharpening his words. "You're making this harder."

She would make it very hard. She would struggle tooth and nail. He might have his wicked way with her, but she'd inflict as much damage on him as she could. She opened her mouth to tell him so and took in another wave of water.

She was coughing and choking as he hauled her out of the pond. Archie ran toward him, barking, but he ignored the dog as he bent her over his arm and whacked her on the back. Water gushed out of her mouth.

She should try to escape now, but she was too busy struggling to get air into her lungs.

"Breathe, damn it," he said.

She'd be happy to. She attempted to tell him that, but apparently air was also necessary for speech. She couldn't even croak.

"Bloody hell. I'm not going to let you die." Suddenly she was flat on her back on the grass and his mouth was over hers. His warm breath forced itself into her lungs.

She didn't know much about rape, thank God, but this didn't seem like a prelude to it.

He lifted his head and air whooshed out of her.

"Aurgh." She started to cough again.

He turned her immediately to her side. "Breathe," he ordered again, rubbing her back and shoulders.

She breathed. Such a simple thing, automatic until one couldn't do it. In and out. Her heart slowed to a normal cadence.

The sun warmed her as the man's hands moved over her . . . naked skin.

She flipped onto her belly.

"Hey, I don't think that will help." He turned her to her side once more, handling her as if she weighed nothing, his hand on her shoulder and hip. Her naked hip.

She might stop breathing again. And now she was facing him, looking at his knees and—

She squeezed her eyes shut.

"What's the matter?" He pushed her hair back from her face. "Does something hurt? You didn't hit your head when you fell, did you?"

"N-no."

"Let me see." His fingers combed through her hair, pressing on her scalp. His touch was gentle, but firm. "Does this hurt? Or this?"

"No." She kept her eyes firmly closed.

He tilted her face up. "Look at me."

"Why?" But she felt a bit like an ostrich with its head in the sand, so she gave up and looked at him.

She must have died. The man staring down at her could only be an archangel. He had eyes as blue as the pond on a cloudless summer day, fringed with long dark lashes any woman would die for. His dark blond hair—if he wore powder, it had been washed out in the water—had come loose from its tie and fell forward to frame his face—high cheekbones, straight nose, firm lips, strong chin.

Who was he? She'd certainly never seen him before.

"Your eyes look clear. I don't think you hit your head."

"I told you I didn't." He certainly wasn't a servant or a farmer or a laborer. He had the tone and diction of a nobleman, but noblemen didn't come to Little Huffington, unless . . .

Oh, dear.

"You aren't with the Duke of Greycliffe, are you?"

A faint flush colored his cheeks. "Ah, yes. I, er, am."

The duke was here already? She hadn't yet formulated a plan to bring him and Ditee together. "But you aren't supposed to arrive until next week."

He shrugged. "We came early."

She was distracted by the movement of his shoulders. Well, not the movement so much as the shoulders themselves. They were very broad; surely too broad to fit into a proper coat. Blond hair dusted his chest; muscles shaped his arms. He was strong; she remembered that clearly from his grasp in the water.

"Like what you see?" he asked. His tone had changed. Instead of concern, it held heat.

"What?" Her eyes flew back to his face. His gaze had dropped to examine . . .

"Ack!" She slapped her hands over her breasts. "Don't look."

The right corner of his mouth turned up—Lord save her, he had a dimple. "*You* were looking."

"I was not."

He grinned—he had *two* dimples. "Liar."

Oh, the man was clearly a rake of the worst sort. She should shove him away, but then she'd have to take her hands off her breasts. She jerked her chin instead. "Move back."

"Is that any way to thank your rescuer?" he asked, but he moved back. "I expected a kiss."

"You deserve a slap—and close your eyes. You didn't rescue me; you almost killed me."

He frowned, but he did close his eyes. "You were drowning."

"Not until you grabbed me. I'll have you know I've been swimming in this pond since I was a girl." She scrambled to her feet. His shoulders and arms could have been stolen from a Greek statue. They certainly were as hard as marble, but they weren't cold. They were warm—very, very warm.

He cracked open one eye. "Am I getting my kiss, then?"

"No!" Where had her wits got to? She sprinted for the nearest tree. Fortunately its trunk was sufficiently thick to serve as a shield. Once she was safely concealed, she peered around the edge. The man was still kneeling in the grass, but Archie had come up to him, blocking her view of his lower parts.

Which was a good thing, of course.

The fellow was scratching Archie's ears, and Archie was licking the man's face.

Who was he? He couldn't be the duke; dukes didn't go about naked like this. They were far too grand. He must be the duke's cousin, Mr. Valentine.

An insect of some sort decided to take a stroll on her bare backside. She jumped and swatted it away. Good God. Here she was, naked as well. She needed to get dressed immediately, but her clothes weren't within reach, and she was not about to expose herself to Mr. Valentine's interested eyes again. Her interested eyes, however . . .

"Mr. Valentine."

The man kept patting Archie. Perhaps he hadn't heard her. She spoke louder.

"Mr. Valentine!"

His head snapped up then, and he gave her an odd look.

What was the matter? She glanced down. No, she was still completely concealed. Perhaps he was just not terribly bright. A pity, but often the most beautiful people were the thickest—which was another reason Aphrodite was such a prize.

She looked at him again. "Fetch my clothes, Mr. Valentine, if you will."

He stared at her a moment longer—was he going to refuse to do her bidding? No, now he was smiling and standing, putting all his male glory on display.

"Where are they?"

"Uh." He *did* look like a Greek statue, all hard planes and chiseled muscles. The blond hair dusting his chest continued down in a narrow line over his flat belly to a nest of curls from which . . .

That part was *much* larger than any sculpture she'd ever viewed.

Good God, she'd swear the organ grew even larger as she watched.

"Your clothes?" His voice sounded a little strained.

She tore her gaze away from his nether regions. "Up." She cleared her throat. Her heart was pounding, and her own nether regions felt oddly swollen and achy. She was very afraid they were even a trifle damp. What in the world was the matter with her? "They are up on the rock."

"Right." Mr. Valentine strode off, giving her a delightful view of his backside in motion. His muscles bunched and shifted as he climbed the rock. Unfortunately—no fortunately, definitely fortunately—when he came back, he carried her clothes in front of him, obscuring her view.

"You may put them down there," she said, pointing to a spot about ten feet away.

"Very well." He laid the clothes down and paused. "May I borrow your bonnet?"

She choked back a nervous giggle. "I don't believe it will suit you, sir."

"I think it will suit me very well." He straightened, holding her hat in front of his male bit like a shield. "Unless you'd prefer to admire my natural state longer?"

Thank God most of her was hidden behind this tree,

because she very much feared all of her turned red. "I see far too much of your person as it is. Where are your clothes?"

"On the other side of the pond." He grinned. "Did you think I made a habit of strolling about outdoors nude?"

"Of course not." His skin was far too pale to have been exposed to the sun.

She *must* stop looking at his skin. "Thank you, sir. You may take yourself off now. Go fetch your things and be about your business."

"Oh, no. I won't leave until I know you are safely clothed." His damn dimples flashed at her. "I wouldn't want some scoundrel to come along and find you this way."

"Some scoundrel already—" Wait a moment. Mr. Valentine was her ticket to the duke. If she managed to gain his friendship, perhaps he would help her bring Ditee to Grey-cliffe's notice. "Very well. Then turn around so I can get dressed."

"Yes, madam." He bowed slightly before giving her his back. His lovely, lovely back. His shoulders tapered down to a slim waist and a pair of beautifully muscled—

"Are you always so managing?"

She shook herself out of her fog of admiration and reached for her clothes. "I'm not managing."

"You are. You're a bit of a shrew, actually."

"I am not. How can you say such a thing?" She snatched up her shift and threw it over her head. At least now she was covered if anyone else happened by. "Is your cousin likely to follow you, sir?"

"I doubt it. He said he wanted to rest from our trip."

"Oh." Damn. "So he is old and gouty?" Perhaps she would have to focus on Mr. Valentine for Ditee.

For some reason that thought was most unappealing.

Mr. Valentine laughed. "Oh, no."

Thank God! She struggled into her stays and dress. But how was she to bring the duke and Ditee together?

She would definitely need Mr. Valentine's assistance. "Mr. Valentine," she said, stepping out from behind the tree. "I have a proposal for you."

He whirled around, her hat still held before him. "You do? Splendid!"

She could see he was teasing her, but she still flushed. "Not that kind of proposal!"

"No? You're certain?"

"Of course I am. You should not joke about such things."

Drew studied the girl—what was her name? She'd raised her chin, but she sounded a little unsure for once.

He bowed again, careful to keep the hat shielding his cock, which was finally resuming polite proportions. "My apologies."

Her long wet hair was soaking her shapeless, colorless frock. He much preferred her naked, but she'd be beautiful dressed in an elegant gown or an old sack.

His cock bobbed in agreement.

"Do you suppose you might gift me with your name, madam?" He stepped closer, into the shade of the trees.

She stepped back. "Stay where you are."

"If I continue to stand in the sun, my entire body, except for the poor bit I'm shading with your lovely hat, will be sunburned."

"Oh." She turned bright red herself. "Very well. You may stand there, but no closer."

"Thank you." Had no one taught this girl any sense? She was obviously not a servant or country miss looking for some friendly sport. "You took a substantial risk coming to such a deserted place by yourself, you know."

"I have Archie with me."

"That vicious animal?" The dog was on his back, wiggling in the grass. "I suppose he might have come to your rescue if I'd tried to rape you."

She drew in a sharp breath and turned an unpleasant shade of greenish white. Well, it was about time she heard some plain speaking.

"But he would have been of very little use if you'd hit your head when you fell into the water."

"I told you I was a strong swimmer."

"Even strong swimmers should not swim alone."

She glared at him; he glared back at her. This time the silence stretching between them wasn't charged with attraction. One of his friends had drowned swimming in just such a pond a few years ago. He had a point to make.

Finally she looked away. "You may say I am managing, but I suspect you can be very overbearing. How does the duke put up with you?"

He grinned. "I don't know." At some point he would have to tell her who he was, but he wanted to put it off as long as he could.

And if someone had told him he'd be standing naked by a pond in bright daylight with only a lady's hat to provide any sort of cover, conversing with a woman about swimming and dogs and not beds and bodies, he'd have laughed himself silly. "Your name, please?"

She looked down her nose at him—while still darting glances at his chest and shoulders. "Miss Venus Collingswood. My papa is the vicar."

"I see." Vicar's children were often rather wild, but not candidates for dalliance. He would probably have to marry her.

At the moment, the thought was more exciting than

dismaying. In fact, a prominent part of him was very excited indeed—thank God for the hat. "And so what is your proposal?"

"My older sister, Aphrodite—"

"What?" Her parents had named both their daughters after the goddess of love?

She flushed. "Papa and Mama are classical scholars."

He laughed. "I hope you don't have a brother."

"Why?"

Miss Collingswood—Venus—was staring at his chest again. A pity she'd put her clothes back on; he'd very much like to study *her* chest, and with more than his eyes. If she was going to carry the goddess of love's name, she should learn a little of love's mysteries, after all.

"Because a boy with the name of Eros or Cupid would be beaten to a pulp in short order."

"Oh." She tore her eyes away from his shoulders to meet his gaze. "I suppose you are right."

"Of course I am. I take it *you* are not a classical scholar?"

She raised her chin. "I can read Greek and Latin as well as anyone, but I am more interested in modern events." She let out a long breath and her shoulders slumped slightly. "If there were any modern events of interest in Little Huffington."

He grinned. "Things here a bit dull?"

"Not if you find tales of sheep and crop-eating insects and rheumatism interesting."

His grin widened. "Oh, well, if anyone decides to stroll by the pond now, Little Huffington would have much more to talk about than animals and ailments. I *am* still naked, you know."

Miss Collingswood jumped and looked around wildly.

"I thought you'd noticed. You did seem to be examining my—"

"Oh, shush! No one ever comes this way."

"So you are here daily?"

"Of course not. What do you take me for?"

He shrugged. "Then this may be an extremely popular spot, for all you know."

She almost hissed at him. "It's on Mr. Blant's—now the duke's—land. Anyone here would be trespassing."

He inclined his head. "True. And that would make you . . . ?"

"You are impossible." She glanced around again. "Do you really think someone will come by?"

"I have no idea, but perhaps you'd best get to your proposal." He fluttered her hat slightly. "Or I could suggest one of my own."

She glared at him. "As I was trying to say earlier—before you interrupted—Aphrodite, my older sister, is very beautiful."

"More beautiful than you?"

Her jaw dropped, and then she frowned. "Don't be silly."

"I wasn't."

"Oh." Her frown turned to a puzzled, almost wary look. "Well, then, yes, she is far more beautiful than I. She has golden blonde hair and the bluest eyes . . . I'm sure she'd be considered a toast in London."

"I see. And how is that a problem? Can she not make up her mind whom to marry? She must have men falling over themselves to offer for her."

"But she doesn't." Miss Collingswood stepped closer to him, her warm brown eyes earnest. "She is twenty-three and, as far as I know, has never had more than a passing conversation with a gentleman. If a man doesn't appear within the pages of a Greek or Roman text, she won't notice him. Mama and Papa seem completely willing to let her live with them forever."

She was close enough to touch now.

He gripped her hat firmly with both hands. No touching. He must keep his hands to himself, damn it.

"And why is that a problem, if your parents and your sister are content?" He wished the mamas in London would be equally uninterested in throwing their female offspring at his head.

Miss Collingswood's frown returned. She looked exceedingly frustrated. "But Ditee is so lovely. It's a sin to have her spend her life tucked away in this out-of-the-way village."

"Why?"

"Because she is meant for greater things, of course. She could be a . . . a duchess!"

Damn. A duchess meant a poor, sacrificial duke, and he was the only duke in sight. He'd have another damsel to dodge, even here in boring Little Huffington.

"Not that I would—or could—compel her to consider the Duke of Greycliffe," Miss Collingswood was saying, "but I thought, since he was in the neighborhood, it would be a shame for them not to meet."

His jaw dropped. He snapped it shut. That's right, she thought he was Nigel.

"Mrs. Edgemoor thought—but I suppose she might have been mistaken . . ." She looked at him hopefully. "The duke isn't married, is he?"

"No." He had a sudden, very inappropriate urge to laugh. He bit the inside of his cheek to restrain himself. "He's not."

She nodded. "That's good, then. And I know you're a man and his cousin, so perhaps you're not the best judge, but is he at least presentable looking? He needn't be handsome, but it would be best if he weren't, well . . ."

"Ugly?" Damn it, he was going to laugh. "Hideous? Nightmare-inducing?"

"Oh, stop it. Now you are poking fun." She paused and looked at him sideways. "He isn't, is he?"

"I believe the ladies of the *ton* don't flee in horror when they see him."

"And it would also help if he were intelligent, perhaps even scholarly?"

"Well . . ." He'd excelled in mathematics, but he'd been only an adequate classics student. Nigel, however, might be almost as mad for Greek and Latin texts as Miss Aphrodite Collingswood.

"Does he at least have many books? I think an impressive library would woo Ditee more than anything else."

"Oh, yes, he has a spectacular library." Which was also true of Nigel. This match Miss Collingswood was suggesting—not the match between him and her sister, but between her sister and Nigel—might work very well.

Miss Venus Collingswood beamed at him. "Splendid. Then do you think you might persuade the duke to invite us to Hyndon House? I'm afraid I can't get Mama and Papa to bestir themselves enough to have you to the vicarage, and you can be sure any invitation Mrs. Higgins, the squire's wife, extends will not include us."

"Mrs. Higgins has a daughter of her own to marry off, does she?"

"Yes, Esmeralda. How did you know?"

He shrugged. "It cannot be easy to have her chick always cast in the shade by the beautiful Miss Venus."

"You mean Aphrodite."

"Do I?"

She looked disconcerted once more and then frowned. "Of course you do. You are being silly again."

"Hmm." He really would have to kiss her. "Right, then.

Unfortunately I do foresee a problem. We are a bachelor household; we can't just have you and your sister to tea."

"Oh. I see your point." Venus chewed on her bottom lip.

"And it might cause comment if we were to single your family out; I suspect this Mrs. Higgins, for one, would take offense."

Venus nodded. "I'm afraid you are right. What are we to do?"

What he should do was tell her who he was, but the temptation to further their acquaintance when she still thought him merely Mr. Valentine was too strong to resist.

"Perhaps an open house for the neighborhood." Something with a number of people where there might be some way to avoid announcing himself immediately. "Or a garden party. Though I'm a little concerned Mrs. Edgemoor will have my—er, the duke's head. We descended on her early with no warning and now propose to entertain the countryside."

"Don't worry. There are not many families to invite. I'll speak to Mrs. Shipley, our housekeeper. She and Mrs. Edgemoor are friends. I'm certain she'll be happy to help."

"Very well. Then I will see what I can do."

"You think you'll be able to persuade the duke?" Venus looked so hopeful and eager.

"I'm sure of it. Now close your eyes."

"Close my eyes? Why?"

"Because now that you are dressed, I should leave, and I need to give you back your stylish hat." He grinned and leaned a little toward her. "Unless you'd like to see once more what it's been hiding?"

She sucked in her breath and turned red again. "N-no. Of course not."

Did she sound just the slightest bit indecisive? If so, she

mastered whatever momentary temptation she'd felt and squeezed her eyes closed.

Could he master his disreputable urges, however? He studied her face.

One of her eyes cracked open. "Come on, then." She held out her hand, careful not to hold it too close to his person. "Give me my hat."

"So impatient. I won't do anything while you are peeking."

"Oh, for God's sake. Very well." She shut her eyes again.

He didn't trust her to be patient. He smiled as he put the hat on her head. He would have to teach her patience. He tied her ribbon beneath her chin, and then leaned forward to brush her lips gently with his before placing a kiss on her cheek.

She sucked in her breath, but he forced himself to turn and run down to the pond without looking back.

Chapter 3

Drew found Nigel reading in the study.

"You were gone rather longer than I expected," Nigel said, peering at Drew over his glasses. One of Nigel's brows flew up. "Is it storming out?"

"No." Drew dropped into the leather chair facing Nigel's and slung his leg over an arm.

"I didn't think I'd heard rain on the windows." Nigel laid his spectacles and his book on the table by his elbow, picked up his brandy glass, and regarded Drew. "Are you going to tell me why your hair is wet or do I have to guess?"

Making Nigel guess might be fun, but he needed his cousin's cooperation. "I'll tell you. I went for a swim."

"Oh, really? You've never struck me as the sort to dive into the nearest body of water, especially water you've never seen before. In fact, I seem to remember you had strong opinions on swimming alone after Bentley drowned."

Damn Nigel, he was far too knowing. "I wasn't alone."

Nigel choked on the sip of brandy he'd just taken. "Ah."

Drew swung his foot back and forth. How could he

tell Nigel about Miss Collingswood? Saying she'd been swimming naked would give a false impression of her character. At least he thought it would be a false impression. He must remember he didn't know her well, even though it felt as if they'd been friends forever.

They *weren't* friends. They were barely acquaintances, but still . . .

He'd always thought tales of love at first sight were complete rubbish, but now he wasn't so certain. He'd felt strangely more alive with Miss Venus Collingswood. Colors had been brighter; smells, fresher; and—damn, now he sounded like a bloody poet. But there was definitely an energy, an enthusiasm about her that was very seductive—almost as seductive as her lovely face and form.

He glanced at Nigel again. Spirits might inspire him. "Are you going to offer me something to drink?"

"It's your brandy." Nigel cocked his head toward a cabinet against the wall. "Help yourself—and bring the bottle over. I have a feeling I'll need some fortification."

Having his cousin in a mellow mood—or, better, slightly inebriated—might be just the thing. Drew got the brandy and handed it to Nigel after pouring himself a glass. "Are you hiding from Mrs. Edgemoor?"

"Of course I'm hiding from the good woman, though hiding is not exactly the proper term," Nigel said, refilling his glass. "I'm merely trying to reduce the number of times she has to encounter me while under the mistaken impression I'm you. I assume—I hope—you've come to your senses and will stop this ridiculous charade."

Drew grunted and looked around the room. "Is Blant's library everything you'd hoped?"

"Yes." Nigel's eyes gleamed, and he leaned forward. "The fellow has an amazing collection of—" He caught himself. "Oh, no, you're not going to distract me. When are you going to tell Mrs. Edgemoor you are Greycliffe? She's put me in the master bedroom, by the by."

"Excellent."

Nigel fixed him with his best older cousin glare. "Drew, you have to tell her who you are."

"I don't see why." Drew sat down again. "In fact, it's rather important Mrs. Edgemoor not know my identity."

"I see." Nigel's eyes narrowed. "Or rather, I don't see. I thought this masquerade was a spur of the moment lark."

"It was." Drew grinned. "But it's a bit more now."

Nigel stared at him, obviously working through the puzzle; it didn't take him long to come up with a solution. "This has something to do with the person—I assume from your lack of candor, a female—you went swimming with."

"I didn't go swimming with her; I rescued her. I thought she'd fallen into the pond."

"All right, but that still doesn't explain why I need to keep being the duke."

Drew stared at the fire. "She knew we were coming, though of course she thought we'd arrive next week."

"As we would have if you hadn't taken it into your head to flee London."

Drew laughed, meeting Nigel's gaze again. "I didn't see you dragging your feet. You wanted to get away from the Widow Blackburn as much as I wanted to escape Lady Mary."

Nigel conceded the point. "True. Damnation, but the woman is mad. Why she thinks I'd marry her—"

"Perhaps because she's respectable, and you've been enjoying her bed?"

Nigel snorted. "She's hardly respectable, and you know I wasn't the first nor will I be the last male of the *ton* to slip between her sheets."

"But you're the richest, and you did seem a bit besotted."

"Besotted? Hardly. Oh, I'll admit I was dazzled by her remarkable"—Nigel made a rounded motion with his hands—"attributes, and she *is* creative in the bedroom, but she has the depth of understanding and the conversational skills of a turnip. I am finished with her." He raised his glass in mock toast and took a long swallow.

"Well, that's good. I can't say I was eager to welcome her into the family."

Nigel raised an eyebrow. "Nor am I eager to welcome Lady Mary."

"There's no chance of that."

"I don't know. Her most recent plot almost worked. If Sherrington hadn't been with you when you found her in your carriage, you might have found yourself standing at the altar."

Drew scowled and slid deeper into his chair. "There's no way in hell I'd marry that harpy, even if she managed to sneak naked into my bed. There are some benefits to being a duke."

"Cranmore is a duke as well."

Damn it, Nigel was right, of course. Lady Mary's father was a dirty dish, but one with a ducal crest. It had been a near thing that night at Vauxhall—which was why he'd fled to this remote section of the country.

He needed some foolproof way to escape the woman's grasping claws . . .

Marriage. Bigamy was against the law, so if he was already married—or at least betrothed—when next he encountered Lady Mary, he'd be safe.

Another good reason to pursue Miss Venus Collingswood.

"To get back to your swimming companion," Nigel said.

"So the girl knew we were coming. That's no surprise. This is a small village; news must travel like the wind. When she saw you, a well-dressed stranger—" Nigel stopped, mouth slightly ajar, and then put one hand over his eyes. "Oh, God, you were in the water. Please don't tell me you were naked."

Drew had no intention of telling his cousin anything.

"I *hope* she saw a well-dressed stranger," Nigel said. "In any event, she must have made the obvious deduction that you are the duke. I would say it's rather late to pretend to be me, unless . . . Oh." He sighed. "I see it now. She thought you *were* me."

"Exactly. Apparently I don't look particularly ducal na—" Drew coughed. "Wet."

Nigel frowned, but thankfully didn't comment on his slip. "Why the hell didn't you correct her?"

"Because I wanted her to think I was you."

Nigel's eyes widened. "Good God, have you lost your mind?"

"Of course not." Drew put his elbows on his knees and leaned forward. "Don't you see? One of the curses of being a duke is I can never tell if women are attracted to me or to my title."

"Does it matter? Most men would be happy to have all the Season's beauties—respectable and not—vying for their attention."

"It's not *my* attention they want; it's the Duke of Grey-cliffe's."

Nigel frowned. "I suppose it wouldn't help to point out you *are* the Duke of Greycliffe?"

"No."

Nigel looked at him a moment longer and then shook his head and sighed. "All right, I'll try to keep this charade going, but you must know it will likely have unpleasant repercussions. I cannot imagine Mrs. Edgemoor will be pleased to have been hoodwinked."

Drew sat back and grinned. Thank God Nigel was willing to play along. And perhaps if Aphrodite was as beautiful and bookish as Venus said, Drew might not be the only one stepping into parson's mousetrap as a result of this visit. "Don't worry. I'll apologize to Mrs. Edgemoor most sincerely if we're discovered."

"Hmm. And you do realize, don't you, that this girl you seem so eager to fool won't be happy with you either when she discovers you're actually Greycliffe? Who is she, by the by? Someone moderately respectable, I hope."

"She's the local vicar's daughter, Miss Venus Collingswood." He hadn't focused on Venus's reaction to his ruse, but he wasn't about to worry. If events proceeded as he hoped, he'd be in a delightful position to soothe her anger. He quite looked forward to it.

Nigel was frowning as if he were trying to remember something. "Collingswood. Venus Collingswood," he muttered. "Now why the devil does that name sound familiar?"

"I can't imagine you've met her. I understood she and her family never leave Little Huffington."

Nigel was still frowning. "I swear I've heard the name before—or at least the last name. Does she have a brother, perhaps?"

"No, only a sister."

"And her name is?"

"Aphrodite, though how you could—"

"That's it!" Nigel snapped his fingers. "Aphrodite Collingswood."

"You know Miss Collingswood?" Damn. There would be no way Nigel could pretend to be Greycliffe if he was acquainted with Venus's sister.

"No. Now I remember. I corresponded with her father

concerning a short treatise he'd written in *The Classical Gazette*. In his reply, he mentioned his daughter Aphrodite had helped him. Aphrodite is not a name one forgets easily."

Venus had said her sister was a scholar, but Drew had thought she'd overstated the case. Perhaps not. "It sounds as if the woman is extremely intelligent."

"Her father certainly thinks so."

"What, was he trying to interest you in a wife?"

Nigel had just taken a sip of brandy; he sprayed it back into his glass. "He was not."

Drew had long suspected Nigel took no interest in the marriageable women of the *ton* because he found them all feather-headed nincompoops. Venus's sister might be just what his cousin needed. "Venus says Aphrodite is also very beautiful."

"It seems the young lady is a veritable paragon." Nigel pulled out his watch and checked the time. "I suppose I've hidden here long enough. I'll go hide in my bedchamber for a while—are you certain you won't take the master bedroom?"

"Of course I won't. I'm determined to play the part of Mr. Valentine as long as I can. And Aphrodite is not so young; she's twenty-three."

"And still unwed?" Nigel laughed. "She must have some fatal flaw, then, since I cannot believe all the local men are blind." He stood.

Drew rose as well. "I suspect none have interested her enough to tempt her to put aside her books." He grinned. "You should understand that."

Nigel's eyebrows shot up. "You can't be saying I spend too much time in my study! I'm here because I'm avoiding the Widow Blackburn, remember?"

"Right. I should probably warn you that Venus is a bit of a matchmaker. She's hoping our arrival in the neighborhood will brighten Aphrodite's matrimonial outlook." Drew headed for the door—best to have a clear path of retreat. "I believe she thinks her sister would make a splendid duchess."

Nigel laughed. "You'd best be on your toes then, Drew."

"Not I. Remember, Venus thinks *you* are the duke."

Drew closed the door on Nigel's impressively imaginative curses.

"Ow!" Venus pricked her finger for the third time. She watched a red bead of blood ooze out of her abused flesh and then stuck her finger into her mouth. At this rate, the handkerchief she was embroidering would be more red than white.

"Did you say something, dear?" Mama looked up from her book; even Ditee glanced up briefly.

Papa was in the study, writing Sunday's sermon. Sermons were not his forte. He called on the devil a shocking number of times while trying to wrestle a moderately uplifting message onto the page, so the women had retreated to the morning room.

"No, Mama. I merely stuck my finger with the needle."

Mama frowned and then returned to her reading. "Perhaps you should go for a walk. You seem oddly agitated."

Venus swallowed a slightly hysterical giggle. Go for a walk? Dear God! Yesterday's walk was the source of her agitation. Not the walk itself, of course, but what had happened at her destination.

She closed her eyes in mortification, but popped them open immediately.

The vision of a naked Mr. Valentine must be burned into the back of her eyelids, because whenever she shut them, she saw him in exquisite detail. It had been almost impossible to sleep last night.

She pressed her lips together, but didn't quite muffle her

moan. Mama gave her a concerned—and slightly annoyed—look, but thankfully forbore to comment.

And it wasn't just Mr. Valentine's image that tortured her: her body remembered all too well the feel of his naked arm around her waist, of his naked chest against her back, of his hands moving over her skin—and the light touch of his kiss.

She shifted on her chair. She must be sickening. She ached all over. Her breasts and her— She flushed. She wouldn't think of it.

The only way she'd found to control the fever eating at her was to consider how she must have appeared to him—and then a different kind of heat flooded her.

She'd been swimming naked! No woman of gentle birth—likely no female of any sort—did such a shocking thing.

And he'd been *looking* at her. He'd seen parts of her *she* didn't examine closely.

"Venus, please. If you don't wish to walk, perhaps you could find some other activity to do—somewhere else," Mama said. "Your sighing and twitching are most distracting."

Mama and Ditee were both staring at her now.

"Yes, Mama. I'm sorry." Venus stood and took her needlework up to her room. There was no point in attempting any more sewing. She was only turning herself into a pincushion.

She put her workbasket by her desk and stared out the window. As luck would have it, her room faced the pond, though of course it was too far away and hidden by the woods to see. But she knew it was there.

She rested her head against the glass. How would she ever face Mr. Valentine again without expiring of embarrassment? And she'd persuaded him to invite them and all the gentry of Little Huffington to Hyndon House. Everyone she knew could enjoy the spectacle of Miss Venus Collingswood turning red as a beet or engaging in her very first fit of the vapors. Mrs. Higgins and Esmeralda would be especially amused.

Venus straightened. No. She was made of sterner stuff than that—she would have to be. She must remember Ditee. Mr. Valentine was merely a means to an end, a way of bringing her sister to his cousin the duke's attention. She could put up with a little personal discomfort for that. Likely a London beau such as Mr. Valentine had seen countless women without their clothing—and had done many things (whatever those things might be) with them as well. He'd probably already forgotten one thin country miss's unremarkable figure.

He hadn't forgotten to arrange the party, had he? Mrs. Shipley said he and the duke weren't expected to stay at Hyndon House long. There was no time to waste.

She would write him a note. Yes, it was shocking—or would be shocking if they had a personal relationship. This was strictly business. She would remind him of the planned event—and if it wasn't yet planned, perhaps that would prod him into action—and suggest he might wish to bring his cousin into the village tomorrow afternoon so he could meet Ditee before the gathering.

She dipped her quill into the inkwell. Getting Ditee into the village would be a Herculean task in itself, but that was tomorrow's problem.

Drew was talking to Mrs. Edgemoor about the party when Mrs. Shipley arrived. Mrs. Edgemoor had taken it much better than he'd expected—certainly better than Nigel, who had stormed around the study predicting discovery and disaster.

Nigel might well be right, but one needed a little excitement in one's life.

"Oh, Lavinia," Mrs. Edgemoor said, "you'll never guess. Mr. Valentine here says the duke is going to entertain the neighborhood." Her voice was an odd mix of horror and excitement. "How shall I ever manage?"

"I'll help you, Maud. Don't worry." Mrs. Shipley removed her bonnet and smiled at Drew. "Let me give Mr. Valentine this message, and then we'll have a nice chat about it." She handed him a twist of paper and led Mrs. Edgemoor off.

He frowned at the paper. There was only one person at the vicarage who might send him a message, but he wouldn't have guessed she'd be so bold. His heart suddenly felt like a rock. He'd thought Venus was different, but apparently he was mistaken. Grasping hussies weren't limited to Town, and they chased anything in breeches, not just dukes.

He should throw the message away unread: Nigel certainly would. Sometimes—oftentimes—he thought his cousin would make a far better duke than he. He crumpled the paper up, but before he could toss it in the flames, curiosity got the better of him. He smoothed it out, read it—and chuckled.

Dear Mr. Valentine,

Please excuse my presumption in writing to you, but I felt I must put myself forward on my sister's behalf as I understand you and the duke do not plan to linger in Little Huffington. I hope you will not take offense at my reminding you that you thought the duke might wish to invite the local gentry to Hyndon House. In anticipation of that, my sister and I will be in the village tomorrow afternoon in case the duke might enjoy meeting her in a less formal setting.

Yours most sincerely,
Miss Venus Collingswood

Certainly not the impassioned missive he'd feared. Her handwriting was so precise, much like a schoolgirl's, and the tone . . . she sounded like someone's old maiden aunt. Had she gone through many drafts to get it just right? He'd wager she had.

His heart—and that other organ—lifted. She looked nothing like anyone's maiden aunt, old or otherwise. He'd spent quite a heated night, dreaming of her: her slim waist, her exquisite breasts, her soft skin and silky hair, warm brown eyes and sharp tongue. Thoughts of her tongue, and ways she might creatively employ it, had almost forced him to take himself in hand, as it were, something he'd not resorted to since he was a lad.

He folded the note and put it in his pocket. It appeared that he and Nigel had some business to conduct in Little Huffington tomorrow afternoon.

Chapter 4

"Couldn't you have left the book at home?" Venus looked over at her sister as they trudged down the hill to the village. How did Ditee manage to read and walk at the same time?

"I'm at a very interesting part." Ditee shot Venus an annoyed glance before she turned a page. "If you'll remember, I didn't want to come."

"Even Mama agreed your blue dress needed some new ribbon to brighten it up."

Ditee snorted. "That dress is perfectly fine the way it is. There's no need to waste time and money fussing with it."

"Ditee, that dress is five years old."

"So? I can't have worn it more than a handful of times."

Venus drew in a deep breath. She would *not* argue, but she couldn't quite bite her tongue. "The white ribbons are yellowed with age."

Why couldn't Ditee be a little more aware of her appearance? She didn't have to be clothes mad—that would be a mistake here in Little Huffington where the latest fashions were simply late, arriving two or three years after everyone in Town had moved on to other things—but a little interest wouldn't go amiss. She was so beautiful; she would be completely without par if she'd cultivate just a modicum of fashion sense.

Ditee's eyes traveled to the next page. "No one is going to be studying my ribbons at this stupid gathering. Really, I don't know why I have to go. I would be happier staying home."

Venus nodded at Mr. Pettigrew, the blacksmith, as they reached the village shops. "Perhaps, but even Papa said you must attend, Ditee." She'd tried everything to convince Mama and Papa to go and drag Ditee with them after the invitation to the duke's garden party had arrived this morning. She'd even pointed out Papa's living as vicar might be dependent on getting into the duke's good graces; Greycliffe could certainly decide to install someone else if he chose, and then where would they be? It was just an accident she'd mentioned Mr. Valentine.

She frowned down at her sturdy walking shoes. Why hadn't Mr. Valentine told her he'd written to Papa? She kicked a stone that was careless enough to be lying in her path and sent it shooting ahead of them. Once she'd mentioned *his* name, Papa's face had lit up. He'd told Ditee she had to meet Mr. Valentine, who was apparently quite a Latin scholar. Of course, Papa didn't know the man was also young and marriageable; he only cared that he was interested in the classics.

Ditee was supposed to be matched with the duke, not Mr. Valentine, but what did it matter? A husband was a husband, and if Mr. Valentine was more appropriate, so be it.

Venus felt very disgruntled.

"You don't happen to have a pencil and a scrap of paper, do you?" Ditee asked.

"Of course not. Why in the world would I?"

Ditee shrugged. "I didn't think you would; I merely hoped you might. I would have brought them myself if I hadn't had to hurry out of the house."

"You didn't hurry anywhere. I had to hound you for the last half hour to get you to leave."

Ditee sniffed. "There you have it. If you hadn't been badgering me, I would have thought to bring them myself. Now I have nothing to make a note on."

"Likely Mr. Fenwick will have paper and pencil in his shop."

Ditee's face lit up. "Of course! I'll—oh!" She'd quickened her steps just as a man came out of Mr. Whitcomb's snuff and spirits shop. She ran full into him, throwing up her hands to brace herself on his chest and dropping her book to the walkway.

The man grabbed her shoulders to steady her. "Are you all right, Miss?"

Who was he? He was slightly above average height, well dressed—Venus would swear his clothes came from London—and moderately handsome. Hmm. Did he look like a duke?

Mr. Valentine appeared behind him.

Oh.

Venus felt rather like she had at the pond, completely unable to draw an adequate breath.

She'd dreamt of him again last night, of his shoulders and chest and, ah, other naked parts. She'd felt his light, brief kiss over and over, and she'd wished—*yearned*—for something more, though she'd no idea what more there was. She'd woken hot, feeling as if her skin was too tight, her sheets all twisted.

And now she saw him with clothes on. He was just as handsome in his snowy white shirt, dark coat, and doeskin breeches.

And with his knowing, laughing eyes.

She snapped her mouth shut as he bent to whisper by her ear. "She's pretty, but not as pretty as you."

Damn it, her jaw dropped again.

"Yes, yes," Ditee was saying. She sounded oddly flustered. Venus swiveled her head to look at her sister more closely. Good God, was Ditee blushing?

"I'm fine," Ditee said, stepping back out of the man's hold. "I'm so sorry, sir. I wasn't looking where I was going. I hope I didn't do you an injury?"

"Of course not, Miss . . . ?"

"I believe this is Miss Aphrodite Collingswood," Mr. Valentine said, "and her sister, Miss Venus." He bowed. "And we are, as you've probably surmised, the Duke of Greycliffe and Mr. Nigel Valentine."

"How do you do, sir—your grace," Venus said, since Ditee seemed to have lost her tongue.

The duke glared at Mr. Valentine, who gave him an odd look in exchange. Then Greycliffe nodded—well, it was more a jerk of his head than a nod—and bent to save Ditee's book from the pavement. He glanced at the title and smiled as he handed it back to her. "You are reading Horace, I see."

Oh, dear. Venus glanced at Mr. Valentine by her side. Would he jump into the conversation and start discussing classical matters, distracting Ditee's attention from the duke? That would be disastrous.

"Oh," Ditee said, taking the book. "Yes. Thank you. Do you know the work?"

"Indeed. Horace is one of my particular favorites. I believe I've read everything he's written many times over."

Ditee's face lit up in a way Venus had never seen before. It made her even more beautiful—as the stunned expressions on the men's faces proved. "Oh, that is wonderful, your grace. Then perhaps you can answer a question that has just occurred to me."

Thank God the duke admired Horace. Now if she could just keep Mr. Valentine out of the conversation, all would be well.

Not that she wished to have the annoying man to herself, of course.

"May we escort you to your destination, ladies?" Mr. Valentine asked. "Then you and, er, my cousin can continue your discussion, Miss Aphrodite."

Ditee glanced at Venus and then at the duke. "Oh, yes, that would be very nice. We were just on our way to Mr. Fenwick's store to purchase ribbon."

This was a day for Venus's mouth to be constantly agape. Ditee hadn't ripped up at Mr. Valentine or told the men how she'd been forced to shop for silly gewgaws. She'd never heard her sister sound so pleasant.

"Splendid. Then let us proceed." Mr. Valentine offered Venus his arm while the duke and Ditee walked on ahead.

Venus's fingers trembled slightly as she placed them on Mr. Valentine's sleeve. She could almost see his naked arm beneath the cloth, and she remembered very distinctly how it had felt wrapped around her in the water—

She waved her hand in front of her face. She could not think about such things.

"Hot?" Mr. Valentine asked.

"Yes. The weather is stifling."

"I don't know. I think there's a bit of a breeze."

Blast it, so there was. Time to change the subject. "I have a bone to pick with you, sir."

"You do? And here I thought I'd been the complete gentleman. What is the problem?"

"Don't pretend innocence." She looked up into his deep

blue eyes with their long, long lashes. He looked like a
choirboy, not the slippery fellow he was.

The sensation of his wet arms slipping over her naked
body was so strong, she shivered. She forced her gaze
ahead—and had the startling sight of Ditee talking in a
distinctly animated fashion to a marriageable male. Good
heavens! Her sister was even smiling.

Venus should be delighted that her matchmaking looked
to be well underway, but she wasn't. She was too . . . annoyed
with the man next to her.

"I'm not pretending," he said. "I sincerely don't know
what has put you in a pet."

She clenched her teeth. "If you'll forgive me, I find that
hard to believe."

They reached Mr. Fenwick's establishment. The duke es-
corted Ditee inside; Venus turned and poked the miscreant
next to her in the chest.

"You acted as though you had no idea who I was when
we met at"—she felt herself flush—"before, but then I
found out you'd written to Papa."

Mr. Valentine's eyes looked decidedly wary. "Er, I did?"

"Yes, as well you know. You wrote him about some arti-
cle he'd written in *The Classical Gazette*. So why didn't you
mention that fact?"

His lips twitched into a half smile. "I was distracted."

"By what?" She crossed her arms, arching an eyebrow.
This should be interesting.

He glanced down the street and took her hand, direct-
ing her away from the shop door. They were in plain view
of anyone passing by, but enough out of the way that someone would have to walk over to them to hear what they were
saying.

His smile had widened and his eyes were gleaming with
mischief . . . and something far hotter. "Do you have to ask?"

"Y-yes." What game was he playing now? He'd kept hold of her hand and was drawing circles in her palm with his thumb. She felt it all the way through her glove to her, er . . . *core* might be the most polite way to refer to the area of her person that was fluttering and growing embarrassingly damp. "I have n-no i—" She sucked in her breath. His thumb had moved to the inside of her wrist, setting her disreputable core to throbbing.

She snatched her hand away from him. "I have no idea why you wouldn't have revealed such an important point."

"Hmm." He appeared to study her face. She'd swear there were little flames flickering deep in his eyes. His gaze dropped to her mouth, and she felt her lips swell. "What are we talking about?" he whispered, his voice rather hoarse.

What indeed?

Her lips ached to feel his touch. Would he—

Good God! She jerked her head back. "Don't try to avoid the question. You were about to tell me how you could have neglected to mention you'd corresponded with my father."

"Oh, that's easy. I wasn't thinking about your father."

"What *were* you thinking about?"

Oh, dear, perhaps that was a bad question to ask. If Mr. Valentine's expression had been warm before, it was scorching now.

"I was thinking how beautiful you were with your long, chestnut-colored hair and lovely creamy skin"—he leaned closer, dropping his voice to a hot, deep whisper—"*all* your creamy skin."

Her knees felt as if they might give out. She put her hands on his chest to steady herself, and his fingers came up to cover them.

"And when most women would have been terrified, you

were so full of spirit." He gripped her hands tightly. "You took an outrageous risk, you know."

"No." She wanted to argue, but her brain and voice weren't functioning properly. She stared up at him; his face stilled, and his eyes focused on her mouth again. Oh. He was going to kiss her here on High Street in front of Mr. Fenwick's shop where the entire village could see them.

She should stop him.

She'd never been kissed. Not really. The brief brush of his lips at the pond did not count. That had just been a tease . . . perhaps a promise?

She tilted her face up, let her eyes drift closed . . .

And heard Ditee's voice behind her.

"Venus, Mr. Fenwick has—*what* are you doing?"

"You weren't going to kiss Miss Venus in the middle of High Street, were you?" Nigel asked as they rode back to Hyndon House.

"Of course not." It hadn't been the *middle* of High Street . . .

Damn it, he *had* almost kissed Venus in full view of any passerby. What was the matter with him? He'd never before lost awareness of his surroundings so completely, except perhaps when he'd been standing naked at that pond.

It was all Venus's fault. There was something about her that made his good sense shut down. It wasn't just her beauty; he'd seen plenty of beautiful women in London. It was her spirit, her determination, her sharp tongue. He felt so alive when he was with her, as if something exciting— likely disastrous—was about to happen at any moment.

But the oddest thing was he also felt very comfortable with her, as if they'd been friends forever.

His mother had died when he was four; his father when

he was thirteen. As duke, he had countless dependents, but he hadn't had a family in a long, long time. Yes, he had Nigel. Nigel was like a brother, but Nigel was seven years older than he. There had always been that distance—and Nigel would eventually marry and have his own family.

Drew had always felt deeply alone—but not when he was with Venus.

"This is only a small, rural village miles from London," Nigel was saying, "but I'll wager my yearly income that gossip flourishes here, too, and rumors that the Duke of Greycliffe is showing a marked interest in a certain country miss will be flying back to Town faster than the wind."

Blast it, Nigel was probably right. Hell, London's biggest gossips could have been standing at his elbow and he likely wouldn't have noticed. But Nigel did have one crucial detail wrong.

"The gossips won't be saying the duke is dallying with Venus; no one here knows I'm Greycliffe. They'll say you were the one misbehaving."

The *ton* wouldn't know what to make of staid Nigel Valentine, so discreet—before Widow Blackburn, that is— acting in such a publicly scandalous way. Not that they'd know what to make of Drew either if the truth got out, but it seemed dukes were expected to behave as if society's rules did not apply to them.

Nigel gaped at him—and then favored him with a long, rather imaginative string of curses.

"I'm sorry," Drew said. "What was that one about the witch's teat? I didn't quite catch it."

"Bloody hell, Drew, I'm going to kill you."

"You can't. Murdering a peer is a capital offense. You don't want to hang, do you?"

Drew could almost hear Nigel's teeth grinding.

"I might risk it."

"Not a good idea." They turned through the gates to Hyndon House and started up the drive. "Don't worry. I'm sure things will sort themselves out." Drew shot Nigel a look. "Perhaps the gossip will give the widow a disgust of you."

"Not likely. I—"

"Good God!" Drew reined his horse in so abruptly the animal tossed its head and sidestepped. They'd just come around a bend, and he could see the front door—and a carriage with the Duke of Cranmore's crest on the side.

"What is it? Oh."

Nigel's words came from behind him; Drew hadn't waited to discuss the matter. Acting on instinct and a touch of panic, he'd kicked his horse down a side path into the trees.

Nigel followed. "You can't hide in the woods forever."

Drew swung off his horse and led it deeper into the shadows. "I can hide until she leaves—and she has to leave. Even a disreputable baggage like Lady Mary knows that she can't stay overnight in a bachelor household." He looped his horse's reins over a low-hanging tree limb and edged up to peer around a large bush. There was no movement either from the carriage or the house.

"After the way she lay in wait for you at Vauxhall, I wouldn't be so certain. And chances are Mrs. Edgemoor hasn't the mettle to stand up to her."

"We can only hope the good woman has a deep well of moral outrage. Sometimes—no, here's Lady Mary now."

Nigel hurried up to look around the other side of the bush. "And another female. It looks like—oh, damn."

"It's the Widow Blackburn." Drew gave a low whistle and looked at Nigel. "I didn't know they were bosom friends."

Nigel was not amused. "How the bloody *hell* could

Cranmore have countenanced his daughter traveling down from London with that woman? Doesn't he care for his daughter's reputation?"

Drew shrugged and looked back at the house. "It's a little late for that; his precious daughter's reputation is almost as black as the widow's. Hey now, who's this?"

A fubsy woman with an enormous hat and an equally fat and squat younger woman climbed into the carriage after the widow and Lady Mary.

"They appear made from the same mold," Nigel said. "They must be mother and daughter."

"Quite likely. The older one looks rather pompous. I'll wager she's Mrs. Higgins, the squire's wife."

Drew watched the coach rumble off. He and Nigel went to their horses to keep them quiet; the foliage was dense enough that unless the women knew where to look, they wouldn't discover them.

Mrs. Edgemoor had a lot to say when they finally entered the house.

"Oh, your grace," she said to Nigel, "we had visitors while you and Mr. Valentine were in the village." Mrs. Edgemoor's face was pinched into an expression of disapproval. "Squire Higgins's wife and their daughter, Esmeralda; a Mrs. Blackburn who, if you'll pardon me saying so, is no better than she should be; and Lady Mary Detluck, the Duke of Cranmore's daughter." Her nose wrinkled as if she smelled something bad. "Lady Mary was very high in the instep, your grace, not at all like you. She and Mrs. Blackburn said they were"—Mrs. Edgemoor flushed and seemed to have difficulty getting the words out—"special friends of yours."

"Oh, no," Nigel said. "They are definitely not that."

"We came down early, Mrs. Edgemoor," Drew said, "to get away from them."

Mrs. Edgemoor so forgot herself as to grin, clearly relieved, and nodded vigorously. "That's just what I thought. Those London women were trying to suggest they were betrothed to you and said I should tell them where you were and what you'd been doing while you were here, which of course I never would—not that you've done anything scandalous, of course. Why, two quieter, better behaved gentlemen I've not had the pleasure to meet, and that's the truth."

Drew was careful not to meet Nigel's eye; Mrs. Edgemoor might not consider having a naked tête-à-tête with the vicar's daughter precisely well-behaved.

"Did they say how long they intended to be in the area?" Drew asked.

"No, but they did say they would see you at the garden party. Mrs. Blackburn has a friend who's a friend of Mrs. Higgins, so they are staying at the squire's house."

"I see," Drew said. At least they had a little longer before they had to face those harpies. "Is everything coming along well for the party? We're so sorry to put you to all this trouble."

"It's no trouble at all, sir. Mrs. Shipley is helping, and I've got some girls in from the village, too. It's not as if there are many people who will come—Little Huffington is, well, little." She frowned, twisting her hands together. "I do hope those London ladies won't look down their noses at us."

"If they do, that is their problem, isn't it?" Nigel said.

"Yes, your grace. That's right." Mrs. Edgemoor gave them another wide smile before curtsying and hurrying off, likely to attend to more party details.

They went into the study. Drew sprawled in a chair and let out a long breath. "Things are going to get complicated."

Nigel snorted. "Quite."

"It will be hard to keep this charade going with the widow and Lady Mary here."

"Hard? It will be impossible." Nigel poured two glasses of brandy and handed Drew one before taking the chair across from his. "You have to tell Venus who you are."

Drew wanted to put that off as long as he could. "I'll get to it."

Nigel stared at him. Damn, he *was* looking as unbending as the Dover cliffs now. "Do what you wish, but I will not continue with this masquerade any longer."

"But . . ."

"No. We have not precisely—not explicitly—lied to anyone yet, but we are sailing very close to the wind. I decided in the village I was done with it. Widow Blackburn's and Lady Mary's arrival on the scene just reinforces my decision."

This wasn't a surprise, but . . . "What happened in the village?"

Nigel frowned. "What do you mean, what happened in the village?"

"What happened to make you suddenly decide you couldn't pretend to be me any longer?"

Were the tips of Nigel's ears red?

"My good sense simply reassured itself," Nigel said, not meeting Drew's eyes.

"And you met Aphrodite." It appeared that Venus's matchmaking efforts were bearing fruit. "She *is* very beautiful."

"And very intelligent." Nigel looked Drew in the eye then, his cheeks definitely flushed. "I do not care to deceive her."

"We aren't exactly deceiving her."

"You are splitting hairs. If she thinks I'm you, she's operating under a mistaken assumption, one I could clarify. If I don't do so, that's deception in my book." He grinned suddenly. "I don't want to think her feelings for me—whatever they are—are influenced by her misperception of my rank. You should be sympathetic to that sentiment."

Blast it, of course he was. Drew took a long swallow of brandy. It looked as if he would definitely have to tell Venus he was Greycliffe sooner rather than later.

Chapter 5

"What were you doing with Mr. Valentine, Venus?" Ditee asked as they studied lengths of ribbon in Mr. Fenwick's shop. The duke and Mr. Valentine had left a few moments ago. "You looked most peculiar."

"Talking about the classics," Venus said. That wasn't a complete lie. She *had* mentioned the man's letter to Papa.

"Oh. But you had your eyes closed."

"I'm sure I must have been on the verge of falling asleep. You know how much I hate that subject." Venus plucked a ribbon from the display and held it up to Ditee's face. "This shade of blue would look very nice on your dress. It matches your eyes."

"It does?" Ditee ran the fabric through her fingers. "Do you really think so?"

"Yes, indeed." Venus pretended to study the other ribbons. "I thought the duke seemed like a pleasant gentleman. Did you?"

"Oh, yes!" Ditee's face lit up again. "He's extremely

knowledgeable. He answered my question about Horace most thoroughly. I was very impressed."

This sounded promising, especially as Ditee's cheeks were quite pink. "He's rather handsome, too."

Ditee's color deepened. "Perhaps."

Venus bit the inside of her cheek to keep from grinning. Her bookish sister was finally showing some interest in the opposite sex. "Perhaps you should get a new comb for your hair as well." She held up one that sparkled even in the dim light of Mr. Fenwick's store. "Something like this."

"That *is* very pretty."

In the end, Ditee got two combs, the blue ribbon, and a length of deep rose ribbon for her walking dress. Venus was delighted with the way things were progressing, until she bumped into Mrs. Fedderly on the street outside Mr. Fenwick's shop.

"Oh, Miss Venus—and Miss Aphrodite. I was so hoping to run into you." Old Mrs. Fedderly was the village gossip, but since her eyesight wasn't very good any longer, people generally took her stories with a large grain of salt. "I saw you chatting with our illustrious new neighbors." She winked at Venus. "Finally doing a little matchmaking for yourself, eh?"

Venus felt herself flush. "No, I—"

"They seemed quite taken with both of you." The woman's thin eyebrows did a little jig. "Perhaps they'll be staying in Little Huffington longer than expected."

"Have you met the duke and Mr. Valentine, Mrs. Fedderly?" Aphrodite asked.

"No, but I am very much looking forward to their garden party. It will be so nice to have social activity at Hyndon House again. You know Mr. Blant used to entertain all the time when he was young." Mrs. Fedderly batted her short, white lashes. "He was quite the rogue."

The thought of Mr. Blant entertaining more than a side of beef was stupefying in itself, but to consider him a rogue of any stripe was beyond Venus's powers of imagination.

The rattle of a carriage approaching filled the stunned silence. They all turned to regard the impressive equipage bearing down on them.

"Now who could this be?" Mrs. Fedderly rubbed her hands in apparent glee. "I swear things haven't been this exciting since Farmer Isley's goat ate Miss Wardley's favorite bonnet."

The coach creaked to a stop, and Mrs. Higgins lumbered out, followed by her daughter and two elegant ladies.

Mrs. Higgins hurried over to them—she could move surprisingly quickly when sufficiently motivated. "Mrs. Fedderly, have you seen the Duke of Greycliffe and his cousin, Mr. Valentine?" she asked, completely ignoring Venus and Ditee.

"Oh, yes," Mrs. Fedderly said with a small, sly smile, obviously delighted to be one step ahead of Mrs. Higgins with village gossip. "But you might better ask the Misses Collingswood. They were actually conversing with the gentlemen."

Venus was surprised Mrs. Fedderly didn't literally crow. The only thing better than beating Mrs. Higgins to some juicy gossip was forcing her to apply to the Collingswood girls for elucidation.

Mrs. Higgins's mouth pursed as if she'd just bitten into a lemon.

"Have you found them, Mama?" Esmeralda asked, coming up.

"No, but apparently the Collingswood girls know where they are."

"Oh?" Esmeralda glanced at Venus's green dress and turned up her bulbous nose. "Why would the duke and his cousin speak to someone so . . . dowdy?"

Venus clenched her teeth. True, her dress was a shade of green popular last year—well, perhaps the year before last—but it was still serviceable. And Esmeralda was hardly a pattern card of fashion. Her insipid pink gown was so covered with knots of ribbons and bits of lace, she looked like a walking haberdashery. She would just tell her—

"Who are these people, Mrs. Higgins?" The older of the two stylish women peered disapprovingly at Venus through her lorgnette. Venus had an almost overwhelming urge to grab the dratted spectacles out of her hand and ram them through her ridiculously elaborate hairstyle.

"Just Mrs. Fedderly and the vicar's daughters, Mrs. Blackburn."

Venus was quite, quite tired of being talked about as if she were deaf and dumb. "Yes, I am Venus Collingswood. This is my sister, Aphrodite. And you are . . . ?"

"Mrs. Blackburn," the woman said, "and Lady Mary Detluck"—she indicated the younger woman—"the Duke of Cranmore's daughter."

Lady Mary sniffed. "So tell me where my betrothed is, if you will. I came all the way from London to see him."

"Your betrothed?" Venus bit her lip. Damn it, she hadn't meant to say that, but shock had got the better of her. Mr. Valentine had said nothing of a betrothed lurking about. Surely he would have said something if the duke . . . But would he have mentioned a betrothal of his own?

Her stomach dropped to her toes.

"Betrothed?" Mrs. Fedderly laughed. "I didn't see any men who looked betrothed."

Lady Mary scowled. "Perhaps your vision is defective. I

assure you Greycliffe is promised to me, and Mr. Valentine is affianced to Mrs. Blackburn."

"My vision is fine," Mrs. Fedderly lied, "and I assure *you* the duke and his cousin looked quite smitten when they were walking and talking with Miss Aphrodite and Miss Venus."

Mrs. Blackburn's eyes were as hard as stones. "Oh, well, a little flirting is to be expected. They are men, after all." She looked from Venus to Aphrodite and back. "I hope no one misunderstood their intentions."

Lady Mary snorted. "Really, can you imagine Greycliffe or Mr. Valentine showing any serious interest in such rustics?"

Mrs. Higgins and Esmeralda sniggered, but Venus would wager all her pin money Lady Mary considered them just as rustic as her and Ditee.

Mrs. Fedderly sniffed. "Mr. Fedderly, God rest his soul, used to say the air—and the women—were cleaner in the country."

The ensuing shocked silence gave Venus her opening. "I believe the duke and Mr. Valentine returned to Hyndon House, ladies. At least, that seemed to be their intention; I can't claim to be in their confidence." *Ha! She was most obviously not in their confidence.* "Now if you'll excuse us, we've been gone far longer than we intended. Are you ready to leave, Ditee?"

"Oh, yes," Ditee said.

"Good day, then." Venus smiled as pleasantly as she could. "And welcome to the neighborhood, Mrs. Blackburn, Lady Mary. I hope you have a"—*dreadful, hideous, horrible*—"nice visit."

"Thank you. We don't intend to stay long, of course," Lady Mary said. "The country is so boring, don't you know?"

"But I'm sure your presence will enliven it." Venus strode off up High Street before she could say more.

"Those women were unbearably rude," Ditee said, falling into step beside her. Her book remained closed.

"Yes, they were."

They walked a few moments in silence.

"Do you think they really are betrothed to the duke and Mr. Valentine?" Ditee's voice sounded uncharacteristically small and sad.

Damn it all, how dare those miserable men hurt Ditee? Venus was so angry she'd like to kick something. No, *someone*, and in a very sensitive part of his damn handsome body. "They said so, didn't they? I can't imagine why they would take it into their heads to lie about something like that."

There was no point in entertaining false hope. Anger, though . . . fury . . . revenge—yes, she'd gladly entertain all those emotions.

They reached the vicarage. Ditee opened the front gate and held it for Venus.

"You go on in, Ditee. I'm going to walk for a while."

"Oh." Ditee frowned as if she was having trouble understanding the simplest concepts. "Are you going to take Archie with you?"

"Not this time." The stupid dog liked Mr. Valentine— but then Archie also liked rolling in dead things. "I'll see you later."

Drew stood in the garden with Nigel, Mrs. Edgemoor, and Bugden, the gardener, a vegetative emergency at their feet.

"What am I to do about these poor bushes?" Bugden asked, appearing to be on the verge of tears.

They *were* a sorry sight. Five or six large shrubs had been picked clean of all greenery. Drew couldn't tell from

Bugden's increasingly emotional speech—and consequent descent into the local dialect—whether the culprit was a giant hare or a hairy caterpillar.

He flinched. Something had hit him in the shoulder. Were there other garden marauders about?

Ah, there—he distinctly heard Bugden say "creepy crawler." It must be the hairy caterpillar who was the villain in the bushes' demise.

Mrs. Edgemoor and Bugden had turned to Nigel for guidance, but Nigel was gazing into space, likely contemplating the fair Aphrodite.

"I'm afraid you'll just have to dig them up," Drew said. "They look very . . . dead."

This unfortunate word choice sent Bugden off on another impassioned speech. Apparently the plants had been flourishing just the day before; the vicious, sneaky bugs had crept in on their many legs in the dead of night to attack the poor, defenseless bushes, devouring them with incredible speed.

"Yes, well, that is a terrible shame." Clearly some sympathy was in order, whether for the denuded shrubbery, which was long past caring, or Bugden, who obviously took the caterpillars' actions as a personal affront, or even Mrs. Edgemoor, who was wringing her hands and almost moaning. "However—*ouch*!"

Some hard missile had definitely collided with his other shoulder. He glanced down; had that large pebble been there by his foot before?

Nigel emerged from his woolgathering. "What is it?"

"Oh, nothing." Drew smiled. He'd go looking for his assailant as soon as he dealt with the plant problem. He was quite certain his attacker was not a hairy caterpillar. "The sad truth is I suspect nothing will resurrect these bushes."

"Aye, yer right there." Bugden looked gloomily at the plant corpses.

"So all we can do is remove the remains."

"But the garden party is tomorrow," Mrs. Edgemoor said. "It'll look a fright."

It already looked a fright, as if fire or drought—or caterpillars—had come through, but Drew felt it wisest not to point out the obvious. "Perhaps a few potted plants would do the trick?"

"Hmm." Bugden nodded. "That might work, and I know just where I can get some. There are too many in the music room anyway."

Mrs. Edgemoor looked unconvinced. "I'm not sure . . ."

"Now, Maud, ye know I'm right. Come, let's see what we can do."

Bugden and Mrs. Edgemoor went off to discover what indoor plants they could dragoon into outdoor duty.

"Well done," Nigel said. "You appear to have averted a major disaster."

Drew laughed. "Yes, well—*ow!*"

Something large and hard hit his arse with enough force to leave a bruise, he'd wager. He looked down. That was no pebble by his feet; that was a rock.

"I think the hedge over there is trying to get your attention," Nigel said.

Drew looked in the direction Nigel indicated. The hedge shook emphatically.

"If you'll excuse me, I believe I'll go commune with nature."

Nigel snorted. "Just be sure you don't come to an unhappy end like these bushes. The garden is obviously full of danger."

Drew caught a quick glimpse of chestnut hair and a green-cloth-covered arm, and then another projectile flew through the air to land at his feet. This one was the largest yet. "Indeed it is."

"She has a good arm, but she must be tiring," Nigel said, choking back a laugh.

"Ah, but I believe this was sent as a warning only."

Another rock landed, this time headed for his toe. He moved his foot quickly.

"The lady grows impatient."

"Yes. I'm off. If I don't return by suppertime, send Bugden out to collect my poor corpse. He can dispose of it with the late, lamented bushes."

Drew strolled over to the tall, green hedge. What wild bee was in Venus's bonnet now? Had she come to punish him for not kissing her in the village earlier?

He wished that were the case; he'd be happy—very happy—to rectify the omission.

And that wasn't the only omission he should rectify. Nigel was right. He should tell her now who he was. The longer he waited, the deeper the hole he dug, making it all that much harder to climb out and into her good graces.

But he didn't want to tell her, not quite yet. He wanted to know if she cared for *him*, for Drew Valentine, before he introduced her to Greycliffe. Once the duke was out of the bag, as it were, he'd never know her true feelings.

He peered cautiously around the hedge. "Did you wish to talk to me, Miss Collingswood?"

"Of course I wished to talk to you, you serpent." She hissed very much like a snake herself.

"About what?"

Her large brown eyes flashed with temper, and it looked as if steam might come out of her ears at any moment. "You know very well what I wish to discuss. And do come here behind the hedge. Do you want to be discovered?"

"Perhaps I fear for my safety," he said, stepping behind the vegetative screen. They were in the beginning of the maze. He'd seen it from his bedroom window, but he hadn't yet had time to explore it. "You were flinging rocks at me, after all."

"Oh, don't be a cabbage-head."

If he remembered correctly, the maze's center had a sizable tree that looked as if it would shield anyone under it from prying eyes very nicely. Chances were slim he could take advantage of it, but hope sprang eternal. Perhaps he could discover how she felt about him now and then steal a proper kiss before confessing his sins. "Do you know the key to this maze?"

"Of course—and don't change the subject."

"I wouldn't think of it. Let's stroll to the center and you can show me the way of it." He tried to take her arm, but she shook him off.

"I'm more likely to show you the way to perdition, you lying blackguard," she said, "not that you need any directions to *that* destination." She strode off.

He followed her, addressing her back. "Here, now, I never actually lied. I may have let you assume—"

"Let me *assume*!" She whirled around and pinned him with a venomous look before turning and continuing her brisk pace forward. Her hips swished back and forth in a very enticing manner. "You more than let me assume. I thought the whole point of this garden party was to further Ditee's match with the duke."

"Er, yes . . ." He cleared his throat. What exactly were they speaking of? Best to proceed cautiously. "That is, yes, of course. I think your sister and my cousin would make an excellent match."

"Ha!"

She walked even faster. She had long legs, but his were

longer. Still, she was obviously used to walking distances in the country; he had to hurry to keep up with her.

"Is there a problem?" A stupid question. Obviously there was a problem, but for the life of him, he couldn't discern what it was.

"Yes!"

They reached the center of the maze. As he'd hoped, there was a bench underneath a splendidly leafy tree. Anyone—or two—sitting on the bench would be completely invisible to someone in the house or on the grounds. Unfortunately, even the most inveterate gambler wouldn't take odds on his chances of persuading Venus to join him for a protracted bit of lovemaking. From the sharpness of her glare, he'd be lucky to emerge with all his body parts intact.

He clasped his hands behind his back, but quickly thought better of it—that position left his tender bits too unprotected—and dropped his hands back to his sides. "I'm afraid I don't follow. Could you explain the difficulty?"

He'd never really thought looks could kill, but he might have to revise his opinion.

"Your London *friends* stopped in the village looking for you," she said.

Damn. "Do you mean Lady Mary and Mrs. Blackburn?"

"Whom else could I mean? Little Huffington is not exactly littered with Londoners."

"Well, I wasn't certain since I wouldn't consider them friends, precisely."

This was the wrong thing to say. If Venus had been angry before, she was now utterly furious. He half expected her hair to transform into snakes and her eyes to shoot lightning bolts. He glanced around the clearing to be sure there weren't any other, more prosaic weapons at hand.

"Oh, no." She spat the words as if they were some vile-tasting tonic. "They are far more than friends."

"They are?" What the hell had those two harpies said?

"Don't try to deny it. Lady Mary told us she is betrothed to the duke."

"She is not!" He saw red for a moment. He'd like to shake that lying jade until her teeth rattled in her head. How dare she say they were betrothed? He might—perhaps— expect her to try such a lie on poor Mrs. Edgemoor: Lady Mary wouldn't see a housekeeper as meriting any respect. But to lie to Venus . . .

Venus waved her hand, as if she didn't really care. "And"—now her voice started to break—"she said Mrs. Blackburn is affianced to *you*!" The last word came out on a wail.

What? But Venus had just said Lady Mary claimed to be his—oh, right, Venus thought he was Nigel.

He'd waited a fateful moment too long before stepping toward her and extending his hand. "Venus—"

She slapped his fingers away. "Don't touch me, you despicable blackguard."

He was not used to being insulted. Anger flared in his gut. He tried to swallow it, but his voice sharpened. "Be reasonable."

"Reasonable?!" She swiped at her nose with her sleeve. "You want me to be reasonable?"

"At least lower your voice. You're shrieking like a fishwife."

"What? Are you afraid everyone will discover what a disgusting, dishonorable liar you are?"

How dare she call his honor into question? If she were a man, she'd be meeting him in a duel. "I haven't lied to you." Perhaps he'd let her assume a few things, but he'd never out and out lied.

She swiped at her face again. Didn't the girl carry a handkerchief? He reached for his.

"So you've always been completely honest with me?" She sounded just a little hopeful.

He froze, his hand still in his pocket. He wanted to say yes. If he said yes, maybe she'd calm down and let him put his arms around her and explain. Maybe they would end up on that lovely bench doing delightful things with their hands and lips.

But the truth was she thought he was Nigel.

She wasn't stupid; she saw his answer on his face. "You, you . . . *toad*." She snatched up her skirts and ran.

He let her go. Catching her would only lead to more shouting. She didn't want to hear him—and, frankly, he didn't know what to say.

He sat down on the bench and dropped his head into his hands.

His life was a complete mess.

He *hadn't* lied to her; he just hadn't corrected her. She'd been naked, for God's sake. He couldn't be expected to think rationally in such a situation. It wasn't his fault she'd assumed he was Nigel.

He leaned his head back against the tree trunk. No, he should be honest with himself for once. He *had* misled her—and he'd do it again in a heartbeat. He'd wanted her to see him, not his title.

Unfortunately now all she saw was a lying rogue, and that bothered him far more than he could have imagined.

Bloody hell.

He must beg her pardon, grovel if he had to—and after their brangle just now, he'd probably have to. Today. He couldn't put it off. If she discovered his identity at the garden party tomorrow—especially with Lady Mary watching— she'd never forgive him.

It was getting late, but there were still some hours of

daylight left. He'd ride over to the vicarage as soon as he left the maze.

He stood, his mind made up, and strode out of the clearing. He turned right and then right again and then—damn it, he was back in the center. Very well, he'd turn left instead. Or . . . left, then right. Or right, left, left . . .

Nothing worked. He was trapped like a rat—Venus would surely find that most appropriate.

He stood in the bloody clearing and shouted for help.

Chapter 6

Venus never cried. Crying was a stupid waste of energy. It made her eyes ache and her head throb.

She sniffed. And her nose run, too, damn it. Of course she didn't have a handkerchief.

She stopped and took a deep, shuddery breath.

What was the matter with her? She pressed the heels of her hands to her forehead. Had she completely lost her mind? She'd certainly lost her temper. Mr. Valentine had been correct. She *had* sounded like a fishwife. He must be laughing at her, the silly rustic who'd fallen in love with—

Oh, God, she wasn't in love with the villain, was she?

Her knees folded, and she sat down abruptly on the grass.

She couldn't be—she'd only just met him. Yes, he was sinfully handsome with his blue eyes and wicked smile and naked—She slapped her hands over her burning cheeks.

He'd haunted her dreams, but it wasn't just his appearance that attracted her. It was everything about him. Just talking to him—arguing with him more often than not—

thrilled her. She was always thinking of him, always wondering what he would say about something, how he would smile . . .

Bah—she'd been building air castles. All this time, he'd been betrothed to Mrs. Blackburn, who must be several years older than he. Not that it was any of her business. He could marry old Mrs. Fedderly with her blessing if he wished.

She stood up, scrubbed her hands over her face to get rid of any lingering tears, and brushed off her skirt. Enough. She must think of Ditee. She needed to tell her Lady Mary had lied: she was not betrothed to Greycliffe. Mr. Valentine had looked genuinely horrified at the notion, and no matter how slimy and disgusting he was, he couldn't be that good an actor.

It was past suppertime when she let herself into the vicarage.

"There you are," Mrs. Shipley said. "Your mama has been asking for you."

"Oh." Venus sniffed and tried to smile. "I was out walking."

"Been crying, have you?"

She ducked her head to avoid Mrs. Shipley's eyes. "Don't be ridiculous. Why would I be crying?"

"I don't know. Maybe for the same reason your sister's bawling her eyes out."

Venus's stomach knotted. "Ditee's crying?"

"I just said so, didn't I? She's been locked in her room since she came home from the village."

"Oh, dear. I'd best go talk to her."

"Good. Shall I tell your mama you're home?"

"Oh, no, no need to disturb Mama. I'll just go up and see Ditee, and then I think I'll go to bed myself."

Venus could feel Mrs. Shipley's eyes boring into her back as she went up the stairs.

She tapped on Ditee's door.

"Go away." Ditee's voice was muffled as if she had her face buried in her pillow.

"Ditee, it's me, Venus. Let me in."

"No. Go *away*."

"Ditee, I spoke to Mr. Valentine." Venus paused; she could almost feel Ditee listening. "He said the duke is not betrothed to Lady Mary, and I think he was telling the truth." *About that at least.*

Silence, and then she heard feet hurrying over the floor. The door flew open so quickly, Venus almost fell into the room.

"You're certain?" Ditee asked. Her face was blotchy and red, but she still looked beautiful.

Venus nodded. "Mr. Valentine was quite definite on the subject."

"Oh." Ditee stared at her for a full minute and then made an odd sound—a cross between a sob and a laugh—and threw her arms around Venus, hugging her so tightly Venus could barely breathe. "Oh, that's wonderful. Thank you so much."

Venus hugged her back. At least one of them was happy.

"Sleep well?" Nigel asked as he strolled into the breakfast room.

Drew looked up from the table and considered winging his slice of ham at his cousin. "Not particularly."

"I did," Nigel said, filling his plate with roast beef, smoked herring, cheese, and eggs. "A clear conscience is a wonderful thing." He sat down next to Drew. "I'm going to tell Aphrodite that I'm not the duke at the garden party today."

"I see." Drew stared at Nigel's breakfast and then looked at his own food. What had possessed him to select this nauseating collection of items? He wasn't the least bit hungry. He pushed the plate away and took a sip of coffee.

He'd meant to tell Venus yesterday who he was, but it had taken a good half hour to get free of the maze. After Bugden had rescued him—and told him the key so he wouldn't get trapped again—he'd dragged Drew off to see how he'd fixed the caterpillar catastrophe. While Drew was talking to Bugden, Mrs. Edgemoor appeared and begged him to come see if he thought the music room now looked too bare. He'd gone with her and assured her it was fine, but then she'd wondered if she should get the duke's opinion at which point he confessed *he* was the duke. That revelation caused her to scream and throw her apron over her head.

By the time he'd got Mrs. Edgemoor's ruffled feathers smoothed and had convinced her the whole scheme had been a harmless, pointless male joke, it had been time for supper. He hadn't been about to further upset her feelings by skipping the meal. Unfortunately, Cook had had an issue in the kitchen, so supper had been delayed, and once they finally finished eating, the light was gone. There was no moon; he wasn't familiar with the terrain; and, really, what would Venus's parents have said if he showed up at their front door so late? So he hadn't gone.

He'd been haunted all night by bizarre dreams of towering hedges, vicious caterpillars, and a beautiful, very naked Venus constantly running away from him. He'd woken painfully aroused, completely exhausted, and deeply depressed.

He was in serious trouble.

"You really should tell Venus today."

"I *know*." Drew pressed his fingers to his forehead. "Sorry. Didn't mean to shout."

Nigel regarded him as he chewed his damn roast beef. "It's very tempting to say I told you so."

"I'm sure it is."

"I won't say it though."

Drew grunted. Damn it, Nigel was laughing at him. "It's not amusing."

"On the contrary, it is. You've got yourself into quite the pickle, haven't you?"

"You're in a bit of a fix yourself."

Nigel swallowed a forkful of eggs. "No, I don't believe I am. I gave the matter much consideration last night. I've only met Aphrodite once and then only briefly. I shall simply apologize for any confusion"—he grinned—"and blame everything on you."

"Thanks so much."

Nigel finally finished consuming his disgusting break- fast. "It *is* your fault, you know, but don't worry. We all make mistakes in our salad days." He grinned. "And you *are* a duke. Much as you might hate it, your title does for- give a multitude of sins." He stood. "I'll see you later."

He went off whistling, the blackguard.

Drew took another sip of coffee. Blech! He spat it back into the cup. It was cold.

No matter what Nigel said, Drew couldn't laugh this off as a youthful indiscretion. Venus certainly wouldn't see it that way.

Hell, he didn't have youthful indiscretions. He'd always been a serious child, but once he'd been saddled with the title, he'd had to grow up all at once—Nigel's father, Drew's guardian, had seen to that. He'd told Drew countless times it was his duty to care for his dependents, invest wisely, take a wife, and have many sons. And to stay out of dangerous places like gambling dens. This was the first time he'd done anything at all foolish.

Damn it, he was too young for this. He should have years before he needed to think of finding a wife and starting his nursery. But there was no point in fighting it. He felt what he felt. Even if he hadn't compromised Venus, he would want to marry her. He only hoped she would have him.

"I'm not feeling well, Mama," Venus said, standing in the doorway to her sister's room. "I think I should stay home."

"Nonsense." Mama pinned up a loose curl of Ditee's hair. "You're never sick."

"I am today." Her head was pounding, and her eyes felt dry and scratchy. She couldn't have slept more than an hour or two last night.

"Oh, Venus, you can't be sick." Ditee twisted around to look at her. "You can't miss the duke's garden party."

"Of course I can."

"Sit still, Aphrodite," Mama said, "or I'll never get this hair pinned properly." She glanced over at Venus. "You'll be fine; it's probably just nerves."

Her stomach twisted. Yes, it was nerves; her nerves had kept her from eating breakfast and would probably cause her to burst into tears the moment she saw Mr. Valentine. Then she could conveniently die of mortification. "I truly feel ill."

Mama lifted an eyebrow. "Is it that time of the month, then?"

"No!" She pressed her fingers to her forehead. She

should have lied, but Mama would have caught her out in that too soon. "Perhaps I am just tired."

"You'll perk up once we arrive," Mama said, finishing with Ditee's hair. "After all, you're the one who's always telling me we should take a greater interest in society, aren't you?"

"Yes, but—"

"You *have* to go, Venus. Please?" Ditee looked beautiful in her old gown furbished with new ribbon, but she looked very anxious, too. "I don't think I can go without you."

Ditee hadn't asked Venus for anything—besides a pencil and scrap of paper—in years. And besides, it looked very much as if Venus's matchmaking plans were going to come to splendid fruition. She would love to see that. She wanted to say yes—but she wanted more not to see Mr. Valentine. "Oh, Ditee, you'll be fine without me."

Mama looked from Ditee to Venus and back again. She might spend most of her time wading through Latin and Greek texts, but she wasn't completely oblivious to her surroundings. "Girls, is there something I should be aware of?"

Ditee paled and opened her mouth, surely on the verge of spilling the entire story.

"No, of course not, Mama," Venus said before Ditee could find her voice.

Poor Ditee looked back at her. Her sister was as white as snow—was she going to faint? She couldn't miss the party; Venus didn't trust Lady Mary not to compromise the duke somehow. And really, sometimes with men it was a matter of out of sight, out of mind. Ditee *had* to go to Hyndon House. Things were still too uncertain to rely on the duke's brief meeting with her to cement the match.

Venus's stomach clenched into a tight knot, but she made herself smile. "I guess I'm feeling better. I'll go get ready."

"Oh, thank you." Ditee might as well have thrown herself at Venus's feet and kissed her shoes, her relief was so obvious.

Mama's frown grew. "What have you two been up to?"

"Up to? What could we possibly have been up to?" Venus asked. She glared at Ditee and gave the slightest shake of her head when it looked as if her sister would explain. "We've only been into the village to buy ribbon, and you know nothing ever happens in Little Huffington. Isn't that right, Ditee?"

Ditee got her message. "Oh, er, yes. That's right. There's nothing to tell. Not really."

Mama's brows met over her nose now. "But—"

"If I'm going," Venus said, "I'd better hurry. We don't want to be late."

Since all Venus had to do was pull on her old dress, Mama might be forgiven if she pursued her for further information, but she apparently decided to leave well enough alone. She just nodded. "I'll come in a moment to help you with your hair."

By the time Venus climbed into the carriage, she'd got a better hold on her emotions. There wouldn't be a huge crowd of people at the party—Little Huffington was little, after all—but there should be enough of a crowd that she could stay on the fringes of it until Mama and Papa were ready to go. And if they wanted to stay longer than Venus could bear—a somewhat unlikely situation as Mama and Papa had never attended a party to her knowledge—she could always walk home.

It was a very short drive to Hyndon House, but there was a long line of coaches waiting to disgorge their passengers.

"Good heavens," Mama said, "where have all these people come from?"

"Demmed if I know," Papa said. He looked distinctly uncomfortable in his best clothes.

When they finally reached the front of the house, Mr. Bugden opened the carriage door and let down the steps.

"What are you doing here?" Papa asked. "I thought you dealt with plants, not people."

"Aye, Mr. Collingswood, but we've many more guests than expected. Mrs. Edgemoor believes the London ladies sent word to their friends."

"The London ladies?" Mama asked as she descended.

"Lady Mary Detluck and Mrs. Blackburn, madam." He leaned a little closer and dropped his voice. "His grace and Mr. Valentine were none too happy, I'll tell ye."

"Maybe you were right, Venus," Ditee whispered, hesitating in the carriage. "We both should have stayed home."

"Nonsense," Venus whispered back. "I'm certain the duke is not the least bit interested in these women. You heard Mr. Bugden; he's not happy they are here." She gave Ditee a little push to get her moving.

"But, Venus," Ditee said once Venus joined her on the ground, "look how beautiful their gowns are." Five or six very elegant women stood in front of them waiting to enter Hyndon House.

"They can't hold a candle to you, Ditee." The other women's dresses might be finer, but the women themselves had not half Ditee's beauty, if Venus did say so herself, and likely none of her sweet disposition.

They made their way slowly over the drive, up the steps, and into the house. As soon as they stepped through the front door, Venus saw the duke catch sight of Ditee. His whole face brightened.

She elbowed her sister. "See?" she whispered. "Greycliffe has been watching for you. He can't look at anyone else."

"Oh." Ditee flushed a deep red. She smiled shyly, and Greycliffe grinned back at her. Angels might as well have broken into song and hearts and flowers rained from the sky. Clearly as far as the two of them were concerned, there was no one else in the room.

It would be rather revolting if Venus didn't love Ditee so much.

Of course Mr. Valentine, standing to the duke's left, hadn't noticed Venus's existence. He was bent over slightly, listening to something Mrs. Fedderly was saying.

And when he did see her—

Panic closed her throat. She couldn't greet him amid all these people, especially after the way she'd left him yesterday.

"I think I'll go around this way," she whispered to Ditee. "I'll see you in the garden."

"All right." Ditee clearly hadn't heard a word Venus said; she was too focused on Greycliffe.

Fortunately, the door to the dining room was just to Venus's right. She slipped through without Mama or Papa noticing—and almost bumped into Mrs. Edgemoor.

"Oh, Miss Venus," Mrs. Edgemoor said, looking more than a little harried, "I'm so glad you're here. I know you're a guest, but I was wondering if you might help me with Cook?"

"What's the problem?" Venus asked, taking her arm.

"Cook isn't used to managing for so many people. One of the village girls I hired in to help knocked over a plate of cheese by accident, and Cook started shouting. She is threatening to quit on the spot. Mrs. Shipley is trying to calm her, but we thought perhaps you could do a better job of it."

Venus would tame wild animals if it meant being somewhere Mr. Valentine was not. "I'll be happy to see what I can do."

Where the hell was Venus?

Drew smiled at the wizened little woman—Miss Wardley?—who was, he hoped, the last guest he had to greet. Nigel had deserted him as soon as the Collingswoods—minus Venus, damn it—arrived. Apparently Venus had come with them; Mr. and Mrs. Collingswood looked dumbfounded when they discovered she wasn't at their side.

A dancing bear could have appeared and Aphrodite wouldn't have noticed; she had eyes only for Nigel—eyes that widened when she realized Nigel wasn't the duke. Nigel wasted no time in reassuring her and starting a discussion about some obscure Latin translation with her and her parents. The four of them then vanished into the study, leaving Drew to do the welcoming by himself for the last fifteen minutes. But the end was in sight, he hoped.

"You're really a duke?" Miss Wardley—or perhaps the name was Woodley—asked.

"Yes, madam, I am." And he was never going to pretend otherwise. If she would just move along, he could find Venus, confess, and, with luck, persuade her to forgive him. He only hoped she hadn't realized the truth already and consigned him to the devil.

"You look too young to be a duke." Miss Whatever-her-name-was blinked up at him suspiciously.

He would definitely have to take to powdering his hair

even if it caused him to sneeze his head off. "I assure you I've had the title since I was thirteen."

"Hmm."

He forced himself to keep smiling. There was no one ascending the stairs behind Miss Wardley-Woodley yet, but the longer he stood here, the higher the odds became someone else would arrive. Damn Lady Mary for spreading the word through her friends in the *ton*. As bad luck would have it, there was an infestation of society sprigs at a house party only a few hours' ride away.

Hopefully those "guests" wouldn't linger. He'd already told one fellow it would be completely impossible for him to stay overnight.

Miss Woodley was examining him as if he were an animal in the Royal Menagerie. If he showed her his signet ring, would that satisfy her? He raised an eyebrow and tried for his haughtiest expression.

That did the trick. She broke into a wide smile and clapped her hands. "Oh, wait until I write my sister. She won't believe I met a real duke—and a young, handsome one to boot!"

With that, she finally toddled off. Drew waited until she'd moved about ten steps away, and then he fled his post.

Where was Venus? It was infernally difficult to look for her. In every damn room someone wanted to talk to him. He endured the twaddle as patiently as he could; he didn't want to raise speculation by dashing around as if he'd lost something . . . which of course he had.

He came within an ambsace of being trapped by Mrs. Higgins and her annoying daughter at the dining room sideboard and had to dodge into the parlor to miss Lady Mary. He did Nigel a great favor by misdirecting the Widow Blackburn when she inquired as to his cousin's whereabouts. Finally he found Venus in the blue drawing room, talking to Mrs. Fedderly.

He paused on the threshold. She was partly turned away from him; he could see her elegant back and profile. Rather more hair tendrils than strictly fashionable had escaped from the knot on the top of her head; she swatted at them as she responded to something Mrs. Fedderly said.

His spirits—and something else—lifted. He must be grinning like an idiot.

But he couldn't smile yet. He still had some very rough ground to get over. He approached cautiously.

Mrs. Fedderly saw him first. "Well, look who's here."

Venus glanced over her shoulder and then turned to face him. "Mr. Valentine."

Venus couldn't see Mrs. Fedderly's expression, but he could. The woman's eyebrows shot up to disappear into her coiffure, and then a look of amusement crept over her face. The blasted female was looking forward to seeing how he got out of this mess.

"Mrs. Fedderly, Miss Collingswood." He bowed. "I was sorry to miss you when you arrived, Miss Collingswood. I saw your parents and sister—what became of you?" Blurting out his identity in front of Mrs. Fedderly wasn't at all appealing.

Venus suddenly looked vaguely unwell. "Mrs. Edgemoor asked my help with a problem."

"Oh? And were you able to assist her?"

"Yes."

There didn't seem to be anything else to say. They stared at each other while the silence stretched out—and Mrs. Fedderly giggled.

They both glared at her.

She cleared her throat. "Sorry." She made a sort of

strangled noise. "I suppose you both are wishing me at J-Jericho." She covered her mouth, but wasn't entirely successful at muffling her mirth.

Drew smiled as politely as he could. He was not going to deny it. "I'm sure there are plenty of other people you should speak with."

"Ah, but none of the other conversations will be half as amusing."

Drew had no reply to that.

As soon as Mrs. Fedderly left, he and Venus both spoke at once.

"Mr. Valentine, I should apologize—"

"Miss Collingswood, I need to beg your pardon—"

They stopped. Venus flushed and looked down at her hands.

Drew grinned. Perhaps this wouldn't be so bad after all. "Miss Collingswood, I will grant you the choice—which of us should apologize first?"

She laughed then and looked up. "Oh, I suppose I should rather get it over with. I—"

"There you are!"

Drew stiffened. Bloody hell, why did Lady Mary have to find him at this precise moment?

He refused to look over his shoulder. Perhaps if he ignored her, she would go away.

And perhaps pigs would sprout wings and fly.

"I've been looking all over for you, your grace." Lady Mary put her hand on his arm in a damn propriety fashion and gave Venus her most condescending look. "Oh, I see you are talking to one of those Collingswood girls." She laughed. "Which one are you?"

Venus looked from Lady Mary to him with wide, shocked eyes. "Your grace?" she whispered.

"What's the matter with—" Lady Mary began.

Drew glared at her, shaking off her hand. "You are interrupting a private conversation, madam. I will thank you to take yourself off immediately."

Lady Mary drew in an indignant breath, but Venus filled the silence first.

"That's not necessary. I was just leaving."

Chapter 7

He was the duke.

Venus pushed her way out of the room, ignoring Mr. Valentine's—no, *Greycliffe's*—call to stop. If she didn't get outside immediately, the walls were going to close in on her.

He was the *duke.*

Oh, God, how he must have been laughing at her all this time. The silly little provincial. The girl so green she could pass for grass. The little idiot who'd fallen in love with him.

She burst through the terrace doors and struggled to get a deep breath. Damn it, her chest was too tight. She panted, looking around.

All the elegantly-dressed strangers were staring at her.

Her eyes met Mrs. Blackburn's. The widow's lips twisted into a smirk, and she bent forward to say something to the tight knot of people around her. Everyone sniggered, and two men pulled out their quizzing glasses to examine her from head to toe.

"You think *this* was what caused Greycliffe to leave

Town so abruptly?" the fatter one asked. His tone left little doubt he found the notion beyond astounding.

"Oh, no," Mrs. Blackburn said. "She's at most a small diversion—a way to pass the time until Lady Mary arrived."

Venus wanted to scratch the harpy's eyes out, but she was shaking too much to do so. And the London people would just laugh at her anyway . . . the way Greycliffe had been laughing at her.

"Oh, there you are, Venus." Mrs. Higgins, a tart in her hand, waved to her from a refreshment table set out farther down the terrace. "Will you tell Mrs. Edgemoor the food is running out here? Esmeralda would like more biscuits."

"Yes, hurry on, do," Esmeralda said, her mouth only partly clear of crumbs.

"You see," Mrs. Blackburn said. "She's really little more than a servant."

Damn, damn, damn. She had to get away, far away, as quickly as she could. She rushed across the terrace and down the steps to the gardens.

"Miss Collingswood! Venus!"

Mr.—the duke—must have got free of Lady Mary. He called to her from the terrace door, creating an even larger spectacle. Mrs. Blackburn and her London friends must be memorizing every detail to relate at all the balls and routs and soirees once they returned to Town.

She would give them one more thing to talk about.

She picked up her skirts and ran.

"Lost something, your grace?" Chuffy Mannard called. He was standing with the Widow Blackburn and the other unwelcome London visitors.

Drew had always thought Mannard a fat boil on the *ton*'s

arse, but he hadn't until just this moment realized how stupid he was. Did the nodcock want him to shove his annoying grin down his throat? He would be more than happy to oblige.

Mannard must have realized his peril when Drew took a step toward him. "Er, no offense meant, of course, your grace."

"I should hope not." Drew swallowed—with great effort—the rest of what he wished to say. His words would not be at all appropriate for mixed company, and in any event he had more important things to do than castigate Mannard. He had to catch Venus.

Lady Mary slipped by him and linked her arm through Mannard's. "Don't mind his grace, Chuffy. He's *in love*." She might as well have said he was insane. She turned to Mrs. Blackburn. "This party is sadly flat, don't you agree, Constance?"

Nigel must have given the widow her congé for she nodded immediately. "Yes, indeed. Such a collection of rustics. I don't know how I've kept from falling asleep."

"We should have room for you at Beswick's party," Mannard said. "What do you think, Nanton?"

"Right-o." Nanton wasn't as cabbage-headed as his companions. "Let's leave now."

"Very good," Drew said. "Don't let me keep you."

Lady Mary sniffed. "I'll have a word with Mrs. Higgins about fetching our things," she said as she and her group of annoying Londoners left.

Thank God. Drew had never been so happy to see the backs of a set of people in his life. Now he could go after Venus. She had quite a head start, but—

"Greycliffe, I've been looking all over for you." Nigel came up behind him, clapping him on the shoulder.

Drew bit back his impatience with effort and turned.

Damn, Mr. and Mrs. Collingswood and Aphrodite were there, too. Why the hell did they have to choose this of all moments to emerge from the study? Venus would be all the way to the Colonies before he could go after her.

He forced himself to smile. "I hope you are enjoying the party?"

"Oh, yes, indeed," Mr. Collingswood said. "Far more than we expected, I'll admit. Mr. Valentine is quite the classics scholar, you know."

"I know. He puts me to shame."

Nigel snorted. "I should tell you that his grace is a far better mathematician than I could ever hope to be."

Drew kept smiling. Surely they were not going to waste precious time trading compliments?

Aphrodite came to his rescue. "But where is Venus? I thought we might find her here with you." She blushed furiously. "I mean, we didn't see her inside."

"I believe I saw her heading into the gardens," Drew said. "I was just on the point of following her to offer my escort."

"Oh." Mrs. Collingswood frowned. "She did say she wasn't feeling well, but I thought she'd improve once we got here. Venus is never sick, you know."

"Perhaps she went home," Mr. Collingswood said. "It's not far."

"Nevertheless, I must make sure she's come to no harm," Drew said. It was unlikely now he'd catch her before she reached the vicarage, but he would knock on the front door when he got there and try to persuade her to listen to him.

"That's not necessary," Mrs. Collingswood said. "Venus is used to walking all over Little Huffington by herself. It is quite safe. She's never met with unwanted attention."

Except when she'd encountered him naked at the pond.

"And you can't leave your guests," Mr. Collingswood pointed out.

"I'm afraid I can and I must," Drew said. "There is something I need to speak to your daughter about. It can't wait."

Mr. and Mrs. Collingswood gaped at him, and even Nigel looked surprised, but Aphrodite smiled broadly.

"Then of course you must go, your grace," she said. "Don't let us detain you another moment."

He was so appreciative he could have kissed her—if it wouldn't have shocked her and likely earned him a drubbing from Nigel. "Thank you." He bowed. "Please excuse me."

He crossed the terrace and descended the stairs, keeping himself to a brisk walk until he passed out of sight.

Then he ran full tilt toward the vicarage.

Venus stumbled down the narrow path through the trees. Branches caught her dress and tangled in her hair, pulling out her pins. Her lungs ached from running, and somewhere along the way, she'd got a pebble in her shoe. Now it was digging into the ball of her foot.

And she was crying. Damn it, she'd cried more in the last twenty-four hours than she had in her entire life. She wiped her nose on her sleeve—she still didn't have a handkerchief—and sat down on a rock at the edge of the woods. She could just see the pond through the tree branches.

She tried to take in the calming scent of water and pine and dirt, but her nose was too stuffed from the blasted crying. All she managed was a dismal snuffle.

She jerked off her shoe and shook out the pebble. It bounced off her foot and vanished in the pine needles. Such a little thing, but it had felt enormous.

Maybe that's what this problem with Mr. Valentine—

no, *Greycliffe*—would feel like in a week or two: a little, insignificant pebble instead of a large, heavy, crushing rock.

It was possible. Time healed all wounds, didn't it?

She swiped at her nose again.

Everything about him, every word he'd uttered from the moment she'd met him, was a lie. So her feelings for him were a lie as well. They must be, no matter how true they felt now. She couldn't love someone she didn't know.

She pulled her shoe back on.

And what about Ditee? Dear God, it was her fault her sister had fallen into the clutches of the duke's cousin. He must be as culpable as the duke; he hadn't corrected them when they'd met him in the village.

Ditee would be heartbroken, and it was all Venus's fault. She was never going to play matchmaker again.

She walked over to the pond. The water looked as cool and calm as it had when she'd met the blackguard duke. Well, calmer, actually. Archie wasn't here to splash around and disturb the birds.

Had it only been—

Damn. Something—someone—was coming. She heard branches snapping in the woods behind her. She whirled around just as Greycliffe, the weasel, erupted from the trees.

Her foolish heart leapt to see him. He had leaves in his hair and mud on his breeches and he had never looked so handsome—except, of course, when he'd been naked.

She took a step back and raised her chin, daring him to even try touching her. "Why are you here, *your grace*?"

He flinched at her tone and stopped a good five yards from her. Her foolish feet wanted to go to him.

She turned to examine the pond instead.

"I'm here to apologize," he said, "and to explain."

Had he taken a step toward her? She would not look.

"You do not need to apologize, and there is nothing to explain. We have young men in Little Huffington. I've seen them play j-jokes before." She swallowed more tears. "Someday I'm sure I will find this all very f-funny."

And if she said another word, she'd burst into tears again and prove she was as great a liar as he.

"It wasn't a joke."

He sounded so bloody earnest. He stepped nearer, but at least he didn't have the effrontery to touch her. She gave him a cold look to keep him in his place and then turned her attention back to the pond. The ducks were upending themselves to feed on the plants and insects under the surface.

"You see, Mrs. Edgemoor mistook Nigel—that's my cousin—for the duke when we arrived; that's what got the idea stuck in my head," he said. "People forget dukes can be young."

She hadn't thought of his age. "How old are you?"

"Twenty-one."

Her heart sank. That was far too young for a duke to marry; even she knew that. He would want to sow his wild oats for many more years.

"And then I came upon you, and you assumed I was Nigel, and I saw a golden opportunity, one I couldn't let pass."

"A golden opportunity?" She sent him a sidelong glance. He'd turned to gaze out over the pond, too, his hands clasped behind his back. He was standing even closer to her, so close their sides almost touched. "What do you mean?"

"A chance to not be Greycliffe for a while."

She tilted her head to look up at him. His face was unlined; his features still had the curve of youth, but his expression had hardened with knowledge beyond his years.

"Everyone thinks I should be so bloody happy to be a rich duke," he said, "but they don't know what it's like. They don't know how often the title feels like shackles."

He turned to face her. His eyes were so blue and clear and . . . honest.

"My life changed when I was thirteen," he said. He snapped his fingers. "Just like that, I was no longer me, Andrew Valentine. I was Greycliffe. Men wanted to befriend me and women marry me—or climb into my bed—just because I was a duke. I could have been mad, old, crippled, vicious—it didn't matter. As long as they could call me 'your grace,' they wanted a piece of me."

He touched her then, just a light brush along her cheek. He'd lost his gloves somewhere between Hyndon House and the pond. His skin was warm and slightly rough as if he used his hands for more than reading and writing letters. "When I met you, I couldn't pass up the opportunity to be me again. Not a duke. Just a man. Can you understand at all?"

She could. She wasn't a duke, of course, but she'd spent her life wanting people to see her as herself, not as the vicar's daughter or Ditee's little sister.

"Y-yes." She moistened her lips. She was suddenly breathless. "I suppose I can, y-your grace."

His brows lowered into a scowl. "Don't."

"Don't what?" He was so close she could see a faint, thin white line at the corner of his right eye, likely a scar from some childhood mishap.

"Don't 'your grace' me."

She put her hands on his chest. "What should I call you?"

"Drew." He bent closer so his lips were only inches from hers. "Call me Drew, Venus. Please?"

His voice sounded oddly husky. Was he going to kiss her?

She should pull away. She was only the vicar's daughter. He was likely playing with her.

But she didn't think so. She could be wrong, but she would trust her heart in this. Better to risk pain now than spend her life wondering what might have been.

"Drew," she said, lifting her chin.

Chapter 8

Drew closed the small gap between them and brushed Venus's mouth with his.

Lightning flashed through him to lodge in—

He jerked his hips back and his head up.

He was not a virgin—he'd accepted more than one invitation to dance in some high flyer's bed—but he'd never felt this overwhelming emotion before. It was more than lust, though it was definitely that, too.

He put a good foot of space between him and Venus. He might not be a virgin, but she was.

Venus blinked at him as if she were waking from a dream. He felt rather proud of himself until she opened her mouth.

"That's it?" She frowned.

"Of course that's it." He frowned back at her. "What more do you want?"

"I—" She blushed. "I don't know. I just feel as if there *is* more."

"Well, there's not." Damn it, the randy part of his brain was picturing in maddening detail all the other things he could do with her. It didn't help that he'd seen her naked at this very pond—which he hoped was just as cold today. Once he deposited her safely at the vicarage, he might have to take a brisk, deflating swim.

"Oh." She bit her lip. "I didn't mean to insult you. It was very nice."

Splendid. Now she was criticizing his lovemaking skills. If only he could show her—

"Do you suppose we could do it again?"

His cock almost jumped out of his breeches. *"No!"*

God give him strength. Here he was, trying to be noble even if it killed him—which it most likely would—and she was tempting him beyond any man's ability to resist. Not that she knew it, of course. She'd no idea the fire she played with, but he could feel it building, and it was hot enough to incinerate them both.

He should jump in the damn pond right now.

Venus's face had gone white. She turned away, but not before he saw the glint of tears in her eyes. "You don't have to shout." She sniffed and then blotted her nose on her sleeve. "I'm not going to attack you or anything."

His cock pleaded with him to encourage her assault. He reached for his handkerchief instead. "When we are married, I'm going to see you have a handkerchief for every day of the year."

Her head whipped around, her jaw dropping. *"Married?"*

His eyebrows shot up. "Yes, of course. What did you think I meant by kissing you?"

Venus's tears dried like magic as anger replaced mortification. She wanted to hit something, preferably this idiotic man standing in front of her, holding out his damn handkerchief and looking at her as if she were the insane one. Now that she'd recovered from the newness

of the experience, she remembered how he'd jumped away
from her.

"You kiss me and find the experience so repugnant you
almost run to the other side of the pond, and now you talk
of marriage?" She grabbed her skirts so as not to grab his
throat and raised her chin to look down her nose at him.
"Perhaps I don't wish to be married to a man who doesn't
enjoy kissing me."

He shoved his handkerchief back in his pocket. "Of
course you'll marry me."

"Of course I won't, *your grace*."

"Don't call me that."

"Why not? You're acting as though you own all you
survey." Venus stepped up to him and poked him in the
chest with her finger. "Well, you don't own me, sirrah."

"For the love of *God*, woman."

His hands shot out and grabbed her, hauling her up
against his body. One hand pressed her into a very large
bulge below his waist and the other urged her chin higher.
His mouth swooped down.

This kiss was nothing like the last. It was hot and wet,
and somehow his tongue found its way past her teeth,
plunging deep, sweeping through her.

Her knees gave out; if he hadn't been holding her up,
she'd have melted into a puddle at his feet. Part of her *was*
melting.

"See?" he said, lifting his head and brushing a kiss over
her cheek. "I like kissing you. Now we should—"

"Again." She stretched to reach his mouth, running her
hands through his hair and wiggling against his body—
and the interesting protuberance—as she did so. "Please,
Drew?"

"No." He straightened, but he didn't push her away.
"We shouldn't."

She could tell it was only his brain protesting; his heart—and other organs—didn't agree. She would persuade him. She kissed his chin.

"Stop that, Venus."

"I don't want to." She nibbled on his bottom lip.

He held out for another moment; then he made a small, guttural sound, almost of pain, and opened his mouth.

She tried doing what he'd done, probing his dark heat with her tongue.

Things got somewhat frantic then. His hands moved all over her—her back, her derriere . . . oh, they slid up to touch the side of her breast. Her nipples hardened into tight little peaks, and she leaned back, silently inviting him to continue his explorations.

He stopped. Damn it, his scruples must have reared their ugly heads again. Well, she would fix that. She slipped her hands down his front, aiming for the bulge in his breeches.

He grabbed her fingers before they could reach their target. "Careful, Venus. We are rapidly approaching the point where it will be impossible for me to stop."

She grinned. "Why would you want to stop?"

"Because you're a virgin, damn it."

"I imagine you can fix that."

His face looked strained, as if he were fighting an inner battle. "We should wait until our wedding."

"No." She loved him with a fierce, true love that filled her with courage. "I don't want to wait."

"But we've known each other only four days."

"It doesn't matter. It could be four days or four years or forty years—I know that I love you, that I will always love you." She searched his eyes. "Don't you feel that way, too?"

"Yes," he said, and she could see he was telling the complete truth this time. "I'm sure everyone will say we are mad, but yes, I feel it. I love you, too."

She laughed, tugging his shirt free of his breeches. She was going to explode with happiness. "Then show me."

Drew was obviously more adept at getting women out of their clothes than she was at getting men out of theirs. She got her arms tangled up with his more than once. Finally he made a growling sort of noise and grabbed her hands.

"It will be faster if you let me do it."

Venus was all in favor of speed so she acquiesced, and in another moment, she was as naked as when she'd first met him. More importantly, he was as naked.

"Oh." Now she could touch everything she'd only seen before. She ran her hands over his hard, warm chest and followed the springy blond hair down to—

He grabbed her hands again.

"Hey!"

"Another time." He picked her up and laid her on their clothes. "If you touch me now, it will be over before it's begun."

She didn't understand, but he sounded as if he knew what he was talking about—and he started to kiss her. Mmm. His clever mouth moved to her shoulder and then to her breast. "Oh!" His lips closed over a nipple. "Should you be . . . ahh."

She didn't care if he should or he shouldn't; what he was doing felt so good. His mouth and tongue played with one nipple while his fingers teased the other and then wandered lower, stroking down her side to her hip.

She moaned. Her body was awash in strange, wonderful sensations. Every part of her that Drew touched grew hot and desperate. But there was one very desperate part of her he hadn't yet touched; his fingers lingered just a few inches away. She spread her legs and arched her hips to encourage him to proceed in the right direction.

He took the hint.

"Ohh."

His finger slowly, delicately, slid around the small point. Her hips jerked.

"You are so wet, so ready for me, Venus." He sucked on her nipple as his finger continued to tease her.

"Ohh. Drew. Please." Her hips twitched and wiggled as if she was doing some very odd dance. She should be embarrassed—the vicar's daughter, naked outdoors, moaning with lust, begging to be taken—but there was no room for embarrassment in her heart.

"Your wish is my command, my love," Drew said, his voice breathy and strained. He lifted himself over her and came slowly into her body.

"Oh!" She felt a brief, burning pain, and then Drew was deep inside her, filling the part of her that had been so empty just moments before.

"Are you all right?"

"Mmm," she said. "Yes." She shifted her hips. Her body had already got over the shock of penetration; now it wanted him to move.

And move he did, being careful to keep his weight on his forearms so he didn't crush her. In and out.

She grabbed his hips. The spot that had been so tense before was tense again. Each time he moved, he pulled her tighter and tighter . . .

"Drew. I-I need—"

Nothing. He slid deep one last time, and she felt something hot and wet pulse into her just before a drenching pleasure took her breath away.

She felt wonderful.

Drew slid free and moved to the ground beside her, pulling her up against him.

"Mmm." His body and the sun were warm on her naked flesh. She could barely open her eyes. "What did you do?"

He chuckled. "Magic, my dear duchess."

"I'm not your duchess yet."

"But you will be shortly. Very shortly. By the time we make it to the vicarage, your parents will be home. You will look well and truly compromised, and I'm sure your father will wish to marry us on the spot."

She drew a lazy circle on his chest. Drew was probably right. Mama and Papa would be terribly shocked.

She waited to feel embarrassment, but she'd become a complete wanton. She felt nary a drop of remorse. "That would be fine."

"Good." He laughed and kissed her nose. "You'll be my duchess, Venus, but more importantly, you are my love."

She grinned at him. "I'll be your duchess of love, and you'll be my duke, no matter how much you dislike the title."

He put a slow, lingering kiss on her lips. "As long as I have you by my side, my dear duchess-to-be, I can bear being Greycliffe." Then he kissed her again.

It was another half hour before they finally made their way to the vicarage.